★ ★ ★

A Journey
HOME

JACKSON'S STORY

Book Three in the Journey Series

A Journey Home
Copyright © 2024 by Alexandra Grace

All rights reserved.

No part of this book may be reproduced or transmitted in any form
or by any means, electronic or mechanical, including photocopying
and recording, or by any information storage or retrieval system,
without permission in writing from the author.

This is a work of fiction. Names, characters, businesses, events, and
incidents described in this publication, except for those known in the
public domain, are the products of the author's imagination. Any
resemblance to actual persons, living or dead, or actual locales or
events is entirely coincidental.

Cover design by GetCovers
Edited by Wonder and Wander Editing Co.

The Journey Series is a steamy, closed-door romance.
Book 3 Content Warnings: Coarse language, suicide of a loved one (off page),
PTSD, loss/grief, rape (off page), and violence (nothing graphic). Jackson's story
has hardships, pain, heartbreak, and raw emotions. But there is even more
inspiration, hope, sweetness, perseverance, and unconditional love to balance out the
heartfelt story. Enjoy!

Follow me on Instagram and Facebook: @authoralexandragrace

Website: https://authoralexandragrace.carrd.co

The Journey Series by Alexandra Grace

The series is best enjoyed if read in the following order.

(Prequel Novella)
A JOURNEY WORTH TAKING

(Jackson's Story)
A JOURNEY SPARED

A JOURNEY TO LOVE

A JOURNEY HOME

(Sydney's Story)
A JOURNEY BEYOND

The Journey Series Spin-off:

(Nora & Jordan's Story)
MAKE YOU LOVE ME

To all veterans.

To wounded warriors and warrior angels.

*To those who have embarked on
a long journey to find their way home.*

A Journey Spared (Book 1) Recap

U.S. Marine Sergeant Jackson Vane and his best friend Will were the only survivors in their unit of an enemy attack overseas. Jackson's extensive injuries resulted in four months of recovery in a London hospital and his unwanted discharge after eight years of service. Needing support, he had no other choice but to return to his childhood home in Richmond, Virginia.

Eleanor, his father's estate manager and the person who raised him, cared for him while he mourned the loss of his friends and career. Their special bond provided the medicine he needed to find a path forward. Avery, Will's cousin and Jackson's physical therapist, had loved him since she was young. She saw his return as their chance to finally be together. Her creative therapy helped him walk again, but he couldn't love her in the way she wanted.

After they broke up, Jackson continued his healing journey on his own until he could run long distances again (his first love). Running and spending time outside calmed his PTSD symptoms and energized him.

Before the explosion, he and his three friends traveled the world, seeking the next greatest adventure. When a mysterious feeling called him to leave Richmond, he thought an epic journey would help him connect with the person he'd been before tragedy struck.

After brainstorming ideas, he decided to run from Richmond to Orlando, Florida in honor of the friends he lost and veterans everywhere. He also hoped the adventure would open the door to his future and mend his broken heart.

Ben, Avery's newly unemployed friend, joined him to manage trip logistics, promote Jackson's mission on social media, and enjoy a long vacation. Despite having to keep Ben out of trouble most nights on the road, the start of his journey was working as he'd hoped and blessed him through the first two stops to visit Eleanor and Will's family.

A Journey To Love (Book 2) Recap

The journey to his third stop, Myrtle Beach, wasn't easy. His PTSD symptoms returned, and his body started rejecting the work. Meeting Emily while out alone on his first night at the beach changed everything. Her light guided him out of the darkness and gave him a new hope for the future. But she didn't enter his life just to save him. He had a role in hers as well. Since both had a past they couldn't escape—his mostly in his head and hers in the flesh—they saved each other.

Besides Jackson, Emily had two other men vying for her attention: Lucas, a doctor at her physical therapy office and Cameron, her ex from college who had returned to Savannah. She wanted nothing from either of them and discouraged them at every turn, yet one was persistent in his pursuit and the other demented. Someone had also broken into her house. No longer feeling safe at work or at home, Emily quit her job and joined Jackson on his journey with Genevieve in tow.

Ben finally got through the titanium walls around Genevieve's heart only to be shut out again as she tried to heal from a traumatic event.

The destination of Jackson's journey is literally right around the corner, and it's almost time to go home.

Chapter One

★ ★ ★

Emily

C ome on, Emily. We've got to go," Ben yelled from outside her hotel room soon after Jackson left for his final run. After nearly 900 miles of running in honor of his fallen comrades and veterans, he'd reach his destination of Disney World in Orlando, Florida in the next couple of hours. She, Genevieve, and Ben planned to be his welcome party.

"Okay. Okay. Hold your horses," she called and opened the door to let him inside. "What's the rush?"

"Trust me. We need to go."

"Fine," she exhaled. "Take Jackson's suitcase." She handed him the luggage before grabbing her own and following him out the door. "Where's G?"

"Already in the car."

"She talking to you yet?"

With a scoff, he pushed the button for the elevator, and the door opened immediately. "Can't touch her either, but at least she doesn't cringe as much. Just avoids me."

"I'm sorry. I thought she was getting better."

"Maybe she is and just doesn't want me to know it." As they stepped out, he stopped at the edge of the lobby and lowered his voice. "Emily, I'm not sure how much more rejection I can take. After today, the trip will be over, and we'll be free to go our separate ways. It seems to me that's what she wants."

"Ben." She rested a hand on his arm and studied his face. The hurt he'd endured over the past several weeks was evident in the bags under his eyes. He hadn't been sleeping—too worried, frightened, desperate, and near his breaking point. "She just needs—"

"I can't do this right now. We have to go." Without waiting for her, he rushed to Genevieve's little yellow sports car parked under the awning.

"Can you please tell me why we're going so early?" she huffed when she finally caught up to him.

He loaded their luggage in the trunk then held the driver's side door open for her. "The keys are in the ignition. Follow me."

Irritated at being ignored again, she sank into the driver's seat and watched him jog to the other car. "Do you know what's going on?" she asked Genevieve sitting in the passenger seat.

She responded by buckling her seatbelt, still silent, distant, and in her head.

With a sigh, Emily started the engine and followed Ben out of the parking lot. In less than thirty minutes, they were parked in the back of a large, packed lot near the Disney World theme park entrance.

"Ben, slow down," Emily huffed. She and Genevieve were having trouble keeping up with him as he hurried through line after line of vehicles. They soon reached the street, and she got her answer—a festival of red, white, and blue as far as she could see.

They stood at the edge of the crowd in awe of the magnitude. Thousands of people crowded the area, holding U.S. flags or balloons, visiting colorful exhibits, and enjoying food trucks, vendors, and a live band. The amusement park could be seen off to the right.

"What is this?" she asked, her hand rising to her heart as she took in all in.

Before he could answer, a thin woman with bouncy blonde curls and porcelain skin waved as she approached them with a wide smile.

"Ben! It's so great to finally meet you in person." She stretched out her hand.

"Yes, it is."

She watched him place his hand in hers and linger for a moment. The woman's big, dark eyes held his gaze without acknowledging Emily or Genevieve standing beside him. Not appreciating their unspoken familiarity, Emily cleared her throat, then forced a grin when they turned to her in unison.

"Hi, I'm Emily, and this is my friend, Genevieve. How do you two know each other?" She looked to Ben for the answer.

"Samantha is the Assistant to the Orlando Mayor. She contacted me through social media several weeks ago and organized all this."

"Speaking of that. What is it?" Impatience smoldered in Emily's belly. Genevieve was disengaged in the conversation, barely making eye contact, and Emily worried she'd read Ben's reaction to Samantha the same way she did.

"He didn't tell you?" Samantha's eyes widened with her playful smile as she tapped Ben on the arm. "Shame on you."

"How about you tell us?" Emily suggested, then narrowed her eyes in disapproval at Ben.

"This is for Jackson. We've been following his journey through Ben's beautiful photos and wanted to give him the finale a hero deserves."

Emily's eyes went blurry with tears. She looked over Samantha's shoulder at the festivities with a new understanding and saw more than she had before. In the distance, she saw banners welcoming Jackson to Orlando, dozens of exhibits for veteran's services, and patriotism abundant in every direction.

"It's absolutely amazing."

"It was our pleasure. Come." Samantha took Ben by the arm, then beamed a smile over her shoulder. "It's almost time."

"Time for what?" Emily yelled as they entered the noisy crowd.

"You'll see."

They shadowed Samantha hasty pace to the edge of the stage where the band played just moments before. Stopping in front as she directed, they watched her climb the stairs and take the microphone.

"Good morning, fellow Floridians." She waited for everyone to gather around before continuing. "Thank you for coming out today to honor our nation's veterans, and especially one special veteran in particular who's on his way here right now." The crowd erupted into applause, and she motioned for them to quiet down. "Jackson Vane fought through near-death, paralysis, and unfathomable loss. He worked hard, refused to give up, and has run over 900 miles to bring awareness and pay tribute to veterans everywhere. He is a true patriot and hero to us all."

The crowd roared again until Samantha answered a call. She had their undivided attention as they waited for an update. If tears weren't blurring her vision, Emily would have been right there with them.

"Good news," she said into the microphone and placed the phone in her back pocket. "He's almost here! You know what to do. Let's give him a hero's welcome to Orlando."

"What's happening?" Emily asked Ben when the crowd began dispersing quickly down the street.

"I'm not sure. She didn't give me any details when we talked on the phone."

With how friendly he and Samantha had acted earlier, she wondered if they flirted more than they'd discussed the event. She turned to Genevieve, who appeared ready to bolt at the first opportunity.

"Isn't this exciting?" Samantha clasped her hands under her chin as she rejoined them, her eyes laser-focused on Ben.

"Where is everyone going?" Emily asked.

"To line the road and cheer for Jackson as he enters this area."

Emotion consumed Emily once again, taking over her body.

"Are you okay, honey?" Samantha placed a hand on Emily's arm and turned to Ben when the tears came.

"She's Jackson's girlfriend. They met during his journey," he explained.

"Oh, my goodness. How romantic! Come on, we have a few minutes. I want to show you something you're going to love."

Samantha led her to a nearby T-shirt stand. There were generic shirts for Orlando and patriotic shirts in red, white, and blue. Then, Samantha pointed to a dark green one hanging high above the rest.

JACKSON, ORLANDO, and USA were intermingled together in a crossword puzzle-like pattern with solid black ink. The U.S. flag decorated the inside of the O in ORLANDO, and a heart replaced the O in Jackson's name.

"It's perfect."

"She'll take two," Samantha announced to the teenager behind the table. "You look like a woman's small, and what size does Jackson wear?"

"Large, I think," she answered, though her voice garbled with new tears.

She handed the shirts to Emily and passed a fifty-dollar bill to the attendant. "These are on me." She shuttled Emily back to the edge of the crowd and motioned for the others to join her. "Right there is the spot where his journey will officially end." She pointed to a roped-off area between the stage and crowd. "You'll be able to see everything from here."

"Thank you, Samantha," Emily said, gathering herself. "For the shirts and for organizing all this. You were right. He deserves this."

Samantha gave her a quick hug before leaving the group to tend to more event logistics. As she walked away, she flashed Ben an *I'll see you later* look, and Emily scolded him with her eyes for not discouraging it. Yes, he was lonely and frustrated, but his lack of concern for Genevieve's feelings agitated her already fragile state.

"I need to get some photos," Ben announced, stepping away before she could ask questions or say something he obviously didn't want to hear.

Speechless, she stared after him until a patriotic balloon, rising at the end of the road, caught her attention. Some members of the crowd yelled, others waved small flags on sticks, and a marching band played an upbeat song.

Jackson must be approaching, and her heart pounded with anticipation. He labored for this moment and endured hardships. He made sacrifices and put others first, all while finding both healing and love for himself. She was beyond happy for him.

In a few minutes, his beautiful journey would end, and she had the best view to see the culmination of it all.

———

Jackson

With just over a mile to go, Jackson checked his watch. Because he had to stop several times to work out cramps or rest his sore knee, he was behind schedule. His body must know he approached the end, and it was revolting— either from not wanting to stop or finally reaching its limit.

What his body wanted was as unclear as what he himself wanted. What would he do with his life when the journey ended?

Marry Emily, obviously, but that was third on the to-do list after proposing and moving her to Richmond. Details for the first task were still undecided since he'd only thought as far as deciding the proposal would happen that night—the perfect exclamation point to his journey's finale. The words he didn't have yet and hoped would arrive in the moment. At least, he had the ring. He made a detour into town after he left Emily's parents' house in St. Augustine and bought the perfect ring to represent Emily and his love for her. All he needed now was the right moment to make it memorable.

Continuing down the main road toward Disney World, he saw several handmade signs stuck in the median grass with a wire frame: *Thank You for Your Service, Welcome to Orlando.* It wasn't until he read the third sign that he understood the signs weren't remnants from a recent patriotic holiday or local event. They were put there for him. In bold, black paint, it said: *Congratulations, Jackson.* He stopped in front of it, his hands dropping to his knees as he tried to make sense of it.

Maybe a friendly resident found his journey on social media and planted a few signs. His heart pounded in his chest, but oddly, he heard nothing else. Less than a mile from an international tourist destination, there should be bustling traffic on that road—lots of it. Standing, he twisted left and right to look down the empty road. Where was everyone?

After snapping a photo of the sign to show Emily, he continued down the road, observing his surroundings for more clues. He passed several more signs, and as he rounded the bend, finally sounds of life—people, movement, action, and excitement. The entrance to Disney World would be just over the horizon.

Emily would be waiting for him by the entrance. They'd embrace, enjoy a day of amusement rides and ice cream, and have dinner together that night to celebrate. The following day, they would head to Savannah as a newly engaged couple, and then to Richmond to start their lives together. He couldn't wait.

He raised his arm to check the time, but something in the distance caught his attention. The haze and humidity from the mid-day Florida sun on asphalt made it difficult to make it out. He shielded his eyes from the glare, the blurry shapes sharpening into vibrant images as he approached.

Thousands of people lined the street, clapping, waving, and cheering—all for him—and it stole the air in his lungs. Overwhelmed, he doubled over, rested his hands on his knees, and gulped for air. The crowd chanted his name, giving him the motivation he needed to straighten and walk toward the dedicated finish line.

Making his way through the aisle of people, he studied their faces, the waving flags, and the hats and T-shirts of veterans proudly displaying their service, and wondered, *Why are they here?* He was no one special to deserve this type of welcome. But if his journey inspired them to come out and support veterans that day, then he'd accomplished mission number one.

Drawing strength from their energy and presence, he crossed under the arch, too surprised by the band revving into a song beside him to think about the significance. Several people patted him on the back or crowded him for photos. Reporters with mics and recorders swarmed him just as suffocating anxiety did.

He needed space, peace, air to breathe, and a moment to regroup. He took a sharp turn away from the commotion, only to be intercepted by a spirited woman with curly, golden hair.

"Jackson! Welcome to Orlando." She offered him a bright smile he couldn't return.

"Thank you, but—"

"I'm Samantha," she yelled over the band and held out her hand. "Please come with me. I'd like you to meet someone."

"Sure, but I need to—"

"Don't worry. This will only take a minute."

"I'm sorry," he began, following her. "Who are you again?"

"Samantha Peterson. I'm the Assistant to Orlando's Mayor. He wanted you to have a hero's finale and was responsible for this celebration. What do you think?" She motioned to the activities behind her.

"It's…"

"Jackson, my boy. Welcome!"

A short man, plump around the middle, waddled towards them with a wide smile. Strands of long hair once secured over the top of his bare head blew wildly in the breeze.

"Jackson, it is my pleasure to introduce you to Mayor Kennedy," Samantha provided.

"Nice to meet—"

"Come. Let's give the people what they want."

Mayor Kennedy removed Jackson's backpack before he could object and thrust it at Samantha.

"I'll take this to Ben," she yelled as he was pulled toward the nearby stage.

That was where he found Emily, standing on the opposite side with Genevieve, and she blew him a kiss over the crowd that had gathered there. He was desperate to hold her and soak in the calm she always gave him.

The excitement had fried his nerves already, and with all the unexpected that accompanied this surprise, his heart rate had yet to stabilize after his run. He paused at the top of the steps leading to the stage to catch his breath.

"Come on. We shouldn't keep them waiting." Mayor Kennedy yanked him onto the stage, and the crowd cheered at the sight of them. "Friends," he said to quiet the group. "It's my pleasure to present to you, U.S. Marine veteran, and our hero, Sergeant Jackson Vane."

A heavy hand fell on Jackson's shoulder.

"We are so happy you chose our beautiful city as your destination. We followed the last half of your memorial run, and it's been exciting to watch. How's it been for you?"

Mayor Kennedy thrust the microphone at him, the motion freezing him with fear. Put him on the battlefield to lead a sea of Marines, but not this. He felt exposed, naked emotionally, and sinking fast. What could he possibly say to the hundreds of people staring at him?

"Just speak from the heart, son," the mayor whispered. "They're here to support you."

With a nod, he willed a hand to take the microphone, wishing he could be anywhere else. "I don't know what to say."

His unsteady hand shoved through his hair. He couldn't think. Being forced to face a silent crowd, hanging on his every word, transported him back to his best friend Will's funeral. As with that day, he felt vulnerable and drowning in the darkness, treading wave after wave of heartbreak and hopelessness. Sweat beaded on his back and stagnant air stung in his chest. He had no idea where to begin, since the words he needed to say kept getting tangled with a dangerous storm of emotions.

"Semper Fi," someone yelled from the crowd.

Those two simple words, weighted with memories, meaning, and purpose, were enough to remind him of why he started this journey and how he finished it.

Will had saved him from the burning Humvee that tragic night in the desert and guided his path from Richmond to Orlando. Because of that, he wanted to honor their fallen friends and fellow Marines, give back to other veterans, and prevent losing any more to mental illness, addiction, or suicide. He thought of Harrison and Eleanor, who raised and supported him when his own parents wouldn't. They, along with Avery, saved him from himself during recovery, allowing him this opportunity. Then, there was Emily and the light she cast over his life.

Without each of these pieces fitting together like a puzzle, he wouldn't be standing there, kicking himself for not having the words to express his gratitude.

"Oorah," he responded, causing an uproar in the audience.

Mayor Kennedy raised his arms to quiet them, allowing Jackson to continue.

"It's been a long journey of recovery since returning to the states. Doctors said I'd never walk again, but Marines never give up." He paused when cheers rippled again. "I lost my three closest friends to war and PTSD. I also struggle with the disorder, but thanks to my family, the support I received on social media, and the amazing people I've met along the way here, my life was saved. This trip may have been mine, but it was for all veterans. If my journey keeps at least one person from giving up the fight, I've accomplished my goal. Thank you for this." He waved over the crowd and toward the festival behind them. "It was completely unnecessary and unexpected, but I'm grateful to share the conclusion of my journey with all of you."

As he handed the microphone back to Mayor Kennedy, reality slapped him across the chest. It was over—the running, the traveling, the mission. All of it had become his life over the last several months. What purpose did he serve without his mission?

While Mayor Kennedy addressed the audience, Jackson looked for an escape and located the stairs they'd climbed earlier. Hurrying off the stage, he stumbled on the last step, stopping his momentum against a nearby tree. He reminded himself to breath deep, think positive, and not focus on the tumbling ground under his feet as his stomach rolled.

"There you are," he heard Emily say behind him.

Straightening, he took her into his arms.

"Everything okay?" she asked, worry sharpening each syllable.

To set her mind at ease and stop his from spiraling, he drew back and pressed his lips to hers. He needed the feel of her to set things right again. To show him how to escape the dark tunnel he unknowingly entered.

"Sorry," he managed and rested his forehead against hers, his eyes still closed to block out the chaos around them.

"Why are you apologizing? What's wrong?"

He felt her eyes searching his face for the answer, but he only had uncertainty and fear to give.

"I have something for you." After reaching into her purse, she held up a T-shirt and watched while he studied the design. "It's perfect, right?" she asked when his emotions cracked again.

"Yes. It's perfect."

"They're selling them at the festival, and all proceeds go to the Warrior Angels Foundation. See?" His eyes snapped to hers, then back to the shirt. She flipped it over and pointed to the word *WARRIOR* printed in black, block lettering on the sleeve.

When he had no words to express how much this gesture of support for his mission meant to him, she softly wrapped him in a hug and ran a hand over his back.

"Sweetheart, there's more." She leaned back to see his face. "They've been fundraising for the Foundation since learning about your mission and raised over $100,000. All of it, along with proceeds from the T-shirt sales, will help so many veterans." She placed a hand on his cheek. "Jackson, the donation will be made in your name. The mayor will make an announcement later."

Consumed with emotion, he reached for the tree to steady himself and slid down the trunk to the ground. Emily mirrored him, kneeling to rest her arms on his knees.

"Jackson, look at me."

He wanted to, but he couldn't find the energy or focus. His mind couldn't focus on any one thing before him or in his head. Everything that happened over the last two years came flooding back, and the world around him twisted like a kaleidoscope. His system faltered at such an alarming rate it felt as though he might shatter if he moved.

"Remember what you said soon after we met," she continued, her voice sounding hollow and distant among the chaos. "You said you find peace in my eyes. Look at me," she instructed gently.

Hoping he could, he slowly lifted his eyes, but they were filled with tears yet to be spilled, blurring his view of her.

"You did it, my love. You accomplished what you set out to do, and it has helped and inspired so many people. What you've done is extraordinary. You deserve this. You and so many veterans didn't get the fanfare that you deserved when you came home." She leaned closer, bringing her face into focus. "If you don't want this celebration to be about you, let it be about them."

She was right, and he wanted to make her proud. He wanted to be the man she fell in love with, not this fragile burden anxiety reduced him to. After all the progress he'd made, learning to control it over the past year, he refused to let it conquer him again, especially on such a special day.

Wiping his eyes with the back of his hand, he stood on shaky knees and pulled her up with him. "Where's that awesome shirt?"

She reached into her bag and handed over his shirt before slipping into hers.

"You look handsome," she said, running a hand over the soft fabric covering his chest. "Now, let's go have some fun."

"Okay." His stomach knotted despite his determination not to surrender to the pressure. "Will you stay with me?"

"Always."

Chapter Two

✲ ✲ ✲

Jackson

Slowly, they immersed themselves in the festival and marveled at the grandeur of it all. There seemed to be miles of activities for veterans, kids, and people of all ages. Nearly everyone wore something patriotic—clothing, hats, beads. Some took it to the extreme and donned costumes. Military personnel and veterans, showcasing their service, could also be seen in every direction.

Making their way from tent to tent, she and Jackson mingled, purchased souvenirs, played games, and met representatives of the organizations present. She did her best to keep him in the moment, but the distractions never lasted long, the commotion happening around them overpowering her gentle efforts.

Along the way, they stopped often for people wanting to meet Jackson or take pictures with him. The attention made him uncomfortable and claustrophobic. He managed to hold it together, but a battle raged inside, and he was losing.

Sensing his unease, Emily did most of the talking, and when his body language shifted to fidgety and reticent she ended the conversation and moved them along, her hands never leaving him.

Hours later, they finally came to the exhibit he looked forward to the most, the Warrior Angels Foundation exhibit, but by then, he'd reached a breaking point. Instead of approaching the representatives, Emily led him to a quiet spot away from the festivities and lowered onto a bench. Sitting next to her, he rested his elbows on his thighs and shoved his fingers through his hair.

"Why was this so difficult? After all the progress I've made, why can't I handle this?"

Tucking a lock of hair behind his ear to see his face, she kissed his shoulder. "You're doing great."

"You're so good with everyone." He turned to her when she reached for his hand. Where would he be if she hadn't been there with him? Hiding from everyone as he was now?

"Talking to people I barely know is eighty percent of my job. I've had lots of practice, and I haven't had to overcome what you have."

He lifted her hand to his lips, then held her palm to his cheek. "If we'd never met, and I somehow made it to Orlando alone, there's no way I could have done this."

Without her, his entire journey would have been different. Eleanor said God had a plan for him. Was meeting Emily that plan? He liked to think it had been Will, showing him where to find happiness. Either way, it didn't matter what caused him to take the first step of this journey or choose the random bar that night in Myrtle Beach. In the end, she'd saved him, and he reached Orlando because of her. Of that, he was certain.

Now, he just needed God, Will, or something else to show him his purpose in life. Although it was enough, loving Emily could not be his only mission going forward. He would gladly do nothing else for the rest of his life if that's what his future held, but he couldn't help thinking there was more.

The highlights of his trip from Richmond to Orlando replayed in his mind. The veterans and families he met along the way—those he helped or kept company for a moment, listening to their story. The money raised in Orlando.

Maybe his journey wasn't over after all. He could do more—*should* do more. And he knew exactly where to start.

He shot to his feet, startling Emily after the long bout of silence.

"What are you doing?" she asked as he patted his pockets and looked around.

"I need my phone." Where was his backpack? Remembering Samantha's promise, he said, "Let's go find Ben."

"Who are you calling?"

"I'll explain later."

Taking her hand, he pulled her through the festival at a pace she had difficulty keeping up with. He apologized but couldn't contain his newfound energy. He continued pushing through the festival until locating Ben, not surprisingly, near the food vendors, and asked for his backpack.

"What's up, buddy?"

Ignoring the question, Jackson accepted the bag, swiftly removed his phone, and stepped away to make the call.

———

Emily

"What's up with him?" Ben asked before taking a big bite of his corn dog.

She grimaced at the sight of the corn dog smothered in ketchup, mustard, and some other substance she didn't recognize. "I have no idea. One minute, I thought I might have to yank him back off the ledge. Then, out of nowhere, he's jumping out of his skin to find you."

Unconcerned, Ben shrugged and leaned over a basket of fries, giving her a clear view of Samantha sashaying with purpose toward them.

"What's up with you and Samantha?"

His head snapped around, brow furrowing at the accusatory tone she used. She'd meant to shade it, but an actress she was not. "What do you mean?"

"I see the way she looks at you. How could you? And in front of G. Does Samantha even know about your relationship?"

"What relationship?" He dropped the half-eaten corn dog onto the paper plate. "Damn it, Emily. I hate what Genevieve's going through, and I tried to be there for her, but you don't know what it's like when we're alone. You haven't heard her scream in the middle of the night, and she doesn't cringe or cower when you touch her. Fuck me." He pushed his hand over his short sun-streaked hair and sighed. "Don't judge me because I'm enjoying the feel of being wanted by a woman that doesn't despise me."

Anger and frustration taking over, he turned to stalk away, stopping when their eyes both landed on Genevieve through the crowd ahead. "Look," he said pivoting back to Emily. "Nothing's happened between me and Samantha. We're just friends, but it doesn't matter, anyway. Seems like Genevieve's already moved on. Why shouldn't I?"

She watched Genevieve talk with a tall, older man by a frozen lemonade stand, sipping and laughing as she used to before Lucas striped away her glow.

By then, Samantha had joined them. *If she stood any closer to Ben*, Emily fumed, *she'd be in his lap.* Despite her disapproval, she participated in small talk while keeping an eye on Genevieve in the distance. When her conversation ended, Emily excused herself.

"Glad to see you're feeling better." Linking her arm with Genevieve's, she led her away from Ben and Samantha. "Who were you talking to?"

"James Hamlett," she answered, and explained that he owned a large chain of fitness centers in Florida. He would he opening new facilities in Georgia, Alabama, and Tennessee within the year and needed a public relations firm for the expansion. "He would be my largest client."

"That's fantastic. So, all it took was a little business discussion to put that smile on your face?"

"It was nice to talk about something other than all the shit we went through. Talking with James, even for the few minutes, made me feel normal for the first time in weeks."

"I get it. What about Ben?"

"What about him?"

"He hasn't been helping?"

"He tried... is trying. I don't know," she sighed. "The guilt is just too crushing when I look at him. And when he touches me..." She shook her head, unable to finish.

"What is it?"

"I want to feel his hands on me again. You know, like it used to be, but it's just too hard to be with him right now and not think of that asshole inside me."

"Oh, G. I'm so sorry. This is all my fault."

Genevieve stopped mid-stride and gripped Emily's arms. "No, it isn't. I told you never to say that again."

She couldn't prevent her head from dropping with the shame she knew Genevieve would lecture her about for feeling.

As predicted, Genevieve yanked off her sunglasses to look her in the eyes. "You had no control over what happened, and there was nothing you could have done to prevent or stop it. He was going to do what he wanted, and it was my decision to allow it. Understood?"

"Yes, I know, but—"

"No buts, and I never want to hear you say it's your fault ever again. I don't regret it, and I'd do it a thousand times if it meant saving you."

"I love you so much." Emily wrapped her friend in a hug and fought back the tears Genevieve wouldn't want to see.

"Right back at you. Now, let's talk about something else, please."

Draping her arm around Genevieve's once more, they resumed their stroll through the packed exhibits.

"Oh, this is gorgeous." Emily picked up a wood carving of a soldier on bended knee when they stopped at a tent with hand-made crafts. The details in the dark glossy wood made her think of Jackson, and she quickly made the purchase.

At the next booth, she bought a chess set in a wooden box with the U.S. flag carved on the top for her father and a beaded necklace and matching earrings for her mother.

"You're going to need a shopping cart if you keep this up," Genevieve teased.

"I can't help it. Everything's so beautiful."

The pair continued along the path until they reached the end, then crossed to the adjacent row of vendors. At the vendor selling photo keepsakes, Genevieve trailed her finger over a black frame with a picture of a happy couple inside.

"G, are you okay?" Emily ventured, noticing her friend had checked out of the conversation. She looked at the frame Genevieve held and recognized the familiarity. It was similar to the one Ben had given them in Savannah. The sweet gesture warmed Emily's heart but only reset Genevieve's stubbornness about her growing feelings for him in reenforced stone.

"Yeah. This reminds me of how we used to be."

"You can get that back."

Shaking her head, Genevieve placed the frame back on the table. "He doesn't seem willing to wait for me to crawl out of the hell I've been in. I think he's done." She kicked at a rock on the pavement and returned the sunglasses to her face, hiding whatever emotion she wrestled with.

"You're healing, and if you just talk to him—"

"I can't give him what he wants, and he's already got one leg out of his pants on his way to that floozy's bed."

"I had hoped you missed the flirting."

"Impossible. They weren't exactly subtle. It was easier to pretend to be in my head than watch him drool over Miss Florida."

"She's not that pretty. You're way hotter," Emily added, hoping the compliment would bring out a smile in Genevieve. It hadn't worked.

"Samantha's willing, and that's what he likes." She continued to inspect the frames before selecting one and handing the merchant a ten-dollar bill.

"He likes *you*," Emily insisted. "He's just frustrated. All he needs is to know that you still want him and your relationship."

"Relationship," Genevieve scoffed, her eyes rolling. "This is why I hate them. They're so needy and unnecessarily complicated." She dropped the frame, now wrapped securely in tissue paper, into her bag and left with Emily on her heels.

"You were happy before, and you will be again. Tell him you want him, and I guarantee Miss Florida will be the last thing on his mind."

"How can you be so sure?"

"I see how he looks at you. He doesn't want to give up. He just feels unwanted."

"I do want him."

"Then you need to tell him before it's too late."

"I can't."

Again, Genevieve exited the booth without a word, and Emily grabbed her arm to prevent her from evading further, her frustration and impatience getting the better of her. "Stop being so stubborn. Why can't you tell him?"

"Because I'm pregnant."

If it wasn't for her still standing upright, she would have thought her heart stopped. She stepped around to face Genevieve squarely. "What?"

"Yeah." Exacerbated by her luck, Genevieve tossed up her hands and let them drop to her sides. "Imagine that. After all my efforts to avoid commitment, I finally give in and poof, a baby. What the hell, Em?"

"Have you taken a pregnancy test?"

"Not since the hospital. It was negative then." Genevieve swatted at the liquid rolling down her cheek. "It won't be now."

"How do you know? Maybe the stress and diabetes are causing—"

"I can tell. This is different than an irregular period or low blood sugar."

"Didn't they give you the morning after pill?"

"Yes, but since it was four days after Luc—" She swallowed back his name and how it made them both feel when they heard it. "The nurses were quick to point out that it might not work."

"Or you were already pregnant from your time with Ben," she suggested, hoping it would set their minds at ease.

"Maybe."

"But I'm still confused about one thing. You've always been over-the-top strict with taking your birth control. Even more than me with my routines."

Genevieve grinned, but it didn't hold. "I don't know. At the time, everything I knew about myself and my life had been flipped on its ass. I'm not surprised something slipped," she sighed. "Of all the things."

"Why didn't you tell us you were dealing with this, too?" Emily asked, then it hit her. "You don't think it's Ben's."

"There's no way to be certain, is there? This is why I can't talk to him. If I have the baby, and it's not his, he'll just leave me then. I'm saving us both the heartache."

"What do you mean, *if*? Are you considering abortion?"

"There's a slight chance it could be Lucas's child. If it is, how can I love it? What if it's a boy, and he has that monster's eyes? How can I look at him every day and not be reminded of what happened?" Tears spilled over and darkened her shirt before she wiped them from her face. "What kind of life would that be for him? For me?"

"You would be an amazing mother, no matter who the father is, and you would love him unconditionally. I know you."

"You're usually right about a lot of things, but you can't know this, Emily." She shook her head. "I'm sorry. This is very selfish of me. You should be with Jackson celebrating and having fun."

"You're not being selfish. I'm here for you, too, always." She looked around. "Anyway, Jackson took off earlier, and I have no idea where he is, or what he's up to. He was acting very strangely."

"Strange, how?"

"We'd taken a break from mingling because he was overwhelmed. He looked like he might break down again. Then, out of nowhere, he was excited and rushing after Ben to get his phone. I haven't seen him since."

"Alright. He can't be far. We'll start where you saw him last and search from there."

"In a minute. I need to tell you something, first. When I left Ben—"

"I saw them, and it's okay. Besides, now's not a good time for us to talk, or I might blurt out that I may be carrying his child." She tried to laugh off the reality of her situation, but it was shaky.

"Not funny, but he does need to know."

"Another time perhaps. Let's go find Jackson. I could use a distraction."

————

After a long search through the food vendors and activities, Emily and Genevieve found Jackson sitting with Ben at a picnic table behind a row of exhibits. The conversation seemed intense, but he looked energized and more animated than she'd ever seen him.

"So, this is where you ran off to."

He stood, picked her up, and twirled her around while she squealed.

"Okay," she managed when the spinning stopped. "Who are you, and what did you do with my man?"

"I did it," he said with a new spark in his eyes.

"I know you did, but I have a feeling we're not talking about the same thing."

"Nope." He kissed her hard, ignoring Ben and Genevieve waiting nearby. "I figured out what I want to do when we get home."

Her eyes watered at the casual mention of their future together. *When we get home.* She couldn't wait. "That's amazing. What is it?"

"I'll tell you all about it later. Right now, I just want to celebrate. Anyone up for dinner and drinks tonight?" he asked the others over his shoulder, his smile wildly beautiful.

"Absolutely," Ben answered before cutting his eyes to Genevieve. She leaned against the nearby tree with her arms crossed against her belly, still ignoring him.

"Good, but I want to talk to a few people first."

"You do?" Emily asked before she could stop herself.

"Yeah. To invite them to join us. Let's make it a party."

"A party?" she asked him, still trying to figure out who stood before her. "Okay. We'll need to find a place that can—"

"I'll ask Samantha," Ben suggested all too eagerly. "She might be able to pull some strings on such short notice, being that she's the mayor's assistant and all."

Emily rolled her eyes and opened her mouth to respond, but Jackson beat her to it.

"Perfect. See if she can make a reservation for thirty."

"Thirty? Who are you inviting?" Emily asked.

"Everyone."

"I'll be right back." Genevieve pushed off the tree and disappeared into the festival.

"We better get started if we're going to invite them all before morning." Emily took his hand, enjoying this new side of him. "Where to first, my love?"

"The Warrior Angels Foundation."

———

It took over an hour, but they found everyone he wanted to invite to his impromptu dinner celebration.

Representatives from the Warrior Angels Foundation, several veteran services and military organizations, and Mayor Kennedy were excited to attend.

As they were finishing their conversation with the mayor, Ben returned with Samantha. "Looks like the festival is winding down. Did you get through your invitation list?" he asked Jackson.

"We did. Were you able to find a restaurant to accommodate us?"

"Yes," Samantha answered. "There's a fantastic steakhouse a few blocks from here with a large banquet room. They are excited to host the hero all of Orlando's been talking about."

"I'm no hero, but I appreciate their accommodating us on short notice." He turned to Ben. "Can you post the location and meeting time on social media? I told everyone to check there for the information."

"No problem, Boss."

"Did you see G while you were out there?" Emily asked and Samantha answered again.

"We saw her talking to James a few minutes ago."

By the tone of her voice, Samantha had figured out Ben's connection to Genevieve, and she wasn't thrilled about it.

"James?"

"James Hamlett. He owns a chain of fitness centers here in Florida."

"Oh, that's right. She was trying to sign him as a client earlier." Emily hoped the explanation would correct the assumptions Ben had jumped to when he saw her earlier.

"We'll find her on the way out," Jackson promised, then asked Samantha, "Will you be joining us for dinner?"

"I'd love to come. Thank you for inviting me."

She smiled before timidly raising her gaze to Ben. Pink quickly flushed over her cheeks, and Emily wondered if more had transpired since she last saw them. After finding out about Genevieve's pregnancy, she was more furious with him than ever.

"Let's go check in at the hotel and get ready."

"Not yet," Genevieve said as she rejoined the group with James at her side. "Jackson, this is James Hamlett. He wanted to see you before you left."

"It's great to finally meet you." James reached out his hand. "My father and grandfather were both Marines, and I have a lot of respect for what you've done."

"Thank you. I hear that you own some fitness centers."

"That's correct. I'm hoping Miss Olsen here can help with the expansion over the next year." James smiled down at her.

"From what I know of Genevieve, she's the right person for the job."

Surprised by the compliment, her head snapped to Jackson.

He winked at her, then gave his attention back to James. "We're holding a celebration dinner tonight. I'd love for you to join us."

"I have nothing but boring responsibilities and a big, empty house waiting for me. So, count me in."

"Great. I'm sure you know Samantha," he motioned in her direction, confident and in control. Emily beamed at him. "She can give you the location. We'll see you there."

As the group walked toward the hotel, Emily stopped outside a boutique.

"I just realized that I don't have anything to wear to the party." She sent a suggestive smile at Genevieve. "Up for some shopping?"

"Like you have to ask."

"We should probably wear something other than T-shirts and shorts tonight." Ben sent Jackson the same smile. "I saw some suits in a window a few shops back."

"That'll work."

"Great. We'll meet you in the lobby in two hours," Emily said and kissed Jackson on the cheek before hurrying inside the shop.

Chapter Three

✭ ✭ ✭

Jackson

Ben and Jackson arrived first to the hotel lobby dressed in sleek new suits. While waiting for Emily and Genevieve, they sat at the bar and ordered drinks.

"I can't believe it's over." Ben propped his elbows on the counter with a loud exhale. "What am I going to do now that I won't be following you down the east coast?"

"Don't you worry, buddy. Everything will work out."

Ben studied him over the bottle before taking a drink.

"What?"

"I'm still not used to this new positive side. When are you going to tell Emily?"

"I'm waiting on one last piece to fall into place first, but tonight. How are things between you and Genevieve? Any better?"

"I think we're done."

"Why?"

"I've hit my rejection limit."

"I've never seen you give up before."

"You saw her earlier. She seems to feel better without…"

"Without what?" Jackson asked, following Ben's stunned gaze to Emily and Genevieve strolling toward them from the elevators.

Seeing Emily like this was like seeing her for the first time all over again. She was stunning in a fitted, light blue-gray dress that matched her eyes. A thin black belt fastened around her slender waist, and the length showed just the right amount of her long legs. The last few weeks of sunshine and beaches had tanned her skin, and it glittered in the light as she walked. Her loosely braided hair draped over one of her shoulders.

She would always be beautiful to him—the perfect picture of grace and timeless beauty—but that night, she took his breath away.

———

Ben

As if in slow motion, Genevieve moved toward him. Her green eyes shone bright and clear, the way they used to, with a touch of matching glittery eyeshadow above her lashes. She left her dark hair natural, wild and wavy, just the way he liked it.

The black dress she wore scooped around her neck, showcasing a mile of cleavage and accentuating every curve as if it were painted onto her perfect skin. *How had she found a dress to fit her like that?*

A wave of possessiveness washed over him. That dress was on a mission, but he surely had no part in her reason for wearing it.

Yanking his attention away, he noticed Jackson standing and pulling out stools for the girls at the bar.

"You look amazing," he whispered to Emily after she settled on a stool next to him and leaned in for a kiss.

"Thank you. I've never seen you in a suit before. I have to say, I like it very much."

"I'll have to remember that. Hi, Genevieve. You look beautiful too."

Ben heard the conversation but couldn't join in. Couldn't force himself to look at the woman currently responsible for pushing his jealousy meter into unsafe territory. He sank deeper the longer they chatted casually beside him.

"Thanks for what you said to James earlier," Genevieve said. "It might have been what convinced him to choose GLO for the expansion."

"No problem. Hey, Ben," Jackson began, attempting to be the wingman he needed in that moment. "Doesn't Genevieve look beautiful tonight?"

"Stunning, actually." Mustering up a little bravery, he turned his eyes to Genevieve. "Can I talk to you? Privately?"

With a sigh, she pushed back from her stool to follow him to a nearby table.

"I meant it," he began, sitting opposite her. "You're absolutely stunning."

"Thank you, Ben. You're—"

"Look," he interrupted, uninterested in small talk. He had to know, and know now. "It's been a difficult few weeks for you, I understand that. I'd have given anything to help you, but you seemed to want anything but me. Despite that and the thousand red flags going off in my head right now, I need you to tell me." He paused when he noticed his hands were shaking and moved them to his lap.

"Tell you what?"

"Do you want us, or are you done?"

His heart skipped when she raised her ball-melting gaze to his. How many hours had he spent begging for that one gesture? For her to talk to him? "What do you want?"

"I asked you first."

"Ben, I'm not sure this is the right time for—"

"I disagree. The way you look in that dress, I need to know." His head spun as more flags shot up inside his brain. He ignored them all. "Is that for me or someone else? Because I'm not sure I can handle other men looking at you in that if we're still together. Not after Jacksonville."

"Excuse me?"

"I'm sorry." Nausea rose into his throat at the devastation on her face—one hundred percent his fault. "I shouldn't—"

"No, you shouldn't have. You have no idea what it took for me to put this on when I want to crawl into a hole and cry myself to sleep. This is a dress I would have worn *before* Jacksonville. Before he stole my confidence and ruined my self-worth. But for your information…" She slapped her hand on the table and rose. "I'm not wearing this for you or anyone else. I need to find myself again, and if a little black dress helps me feel normal for a few fucking hours, then I don't care if you can handle it."

Pivoting, she stalked to the bar and yanked her purse off the counter. "I'll be outside when you're ready," she said to Emily and Jackson and fled before any questions could be flung in her direction.

Just when he thought things between them couldn't get any worse, he turns into the world's dumbest asshole and disintegrates any chance of getting her back.

"What did you say to her?" Emily demanded when he joined them, guilt and regret surely written all over his face.

"Nothing. Shit." Running his hand through his hair, he wished for a magical do-over. With a second chance, he'd tell her how much he missed her and not let his emotions cloud the conversation. He'd confess his love for her— something he'd never admitted—and beg her to come back to him. But to his detriment, that tight dress turned his brain to mush, allowing colossal asshole Ben to step forward and ruin everything, including magical do-overs. He doubted she'd ever talk to him again after what he said.

"Is this about Samantha?" she asked.

"What about her?" Jackson's eyes snapped eyes to him and without waiting for an answer, he said, "Tell me you didn't."

"No. Of course not."

Emily's temper matched Genevieve's, adding to his remorse. "With everything she's been through, she doesn't need this stress. And this is Jackson's special day. What are you doing?"

He snatched his beer off the bar. He screwed up. He knew that already and didn't need a scolding from either of them. "I didn't mean to upset her."

"You obviously did. You're being selfish."

Unable to argue with her, he scrubbed his hand over his face before placing it on Jackson's shoulder. "I'm sorry."

"It's alright, buddy. You're both in a difficult situation, and emotions are high. Let's try to enjoy tonight, and you two can talk it out later."

"Okay, but I doubt that's possible."

————

Jackson

The first to arrive at the restaurant, the foursome found the manager and discovered the dinner menu, bar selections, music, and services had already been set. Samantha had taken care of all arrangements and even decorated the room.

"She's something, isn't she?" Ben said absently, surveying the large room.

Each round table was covered with white linen tablecloths and patriotic centerpieces. There were also red, white, and blue balloon clusters in every corner and carnations of the same colors on serving tables. She had thought of everything.

"Now, all we have to do is wait for everyone to arrive."

"No. I want to talk to you first." Jackson closed the door and motioned for them to sit at a nearby table. "I can't tell you how much I appreciate all three of you. Yes, even you, Genevieve," he confirmed when she furrowed her brow in response. "You are my three closest friends, and for your help in getting here, I have something for each of you."

"Jackson, that's not necessary," Ben began but didn't say anything more when Jackson raised his hand to stop him.

"Yes, it is. Especially you. You've been with me since day one. From rescuing me from a storm, to shoveling horse manure, to tractor shopping—"

"And taking amazing pictures," Ben added.

"Yes, of course. Because of your brilliant idea, skill, and artistry, we reached more people. For that, I will be eternally grateful."

"*And* I made sure you had some fun on this trip."

"If getting into trouble around every turn is your idea of fun…"

"You know it."

Changing the subject to the purpose of his speech, Jackson removed a white envelope from his inside jacket pocket and handed it to Ben. "This is an investment in the business you want to start when we get back."

Ben checked the contents inside, his eyes widening in shock. "I can't accept this."

"Yes, you can, and you're keeping the car, too. It prefers your driving, anyway."

Pushing from his seat, Ben rounded the table, and wrapped him in a hug. "I love you, man."

"I love you, too, buddy."

After Ben stumbled back to his seat, Jackson turned to the girls. "Genevieve, your surprise is coming with my announcement later this evening."

"Oh, goodie. I love surprises."

He smiled then reached out for Emily. "My love." She rose to stand in front of him, and he instantly started sweating from the engagement ring burning in his pocket. Stalling, he bent for a kiss and a moment to reassemble the words that jumbled the second her adoring eyes met his.

"Excuse me, Mr. Vane," the waiter interrupted. "Your family's here."

"My what?" he asked, confused.

Instead of explaining, he held the door open

"William?" Jackson stepped around Emily to kneel in front of the child, who had stopped short when he noticed strangers in the room. "William, my boy. Come here."

His little lip puckered, then he let out a squeal before waddling into Jackson's open arms.

"Oh, I've missed you so much. Where's your mother?"

"Hi, stranger," Sydney said on cue, entering the room.

Shifting the child to his hip, Jackson hurried to her, and hugged her tight. "What are you doing here?"

"We were following your journey and didn't want you to be alone at the end." She leaned back to see him, her arms still secured around his waist. "Will would be so proud of you."

"Thank you. I'm so glad you came, but I'm not alone. Come. I want you to meet a few people."

Taking Sydney's hand, he led her to the others.

———

Emily

"I'd like you to meet Sydney," Jackson said to the others. "She and my best friend Will were dating before he passed."

He paused to swat at his forming tears, surprising Emily. Except when he struggled with anxiety or fought against memories, he rarely showed emotion—always calm and controlled. Seeing him cry in front of Sydney within moments of her arrival, pricked at her heartstrings with conflicting feelings.

"Sydney, meet Ben."

"It's so great to finally meet the man behind the camera." Sydney held out her hand as Ben stood to greet her.

"And this is Genevieve and Emily. We met in Myrtle Beach and have been traveling together these last few weeks."

"I see." Sydney's eyes took them both in before saying, "Nice to meet you both."

Emily smiled back, despite feeling Genevieve's suspicious glare on her. She knew what her friend was thinking. She saw Sydney's reaction to Jackson and her shock to find him with female company. He hadn't told Sydney about his new girlfriend, and Genevieve wasn't the only one wondering why.

"It's great to meet you, Sydney. I've heard so much about you," Emily finally said.

"And this is William, their son and my godson," he continued proudly and kissed the child on the cheek. "I found out that Will had a son when I stopped by to visit his parents on the way to Myrtle Beach."

"They have a special bond," Sydney added. "From the moment William saw him, his love for Jackson was undeniable."

Genevieve leaned in to whisper, "And so is Syd—"

"Mr. Vane," the waiter interrupted before Emily could tell her friend to shut up. "The guests are starting to arrive. Shall I send them in?"

"Give me a few more minutes, please."

With a nod, he closed the door behind him.

"Will you stay for dinner?" he asked Sydney.

"I wouldn't miss it for the world. I'm so happy for you."

Sydney rested a hand on Jackson's arm, looking up at him with her big, green eyes, and Emily and Genevieve shared a knowing glance. A nagging tingle slithered up Emily's spine at the exchange, but she chose to ignore it. No one could change Jackson's love for her. Not even a stunning redhead with ivory skin, an hourglass figure, and sexy Irish accent.

Then again, whenever he interacted with William, his devotion to the child was something she hadn't seen in him before. A part of her couldn't help wondering if his desire to be a father to William would push him into Sydney's arms.

No, she scolded herself and shuddered. She would not let her insecurities ruin this moment. That night, they were celebrating Jackson, his journey, and his exciting announcement—whatever that was. Nothing else mattered or deserved her energy.

He handed William to Sydney and clapped his hands together. "Are we ready?"

———

The room continued to fill steadily over the next hour, and Emily watched Jackson confidently greet each guest from afar. He was poised, professional, attentive, and incredibly attractive. To keep her mind from going off the deep end again, she scanned the room for a distraction, frowning when she found Samantha and Ben huddled together at a corner table. They were only talking, but an unmistakable spark of chemistry bounced between them. To their left, she saw Mayor Kennedy and representatives from the Warrior Angels Foundation.

From there, her eyes cut to Sydney and William as they approached Jackson. He lifted the child and tossed him into the air, making them all laugh. To the unaware, they looked like a family—a very happy family.

Emily's stomach churned at the thought. As a server approached, she flagged him down and selected a glass of red wine from the tray he carried.

"Everything okay?" Genevieve asked, reminding Emily that she wasn't alone.

"Yes, of course. Why wouldn't it be?"

"Oh, I don't know. Just like mine, your man's time and attention seems to be tied up with another woman."

"You're not helping."

Genevieve shrugged. "All I'm saying is little Sydney has something on her mind, and it has everything to do with stealing your boyfriend."

"I doubt she even knows he has a girlfriend," she admitted aloud against her better judgment.

"You're probably right, but if she does, she apparently doesn't care. She has that baby, and Jackson's already in love with him."

"G, please, I'm begging you. I'm already hanging on by a thread." She pushed back the tears straining to be set free. Jackson had been so busy with his guests, Sydney, and William that he seemed to have forgotten she was even there. Before Sydney arrived, she felt like the center of his world, and insignificant ever since. "I don't need you to point out what's blatantly in front of me."

"You're right. I'm sorry. I'm just so pissed all the time these days."

She touched Genevieve's arm. "I'm sorry too."

"I wish I could have a drink." Instinctively, she touched her stomach.

"Mmm. You are missing out. This wine is fantastic."

"I hate you," she growled as Emily taunted her with a sip. "Have you ever wondered how Jackson paid for this trip? The hotel rooms, the food, this party? Tonight, he's made a considerable investment in Ben starting a business and gifted him the car."

"It's crossed my mind, but it's none of my business. I just figured he had sponsors or savings or something. Why do you ask?"

"I'm just curious, that's all. I do wonder, though, if Sydney—"

"Ladies, it's so nice to see you again," James interrupted, stepping up to them with two glasses of wine and a big, toothy smile.

"Hello, James. You're enjoying the wine, I see," Genevieve teased, matching his energy.

He laughed, then held up the full glass in his left hand. "This one is Samantha's. We were talking with Jackson's companion, Benjamin, I think, when she realized she forgot something in her car. She asked me to guard her glass until she returns."

Emily watched Genevieve hold her smile with determination, but her skin paled around it. When someone stole James' attention, her eyes darted around the room and Emily's followed, knowing she searched for Ben. He was also absent.

"She's a real go-getter," James continued to praise, his attention returning to their conversation. "Organized that entire event on her own. Are you feeling all right, Ms. Olsen?"

"We really appreciated all she and the City of Orlando did for Jackson today," Emily interrupted to distract him and give Genevieve time to compose herself. She looked as though she might empty her stomach at any moment. "I've never seen him so energized. The celebration really seemed to inspire him. Oh, there's Samantha now."

As James turned around, she grabbed Genevieve and fled toward the emergency exit in the back of the room.

At the first brush of the cool evening breeze outside, Genevieve leaned back to enjoy it, then doubled over to vomit in the shrubbery.

"Great. Just what I needed," Genevieve stood, wiping her lips with the back of her hand. "Morning sickness, at night, mind you, while I'm wearing this fabulous dress. Sounds like my life right now. A shit show of dysfunction."

"Oh, G. You're not having morning sickness. It's too soon. It's probably your blood sugar. What have you eaten today?"

"You don't want to know."

"I figured. When we get inside, you're going to check your glucose and get some food or orange juice if you need it." She patted her gently on the back.

"I can't believe this is happening."

Emily passed her the small cocktail napkin she was given along with the glass of wine, but by then, Genevieve was sick again.

"I understand that you're dealing with a lot, but you've got to take care of yourself. It's not only about you anymore. This is serious."

"I know." Agitated by the lecture and unexpected ab workout, Genevieve rested her hands on her knees. "Was he with her?"

"What do you mean?"

"You know what I'm asking."

"Yes. But we don't know what, if anything, happened between them," she added quickly when Genevieve dropped her head.

"Don't be stupid, Emily."

"G, what happened with Ben earlier, before we left the hotel?"

Straightening, Genevieve yanked open the small purse dangling from her wrist, removed a container of mints, and tossed one into her mouth. "I don't want to talk about it. Let's go back inside. We should be having a good time like everyone else. We deserve it."

———

Jackson

"Attention everyone," Ben called over the music, playing through the ceiling speakers. "Please take a seat."

Sydney and William, Mayor Kennedy, James, and Victoria from the Warrior Angels Foundation and Emily encompassed Jackson's table at the front of the room. It was the perfect spot for seeing and addressing the other six tables, now full of his special guests. For once, he didn't want to run from this moment in the spotlight. He embraced it and relished feeling whole again, like that final puzzle piece had been set into place. He knew finding his purpose would give him that peace and inner strength, which was why he fought so hard to find it.

After dinner, Ben stood and clicked a knife against his glass. "I'd like to make a toast in honor of Jackson, my friend and someone I greatly admire." He raised his glass, and everyone followed. "To attaining impossible goals, working hard, making new friends, and reaching for our dreams. Congratulations, Jackson."

The room erupted with excitement until Jackson stood to speak. "I want to thank everyone for coming tonight and for the unbelievable welcome today. Mayor, Samantha, thank you and your amazing team for organizing the festival."

The duo raised their glasses in response.

"I'm not the type of person who seeks out or enjoys attention. In fact, I usually avoid it. As you can imagine, today was very difficult for me, but I am so grateful for every second and the inspiration it gave me. You see, throughout this three-month journey from Richmond to Orlando, I searched for an answer to one question: What will I do with my new civilian life to gain the same fulfillment I got from serving? Not one idea came to mind until I came here."

"Tell us, Jackson," someone yelled from the back of the room, causing the group to laugh.

"Sorry. I don't usually talk this much." Embarrassed, he smiled down at Emily for a little added courage, and like a battery, her light fueled him. "Okay, here it is. I want to start a non-profit fitness center for veterans. The facility will offer free services for those who can't afford it or don't have insurance for things like physical therapy, PTSD counseling, wellness, and more. If possible, I'd like to partner with the Warrior Angels Foundation, and anyone else who'd like to get involved. Mr. Hamlett, I could use your expertise for the fitness room. Genevieve, I'd like you to handle all the marketing and promotion, if you'll take it on."

"I'd love to," she agreed.

"Count me in, too," James said. "This sounds like a worthwhile and exciting project."

"Where will you build it, and what will you call it?" Mayor Kennedy asked.

"I'll build it in Richmond, of course, and name it VETS for Veteran Exercise and Therapy Services."

"That's amazing, Jackson. I'd like to get involved and make an investment. Hell, maybe one day you can expand to Orlando."

"Great idea. Thank you, Mayor."

By the time everyone started mingling again, he'd secured four more investors and a partnership with the Warrior Angels Foundation. He'd already spoken with his attorney about setting up the non-profit, and Harrison agreed to help search for possible locations to consider when he returned.

Everything was coming together, but he still had one more important mission to accomplish.

Chapter Four

☆ ☆ ☆

Emily

S o, you knew about Sydney and William?" Genevieve
asked while Jackson mingled with the few remaining
guests an hour later.

"Mostly. He told me that Sydney will be moving back to
Richmond so he can help raise William."

"Wow. That complicates things. Especially since she's
moving to be with Jackson."

"We don't know that."

"I know you saw the same look I did."

Emily looked away, wishing she hadn't seen the longing
in Sydney's eyes. She had more than a friendly appreciation
for Jackson, and he was so blinded by his love for William
he couldn't see it, too.

"Maybe more happened between them than he told you," Genevieve suggested, adding more coal to the fire rekindling in Emily's gut, whether she believed it or not.

"I didn't get that vibe, but whatever they went through together, it was enough to give her hope." She glanced down at her hands, now trembling in her lap. "She gave him a bracelet with William's initials on it. He never takes it off."

"Interesting."

"I'm sure we're reading too much into it."

Genevieve's shoulders popped up. "I hope so, but how does Jackson read it?"

"Who knows? He doesn't seem to notice the ogling of literally every woman that lays eyes on him."

"Not every woman," Genevieve boasted.

"You're right. Thank God, but even you can't deny how gorgeous he is."

"I'm not blind. It's just my eyes don't go all *googly* for him."

"Good to know." With a laugh, Emily set her glass aside. She'd drank too much already, the buzz only adding more color to her overactive imagination instead of muting it.

She glanced across the room in time to see Samantha place her hand on Ben's knee and lean close to whisper in his ear. A disgusted sigh leaked out—another side effect of the wine—and she instantly regretted it. Genevieve's curiosity had her following Emily's gaze and catching the intimate interaction.

Ben smiled in response to whatever Samantha had whispered, and Emily longed to throw her shoe at him. He acted like Genevieve had meant nothing to him for the past month, and it clearly hurt her.

"You really need to talk to him," Emily tried again despite her frustration and previous failed attempts.

"What for? He's made his intentions clear."

"What about the baby?"

"What about it? I still have time to decide what I want to do."

"I know what you're thinking," she said when Genevieve's distant gaze glazed over. "You'd make a wonderful mother. Don't believe otherwise."

Genevieve turned up the corners of her mouth in appreciation for Emily's faith in her but said nothing.

The friends sat in silence and watched the room slowly empty as more people said goodbye to Jackson. Emily watched him hug some and shake hands with others, but her breath caught in her chest when Sydney approached, handed him William, and led him out the door.

With a sigh, she reached across the table for the wine bottle and refilled her glass. She hadn't planned on having another drink, but the evening had taken an uncomfortable detour.

———

Jackson

"It means so much to me that you were here tonight," Jackson said while escorting Sydney outside.

"I wouldn't have missed it for anything. Plus, William wanted to see you."

Brushing his hand over the child's soft auburn curls, he kissed him there. "I missed you both, too."

"Jackson," Sydney began and took a deep, shaky breath. "I didn't just come here for William. I came to… I wanted to tell you that I…"

"What is it, Sydney? Is everything all right at home?"

He took her hand and felt the friction in her pulse. "Yes, it's fine," she answered, letting her eyes fall to their hands. "I came to tell you that William wasn't the only one who missed you. I can't get you out of my mind, and I need to know if you feel it too."

"Sydney, I—"

"Are you are seeing one of those women traveling with you? If you are, it doesn't matter. I have to know if there's a chance for us."

"I'm in love with Emily," he said quickly. If he learned anything from his failed relationship with Avery, it was that being direct and upfront prevented confusion, false hope, and broken hearts. "I want to marry her."

"I see."

Wrapping his free arm around her shoulders, he pulled her close. "I appreciate you telling me how you feel, but don't you think these feelings you're having are more about Will?"

Sydney's head fell back to meet his gaze. "What?"

"You don't have feelings for me, Sydney. Being with me just reminds you of Will and brings him closer, like it did in Murfreesboro?"

Tears flooded her eyes and her knees buckled under the weight of her grief. Kneeling, he repositioned William on his hip to try to soothe and support his mother.

"Sydney."

She buried her face in his chest, and he held her while she cried. He'd give anything to take away her pain, to add it to his own so she could remember the good times with Will before the grief. While he harbored his own emotions to focus on helping Sydney through hers, movement behind the restaurant window caught his attention. He turned in time to see Emily walk away.

"Sydney," he tried again, his heart aching from being pulled in two directions. He wanted to be Sydney's foundation, but he also needed to ensure Emily hadn't misinterpreted what she saw.

She wiped her eyes with the back of her hand and allowed him to help her stand. "I'm sorry. I didn't mean to ruin your celebration."

"You didn't. Seeing you and William made it even more special. I adore you both."

She closed her eyes and forced a smile. "You're right, by the way. This is about Will. Everything is about Will." She twirled the end of her shirt around her finger, unable to look at him. "Whenever you're near, I can feel him, and seeing the way William responds to you... I felt whole again when you and Will were with me in Murfreesboro, and so empty when you weren't. I'd do anything to feel that again, including throwing myself at you and potentially ruining our friendship."

Reaching out, he pulled her close. "Nothing's changed on my end. I will always be here for you and William, no matter what, and you will find happiness again. He would want that for you."

Although, she nodded she didn't seem convinced.

"Sydney." With a finger under her chin, he lifted her face. "You will be happy again if you don't give up. Take it from someone who hit rock bottom and is now happier than he ever thought was possible. You will be, too."

"Thank you, Jackson. I'm happy for you. Truly. Emily's a very lucky girl, and I'm glad you found your person."

———

After helping get William into his car seat and saying goodbye, he rushed through the restaurant to the back room where only a few party guests remained. He located Emily immediately, but with her back to the door, she hadn't seen him re-enter the room. He didn't like how her posture drooped, like she'd been upset and the aftermath drained her of energy. Anxious to talk to her and set her mind at ease, he picked up speed on the shortest route to her.

"Jackson." Mayor Kennedy intercepted him and placed a heavy hand on his shoulder. "Thank you for choosing Orlando for your destination."

"I couldn't imagine being anywhere else." Glancing over Mayor Kennedy's head, he watched Emily and Genevieve leave through the back door. Where was she going?

"I look forward to seeing VETS come to life and working with you soon. Be safe going home."

"Thank you again for the amazing welcome. I'll be in touch soon about VETS." Finally free, he started toward the exit.

"Jackson! Over here," Ben called.

"I can't. I need to find—"

"Come say bye to Samantha first." He grabbed hold of Jackson's arm and pulled him toward the bar. "Didn't she do an amazing job with the festival?"

"Yes, she did," he surrendered, understanding that Samantha deserved his attention after all she'd done for him.

He accepted the shot Ben passed him and held it up in salute. "Thank you, Samantha. I'll never forget today."

"It was my honor. I can't wait to tell everyone that I got to meet you and your team." Hopping off the stool, she wrapped him in a hug before returning to Ben and placing a hand on his leg.

He glared at Ben and Samantha, wondering what in the hell was happening between them and if he should say something. He settled on the safer and more pressing matter, "Do you know where Emily went?"

"I think she went back to the hotel," Ben answered.

"Why?"

"She didn't say, not that she's speaking to me right now."

Was this new development why Genevieve got upset earlier, and why Emily wasn't speaking to Ben? Jackson couldn't blame either woman for their reactions if Ben had moved on so suddenly.

With a sigh, he tossed back the shot. Hopefully, a little liquid courage would help him get through his conversation with Emily. He had no idea what to expect or what she was thinking. He'd been so busy that night, he barely spoke to her, and it was his only regret. Without her, he wouldn't be there. Wouldn't feel so healthy, happy, and whole.

He thrust the glass at Ben and motioned for a refill.

"I'm heading back to the hotel. You should come with me."

"There's nothing there for me." Ben's voice quivered with the confession, giving Jackson hope that he hadn't forgotten where he'd laid his heart. "Thank you for taking me on this trip and giving me a fresh start. I'll never be able to repay you."

"I don't expect you to."

He smacked Jackson on the back and pulled him into a tight hug to whisper, "Love you, buddy. Please tell Genevieve I'm sorry."

"You should tell her yourself."

He nodded in understanding as he pulled back but couldn't look Jackson in the eye. "Have a safe trip home."

"Take care, Jackson. I wish you all the best," Samantha added before following Ben out of the room.

Shaking his head, he watched them leave. The trip had officially ended, and Ben was no longer his responsibility. Taking off toward the hotel, he reset his mind to repairing his relationship with the love of his life.

If she'll listen.

Entering their room, he called for Emily, his voice echoing through the empty space. He tried Genevieve's room next.

"Jackson," Genevieve greeted flatly after opening the door. She leaned on the handle with pinched lips and raised eyebrows.

"Already declared me guilty, I see."

"How's Sydney?"

Annoyed, he looked over her shoulder. "Is Emily here?"

Ignoring the question, she crossed her arms. "I'm so tired of you men. You're all so fucking fickle."

"Just tell me where she is. I can explain everything."

"She's in the bathroom. Sure, come in," she deadpanned, letting the door slam shut as Jackson pushed into the room.

"G, who's here?" Emily asked, stepping into the room and stopping mid-stride when she saw him. "Hi," she said cautiously, noticing the grim look on his face.

Words were suddenly lost to him. On the walk over, he'd compiled all the things he wanted to say, but seeing her eyes red from crying had him forgetting every word. He expected angry suspicion, not tears, and it broke him.

"I'll be back in a few," Genevieve announced, though no one paid her any mind.

"Emily, I know you saw me with Sydney outside the restaurant. You must know, it's not how it looks."

"Jackson, I—"

"We have a history, yes, but it's not the one you think. I'd never lie to you, and everything I've told you is the truth," he continued, desperate to make her understand. "We met at the beginning of my journey. She asked me to be William's Godfather because she thought it was what Will would want, and I left. There is no romantic connection, and nothing happened between us the night I stayed there. The only history we have is our mutual love for Will and their son."

"Jackson—"

"I care for her. She's Will's family, and I want to be there for her, but I don't love her in that way or want to be with her. It never once crossed my mind, even before you and I met. You're the only one I want." He felt exposed, stripped down and beaten. They should be celebrating a new ring on her finger, but at that point, he was simply grateful she hadn't thrown him out.

"When you saw us, she was overcome with emotion about Will, and I was comforting her," he explained, trying anything to end the awkward distance between them.

He crossed the room, took her hand, and gently pulled her down to sit on the bed beside him.

"I want to be a part of William's life and help her get on her feet. Will would have done the same for—"

"Jackson," she placed a hand on his cheek to stop his rambling. "I know."

"You do?"

"I know you love me. I know you would never stray into another woman's arms. I know you are the sweetest, most generous, devoted, caring man I've ever met. You'd give the shirt off your back, the money in your wallet, and every ounce of energy you had and then some to help anyone. I didn't think something happened between you and Sydney earlier." She smiled when he frowned in confusion.

"Then, why did you leave the party? Why were you crying?"

She lifted both his hands to her lips, and her eyes softened, telling him what she wanted. With relief pouring through him, he kissed her gently.

"Thank you, my love. I needed that," she said with her eyes still closed.

"Why?"

"I had a little too much to drink tonight, and my insecurities did get the best of me." She grimaced. "You were busy with Sydney and the other guests, I let that toy with my emotions. I'm a fool."

"I'm so sorry I didn't make more time for you."

"Don't be. I understand, and I'm so proud of you. You deserved all that attention and were setting the foundation for your dream. I get it."

"Then, why were you crying?"

"Funny story." She smiled. "G wanted to leave, so I walked back with her to the hotel. I figured you'd be a while still, and I'd planned to come back for you, but—" A laugh slid out, surprising them both.

"What happened?"

"G's heel broke in the parking lot. It would have been hilarious, especially with all the wine I drank." She stifled another giggle. "But her arm flew up when she tried to catch herself and hit me square in the nose. It burned something awful, and after it stopped stinging, I laughed so hard I cried… All the way to our room." She laughed again at the memory. "G wasn't happy, though, with my amusement or the shoes. She'd just bought them this afternoon."

"Happy tears?"

"Silly, drunk, foolish, happy tears." Climbing into his lap, she draped her arms around his neck. "I was a little anxious about Sydney. She's so vibrant and beautiful, and seeing her in your arms wasn't the highlight of my day, but I know you. Deep down in my soul, I know us."

"I would never, ever hurt you. My heart is so full of love for you that you're the only woman I see."

"I can feel that and hope you know you're it for me."

Drawing her close, he held her until her soft lips found his.

"Can you two do that in your own room?" Genevieve asked, more annoyed than before. "You're making me want to puke, and it's not the baby this time."

"Baby?" Jackson shot up, setting Emily on her feet beside him. "You're pregnant?"

Her hands flew out in frustration and dropped at her sides—the only confirmation he needed.

"Does Ben know?"

"No, and you can't tell him. I haven't decided what I want to do."

"He has a right to be a part of that decision."

"His right was forfeited when he slept with another woman."

"G, you don't know that's happened," Emily circled an arm around Genevieve's waist, attempting to soothe her mounting agitation.

"Come on, Emily. Don't be so naïve. You saw them tonight, and I know how he looks after he's had sex. It was written all over him." Crossing her arms, she dropped onto the couch. "I'm sure he'll say I drove him to it."

"He's just trying to soothe his heartache." Emily sat beside her. "All he needs is to hear that you want to be with him, and Samantha would disappear."

"If that were the case, why did he pack his things and leave already?"

"He did? I can't believe—"

"Why don't you two go and celebrate? I want to be alone anyway."

"G. Don't be like that."

"Please, Emily." She lifted her glistening eyes. "Please."

Emily glanced at him, looking for him to provide another excuse for them to stay. Not wanting this burden, he said nothing. He and Ben were friends. How could he keep this from him? Thinking of Will and the news of William he didn't hear in time, he vowed to tell Ben if Genevieve didn't come clean soon.

"Okay, but we're just a few doors down if you need us." Emily stood and kissed Genevieve's head. "Love you."

"I hate leaving her like that," Emily confessed when she and Jackson entered their room.

"I know, but she's tough, and we have unfinished business." Crossing the room, he picked her up, and tossed her on the bed before yanking off his shirt.

She squealed when he jumped on top of her, fitting her body to perfectly with his. As she wrapped her arms and legs around him, all that had happened that night suddenly became irrelevant.

———

"I have something to ask you," Jackson said later when her eyes opened and found him. He'd been watching her sleep, impatience poking at his nerves.

"Yeah?"

"You can think about it if you want. No pressure and no is an option."

"Okay. You've caught my curiosity. Ask away."

"I was hoping you'd head up the physical therapy program at VETS." When she continued to stare at him, he couldn't read her.

"Are you serious?"

"I am. But I know how much your career means to you and want you to do what makes you happy. If working at a private practice would be more—"

She flung herself into his arms, her heart beating fast against his chest. "Nothing would make me happier than working on this amazing project with you. I have so many ideas already." She kissed him hard. "I love you so much. Thank you for trusting me with this. I can't wait to get started."

"Me either. But right now, I want to keep celebrating." He rolled Emily onto her back and kissed her with all the passion he had left. "We deserve it."

———

"What are you thinking about?" he asked to distract himself from her fingertips tracing lazy circle over his chest.

"Richmond. I was just thinking about our life there and all the unknowns."

"Like what? Are you concerned about something?"

"I've always been a planner. Until meeting you, I mindfully considered everything before acting. Soon, I'll be moving to a city I've never visited and know nothing about. It's so unlike me. I have so many questions."

"And I have answers."

With a giggle, she sat up and waited for him to join her. "Okay. We'll need to pack my things in Savannah before moving, but where will we live? How will we support ourselves and pay our bills while we're building VETS? Neither of us has a job, and I figure rent is more expensive there." She stopped when he smiled. "What?"

Relieved, he took her face in his hands and kissed her. "*That's* what's bothering you?"

"Yes. You don't worry about that?"

"No, and neither should you."

When Emily stared at him, confused and still concerned, he was grateful for a reason to have the conversation he'd been struggling to start. He briefly told her about his inheritance.

"I thought you and your father had a strained relationship."

"We did, and believe me, no one was more shocked than me. You have nothing to worry about. We will have everything we need."

She kissed him softly. "I trust you, my love."

"I love it when you call me that."

———

Later that morning, when Jackson returned to the room after a shower, all the tension he'd washed away filled his chest again. Emily sat on the edge of the bed in her robe, her head down and shoulders slumped.

He knelt in front of her, and a sudden rush of panic shot down his spine as he brushed the hair from her face. Flashbacks of Jacksonville and when she told him about the break-ins consumed his thoughts and suffocated him. "What happened?"

"G's gone."

"What do you mean?"

She held up a piece of paper. "She must have slid this note under the door while we were sleeping. All it says is she needed to go home and that she's sorry."

Relieved to know her gloomy mood wasn't because of a new development in her real-life nightmare, he let the tension seep out of his body with a long exhale. "I know she was upset last night, but she seemed okay at the party."

"You didn't see everything. It's one thing to know your relationship is over. It's another to watch the man you love blatantly flirt with another woman in front of you. She's convinced that Ben and Samantha started whatever is happening between them long before yesterday and that they had sex during the party. We saw them leave together, and the flirting was over-the-top when they came back."

"And now she thinks he spent the night with her."

"Yes."

"He's frustrated with where they left things, but there's no way he lets her go that easily."

"I thought so too, but now I'm not so sure. Yesterday, he told me he couldn't take much more and that he enjoyed feeling desired again."

"He's being selfish."

"Agreed." She shook her head and tossed the letter aside. "I hate that she's having to go through all this alone. Ben is one thing, but she still struggles with her memories, and now, she's having to think about the baby."

"The letter sounds like she wants to be alone." He joined her on the bed and took her hand.

"I know, but that's what she does. I feel like I'm letting her down when she needs me the most."

"You could never let her down, but if you want to see her, let's go."

"What?"

"If you think Genevieve needs you, you should be there for her. Plus, the sooner we get out of here and pack up your things, the sooner we can get started on building our life together."

She leaned in and kissed him softly. "Those Disney princes have nothing on you, my love."

"Come on." He stood and reached for her hand. "It's time to go home."

Chapter Five

✩ ✩ ✩

Jackson

He and Emily stood outside her little Cape Cod home while she prepared herself to go in. The late afternoon sun had fallen behind the trees, casting an eerie shadow over the house and horror waiting for her inside.

"Ready?" he asked and squeezed her hand to remind her she didn't have to face this alone.

When she forced a nod, he led the way inside. At first glance around the living room, his heart broke for her. The home she'd mindfully created for herself was unrecognizable. Someone had gone to extreme measures to destroy every inch, crafting a message to her. Seeing the damage would cause her more emotional trauma, and he could not wait to get her out of there.

He watched her closely as she took in the room—her face now stone white. Her breathing was erratic as her wide, dilated eyes jumped from the broken bookshelves to the gashes in the couch to the torn curtains and black graffiti on the walls.

"Are you okay?"

"It's far worse than I imagined," she whispered behind the hand covering her mouth.

"Emily, my dear," Charlie said, entering the room and rushing to her side. "I didn't hear you come in."

She fell into his arms. "Have you been here all this time?"

"No. I went home for a bit last week. We got back this morning."

He released her and turned his attention to Jackson, standing by the door. "Great to see you, son."

"Mom's here, too?" she asked. "Why?"

"G called on her way home. Your mother wanted to be here when she returned. They're together now."

"Good."

"I'm sorry you had to see the house like this. We've been searching for evidence and didn't want to clean yet."

"Did you find anything?"

"No. I was hoping you could determine what's missing and if the graffiti means anything to you. It may give us clues."

With trepidation, she began moving around the room. Jackson followed closely behind for a second pair of eyes. The black markings on the walls seemed to be just that, random markings. Nothing forming words or pictures. They stepped carefully over the broken glass and books on the floor below the bookcases. Under ripped out book pages, she found the picture frame Ben gave her when they detoured to Savannah on their way to Orlando—the photo he'd taken of her and Genevieve on the beach absent behind the shattered glass.

"We'll get it reprinted," Jackson said, knowing it wouldn't make this experience any more tolerable.

Dropping to her knees, she searched and sifted through the clutter, desperate to find something to salvage.

"What is it?" he asked when tears slid down her cheeks and knelt beside her. She held what looked like a pile of kindling.

"Our clock." Sobs burst from her as her head dropped to his shoulder.

To control the fury smoldering inside his chest, he refocused on what she needed from him and kissed her hair. He wasn't angry about the broken sentimental trinket. That could be replaced easy enough. It was how the damage to that little beach clock added salt to her reopened wounds after she'd worked so hard to heal them.

"You don't have to do this right now. We can come back tomorrow," he said, pleading with her to not force more on herself than necessary. Pulling from his own experience, he worried about setbacks and the complications they cause long-term.

She shook her head and stood. "No. I need to get it over with."

He could almost see her shutting off her mind to complete the job in front of her. The woman was unbreakable. Turning from him, she roamed about the room on her own internal autopilot.

"How was Orlando?" Charlie asked once Emily moved to her bedroom.

"It was amazing. Thank you."

"Sorry we couldn't be there."

"I didn't expect you to come. Especially with this." He glanced over the room again, hoping a clue would catch his attention. "Find anything to help identify the asshole who did this?"

"No, and it's starting to piss me off." Charlie ran his hand over his bare head. "What do you two plan to do next? I'm worried about her being here."

"Me, too. We're here to get what she needs, and then we're heading to Richmond."

"Good." Charlie turned to walk away, then stopped, curiosity alive in his dark eyes as he whispered, "Did you propose?"

"I started to but got interrupted." He sighed when Charlie's excitement switched to confusion. "It's a long story. I'm waiting for the right moment now."

"Make sure it's memorable. She deserves that."

"What are you two whispering about?" Emily asked, entering the room. She grabbed the laundry basket sitting on the dining room table and studied them.

"Nothing, dear." Charlie winked at Jackson before facing his daughter. "Just guy talk. You almost finished? You shouldn't linger."

"I won't. I need to grab a few more things and look through the mail. Then, I want to go check on G." She looked to Jackson. "Do you mind?"

"Of course not. Whatever you want."

"I gathered all the mail and personal documents I found throughout and set them on your dresser," Charlie said.

With another forced grin, she returned to her disheveled bedroom. Jackson hoped to see a genuine smile return to her beautiful face as soon as they got the hell out of Georgia.

"I'll find some boxes for you tomorrow morning," Charlie promised. "When will you leave for Richmond?"

"We don't have a plan. We'll leave when she's ready."

"You're not in a hurry to get back after your long trip?"

"I am. There's a lot to do, but I want to make sure she's comfortable first."

"You're a good man." He dropped a hand on Jackson's shoulder and smirked. "I'm glad to hear that you two at least decided where you'll live."

"We did, and we'll be working together on a new project when we get back."

"That's great. Glad it's all working out for you both. You'll have to tell me about it when all this is done."

"Sure. Hey, Charlie," he began and shoved his hands in his pockets. This would not be an easy to question to ask, especially since he wasn't sure he wanted the answer. "What did Genevieve tell you about the trip?"

"What do you mean?"

"I'm just wondering what you heard."

"Jackson, are you asking if I know about what happened to my two girls in Jacksonville?"

He nodded and swallowed hard, afraid Charlie blamed him for what happened as he blamed himself.

"If I ever get my hands on that bastard and the one doing this shit, I may end up in jail right alongside them." Then, he looked over his wire-rimmed glasses and winked. "But it would be worth it."

"Yes, sir."

"Don't worry, son. I know you did everything you could. Thank you for taking such good care of them."

Relief melted the tension in Jackson's frame as Emily rejoined them. She held the basket, now full of clothes and items she'd salvaged from the wreckage.

Jackson accepted the heavy load, but she stared through him as if he wasn't there, her face void of color. "Emily?" Concern for her mental state reactivating the tension throughout his system like it came through an IV.

She said something, but her voice was shaky and barely audible.

He set down the basket. "What's wrong?"

She held up a piece of paper with a trembling hand before collapsing into his arms.

———

"Hi there," he said softly when her eyes fluttered open.

Disoriented, she reached for the cold cloth on her forehead and sat up.

"You fainted," he said, reading the questions he saw in her eyes.

"I did? Why?"

"You don't remember?"

"No." She snapped her head around to check the room around them. "Where's Dad?"

"He left. Can I get you anything? Some water?" When she nodded, he slid out from around her and jogged to the kitchen.

"I can't believe this happened." She took the glass of ice water he handed her, her gaze dropping to her lap. "I thought Lucas getting locked away meant I was free of all this."

"You will be as soon as we get home."

"You don't think this psycho will find us there? Lucas found me in Jacksonville with no problem."

"I'd hope so, but if you're worried about being in pictures or promotions for VETS, you can lay low for a while."

"No," she said immediately and shook her head. "Absolutely, not. I don't want to miss anything."

"Are you sure?"

"Yeah." She sipped the water, then set the cup down on the dusty coffee table. "I hate that my problems are causing you more hassle and delays."

"Emily, your hassles are *ours* now. Your pain is mine, too." He placed a hand on her cheek. "Whatever you're dealing with, we face it together."

Closing her eyes, she took in a deep breath as if to let the worry go before finding his face again. "I'm sitting here in the shambles of my former life, and all I see is you." She laced her fingers with his and held his hand to her chest. "Make love to me, Jackson."

"Emily." Her request caught him off guard. "I don't think that's—"

"Please," she said on a sigh and kissed his fingers. "I want to forget this ever happened. Even if it's just for a little while. You can make me forget."

His heart stopped when her tears spilled over, and sobs jammed in her chest. He'd do anything she asked, not only to stop her tears but because her plea was painfully familiar. He remembered what it felt like to be willing to give anything for one moment of peace—just a few minutes to feel something other than heartache and sorrow. He couldn't deny her that.

Cupping her face in his hands, he kissed her where the tears coated her cheeks before scooping her into his arms and carrying her to the bedroom. While she sat on the bed, he lit the candles she kept on the furniture as she'd done their first night together there. Quickly, he removed the dusty quilt and debris from the bed, then pulled her to him.

She trembled as she always did when he removed her top, and again when his hands slid down her arms. He'd grown accustomed to the way her body reacted to him, and he'd learned her cues, sounds, and shudders. When her eyes, blurry and soft, locked on his, he knew she was ready. In that moment, nothing else mattered but giving her what she needed.

"I love you," he whispered, before pressing his lips to her neck.

"Take me, Jackson. I need you."

Chapter Six

★ ★ ★

Emily

"Do you see stars floating on the ceiling?" Giggling, she couldn't tamp down the giddiness still bubbling through her. Draped lazily across Jackson's lap with the rest of reality tucked away in the darkness was exactly where she wanted to be.

He trailed a finger down her torso. "That happens to me every time I touch you."

"Mmm." She raised an arm and placed her hand behind his neck, drawing his lips to hers.

"This reminds me of my first night here," he admitted and combed his fingers through her hair. "We didn't get out of bed for days. Every touch ignited something new."

"From what I recall, and I remember everything about that weekend, it didn't take much to get us going."

"A glance from your smokey blue eyes. A smile. A touch." He leaned down to kiss her collarbone, glowing in the moonbeams from the curtainless window. "All we had to do was think about it."

"I can't wait to have lazy Saturdays in Richmond."

"Me, too. I'll have to give Ms. Beasley the weekends off so we can be free to make love whenever and wherever the mood strikes."

"I love the way you think. Does your kitchen have an island?"

"*Our* kitchen," he corrected. "And yes, it does."

"Good. Tell me more about our house."

"It's two stories with a basement and was built in 1902. The stone on the outside matches the fence surrounding the property, about thirty acres. The sunset is the most beautiful thing you'll ever see when it reflects off the lake out back. Especially in the fall. We have a few apple trees and a grapevine that Ms. Beasley uses to make the best apple pies and homemade wine."

"How many bedrooms?"

"Six. Four upstairs and the two downstairs are for Ms. Beasley and Brian."

"Brian?"

"Sorry. Ms. Beasley's grandson. He helps with maintenance and mowing. He's still in college, so he's only there on weekends." He looked down and cast her a sly smile. "We'll have to figure out a new schedule for him, too."

"Good thinking. What else?"

"There are wood-burning fireplaces in the living room, office, dining room, and main bedroom. They come in handy during the cold Virginia winters. Wait. Have you ever seen snow?"

She shook her head. "Will you show me how to build a snowman?"

"Absolutely. There's also a great hill on the west side where we can go sledding. It's a little fast, but you'll love it"

"I can't wait." She took in a deep breath, letting it out slowly. "How about a nice hot shower before we go to G's? I miss your hands on me already."

"When you say things like that, you could ask for anything and get it."

"Noted."

————

"You make my insides melt," Emily all but purred as Jackson thoughtfully dried every inch of her skin with a towel.

"Yet another mission accomplished." He smiled, and his gentle blue eyes whisked her troubles away like a Caribbean ocean breeze.

"We're never going to get out of here... if you... don't..." Her sighs slithered into moans when his lips traced her navel. "When you touch me like that, the house could be ripped out from around us, and I'd never notice."

"I'm happy to oblige whenever you like."

Her cheeks flushed at the thought of their living together and enjoying more moments like this. "Good. I suspect I will be liking a lot soon."

He wrapped her in a towel and held her against his smooth skin. "Let's get out of here so we can go home. I'm ready to christen our kitchen island the same way we did this one." He kissed her cheek. "And our shower." Then moved to her neck. "And our couch."

"Every inch of that house, I hope."

"It's a big house. It might take a while."

"Is that a promise?"

"God, I love you."

After they dressed, Jackson had her close her eyes to the chaos so she could leave with only the bliss they created in her thoughts.

"How am I going get out if my eyes are closed?"

"Easy."

Lifting her into his arms, he carried her through the wreckage while her face stayed buried in the hollow curve of his shoulder.

———

"What are you two doing here?" Genevieve asked after she let them inside and hugged them both.

"Sorry for stopping by so late, but we wanted to check on you since you left Orlando without saying goodbye," Emily scolded.

"I said goodbye, just not in person."

"I hear Mom's here, too."

"Yes, but she ran to the store. I've been sick all day, so she went to get some ginger ale and crackers."

"I thought you looked a little pale. That's going to keep happening until you start taking care of—"

"I know. I know. But getting my brain to cooperate with my new body is a skill I haven't yet mastered."

Emily sat on the living room couch next to Genevieve. "Talking with Ben would go a long way in helping with that."

"I doubt it. I thought getting away from the reminders would help, but it's been relentless ever since I left Orlando, like I'm being punished."

"You're not being punished." Emily stood when she heard the front door open and close, excited for another reunion.

"They didn't have any Ritz, but I found some—" Eden stopped when she entered the living room and dropped the bags at her feet. "You're back!"

"Hi, Mom." Emily's eyes filled with tears as she made her way into her mother's arms. She, too, needed her mother and found comfort in her embrace. "I've missed you."

"I'm so glad you're here." She held her daughter at arms-length and looked her over. "You're practically glowing, and I know why." Looking over Emily's shoulder, she winked. "Hi, Jackson. Congratulations."

"Thank you, Mrs. Robertson."

"Come help me put these groceries away. I want to hear about the trip." She handed Emily a bag and picked up the other before entering the tiny galley kitchen.

————

Genevieve

"I guess I owe you another apology," Genevieve said, folding her legs under her to face Jackson.

"For what?"

"You know. I'm sorry for accusing you of cheating on Emily. I know you wouldn't do that to her. I was just so angry at your species."

"I got that message loud and clear." He smiled, but it didn't soothe her guilt. "But I don't blame you. I would have been suspicious too, and you have a right to be angry."

"Thank you." Surprised by his support, she didn't know what else to say.

"For the record," he began, "the last time I talked to him about you, he was distraught over how to make things right."

She puffed out her frustration and reached for her water bottle sitting on the coffee table. "That seemed to pass rather quickly."

"I don't know what happened with Samantha. I didn't see them together until after the party."

Her eyes cut to his. Although she saw the truth there, she asked anyway. "They were still together after everyone left?"

"Yes. They were the last to leave. I'm sorry."

She nodded. "I guess that's where he stayed last night."

"Maybe, and if he did, maybe she was just someone he could talk to."

"Jackson, I know you aren't that stupid. You know him as well as I do."

"Yeah, and that's why I beg you to tell him about the baby."

"I haven't decided what I want to do, and I doubt he will care."

"Come on. You don't believe that."

She shrugged, unsure of what she believed about so many things. "If he wants any part in raising it, how will that be possible? He'll be up there, and I'll be here." With the devastating hopelessness she felt, it took everything she had to fight the liquid sadness stinging her eyes. "I hate this. I didn't want it to be this way."

"I know." He shifted closer and draped an arm around her. "It's hard, and it hurts, but he deserves to hear it from you. Trust me, he'll want to know."

More despair consumed her, and she was helpless to fight it. His tender empathy, coupled with a healthy dose of reality, was more than she should take. "What if it's not his?"

"Only he can know if that will be a factor, but you'll figure it out together."

"It's too late, Jackson. He's with Samantha, and I can't blame him." She sniffed. "Do you…"

She couldn't form the words and collapsed onto his lap, letting her emotion flow through her body before it destroyed her. She was tired of being strong, sick of the drama and nightmares, and so damn sick and tired of seeing Lucas's demonic face or Ben with Samantha every time she closed her eyes.

"Want me to grab that for you?" he asked when her phone, sitting on the coffee table, lit up with an incoming call.

She shook her head and covered her face. "What if it's him?"

"Wouldn't that be a good thing? You two need to talk."

"I can't."

Leaning forward, he checked the caller ID. "It's not him."

She hadn't planned on answering, but it still didn't stop disappointment from adding itself to her emotional chaos. Her life felt like the aftermath of a tornado—so much wreckage to cleanup and no clue how to start.

"You going to get that?" Emily asked, entering the room with her mother and rushing closer when she saw Genevieve curled up in Jackson's lap. "Oh, no. What happened?" She knelt in front of her and pushed the hair out of her face. "Was that Ben?"

She looked to Jackson for the answer when her question was ignored, and he shook his head.

"Oh, honey." Eden joined them on the couch.

She wanted to be strong to keep Emily and Eden from worrying, but it felt too good to be held and comforted.

Protected. Safe. She waited until the sobs stopped choking her to sit up. "I had some spotting this morning."

"Is that what's bothering you?" Eden asked. "I see patients all the time who experience that, and it doesn't always mean something's wrong. Have you been cramping?"

"Some, but it's hard to tell if that's from the bleeding or from puking constantly." She tried to laugh but didn't have the energy.

"You should see your doctor," Emily suggested. "If for no other reason than to confirm what you think you know and make sure your glucose numbers are okay." She turned to her mother. "She shouldn't be this sick already. I'm worried it's something else."

"She doesn't have a fever or any other symptoms. Could be from stress, and if she is pregnant—"

"I'm pregnant."

"*If* you're pregnant, your body is trying to manage a lot of recent changes and is probably struggling to keep up. The saying about worrying yourself sick is real for some people."

Emily placed a hand on Genevieve's leg. "You're going to the doctor."

"Fine."

"It could be days before you get an appointment. Can you stay with her?" Emily asked her mother.

"Genevieve, sweetie, you know I would if I could, but I must get back. We have some work scheduled at the house, and it can't wait. The last storm ripped a decent hole in our roof. I'm sorry, dear."

"Dad can't do that?" Emily persisted, her frustration showing.

"He's working with the S.P.D. right now on your case. He thinks he's made progress and—"

"He has? Did he find something?"

"Emily," Genevieve interrupted. "It's okay. I can take myself to an appointment. I'm not helpless." Suddenly feeling claustrophobic, she stood and strolled to the sliding glass door overlooking her balcony and the city beyond.

The others continued to whisper behind her, fussing over *poor Genevieve* like she wasn't a grown ass woman. She had a moment of weakness and cried. So what? It didn't mean she was incapable of simple, everyday tasks.

But despite herself, she didn't want to see the doctor alone. She didn't want to hear that all the stress she'd been under had hurt her baby or that he'd been conceived against her will in the woods. If that could even be determined yet. It's not like she had any prior experience growing a human.

Whether she found out soon or months from now, she didn't want the countless number of hours she spent convincing herself the baby was Ben's to have been wasted. She was ninety-nine percent confident in the rationalizations she'd done. It was the one percent of doubt that kept giving her regular nervous breakdowns.

"Shit," Genevieve pushed out through gritted teeth. Why couldn't she handle this? She'd never had trouble controlling her emotions or her life. Never had she lost it as she was doing at that moment. "Fuck me," she said to herself. Gripping her stomach with one hand and her mouth with the other, she took off toward her bedroom and slammed the door behind her.

———

Emily

Emily sighed and rested her elbows on her knees. "I can't leave her like this."

Jackson ran a hand over her back. "We can stay however long she needs."

Turning in her seat, she took his hand. "I really hate to say this again, but you should head back without me. It will be for just a few days," she added when he pulled his hand away and stood.

"I'll go check on G and give you two some privacy," Eden announced and rushed out of the room.

"My love," Emily began and went to him. "We've caused you enough trouble and delay on your journey. You need to take advantage of the momentum you gained in Orlando."

"I'm not leaving you here alone."

"You're not. I'll be with G, and Dad is nearby. Sweetheart." She placed a hand on his cheek. "I love and appreciate how you want to protect me, but you can't be with me every minute of the day and night. At some point, we'll have two different schedules and responsibilities even when we're in the same city."

"It's too soon and not here. Anywhere but here."

"I know, but I'll never forgive myself if you miss out on something for VETS because you stayed. Neither will G."

"And I'll never forgive myself if something happens to either of you."

"It won't. I wouldn't ask you to go if I thought we were in any danger. Please."

He let out a long breath and paced to the window. "My final run to Orlando was supposed to be the last time we ever said goodbye."

She wrapped her arms around him from behind and listened to his jagged breathing. "I love you."

His muscles went lax with the words, and he turned to hold her, kissing her forehead in surrender. "I hope she knows how lucky she is to have you."

"She has us now." When his face revolted, she laughed. "I saw you with her earlier. You can no longer deny your care for her."

"I don't know what you're talking about."

"The way you comforted her earlier was incredibly sexy."

"Oh really?"

She nodded and bit her bottom lip—an invitation he never refused. As he bent down for a kiss, the others returned.

"I'm sorry," Genevieve said, shuffling toward them, looking weaker than before.

"You have nothing to apologize for, and you won't have to do this alone," Emily said. "I'll stay with you until you're feeling better."

"I can't ask you to do that."

"You didn't. I volunteered, and the decision has been made." She crossed the room and took Genevieve in her arms.

"Since when do you get to make all the decisions?"

"Since right now, and you have to listen to everything I say." She leaned back and pointed a finger at her friend.

"Ha. Good luck with that." Genevieve let out an awkward laugh until she found herself sandwiched between Emily and Eden, their arms wrapped around her. She leaned in for support, her body trembling.

"What's wrong?" Emily asked, holding her friend tighter as she sobbed. The idea of Genevieve crying was enough to send her in a tailspin, much less witnessing it.

"I love you both so much."

"Oh, G. We love you, too. And you know who else loves you?" Emily leaned back with a smile, hoping to lighten the mood. "Jackson. Isn't that right, sweetheart?"

Genevieve, Emily, and Eden whipped their heads around, catching him off guard and making him noticeably uncomfortable.

He cleared his throat and nodded. "Yes, of course."

All eyes were fixed on him until Genevieve burst into uncontrollable laughter. Mission accomplished.

"It's okay, Jackson. You're not going to spontaneously combust from it." Genevieve crossed the room and rose onto her toes to give Jackson a hug. "I love you, too."

———

It took most of the next day and a team of people to pack up the items Emily salvaged from her house. Jackson switched the rental car with an SUV to take more of Emily's things to Richmond. Since most of the furniture was damaged, they hired a local moving company to haul it away.

Looking around at the now empty house in the daylight, the dents, holes, and graffiti on the walls seemed to scream louder, and it no longer felt like home.

"Honey, we need to hit the road," Eden said, breaking into Emily's thoughts as she stood motionless in the living room.

"We're coming. I just need one more minute." After her parents left, she leaned back against Jackson, his arms coiling around her. "I had so many amazing memories here, many of them with you."

"I'll never forget." He kissed the top of her head, and she basked in his comforting scent and touch. "We enjoyed every inch of this house, and I fell even more in love with you here."

"Me, too, but the funny thing is, I'm not going to miss it. I've never been so ready to start over."

"I can't wait to have you in Richmond. For my sanity, please be careful and hurry back."

She looked up, and the love and care in his eyes made her knees go weak beneath her. "Nothing could keep me away."

Chapter Seven

✯ ✯ ✯

Emily

Genevieve's doctor squeezed her into the schedule for an appointment in two days. While they waited, she and Emily rarely left the apartment. They ate what little food they found in the kitchen and ordered delivery for dinner.

When Genevieve wasn't working, they watched movies—anything but sappy love stories. Whenever there was a hint of romance in the storyline or the movie looked to be heading in that direction, Genevieve switched it off and searched for a new one.

"You can't avoid it forever," Emily complained. Sappy love stories were her favorite.

"Watch me. I'm very stubborn."

"Tell me something I don't know."

"Ha. Ha."

Other times, Genevieve would rest for hours after getting sick, giving Emily time to research local construction and home repair companies or make phone calls. She selected a contractor that could start the following week. Her neighbor Harry offered to oversee the repairs and lock up each night.

Within a few months, she hoped to have the house looking like new again and listed on the market, priced to sell. It didn't matter how much she got for it so long as she could pay off her mortgage and get rid of it quickly.

———

"I'm nervous. I don't get nervous. Why am I nervous?" Genevieve rambled as she and Emily waited for the doctor in the examination room.

Emily reached for her hand. "Because you want your baby to be okay. Your mother's instinct is already kicking in."

"I don't want him to suffer, but I'm still not sure being born is the best thing for him."

"It's your decision, and I will support you no matter what. But you don't have much time left. The ultrasound can determine when you conceived, but the abortion law says you can't—"

"Yeah. I looked it up. Do you remember Crystal Lovett from high school?"

"I think so. Didn't she live at the group home with you?"

"Yeah. She had the room next to mine and got pregnant our senior year."

"Why are you thinking about her now?"

"She was raped."

"Oh, no. That's terrible."

"Her boyfriend Toby was a couple years older and had a gambling problem. So, when he mounted a debt he couldn't pay, he offered her up." She puffed out her disgust and shook her head. "She tried to fight back but was either held down or beaten until she couldn't. He did that to her more than once."

Emily gasped, unable to fathom the horror, then remembered she'd come very close to experiencing a similar fate.

"Her crying used to wake me up at night. She didn't know who the father was, of course. She had no family to help, and you know how useless the staff were at the home. We could have walked around naked and bleeding and no one would have cared. She eventually told him about the pregnancy, and you know what he did?"

"I'm scared to ask."

"He called her a whore and walked away."

"G, why are you telling me this?"

"Her story is eerily similar to mine, and she decided to have the baby. It wasn't Toby's."

"None of that means you'll have the same outcome. Yes, you both endured horrible things, but Toby was a coward and obviously didn't care about Crystal. You have people to support you." Emily reached into her purse and handed Genevieve a tissue when tears pooled in her eyes.

"What if Ben doesn't want to be a father, especially if the child isn't his? What if he no longer cares for me?"

"That's not possible," Emily corrected. "And if you needed him, whether you were together or not, he would be there for you." She pulled Genevieve into a hug. "I know it."

Genevieve rested against her until footsteps were heard outside the door. She sucked in a nervous breath and sat up.

A tall, slender woman with blonde hair and kind eyes entered the room, and shook Genevieve's hand, patting the top as she smiled. "It's so nice to see you again. How are you?"

"I've been better."

"Then I'm glad you're here. We'll try to fix that." She turned toward Emily. "Hi. I'm Dr. Lacey."

"Nice to meet you. I'm Emily, the best friend," she said and pointed a thumb at herself.

"OB-GYN," Dr. Lacey said with a broad smile and pointed to her name and title embroidered on her white coat.

They shared a hearty laugh before getting back to Genevieve.

Dr. Lacey set her laptop on the nearby counter. "Your pregnancy test from today was positive. Based on what you included in your paperwork, that's not a surprise."

"It's not. I've suspected it but haven't taken another test."

"I saw in your chart that you experienced a traumatic event last month."

"Yes."

"I'm sorry that happened to you. Did the hospital complete the rape kit?"

"Yes. The tests were negative."

"Did you have unprotected sex before then?"

Genevieve nodded and dropped her gaze.

"When was your last cycle?" Dr. Lacey checked the information in her chart.

"Almost two months ago. But they've been irregular for a while now, so I didn't think anything of it."

"Were you taking your birth control every day?"

Regretting the unfortunate oversight, Genevieve shook her head, causing Dr. Lacey to pinch her lips in disapproval.

"I'd like to run a few blood tests since it's been…" She checked Genevieve's chart. "About a month since your last glucose tests to be sure nothing's gone awry."

"Okay. Do you think he's okay?"

"Who?"

"The baby."

"She's convinced she's having a boy," Emily explained, tilting her head with a smile when Genevieve frowned at her.

"I see. Does that mean you don't want to discuss your options? We'll be able to detect a heartbeat at around six weeks. Georgia law says you have until then to decide, but since we don't know when you conceived…"

"I understand. No. We don't need to discuss it."

"Alright." She closed the laptop and pushed it aside. "I'll send you the results of the bloodwork and any instructions. Be sure to set up your next appointment before you leave, and we'll check the heartbeat then." She took Genevieve's hand and patted the top. "Now, Momma, all you have to do is take care of yourself and keep the stress to a minimum. If you do that, he'll have the best chance to grow healthy and strong, like his mother."

"Thanks, Doc."

————

"You were quiet on the way home," Emily mentioned after they sat down to dinner. They'd picked up Thai food on the way back to the apartment.

"Got a lot on my mind." Without looking up, she served herself some noodles and steamed broccoli.

"Want to talk about it?"

"Not really."

"G." Emily glared down her nose at her friend. "You don't have to go through this alone. I'm here."

"I know, and I appreciate you."

"You seemed to do a one-eighty during the appointment. When you were talking about Crystal, I thought you were leaning toward ending the pregnancy. What changed your mind?"

"It wasn't as sharp a turnaround as it seemed. I think I always knew I would keep him. I just wasn't ready to face it."

"You were scared."

"There's no past tense to it, Em."

"My bad. I get it." She reached across the table for Genevieve's hand. "It's still wonderful."

"I'm not so sure about that. What if I'm a terrible mother. It's not like I have any experience. I've never even held a baby."

"I'll help you, but your instincts will kick in and all this worrying will be for nothing."

"I guess we'll see."

Emily sat back and stabbed a bite of chicken with her fork. "We will. You know what else I see?"

"I'm afraid to ask."

"Your color is back. Have you had any nausea today?"

"Not since we left the doctor's office."

"Then that confirms it."

"Confirms what?"

"You were making yourself sick with worry. Once you made a decision, it went away."

"That's very scientific of you, Doctor Robertson." She took a long drink of water and tried to ignore Emily observing her.

"Ha. Well, this doctor prescribes lots of rest and healthy—"

"I need to close the chapter with Ben," Genevieve said suddenly, almost as if the realization just occurred to her. "I'll never get the closure or peace I need until I do."

"You're right. He's too much a part of this to ignore." She set down her fork, ready to plan, discuss, plot—whatever Genevieve needed to take this necessary step. "What are you going to do?"

"Tell him everything."

"Good. He may be shocked at first, but he'll be thrilled to see you."

Surely thinking the worse, Genevieve shrugged then sighed. "I also have to believe the baby is Ben's, and for that, I can't give him up. We were happy then, and it's not his fault that his parents are no longer together."

"Do you still have feelings for him?"

Genevieve twirled noodles with her fork while she considered. "Yes. Probably always will. He was my first." When Emily's hand went to her mouth and tears filled her eyes, Genevieve shook her head. "Don't get all sappy. This may not have the fairytale ending you're conjuring up in that overly romantic brain of yours."

"It also could be better than a fairy tale."

"What's better than a fairy tale? Isn't that the cream of the crop?"

"It's better when it's real," Emily said with confidence.

"And you have first-hand knowledge on the subject, I gather."

"I do. So could you if you set aside your ego and be honest with him."

"I don't plan to hold back… Unless he's with someone else."

Emily leaned in to make her point. "Even then, G. He deserves the truth. All of it. Let him decide what he wants with all the facts."

Genevieve went quiet, fears and doubts taking over her thoughts, so Emily changed the subject. "I've been meaning to ask you. Why do you think you'll have a boy?"

"Look at how much trouble he's caused me already." She laughed at that, settling Emily's concerns. "Plus, the irony that I should have a boy is too entertaining. How could God pass that up?"

"You're probably right." She patted Genevieve's hand, proud of her friend for facing her fears. "Now, eat something."

"Yes, Mom." Smiling, she picked up her fork, now tangled with a pile of noodles, and stuffed it all in her mouth.

"Good girl." Although the misdirection worked and Genevieve was smiling again, Emily couldn't keep herself from circling back to Ben. "When do you plan to call him?"

"Oh, I don't do phones, as he's well aware. We're going to do this face to face." She watched, her smile hidden behind a bite of broccoli, as Emily processed what that meant.

"What? How do you…? Wait a minute. Are you going to Richmond?"

"If he's there. If he stayed in Orlando with her, then hell no. I need you to find out for me. Discreetly."

"Okay. Jackson should know or at least be able to find out without suspicion. Why don't you want him to know you're coming?"

She shrugged. "I just think it will be better if he doesn't have advanced notice. It will be an honest reaction that way."

"Like when you surprised him in Florida."

"Yeah."

"He's going to be excited to see you. Maybe confused at first, but if you tell him how you feel, he'll welcome you back with open arms," Emily said, attempting to set Genevieve's mind at ease.

"You keep saying that, but I can't believe it."

"You have to, or you'll hold something back and regret it later."

"If he'll give me the time of day, I'll apologize for how I treated him. Maybe it isn't too late for us."

"That's better, but I have to ask. Why you are ready to talk now? What changed?"

"Last night, I laid awake thinking about all that's happened and this new life growing inside me." Instinctively, she touched her belly. "I may not be ready or a good mother, but I'm *his* mother and that's what matters. He also deserves to know his father, whether we end up together or not. I'm choosing to believe he's Ben's until I learn otherwise. *If* I learn otherwise. I'm still not sure I want to know."

"You can figure that out later, but I'm glad to hear you've come to your senses about Ben. One thing's for sure, your little boy will be adored and have the best aunt ever." Emily tossed her hair off her shoulder with flair.

"Absolutely."

"So, tell me." She scooted to the edge of her seat and propped her elbows on the table. "When do we leave?"

"I'm having déjà vu. Have we had this conversation before?"

"Yeah. My best friend needs a kick in the butt every once in a while."

"I'd like to kick—"

"Anyway," she interrupted, knowing what Genevieve planned to say. "I'll ask again. When can we go get our men for the second time?"

"Alright, alright. You don't have to be so pushy," Geneveive laughed. "I have a few things I need to do for VETS and another client before I can leave. How about Friday?"

"I can wait a couple more days. Then, we go claim our happily ever after."

"Oh, no," Genevieve groaned. "I think I'm going to be sick."

Chapter Eight

✭ ✭ ✭

Jackson

Twenty minutes to ten on Friday morning, Jackson left the house in the white BMW sedan that had been collecting dust in the garage. Since he'd returned to Richmond alone, he'd attempted to stay busy with endless maintenance projects at the estate and preparations for VETS.

Ms. Beasley and Brian had done what they could, but the large, old house and thirty-plus acres of land and lake took more effort than a 62-year-old and a college kid could manage on their own. He wasn't complaining. The long to-do list and physical work kept his mind occupied and focused so it wouldn't nose-dive into the familiar darkness.

Without Emily by his side, his mind threatened to take a road trip down memory lane, but so far, he was still upright and in control. Maybe he was getting better at managing it. Maybe the journey to Orlando had helped more than he realized. And just in time since preparations for VETS were underway.

When he wasn't working at the estate, he completed paperwork—so much paperwork it made his head spin—and made connections around town. He researched services and set up meetings with local doctors, construction companies, and other service providers. The most daunting task was finding an architect, but he was confident he'd found the right one after a host of interviews.

With all that taking up his days, he hadn't had a chance to visit Eleanor and Harrison, which was something he looked forward to correcting that morning.

He pressed on the gas to head down the driveway, pausing at the roundabout to look over the grounds. The newly planted annuals around the fountain. The thick evergreens lining the yard and the wooded area on both sides. The old stone house that provided a mix of both fond and dreadful memories growing up and when he returned broken two years ago.

For the first time since learning his father had left it to him in the will, he was grateful and honored to call the estate his. It was the perfect place to start his own family and be the father Grayson had never been. Soon, Emily would join him, and the estate would become theirs.

Knowing her, she would gravitate toward the living room fireplace for a cozy reading spot or the back porch.

She would love the view of the lake at sunset the most, and he couldn't wait to show her.

He also couldn't wait to receive an Eleanor Brown signature hug. Thankfully, her new house was only a short distance away, and he arrived within minutes.

Pulling up to the classic two-story home, pride filled his heart. The light gray wide-planked siding and black shutters gave it an elegant and timeless look. Although he expected Eleanor to prefer stone, the house suited her. Perched behind a manicured front yard, he could picture her tending to the flower boxes under the windows, loving the simple task. Funny how she despised the summer heat and bugs unless she was tending to her flowers. The wreath on the burgundy front door welcomed visitors as she certainly would.

As he pulled into the driveway, the door flung open, and he climbed out of the car in time to catch Eleanor's grandson, leaping into his arms.

"I'm happy to see you, too," he laughed, ruffling Ethan's soft, dark hair. "Man, you've grown. What are you, six-feet tall now?"

"Not as tall as you."

"Not yet, but you keep growing like that, and you'll be taller in no time." The boy beamed a wide smile. "Where's your grandma? I'd like to say hi."

"She's in the back yard in her garden."

"Garden, huh? I'll have to check that out. Lead the way." He followed Ethan through the fence gate and across the sizeable backyard lined with tall pines and fruit trees. A new swing set with a slide and playhouse sat a few yards from the back patio which had an outdoor table set and umbrella. *Looks familiar*, he thought. *Looks like Eleanor.*

"Watch this." Ethan ran up the slide, turned around, and slid down before running back and slapping the hand Jackson held out for him.

"You're fast. Do you like to run?"

"Yeah," Ethan huffed. "Like you."

"Yes, I do. Maybe we can go running someday."

"Can we go today?"

"Not today, but soon. I promise." He couldn't ignore the disappointment on the boy's face tugging at his heartstrings, so he changed the subject. "How do you like your new house?"

"It's so big! I've got my own bedroom and bathroom. No more sharing with all my smelly sisters."

"Smelly? I didn't think girls were ever smelly."

"Yes, they are, and messy too. There's always lotions and makeup and fancy soap laying around. It's all so yucky smelling."

"Got it. They do usually come with a lot of that, but you'll like it one day."

"No way! Girls are gross."

"You'll get to meet a girl that's special to me soon. Her name is Emily."

"Is she smelly?"

"I don't think so. I think she smells good."

"Well, if you like her, I guess I will, too."

"Good boy. I know she will adore you and your sisters." He pinched Ethan's chin between his forefinger and thumb. "Now, where is our favorite gardener?"

Jackson followed where Ethan pointed and spotted Eleanor huddled over a large, raised bed of tomatoes and other vegetables, her back to the rest of the yard.

"Grandma," Ethan yelled and took off in her direction, but Eleanor didn't answer.

Odd, Jackson thought. She heard every noise he made inside and out when they lived together.

She stood and wiped her hands on her apron before walking around to the opposite side of the planter. Finally, Ethan caught her attention, and she smiled.

"What's up, sweetie?" she asked after removing the earbuds from her ears.

"He's here," he puffed, breathing hard from sprinting across the yard.

"Who's here?" Her face twisted in confusion before she noticed Jackson walking toward them. Her hands sprang to her lips as tears swelled and sparkled in the sunlight. Holding out her arms, she crossed to him and accepted his embrace.

"Oh, I've missed you." Pulling back, her eyes traveled over him. "You look incredible. So healthy and handsome. Are you happy? How are the migraines?"

He smiled at her inescapable habit of worrying about him. "Yes, I'm happier than I ever thought possible, and I haven't had a migraine in a while."

"Ahh, Emily's helping with that, I bet. Where is that angel?"

"She's on her way to Richmond now. Hold on. Did I see you using earbuds?"

"Yes, the grandkids said I had to get with the times."

"Funny. I'm picking up Emily and her friend this afternoon at the airport. I can't wait for you to meet her."

"Me either. I love her already. Look at that smile on your face." She placed a hand on his cheek then hooked her arm with his and led him toward the house. "Is she coming up for a visit or to stay?"

"Stay. She's moving in."

"Wow! Looks like we have a lot to catch up on. Let's get some tea, and you can tell me all about it."

After filling Eleanor in on the events that happened since they last spoke, he threw the football with Ethan and gave Eleanor's two granddaughters a hug before leaving for the next stop.

With it being Friday, he knew Harrison would be working from home and took the quickest route there.

"Jackson, my boy. You're home." Harrison wrapped him in a tight hug and patted him hard on the back. "My goodness, it's great to see you. Come in." He called for his wife, who was cooking in the kitchen. "Sweetheart, look who's here."

Sophia turned from the stove and with a wide smile, rushed to him for her own hug. "I'm so glad you're home and all in one piece. We've been so worried."

"I'll admit it was tough getting through at times, mental state being what it was, but I'm a whole new person now. There's so much to tell you."

"Have a seat and fill us in. Lunch is almost ready. Will you stay and eat with us?" she asked.

"I'd love to." He claimed a stool at the counter and accepted the glass of lemonade she poured for him. "Thank you."

"Start from the beginning."

"Alright. You already know that I stopped along the way to see Eleanor in Stony Creek and then Will's parents in Murfreesboro. I just left Eleanor's new place. She's so happy. And as you know, Sydney and William will be moving back to Richmond next month."

"Yes, we close on her house in a couple weeks," Harrison said. "I don't think you'll need to be there since the account you set up for her is ready. All she has to do is write the check."

"Will must be so thrilled." Sophia set down the spoon she'd used at the stove and leaned against the counter. "It's wonderful what you're doing for them."

"Will would have done the same for me. He loved Sydney and if he had known she was pregnant…"

"We can't think about that anymore. No more living in the past for any of us. We can only move forward and be grateful for the time we had with them."

"You're right," he agreed, but it still hurt and probably always would.

"I still can't get over the fact that Will had a girlfriend," Harrison added.

"Really?" Sophia glared at her husband. "Out of everything that's happened, that's what you're amazed by?"

"What? You remember Will's untamed loins. I'm frankly shocked he doesn't have more children."

Jackson choked on the lemonade he was sipping, and it dribbled down his chin.

"Men," she sighed with affection and tossed Jackson a towel.

"Anyway. You still have a spot for Sydney in your finance department, right?" he asked Harrison.

"Sure do. Just waiting on her to finish her degree. One of our accountants is retiring next year, but if Sydney finishes before then, we'll use that time to get her up to speed."

"Thank you. I owe you for that."

"No, you don't. As with you, Will was like a son to us, and we're happy to help his family." He dropped his hand on Jackson's shoulder and squeezed. "We loved all three of you, and we'll love Sydney and William just the same."

Jackson nodded, overcome with adoration and appreciation.

"So, tell us. What happened when you reached Orlando?"

He told them about the festival and celebration afterward.

"That's so amazing. I wish we had known. We could have flown down and joined you," Sophia said, checking the pot on the stove.

"It was a surprise. Ben was the only one who knew and shockingly, he kept it secret. Sydney and William were there."

"How did they know?"

"Pure coincidence. She came so I wouldn't be alone at the end and found us at the after-party."

"How sweet of her, but please tell me you weren't alone."

"No. Ben was there, of course, and Emily and Genevieve had joined us a few weeks prior."

"Oh, really?" Sophia tried not to show her amusement and gave her attention to the boiling potatoes on the stove.

"How did that happen?" Harrison asked. "When you called from Savannah, you were worried about continuing the trip without her. Did you ask her to join you?"

"No. Some things happened at work, and she ended up resigning. It wasn't planned. Her friend Genevieve and Ben had a thing for each other, so she came too."

"Wow. I'm glad to hear it worked out. I was worried about you two."

"It did more than work out. I want to marry her, and she's moving in today."

Harrison smacked him on the arm. "No way! She's moving to Richmond?"

"Are you engaged?" Sophia joined them at the bar, excitement bright in her eyes.

"Not yet. I'm still working on that and finding the perfect moment."

"If you love each other, the moment will be special no matter what."

"I know, but she deserves that and more."

"You don't have to convince us, dear," Sophia said as she grabbed several plates from the cabinet. "We can see how much she means to you. Love is written all over your face." She smiled over her shoulder. "If we can help, just let us know."

"Thank you. Your support means everything to me."

"Are you going to give her your mother's ring?"

"No. I bought a ring right after I talked with her father."

"Why? She wanted you to give her ring to your future wife."

"I can't. Not after everything Dad said."

"What did he say now?" She returned to the island and leaned against it, her arms crossed with frustration.

"It doesn't matter."

"Yes, it does. Jacqueline was my friend, and I knew her well. I want to know what lies he told you."

"Easy, dear," her husband warned. "They're both gone, and he's forgiven them."

"I don't condone anything she did regarding the affair. That was wrong, but she loved you, sweetheart." Resting her elbows on the counter, she took Jackson's hand. "Please tell me. I only want to set your mind at ease if I can."

He sighed. "He said that it was my fault their marriage fell apart. She didn't want me, and he had to stop her from having an abortion. After I was born, they both kept busy with their separate lives rather than having to deal with me."

"You don't believe that do you?" she asked, her eyes full of despair. "What does your heart tell you?"

"It's torn. His stories and my memories don't match up, but he wasn't lying. I could always tell when he was." He thought about how the devastating conversation ruined the only good memories he had of his mother and instantly wished he hadn't. "He later mentioned that she changed her mind after I was born, but it still wasn't enough to make her want to be a real mother to me."

"Thank God for Eleanor," Sophia added.

"And you," Jackson added and covered her hand with his own. "I wouldn't be who I am today without you—both of you." He turned toward Harrison. "You were the father I needed when Grayson shut me out. I love you both, and I'm grateful for all you've done for me."

"We love you, too, sweetie. And your mother loved you, even if she wasn't there much," she added. "Are you sure you don't want to give Emily her ring?"

"I think so. I don't want any lingering reminders and questions of the past when I see it on her finger. I want it to be hers and hers only."

"I get that."

"It sounds like everything is coming together for you, son. We're proud of you." Harrison tapped him on the back. "Speaking of things coming together, do you have any new developments for VETS since we last talked?"

"Why don't we fix our plates first?" Sophia suggested. "Then you can tell us all about it."

When seated at the kitchen table Jackson told them about the Orlando investors he secured, his partnership with James Hamlet, and Emily agreeing to run the physical therapy division. He also listed the amenities he wanted to offer and how he envisioned the completed facility.

"You never do anything halfway, do you?" Harrison set down his fork and leaned back in his seat to study him. "I should have told you this when you called last week... I want in."

"You do?"

"I want to help you get VETS started. I have four sons who served and two that struggled when they came home. I want to help."

"Me, too," Sophia chimed in. "I want to volunteer. Put me to work wherever you need."

Touched by their instant support, he nodded. "Okay but be careful what you ask for. There's a lot to be done."

They continued to discuss the tasks needed to get VETS up and running until it was time for him to leave for the airport.

"I can't wait to meet this amazing woman who put that gorgeous smile on your face." Sophia kissed his cheek before he headed out.

"She did more than that. She healed me."

"Well, I love her like a daughter already."

"Go bring her home, and I'll line up some showings for us next week," Harrison promised.

"Speaking of that, there's an old warehouse on Smithfield Avenue. Can you check on the status of that one for me?"

"Smithfield? Really? Jackson, that's not the best—"

"Trust me. There's something about it. I saw it right before I had the idea for my trip. I think it's meant to be a part of this."

"Whatever you need," he agreed with hesitation.

Chapter Nine

☆ ☆ ☆

Genevieve

I f you two don't take a breath, it's going to make me start puking again," Genevieve complained. Grumpy and the third wheel, she waited while Jackson and Emily had an agonizingly long and passionate reunion at the airport terminal.

"Puke all you want," Jackson obliged, without taking his eyes or hands off Emily.

With an audible sigh, Genevieve crossed her arms and busied herself by surveying the busy terminal. She was bored, which meant hyper-focusing on her sick stomach which got more agitated the closer they got to Richmond.

Although, she was ready to get out away from the interesting airport aroma of fried food, burnt coffee, and pleather, she wasn't looking forward to the backseat ride to

Jackson's house. Even worse, she had a week of their disgusting bliss ahead of her. If she hadn't already been nauseous, their perfect love story and gushing happiness was enough to make her stomach churn. She hated herself for being jealous, but it sure would be nice if some of Emily's good fortune would rub off on her.

"Ready to go?" Emily asked, interrupting her self-loathing.

"Good Lord, yes. You're causing a scene."

"Since when are you against making a scene anywhere?"

"Since I started wearing sweatpants and throwing up everything I eat."

"Whatever. Let's go home," Jackson said and kissed Emily's forehead like the dashing prince she saw him to be. *Disgusting.*

Pushing from the wall that had been keeping her upright, Genevieve rolled her eyes and followed the happy couple through the airport and parking lot.

"Did you get a new car?" Emily asked when they were seated inside.

"No. It was my father's. I like it because someone once nicknamed my three friends B.M.W."

"Why?" Genevieve asked, trying desperately to not to ruin the fancy leather seats in his fancy car.

"Barnes, Mason, and Wilson were their last names," he answered, looking at Genevieve through the rearview mirror.

"Clever."

"Are you going to be okay back there?" he asked.

"Just keep driving."

"Message received."

———

Jackson

Within half an hour, he pulled up to the entrance gate at the estate and entered the code on the keypad.

"This is yours?" Genevieve leaned between the two front seats for a better view.

"Yep." He smiled at the shocked looks on their faces. He'd lived there all his life, and it had always been just a house to him. But he could appreciate the remarkable impression the estate made on those seeing it for the first time. He, too, had a similar experience when he returned from Orlando with fresh eyes and a whole heart.

He parked the car beside the little red sports car his father had preferred and turned off the engine. "Want a tour?"

"Absolutely," Emily answered for them and hopped out of the car.

He led the way into the house and down a long hallway, passing his old room where Brian now stayed on weekends, then into the kitchen.

"Mr. Vane! I didn't hear you drive up." Ms. Beasley crossed the room to them. "I see our guests have arrived safely."

"Ms. Beasley, this is Emily and Genevieve." He stepped back to watch her kiss them both loudly on each cheek.

"Such stunning girls you are. Genevieve, my dear. I have just what you need. Come with me."

Confused, Genevieve cut her eyes to Jackson and Emily before following.

"What is she doing?" Emily whispered to him when the others disappeared into a nearby room.

"Must have something to do with her nausea. Ms. Beasley has a homemade cure for every ailment."

"Amazing how she knew."

"She knows and sees everything. It would be good to remember that," he joked.

"Got it. Your home is so beautiful."

"*Our* home," he corrected, placing a hand on her cheek and kissing her softly.

"Our home. I love it already."

"You'll feel better in no time," Ms. Beasley said as she escorted Genevieve back to the kitchen, an arm around her waist.

"Thank you, Ms. B."

"Will Brian be here tomorrow?" Jackson asked her. "I'd love to catch up."

"Far as I know. He's got a lot of mowing to do. It's rained a lot this week." She shook her head.

"A little grass never hurt anything." He shot her a quick grin. She always fussed over every detail with the landscaping since it was the first thing everyone saw when they came to the estate. And since she was responsible, she made sure it was perfect.

"After his chores are done, I'll send him your way. He'll be excited to see you."

"Thank you."

"Do you ladies need help bringing in your luggage?" Ms. Beasley asked.

"I'll take care of it," he told her. "But first I want to show Emily and Genevieve to their rooms."

"Alright. I'll call you when dinner's ready."

He pulled Emily by the hand into the hallway leading to the foyer, and Genevieve followed closely behind.

They peeked inside the living room with the large stone fireplace he knew Emily would adore and sliding glass doors overlooking the lake, his father's office, and front parlor. They climbed the rounded staircase leading to a balcony overlooking the two-story foyer and ornate crystal chandelier. The large area, complete with antique fixtures, oil paintings with ornate gold frames, and a deep red and beige Oriental rug, was fit for a princess making an entrance at a ball. As predicted, Emily swooned.

At the top, Jackson crossed the landing to a guest suite. "This is your room," he told Genevieve. "The bathroom is through that door, and feel free to use the closet or dressers for your things."

"This is gorgeous." Absently, Genevieve walked around the bed, dragging a hand over the carved wood frame and handmade quilt.

He tilted his head toward the door and led Emily across the hall. "And this is our room."

She moved about the room, her eyes taking in the stately room, four-poster bed, and two red and blue plaid chairs Ms. Beasley added to the sitting area near the double windows and fireplace while he'd been away.

"What?" she asked, noticing him watching her from the doorway.

"You take my breath away in any situation, but seeing you here, it's different and so much more." Sitting on the bench at the foot of the bed, he pulled her onto his lap.

"Why?"

"It feels like I've been waiting for this moment my entire life without even knowing it. For so long, I thought I'd never settle down or have a family. Now, it's all I want. You did that to me."

"Good. It's all I want, too." Shifting her legs, she straddled him and kissed him with the same passion she brought out in him. When she looked at him like that, with absolute love in her deep blue eyes, he always came undone.

Just as lost as she, his hands meandered around her waist, his thumbs brushing over her skin under her shirt. That was all it took, he knew, to get her going. Rising to her knees, she pushed him back against the bed.

"I missed you so much," he managed before she covered his mouth with hers.

A knock on the door had Emily spinning off his lap and leaving him wanting.

"Don't stop on my account." Genevieve leaned on the door frame with her arms crossed and a mischievous smirk on her face.

"What can we do for you, Genevieve?" he asked, trying not to let her impeccable timing get to him, but certain parts of him couldn't get on board with that plan.

"I'm famished. Can we eat that delicious food I smell?"

"Sure. Be right there." He turned to Emily after Genevieve headed downstairs. "Who invited her, again?"

"I think she invited herself."

"Sounds about right."

"Come on," Emily pecked him on the shoulder and stood. "Let's go be social."

He groaned in complaint but allowed her to pull him to his feet.

"Don't worry," she said and wrapped her arms around his waist. "We'll continue this later. Better yet, is there a tub in there?" She pointed toward the bathroom. "If you'd like, we can make new bubble bath memories tonight."

"Yes, there is a tub, and I like how you think."

———

After dinner, Ms. Beasley served the special dessert she'd made for Emily and Genevieve's arrival then returned to the kitchen to clean up.

Genevieve took a bite of the chocolate souffle. "Oh, my God. She's incredible." She closed her eyes and moaned.

"Looks like you're feeling better," Emily observed aloud.

"Whatever she gave me earlier destroyed my nausea and brought back my appetite. At this rate, I'm going to gain fifty pounds while I'm here."

"Speaking of that," Jackson ventured. "How long do you plan on staying?"

Genevieve set down her fork on the empty plate. "That depends. Do you know if Ben is dating that witch or someone else?"

"I haven't seen him since Orlando. We've both been busy."

"When are you going to talk to him?" Emily asked her.

"I don't know. I can't just show up at his house. I need to casually run into him or something."

"Seriously?" His patience waned already, and if he didn't get a grip on it, the week would be a long one.

Emily placed her hand on his arm—a gentle reminder to be patient with their stubborn and still healing friend.

"How about a party?" Jackson suggested for an olive branch and to prevent Genevieve from stalling indefinitely.

"A party? Do you have something else to celebrate?" Seemingly liking the idea, Emily leaned her elbows on the table.

"We should celebrate the creation of VETS with friends and potential donors up here."

Emily clapped her hands. "I love it. G, you know Ben will come to a party."

"I'm in, but I'll need to go shopping," she laughed. "I've outgrown all my dresses."

"How about we schedule the party for next Friday evening? That would give us a week to finalize a few things and get ready."

"Perfect. G and I can work with Ms. Beasley on the decorations, food, and invitations while you focus on VETS," Emily told him.

"Deal. We'll get started tomorrow, but tonight…"

"I know, Jackson." Genevieve stood and grabbed her plate. "You want me out of the way. It's fine. I need to unpack, and I'm feeling a little worn out anyway."

"Thanks, G." Emily watched her disappear into the kitchen then twisted in her seat. "So, my love. Ready for that bubble bath?"

———

Emily

On Saturday morning, Emily, Genevieve, and Ms. Beasley huddled around the kitchen table with coffee and homemade croissants to brainstorm party logistics. After discussing several options, they decided to corral everyone in the living room, the largest area of the house. It also had direct access to the back porch and yard for overflow. The bar could be located there as well, and Ms. Beasley volunteered Brian to be the bartender.

"He's had lots of practice," she said, rolling her eyes. "Speak of the devil."

"Hi, Grammie." Brian crossed the kitchen to give his grandmother a kiss on the cheek. "Whatcha doin'?"

"Planning a party." She patted the empty chair next to her, and he sat as instructed. "I'd like you to meet Ms. Robertson and Ms. Olsen."

"Nice to finally meet you," he said with a wide, friendly smile. "Mr. Vane's talked a lot about you."

Emily reached her hand across the table. "Nice to meet you, too, Brian. Please call me Emily."

"I'm Genevieve," she said and waved.

"What's the party for?" he asked his grandmother.

"Mr. Vane wants to celebrate his new project. We've assigned you to bartend."

"Oh, I can definitely do that. When is it?"

"Friday."

"Alright. I'll be there."

"Thank you, dear. We have a lot to do, so get going. Mr. Vane wanted to see you."

"He does?"

Excitement and admiration graced his sweet face, and Emily swooned. After he rushed out the door, she propped her elbows on the table and leaned in. "He's adorable."

"Isn't he?" Ms. Beasley beamed. "And such a good boy. Took too long to figure out what he wanted to study in school, and it set him back at least a year. Parties too much," she added, shaking her head. "But he has a huge heart."

"When does he graduate?"

"Next spring, hopefully, and by the grace of God."

———

Jackson

"You wanted to see me, sir?"

Jackson looked up from his laptop and smiled. "Brian! How are you?" He crossed the room and wrapped Brian in a hug.

"I'm good. I hear you're having a party."

"Yep. Are you able to make it?"

"I am. Grammie's already assigned me to the bar."

"Uh oh." He laughed at Brian's mischievous smirk. "Make sure you serve more than you drink."

"Of course. I don't know what you're worried about."

"Right. Anyway." Jackson sat back in his chair, and Brian took the one opposite him. "I have an offer for you."

"Yeah? What's that?"

"You're finished with your classes now, right?"

Proud of himself, Brian smiled wide. "Mostly. Just need to do an internship. Not a lot of animal-related opportunities in the city. Not farm animals, anyway." His excitement slowly faded. "But I can't graduate without it."

"I know someone that can help, but you'll have to leave Richmond to do it."

"I was hoping not to, but at this point, I'll go anywhere."

"Good to hear, but it's not far. Less than two hours."

"Is it at a farm?" Brian's enthusiasm consumed his body once again. The kid wore his heart on his sleeve, and Jackson adored him for it.

"Yes. The farmer's name is Griff, and I met him during my trip. He has cattle, goats, chickens, horses, and wheat and corn fields. There's also a very smart dog named Rex."

"That's awesome. And he's looking for help?"

"Definitely. He's third generation, so you could learn a lot from him."

"What do I need to do? It sounds perfect." Brian slid to the edge of his seat.

"I talked with him this morning. All you need to do is pack and head to southern Virginia."

"Holy shit." He shot to his feet, then quickly sat back down. "I mean, thank you, Mr. Vane."

"It's my pleasure. You deserve it, and you're going to do great."

"Thanks again. I can't wait to tell Grammie."

"Well, go ahead. She'll be excited, too."

He rose, and Jackson followed, but before Brian reached the door, he stopped and turned. His face now drooping with concern. "Mr. Vane?"

"Yes?"

"Please don't tell Grammie I cursed. She wouldn't approve."

He grinned but quickly tucked it away. This was serious, he knew. "Of course not. That will stay between us."

"Thank you."

Man, he was going to miss that crazy kid.

Chapter Ten

☆ ☆ ☆

Emily

For the next several days, everyone worked together to plan a party fit for both Richmond's most powerful investors and Jackson's friends. It had to be timeless, fun, and professional; have great music and a diverse bar; and based on the number of invitations Emily and Genevieve addressed, enough food to feed all of Richmond.

"I'm heading to town to pick up the rest of the food and decorations we need for the party," Ms. Beasley told her as they finished putting away the breakfast dishes.

"You're a Godsend. We'll help carry everything in when you return. Drive safe."

She gave Emily a hug before grabbing her purse from the counter and rushing toward the garage.

"Was that Ms. B I heard leaving?" Genevieve asked, stumbling into the kitchen, her long, dark hair tossed wildly over her shoulders. And since she was comfortable with her new roommates, she'd yet to change from the skimpy shorts and T-shirt she wore to bed the night before.

"Yes. She's running some errands for the party."

"Damn. I smelled bacon and pancakes and was hoping she was still cooking."

"We ate about half an hour ago but saved you some. Check the warmer over there." She waved to a silver container by the stove.

Genevieve padded across the room and lifted the lid. Leaning over the leftovers, she took a deep breath and sighed. "I love that woman."

Laughing, Emily sat at the island with her coffee mug in hand. "Sleep well?"

"Like a baby." She winked over her shoulder before searching the cabinets for a plate. "Where's Jackson?"

"He's working in his office."

"Is he excited for the party?"

"I think so. You know he doesn't show a lot of emotion."

"True, but there's a lot riding on it."

"It's going to be great. I'm not worried."

"That's surprising. You over worry about everything, and we've never planned a party this elaborate or important. Oh! There are." Genevieve clapped her hands together then selected a plate from the stack. She piled on enough pancakes and bacon to feed two before joining Emily at the island.

"This time I'm not."

"Good. How'd you sleep in your new fancy bed?" Genevieve teased, picking up the syrup and pouring it on thick.

"Who said we did any sleeping?"

"Nice. Can you believe this house?"

"No. I really can't. He told me a little about it, but there are no words to adequately describe it."

"How wealthy *is* he, really?" she asked with a mouth full of pancakes.

"I have no idea, but he said his father left him everything, including his business, but he sold it. All he told me was that we had enough money to pay our bills while we concentrated on VETS."

"I would say he has more than that. There's live-in staff, Em."

"I know. It's crazy."

"And thank God for Ms. B." Genevieve licked her fingers before leaning over the counter to grab the pitcher of fresh-squeezed orange juice and a glass. "Her cooking is better than going to a restaurant."

"How would you know? You ate that pancake so fast I doubt you tasted it."

"I have heightened senses now."

"Right. I forgot."

Later, as Genevieve changed upstairs, Emily cleaned the kitchen, then checked on Jackson. For a moment, she stood in the doorway and watched while he worked.

He looked out of place with his long hair and T-shirt, sitting at the formal walnut desk. The floor-to-ceiling matching bookcases on the left wall were filled with books, vases, and small statues, but no photos. The red leather chairs in front of the windows looked as though they belonged in a 1950's smoking room rather than an office of her sweet, cinnamon roll of a boyfriend. He obviously hadn't changed any of the decorations since his father died, and the stuffy room didn't match his personality.

"You're very sexy when you work," she said, startling him. His eyes met hers, and she smiled.

"Good to know. Everything okay?"

"Of course." She stepped into the room and ran her hand over a bookshelf. "G and I are going for a walk. I'm dying to check out the grounds."

"Great. How's she feeling today?"

"Better, but not as good as I do after last night." She sat on his lap and draped an arm around his neck.

"I love having you here, and it's even better knowing that you're here to stay." He cupped her face with his hands and kissed her gently at first. When her lips begged for more, he gave it willingly.

"Any chance you two could control yourselves in my presence?" Genevieve said from the door. "It's making me nauseous again."

"We need to get her a bell," he whispered and dropped his forehead to Emily's shoulder.

"G, your timing is unreal." She gave Jackson a loud kiss on the forehead and stood. "Ready to go?"

"Why do you think I'm here wearing sneakers and not downing more pancakes?"

"I want to grab my coffee from the kitchen first. Should I bring you those pancakes?" she teased with a sly grin.

"Don't tempt me."

Before Emily could cross the foyer, a knock on the door surprised them. Genevieve opened it to reveal a woman with big brown eyes and matching hair that brushed the tops of her bare shoulders.

"Can I help you?" Genevieve gawked at the woman as she stood speechless on the stoop, gawking back at her.

"I'm here to see Jackson. I heard he was home from his trip." She tilted her head and frowned, noticing Emily behind Genevieve. "I'm sorry. Who are you?"

"I was going to ask you the same thing," Genevieve countered, her voice laced with suspicion. The woman's low-cut tank, tight miniskirt, and sexy heels accentuated every asset with the sole purpose of grabbing attention—apparently, Jackson's.

"My name is Avery. I'm a friend of Jackson's. Is he here?"

Emily stepped up. "Avery Mason?"

"Yeah." Suspicion had her drawing out every syllable as she accepted Emily's outstretched hand.

"It's so nice to meet you."

"You know who she is?" Genevieve asked, pointing at Avery.

"Yes. I'll explain later," she whispered. "Avery, please come in. I was hoping for the opportunity to thank you for what you did for Jackson."

Too stunned to respond, Avery stepped inside.

"Jackson's in his office. I can let him know—"

"I'm sorry, but who are you two to Jackson?" Avery finally asked.

"Not sure it's any of your business," Genevieve informed her with a touch of her usual sass, "but Emily is Jackson's girlfriend, and I'm her best friend."

"Girlfriend?"

"Yes. And why are *you* here?"

"I…"

"I heard voices, what's—" Jackson entered the foyer and froze when he saw the three women. "Avery?"

"Hi, Jackson." Her eyes met his and lingered, as all do, but this was different. While Avery appreciated the view like all the rest, hers came with longing and ache. "I heard you were back in town and…" She glanced at Emily and Genevieve watching them. "Can we—"

"We were about to leave for our walk," Emily announced. "We'll get out of your way and let you two catch up." She grabbed Genevieve's arm, pulled her outside, and closed the door behind them.

"You were way more understanding than I would have been," Genevieve said as they stepped off the porch and into the grass. "That woman wanted something from Jackson, and it wasn't to talk. Who was she?"

"She's Will's cousin, his first physical therapist, and his ex-girlfriend."

"I knew it. She still loves him, you know."

"Yeah. I saw it."

"And you're okay with them being alone?" She watched Emily closely.

"It doesn't matter how she feels." If the incident with Lucas taught her anything, it was that nothing and no one can alter what she and Jackson share. "He loves me, and I trust him."

"First Sydney and now Avery. You're a bigger person than me. I wanted to drop kick her, and I know nothing about her."

Emily giggled. "Guess it's a good thing I'm here. But I can't fault her for trying. He would be hard to get over. I feel sorry for her."

"You do? Why?"

"Her eyes said it all. She's loved him for a long time, probably always will, and she'll never have him."

———

Jackson

Jackson led Avery to his office and offered her a seat by the windows. "How have you been?"

"Okay. I followed some of your journey on social media. Looks like you accomplished all you set out to do."

"I did. Have you seen Eleanor since she moved back?"

"She called me after she closed on the house. I helped them unpack on my days off."

"That was nice of you." Damn, this was awkward. He hadn't seen her since his father's funeral and their conversation ended with him hurting her again. He expected her to never speak to him again.

"I heard about what you're doing for Sydney."

"Will would have done the same for me."

"Yes, he would."

He took a deep breath, glancing at Emily and Genevieve as they crossed by the window, before coming back to her. "Avery, why didn't you tell me Sydney was pregnant?"

She looked down at her trembling hands. "Fear."

"Of what?"

"Jackson, I'm sorry."

"Why? What did you do?"

"I was insecure about our relationship, and she's stunning and fun and has all the qualities guys easily fall for. And she has a piece of Will. I was afraid of losing you to her."

He shot to his feet and stalked to the window before he said something he might regret. "You should have told me."

"But you would have gone to her immediately, and—"

"Yes. I would have. She needed me and maybe I needed her. We could have helped each other grieve."

"What about what I needed, Jackson. Did that ever matter to you?"

He spun around with a fire burning in his gut to match what he saw in her. "It was all that mattered. It mattered so much that I set aside doing what was right for too long."

"And what was that Jackson? Breaking up with me? Was that the right thing to do?"

"Neither of us wanted to face it, but yes." He stood firm until a tear slid down her cheek. A familiar guilt had him stepping around the chair to sit across from her. "Avery, I didn't want to hurt you, but it was the only way to get you to move on. Please tell me you've done that."

She gave him a noncommittal and unconvincing nod.

"Where did you and Emily meet?"

"In Myrtle Beach during one of my stops."

"Is that where she's from?"

"No. She lived in Savannah."

"Lived?"

"She's moved in."

"Wow. That was fast."

"Avery, I don't—"

"I'm happy for you." She met his gaze and noticed his mistrust in the declaration. "I mean it. Of course, I wished things could have worked out differently between us. I've loved you for as long as I can remember, but I'm glad you're happy. I assume you're happy."

"I am."

She sighed before standing and he did the same. "I'm sure you're busy, so…" She shoved her hands into her back pockets but didn't move.

"Avery, why are you here?"

She shrugged. "I don't know. I just had to see you."

"Does Michael know you're here?"

"What?"

"Before we left, Ben mentioned that you were seeing him."

"I don't care if he knows where I am." Resentment and hurt flashed across her face. "We broke up about a month ago."

"I'm sorry."

"Thanks, but he proved to be the person you thought he was at the gala."

Something he couldn't read flashed in her eyes, causing his blood pressure to spike. At the gala, Michael had been annoyingly assertive in his pursuit of Avery and an arrogant ass when Jackson challenged him. There were no redeeming qualities in that sorry excuse for a man, and he took advantage of Avery's heartache to slither closer. Once he had her, the real Michael undoubtedly showed his ugly face. "He didn't hurt you, did he?"

Her gaze fell to the rug but not before he caught a glimmer of tears forming. "No. Not physically, anyway. He just cheated on me multiple times, and he's a master manipulator, but you already know that."

"You have terrible taste in men," he said in hopes of lightening the somber mood now suffocating the room.

"I really do."

A brief silence lingered between them. "Have you seen Ben since we got back?"

"No. Is everything okay with him?"

"I'm not sure. I haven't seen him either."

"That doesn't sound good."

"It's a long story. I'm having a party here on Friday. If you don't see him before then, you should—"

She squinted at him and tilted her head. "I thought stuffy dinner parties were not your style."

"Still aren't. Plus, this one won't be stuffy if I have anything to say about it, and I have something to celebrate."

"Oh?" Her smile quickly faded.

"I'm starting a non-profit for veterans and want to celebrate with those who will help make it possible. You should come. Without you and Will, VETS would not exist."

"VETS?"

"That's the name of the non-profit. It's short for Veteran Exercise and Therapy Services. I want to help those who are suffering from injuries or PTSD."

"Jackson, that's wonderful."

"So, you'll come?"

"I'll think about it."

He nodded, understanding her hesitation. "If you're interested, I'd love for you to be a part of the physical therapy division. Emily is heading it up and will be looking for volunteers."

"She's a physical therapist, too?"

"Yes." When she smirked, he tossed up his hands. "I know. Apparently, I have a type." Together they laughed, and it was comfortable—like it used to be before a relationship that never should have happened complicated everything.

"This is nice," Avery said, matching his thoughts.

"It is. I hope we can be friends again someday."

"Me too. Someday."

He nodded, pretending he didn't see love still lingering in her eyes. "I'll see you on Friday, then."

———

Genevieve

While relaxing in the shade by the lake, Genevieve had checked out of her conversation with Emily and sunk into her thoughts.

"What are you thinking about?" Emily asked.

"The usual."

"Does the usual happen to be Ben?"

"What if he brings a date? What if he hadn't given me a second thought since he got back? What if he wants to marry me after he learns about the baby?"

"Whoa! One question at a time. First of all, since when did you ever care about another woman when you see a man you want? Second, I bet he's thought about you every second of the day. You're pretty unforgettable. Third, I'm beyond confused by that last question."

She sighed. "What if he's moved on and happy but feels obligated to marry me because of the baby? I don't want him to settle and be all honorable and shit. I want him to want us."

"G, being with you would not be settling, but say he does want to step up. You don't have to say yes. Let me ask you this: What if he wants to marry you because of the baby *and* because he loves you?"

Genevieve fell back to lie on the grass, her hands resting on her growing belly. "I never imagined myself married."

"Or being a mother, I bet. Things have changed. It's time you start thinking about what you want in this new reality."

Lifting her eyes to the blue skies above, Genevieve flipped through the cards she'd been dealt in her mind. She thought she knew what she wanted when she went to Richmond, but it was so like her to jump in without thinking it through first. What if he did want to marry her? Or worse yet, what if he wanted nothing to do with raising their baby? A tear escaped before she could stop it, and she sat up quickly.

"What is it?" Emily asked, following her.

"I love him, and it will crush me if he says he doesn't want me... Doesn't want us."

Proud of her, Emily smiled sweetly. "Do you realize that the old Genevieve would have run away before ever admitting that?"

"I know, and along with that, comes me imagining all the things he could have been doing since I last saw him. The old Ben resurging with vengeance and happy to be free again."

"What do you mean?"

"I just don't want to hear he's completely over me."

"It's only been a week, and there's zero chance of that happening."

"I want to believe you, but—"

"No buts. Believe it until you hear otherwise. Now, let's go shopping and find a dress that will render him speechless."

"Ah. Yes. The perfect therapy."

Chapter Eleven

✶ ✶ ✶

Jackson

"Have you seen my brush?" Emily asked him while blindly searching through the bathroom drawers and cabinets. "How could I lose something that never leaves this room?"

He leaned against the door frame and watched the spectacle. "It's probably right where you left it."

"I've looked everywhere. It's not here."

"Did you look in the top drawer?"

Without a glance his way or pausing, she said, "Multiple times."

"Do it again."

She moved to the drawer he mentioned, and her shoulder's dropped on a sigh as she grabbed the brush. "It's mocking me."

"No. You were just too nervous to see straight." He crossed the room and took her in his arms. "She's going to love you, no matter what your hair looks like."

"This is a big day. I'm meeting the famous Eleanor. I want it to go well." Her body soon melted against his as she took comfort in his arms, her head dropping to his shoulder.

"It's impossible for it to go any other way. I love you, and she will, too."

"Thank you." She leaned back and waited for a kiss.

He gave her what she requested but didn't linger as he normally would. "Here." Stepping back, he pulled the stool out from under the vanity and motioned for her to sit.

"What for? I need to finish getting ready."

"You look beautiful."

"My hair is still wet."

"Sit."

She let out a long breath and plopped onto the cushioned stool. "What are you doing?" she asked when he opened another drawer.

He gently slid the brush from her hands and collected the hairdryer. "Helping you get ready."

Melting, she watched him through the mirror. When her hair was dry, he set the items on the counter then pulled her hair back, running his fingers lightly through it.

"Jackson…"

"Shhh. Just relax." His hands massaged her shoulders before moving up her neck and scalp. "Think about what makes you happy. Banana splits," he whispered, making her giggle. "Sunsets, beaches, porch swings, baths."

"Mmm. You."

"Goes without saying."

"This may be sexier than when you braided my hair," she told him, meeting his gaze in the mirror. He responded with a wink without missing a stroke.

Collecting her hair, he draped it over one shoulder and kissed the newly exposed skin on the other side. "Ready?"

"For more of that? Yes, please."

"She's here."

"What?!" She shot up, knocking over the stool, and he had to jump to the side to avoid it hitting his shins. "How do you know?"

"You didn't hear her? Her voice travels like a—"

"Of course not. Someone was seducing me."

He wrapped an arm around her waist and pulled her lips to his until her nerves resettled. She'd done that for him more times than he could count. He was happy to return the favor. "Finish up. We'll go down together."

Minutes later, they were standing together at the bottom of the stairs while Emily took a moment to breathe.

"It's just Eleanor," he said, attempting to set her at ease.

Her head snapped to him. "I can't believe that sentence came out of that gorgeous mouth of yours."

"Come on." He led her to the kitchen where Eleanor and Ms. Beasley could be heard in an animated conversation about their latest recipe finds.

"Hi, Eleanor," he greeted when they entered, realizing his hand had gone numb from Emily squeezing it.

Eleanor spun around and rose out of her seat, her hands immediately springing to her lips. "Is this—" Tears sparkled in her eyes as she crossed the room.

"Eleanor, I'd like you to meet Emily."

She took Emily's hands and searched her face. "You, my dear, are God's beautiful answer to my prayers. I will be eternally grateful for you."

Sobs burst out of Emily's chest when Eleanor pulled her into an embrace and the pair cried together. Ms. Beasley joined him as they watched the emotional moment, and he draped an arm over her shoulders.

"What a special moment," Ms. Beasley said, dabbing at her own tears with a napkin.

"As expected."

Eleanor pulled back and framed Emily's face with her hands. "Now, it's time we celebrate. Jackson, where's the wine?"

"Coming right up."

———

By the time dinner was served, Genevieve had joined them, and the entertaining stories continued to roll one after the other.

"Those two are hilarious," Genevieve said when Eleanor left to help Ms. Beasley gather dessert.

"Oh, yeah. Especially when there's wine. See—" He leaned on the table and patted Emily's hand. "I told you there was nothing to worry about."

"She worries about everything," Genevieve complained.

"I know, but this shouldn't have been one of those times."

"Couldn't help it. She's so special to you and—"

"So are you."

Touched, she rose off her seat to press a kiss to his lips.

"Will you two give it a rest until I've had my dessert?" Genevieve's eyes rolled, her usual reaction. "I don't want to lose my appetite before the best course."

"Deal with it." Emily leaned in for another taste but stopped when his phone rang. "Ugh. Better check that in case it's something to do with VETS."

He gave her a peck then reached into his pocket. "That's odd."

"Who is it?"

"It's Olan. I didn't expect to hear from him until after the party."

"Answer it. Must be important."

After stepping into the hallway, he answered the call. "Olan, is everything okay?"

"It's me."

"Callie? What's wrong?" She was crying, making it hard to understand her. "Sweetheart, what's the matter?"

"It's Grandpa. He won't wake up."

"What?" He jogged to the office.

"He's on the floor and won't open his eyes."

"Callie, I need to you listen to me. Go to Aunt Sara's house next door and have her come over. She knows CPR. Go quick."

"Okay."

While he waited, he opened his laptop, searched for the local police department's number and called it, using the house phone. He gave the dispatcher Olan's address and checked his watch. They were running out of time.

"Sara's here," Callie said between heavy breaths.

"Good. Now listen to me. Stay outside and wait for the ambulance. They will be there soon."

"Okay. I'm scared."

"Me, too, sweetheart. Can you tell me what happened?"

He paced while Callie recounted finding Olan on the kitchen floor. "I heard a noise like he dropped a pot or something and went to help."

"You're a good girl. Has he been sick or tired lately?"

"He's always tired."

"Has he been complaining of any pains?"

"I don't know." Callie began to cry harder. "I hear it."

"Hear what? The ambulance?"

"Yes."

"Good. Now, do what they say and stay outside while they help your grandpa. Okay? Promise me you won't go inside."

"I promise."

He heard her talking to the paramedics and the door closing behind them.

"Is everything alright?" Emily asked, appearing in the doorway, then rushing to his side when she noticed his worried expression.

"Something's happened to Olan. I have Callie on the phone."

"Oh, no. Is she okay?"

"Yeah. The ambulance just got there."

They switched the call to video to distract Callie from what was going on inside the house. She showed them the new flowers Olan planted, her big girl bike, and the new tire swing in the back yard. After climbing inside the tire, she held the phone out and pushed it into motion.

"Whoa! You're making me dizzy," he joked and laughed along with her until Sara joined them.

"Hi, Jackson." She took the phone from Callie and stepped away.

"How is he?"

"Alive. Another minute longer and we wouldn't have been able to get his heart going again."

"Oh, thank God." He leaned against Emily for support and let the tension melt from his body. It had been a grueling twenty minutes. "What happened?"

"Heart attack, it appears. He's been stressed lately with his son getting out of jail and threatening to sue for custody."

"Why would Chris do that? She's happy and safe with Olan."

"Who knows why he does anything? He's messed up and using again already. Oh. Callie wants to talk to you."

"Hi, sweetie," he greeted when she reappeared on the screen.

"Who's going to take care of me? I don't want to go back to live with Rachel."

Tears reflected the sun in her big blue eyes, and it broke his heart.

"That will never happen. I promise."

"Pinky swear?"

"I pinky swear promise."

She nodded, blew a kiss into the phone then handed it back to Sara.

"Jackson, you can't guarantee that."

"Watch me."

"Well, I hope you find a way, but she can stay with me until Olan's feeling better."

"Talk to him, Sara. As soon as he's able, he needs to plan for her, legally, if something happens to him. He has my attorney at his disposal."

"I will. Thank you, Jackson."

Hanging up, he tossed the phone on the nearby chair and collapsed into Emily's arms, the bottled tension weighing him down.

"Is there something else we can do?" she asked.

"I don't know. But as soon as he can have visitors, I want to go see him."

"You should. I'll go with you."

Chapter Twelve

★ ★ ★

Emily

Two hours before guests were due to arrive on Friday evening, Emily and Genevieve went upstairs to get ready. It had been a long day, and Emily was excited for a little pampering.

She and Jackson spent the morning with Callie and Olan at the hospital. After lunch, while Jackson talked with Olan, she took Callie to the nearby park. She swung, played tag, and helped her climb for over an hour. While she had a great time acting like a kid again and getting to know Callie better, she returned to Richmond sore and exhausted.

But she couldn't ignore the final party preparations. After mustering some energy to check all last-minute tasks off the to-do list, she got ready with Genevieve in the guest bedroom to add a little mystery to her grand entrance.

She couldn't wait to descend those beautiful stairs like Cinderella at the ball in the white cocktail dress she bought earlier in the week. She'd move in slow motion, allowing Jackson to take in the complete picture of her in all her sparkling glory. A laugh snorted out as she thought about it. *All her glory. Ha!*

"What's so funny?" Genevieve asked, eyeing her from across the room.

"Oh, you know me. Just over-romanticizing."

"What else is new?"

"Isn't this fun?" she asked, bouncing over to Genevieve and dropping to sit on the edge of the bed.

"What?"

"This. We haven't hung out like this since Myrtle Beach. I've missed it."

"Me too, but I'd be able to enjoy it more if I didn't want to vomit every time I thought about going downstairs."

"You've got this. Ben is going to be beside himself when he sees you."

Genevieve puffed out her skepticism.

"Are we ready?" she asked, knowing Jackson was already downstairs waiting for her. She could hear him talking with Ms. Beasley and Brian in the foyer.

"You are. Go make your Cinderella entrance, and I'll be down in a minute."

"How did you—"

"Like you said, I know you, and I know you've been wanting to do it since you saw those stupid stairs."

"True, but you better be right behind me."

"Yeah, yeah."

Emily started toward the door, then returned when she noticed Genevieve had gone pale. "Are you sure you're doing okay?"

"No." She let out a shaky laugh. "But I will be. I just need a little more time to build up my courage."

She placed her hands on Genevieve's shoulders and looked at her through the mirror. "You have a plan, you know what you want to say, and you are the strongest person I know. You can do this."

"I love you. Now, go. Your handsome prince is waiting."

She let out a little squeal, the exciting evening to come refueling her energy. "See you down there."

At the top of the stairs, Emily's eyes locked on Jackson as she slowly started her descent. He turned instantly, feeling their connection first. His gaze fell on her and the power it had over her made her knees waver. Resting a hand on the rail to steady herself, she basked in the way he watched her every step, his eyes roaming over her and saying more than words ever could, boosting her confidence.

On the last step, he placed a hand on her bare back, leaning in to kiss her cheek. "You're stunning."

"You don't look so bad yourself, soldier." With her hand in his, she turned to Ms. Beasley and Brian. "The house looks amazing. Thank you both so much for your help this week. Is there anything left to do?"

"Everything is under control, Ms. Robertson. Don't worry about a thing. Enjoy tonight." Ms. Beasley pushed

Brian toward the kitchen, giving the happy couple some privacy before the guests arrived.

Almost eye level with Jackson in her strappy, silver heels, Emily draped her arms over his shoulders and enjoyed the view. His tailored, dark blue suit and long hair, silky smooth and pulled back, accentuated his eyes and she couldn't take hers off him.

"Your beauty never ceases to amaze me," he began, "but tonight, I think my jaw hit the floor."

"Isn't that the purpose of a dress like this?" A giggle bubbled up, but it fizzled when he pressed his lips to her shoulder.

"Another mission accomplished." He leaned in for a kiss and swore when the doorbell sounded through the foyer, ruining the moment.

She giggled. "It's time. I'm so proud of you."

———

Soon after the first guests arrived, the non-stop flow of guests jammed the house with an excitement that seemed to pulse through every room. Most of the early arrivals were Jackson's friends, more interested in Emily than the party. It was the glimpse into his world she'd been hoping for.

While he entertained current and potential donors, she chatted with Harrison and Sophia.

"Have you met the other woman in Jackson's life yet?" Harrison asked with a sly grin.

Emily's thoughts jumped immediately to Sydney and Avery, but she hesitated to answer. "I'm not sure. I've met so many people. To whom are you referring?"

"Eleanor, of course."

"Oh, yes. She came for dinner a few nights ago."

Over Harrison's shoulder, she saw Ben enter the room and realized with concern that Genevieve had yet to make an appearance. Excusing herself, she raised a hand, and called for him over the music and conversations. His eyes found her thought the crowd and he rushed closer, lifting her off her feet with a tight squeeze.

"It's great to see you," she began, "but I also want to punch you in the nose."

"Now, Emily. Would you really want to mess up this face? It's almost as perfect as that dress you're wearing." He clicked his tongue and let his eyes wander over her. "Your beauty is making my heart stutter."

"Flattery will not get you off the hook. I'm still furious with you."

Shoving his hands in his pocket, he smiled sweetly. "Come on. You know you can't stay mad at me for long."

Yielding, her disapproving glare softened. "You're right. You're too frustratingly adorable. How've you been?"

"Busy. I've been setting up my photography studio. Jackson loaned me his attorney, so it's going quicker than if I was doing it on my own."

"That's great. Have any clients lined up yet?"

"Actually, yes. I have a couple clients in Orlando ready to sign when everything's finalized." He grabbed a bottle of champagne from a tray when Ms. Beasley passed by and winked at her. She scowled, then flashed him a playful smile.

"One of those clients doesn't happen to be the Mayor's Office, does it?"

"Emily." He glared down his nose with a sly smile. "What are you really asking me?"

"Fine." She huffed. If he wanted to aggravate her by evading every question it was working. "Are you seeing Samantha?"

"How would I do that? She lives in Florida."

"Ben, you're not answering—"

"Buddy!" he yelled over Emily when he saw Jackson heading their way and swallowed him in a hug.

While they caught up, she slipped away. In the hallway, she found Ms. Beasley with a fresh tray of full champagne flutes. "Have you seen Genevieve?"

She tipped her head toward the kitchen behind her.

"Thanks." Hurrying in that direction, she entered and joined Genevieve at the island. An unopened can of ginger ale and a wine glass sat on the counter in front of her. "Why are you hiding in here?"

"I'm not hiding."

"The hell you aren't. He's here."

"I know."

Emily leaned her elbows on the cool stone. "I asked him if he was seeing Samantha."

"And?"

Instead of answering, she reached across the counter for the opened champagne bottle and lifted it to her lips. She drank deep then slouched with a hand on her belly. "I can't breathe in this damn dress." Sucking in some air, she let it out, then took another long pull from the bottle. "That one was for you."

"You ignored my question."

Taking a page from Ben's book, she said, "I don't know what you're talking about," and patted Genevieve on the arm. "Just kidding. He was being very mysterious, but I don't think so. Come on. We worked hard for this party, and it's time to enjoy it."

With a groan, Genevieve slid off the stool and wiggled the tight yellow dress back into place around her hips. "How do I look?"

"Like a woman on a mission."

"Good. I was afraid you were going to say I look how I feel."

"How's that?"

"Like shit."

"Not possible."

———

Genevieve

The friends strolled arm-in-arm into the living room, where the celebration was in full swing, and Emily introduced her to the people she'd met so far. Although Genevieve attempted to participate in the conversations, she couldn't stop herself from surveying the room for Ben. She wanted to stay one step ahead of him and in control of the situation, but how could she do that when she had no idea where he was.

As her nerves revved, wondering when he'd show up and how she'd feel seeing him again, he walked through the patio doors. Something seemed to lasso her lungs and pull them out of her body because she couldn't breathe.

The gray suit he wore contrasted against his light brown hair and tan skin. He looked more handsome than she'd ever seen him, happy and carefree. Her stomach twisted into knots.

He stopped by the bar beside the back door and talked with Brian. The sweet sound of his laughter hovered over the music and conversations happening around her as he accepted the beer bottle Brian handed him. He turned and his relaxed smile dropped into a scowl at the first sight of her, confirming her fears. She suddenly second-guessed her reasons for going to Richmond. She had no business being there. His expression said it all.

———

Ben

The moment he laid eyes on her, his muscles hardened and burned. He blinked hard and tried to focus on the vision in yellow across the room. The tight dress framed the body he'd dreamed about, ached for. She watched him as though they were the only two people in the room, rays of sunshine radiating out from around her.

He must be hallucinating. She couldn't possibly be there in the flesh, not after all that had happened between them. The dreams that haunted him after Savannah began replaying in his mind. *Not again.* He sighed, frustrated that after all he'd done to keep her in the past, his mind had yet to follow his lead.

He lifted the bottle to his lips, pausing when she moved. Her voice sailed across the room like an arrow through his chest. With the base of his palm, he rubbed the soreness there. *What the hell?* Needing to confirm his sanity, he set the bottle on the bar and spun around. She was gone. Rising to his toes, he searched over the clusters of guests and came up empty.

"Shit." He pushed a hand through his hair and laughed. "I'm going crazy."

"Excuse me?"

"Sorry," he said. "Can I have a beer?"

"You mean the one I just gave you?" He pointed to the full bottle sitting on the counter.

"Guess so. Thanks." Draining half the contents, he decided it was time to get back to the basics. He immersed himself in the crowd and socialized as he used to, but it wasn't long before the busy room began to suffocate him. Reconciling the person he'd been before and after Genevieve didn't make any sense, especially after seeing her—real or not.

He stepped outside for a shot of oxygen, closing his eyes when a breeze hit his flushed face.

"Hi there, handsome," a woman said from beyond the shadows, and he jolted.

He squinted through the darkness at the feminine shape in a light-colored dress, heading his way. As his lungs closed again, he choked out, "Genevieve?"

"Nope. It's me," Avery announced, gliding into the light.

"Oh. Hi, Avery. You scared me." He slapped a hand over his chest, grateful to be breathing again. "I thought you were... Never mind."

"Genevieve? Are you two seeing each other?"

"Yes. I mean, no. I mean, do you know her?"

"We've met," she answered flatly.

"How?"

"What do you mean, how? I stopped by the other day to see—"

"She's here?" Maybe he wasn't crazy after all, but shit. If she was there, what would he say to her? Did she even want to talk to him, or was that why she avoided him earlier? Damn, she looked so gorgeous and—

Avery rested a hand on his arm. "You're acting really weird. It's unlike you to be uncomfortable at a party with it being your natural habitat and all." She laughed at the joke, but he didn't join in. "What's going on?"

"I don't know. I saw her inside, but she disappeared."

"Disappeared? She's not a ghost, Ben."

With the way her face haunted his dreams, he wasn't so sure about that. Running his fingers through his hair again, he grabbed a fist full then dropped his arm in frustration.

"What's up with you? Everything about you is...off." She stepped closer and looked him over.

"I just need some air." And to remember who he was. He sat on the patio couch and rested his elbows on his knees.

"Do you want to talk about it?"

"I don't think so, but thanks."

"Are you sure? You look like you could use a friend, and so could I. I'm going crazy roaming around this party by myself." She sighed and circled a fingertip around the top of her wine glass. "Jackson's moved on. It's miserable seeing him so happy. I mean, I'm happy he's happy, but he still makes my insides boil. It all sucks. It sucks that every other man I meet is such a prolific asshole. And if I'm being honest, I think I subconsciously seek out Jackson's complete opposite. All I want is to be loved. Why is that so—"

"I need to find Emily." Shooting off the couch, Ben rushed back inside.

"Great talk," she called after him, but he paid her no mind.

"I need to talk to you," he blurted, interrupting Emily's conversation and pulling her by the hand into the hallway.

"Ben. I was in the middle of—"

"Where is she?"

"What? Who? You're sweating."

He grabbed her arms and leaned down to meet her gaze squarely. "Who else? I know she's in this house. Where is she?"

"Are you feeling all right? Maybe you should sit down."

"Just answer my question, Emily." He didn't feel the least bit sorry for his sharp tone. If he didn't find Genevieve soon, he might scream, interrupting more than just conversations in this suffocating house.

"She stepped away when I was talking. I don't know where she went."

The words echoed in his ears, and he stumbled backward, his eyes glossing over and blurring his surroundings. Until Emily confirmed it, he hadn't allowed himself to fully believe she was there. Hadn't truly trusted his eyes or ears.

"Ben, are you—" She stopped when the music went silent mid-song, and Jackson addressed the crowd, gathering everyone together for an announcement. "I'm sorry. I have to go." She rushed back to the main room.

The commotion snapped his thoughts back into place. Genevieve was there. He hadn't been seeing things. Now, why in the hell was she avoiding him. The only logical answer: she wasn't there for him. She'd come to support Emily and Jackson.

He slammed his hand against the wall, frustration and confusion flaring inside him, then took off for the office. Jackson kept brandy in the sitting area, and a strong drink, or several, was precisely what he needed to settle his short-circuiting nerves. Beer just wasn't getting it done.

When he reached the edge of the staircase, he hadn't noticed Ms. Beasley coming around the corner and almost knocked over the large tray of champagne glasses she carried.

"Benjamin, you scared me!"

"I'm sorry, Ms. B." He held on to the tray until the glasses stopped wobbling.

"Where are you going? Mr. Vane is about to make a special announcement."

"I needed a stronger drink and a quiet place to think for a bit."

"You want to be by yourself and think? Are you not enjoying the party?"

"I was, and I'll be right back. I promise." Stepping to the side, he allowed Ms. Beasley to pass then called after her. She stopped, careful not to jar the tray, and looked over her shoulder. "Have you seen Genevieve?"

"No, but I've been busy." When he frowned, she continued, "Feel free to look around after you've done your thinking."

Irritated by his weakness, he paced in front of the glossy wooden doors of Jackson's office. What in the hell was he doing? If Genevieve wanted to see him, she wouldn't be avoiding him. And why should he care? She'd made it very clear in Orlando that she wanted nothing to do with him.

What happened to moving on and getting his life back? Why wasn't he enjoying a hot party, which he remembered from experience, was the best way to feel alive? He should be having fun that night, not wandering around alone, worrying about seeing the woman he was unsuccessfully trying to forget. A woman that rejected him repeatedly and shattered his heart. The woman that would ruin all attempts to ever enjoy sex again. A woman he still loved.

"Fuck me."

Seizing both doorknobs, he pushed open the double doors with more force than needed and flipped on the light. His eyes zeroed in on the decanter sitting where he knew it would be and stalked to the small table. With a groan, he yanked out the crystal stopper, filled a glass to the top, and took a long sip. The smooth liquid coated his scratchy throat as he'd hoped. Now, if only it would switch off the electric current flowing through his veins.

Chapter Thirteen

★ ★ ★

Ben

W hat's got you so frazzled?" someone asked behind him. Why did this keep happening to him that night? He spun around, fumbling the glass and spilling brandy over his hand when his eyes landed on Genevieve. The real one.

"Shit!" Tossing the dripping glass onto the table, he shook his hand and looked around for something to wipe up the flustered mess he'd made.

"I'll get a towel."

Thankfully, she rushed out of the room before he could form anything resembling a response. He could use this time to gather enough control to face her like a man, if she hadn't melted his brain in that dress. She looked so beautiful, glowing in yellow, her hair down and wavy. He loved how her thick mane curled when she left it natural. That was how he liked her best. No makeup or walls to hide behind. Just Genevieve.

"Here," she said, re-entering the room and handing him the towel without looking into his eyes.

"Thank you." Carefully, he reached for the towel and his fingers brushed against hers, sending another wave of shock up his arm. She recoiled, as he'd come to expect, and it gave him courage to demand the answers and closure he needed to finally move forward.

"How are you?" she asked and added more distance between them.

"It's weird being back, but I'm good." He watched her while drying his hand and analyzed every movement, glance, breath. "How have you been?"

"I'm okay."

"You look stunning tonight." He couldn't help himself, and he was a fool.

She tossed him a tight-lipped grin and hooked her hair behind an ear. "Thanks."

"I've always loved you in yellow."

"I know." She looked down at her trembling hands, then back up at him. "It's your favorite color."

"You're the only person I've ever told that to."

"Ben, I—"

"Why are you in here and not enjoying the party?"

"I could ask you the same thing." When he scowled, already weary of her evading, she continued. "To be honest, it hurt more than I expected it would. So, I came in here to think."

"What hurt?"

"Seeing you."

"It hurt to see me?" he asked, too stunned to think though his response first.

"Yes."

"Why?"

"When you walked into the room, you looked so happy. Like you'd moved on. But then you saw me, and all that joy and excitement left your face. I saw only pain." She turned her back to him and strolled to the bookcase. "I know I did that to you."

"Genevieve."

"I'm sorry I hurt you." She began to pace, showcasing her nerves. "I'm sorry I pushed you past your limits."

"You were dealing with a lot."

"It's no excuse. You were there for me, and I treated you like shit."

He couldn't argue with that but hearing her say it, he forgave her instantly.

"Can I ask you something?"

"Sure."

"I know I drove you to it, and I don't blame you if you did…" She paused and fidgeted with her fingernails.

"You want to know if I slept with Samantha."

Surprised, her gaze whipped to his, and she nodded.

"I didn't." He watched her chest slowly deflate with a long exhale and knew it was the answer she'd hoped for. But she needed to hear everything. "I wanted to, though."

She closed her eyes before meeting his gaze with determination. "Like I said, I don't blame you."

"I wanted to only because I thought it would make me feel better and forget. When I was in her bed..." Tears filled her eyes at the casual mention, and he was lost. He longed to hold her and tell her everything would be all right, but he couldn't make that promise. Not yet. "I couldn't go through with it."

"Why not?"

"She wasn't you."

Sobs burst from her throat, the force of it crippling the courage she showed him moments ago. She slapped a hand over her mouth, unable to contain the raw emotions bombarding her, and she turned them loose.

He had no idea how to handle the uncharacteristic reaction. During their short relationship, he'd seen so many different sides of her—angry, irritated, electric, happy, dismissive, depressed. He'd even seen her cry before, but this was different.

"Genevieve," he exhaled, desperate to soothe her pain. Stepping closer, he reached out, then remembered how she used to cringe when he touched her. Every cell in his body wanted to hold her and never let go, but those wounds were still sore. He held back. "Genevieve, I'm going crazy seeing you upset. What's wrong?"

She drew in a long breath and swatted the tears from her cheeks. "Can we sit?"

"Sure." He followed her to the matching chairs near the window, and they sat opposite each other. While she gathered her thoughts, he committed the way she looked to memory in case their conversation ended in another eruption. Even with broken tears, she was breathtaking.

"Ben," she started but had to pause to regather herself. "I wanted to tell you…"

"Genevieve, what's going on?"

"I really don't know how to answer that."

"Try."

"Okay. I need to know what happened between us. We never officially ended our relationship—we just walked away. We hurt each other and never talked about it. I want to talk about it."

"Alright. Let's talk." With this new twist, he was more confused than ever. "Where do you want to start?"

"I hadn't fully realized how far I pushed you away until I saw you with her. I was angry at you for giving up and frustrated with myself for accepting it without a fight." Irritated, she wiped the stream now flowing freely down her cheeks.

Studying her, he struggled to understand. Everything he'd experienced with her prevented him from processing her words as black and white. She'd never been straightforward and predictable. "Did you want to fight…for me?"

"Yes, but I was being stubborn, and I was scared—more unchartered territory for me. I didn't know how to handle it."

"I wish you would have told me this in Orlando or before." So much heartache could have been avoided had she simply come to him weeks ago.

"Like I said, I'm stubborn."

Hope poked at his core. "And hardheaded," he added with an unsteady grin.

"And hardheaded. I convinced myself that begging you to choose me would have caused too much—"

"I would have." He held her gaze to show her how dead-serious he was. "I would have," he repeated. "Without hesitation."

"I don't believe you."

"Why not? I could be getting drunk on free booze with many single women at an incredible party," he pointed sharply toward the music and crowd noise coming from down the hall.

"Is that what you want?"

"No. It's not what I want. Shit." He rose and stalked to the bookcase, praying he could breathe if he put some space between them. Her questioning his devotion had him in a choke hold.

"Then, what *do* you want, Ben?"

"Seriously, Genevieve?" His voice was rising with his blood pressure. "Do I really have to spell it out for you?"

"Yes."

"I love you, damn it. I have since the first time we kissed. Are you happy now?" He yanked his hands through his hair and wondered why he was so angry. Why couldn't he tell the woman of his dreams that he had feelings for her? No. It was more than that. It was love, his first and probably his last. How could he ever love another after her?

Reaching his limit, he wished for another drink to keep him from imploding, but he couldn't force his legs to take him back to his glass. Instead, he stood frozen in fear, wondering why she was staring at him and saying nothing.

"I love you, too," she finally whispered and lowered her eyes.

"What?" The woman drained him of all sanity.

"I said I love you, too, and I meant it."

"Why now?"

The overhead light burned like a spotlight around them, showcasing every insecurity—the tension as thick as black smoke in the air.

"I'm a fool. I didn't know that about myself until you left me," she said.

"I didn't leave you."

"You left," she confirmed, "and I deserved it. I practically pushed you out the door, but I was hoping you could look past all my stubborn, hardheaded ways." She stood and strolled toward him as she spoke. "Not just tonight or for the weekend. Not just in bed or on a date."

"What exactly are you saying, Genevieve?" Hope was rising against his better judgment.

She reached for his hand and dropped to one knee. "Benjamin Robert Stevens…"

He smiled when he realized what she was doing, then stifled it to play along. To hell with corralling his hopes. "That's not my name."

"I know." She batted her long lashes, and it still shot inescapable need through his body the way it always had. "Benjamin Stevens, will you be my boyfriend?"

"I'm not sure," he teased, pleased to see her deflate with disappointment a little. "I'm not sure this wild stud is ready to be tamed and put out to pasture. I'll have to think about it and—oww," he yelped when she smacked him on the thigh and stood, crossing her arms—so righteous and annoyed with his foolishness, and oh so Genevieve.

"What I meant to say was, yes, my beautiful Genevieve. I can't wait to be with you tonight, this weekend, and for as long as you'll have me." When her eyes swooned and filled with tears again—strange how she kept doing that—he decided to venture further. "May I kiss you?"

It took a moment for her to process what he said, but she managed a nod, unable to speak through her emotions.

He was cautious and careful when he lifted a hand to her cheek. She didn't pull away or tense with anxiety under his touch, and he melted with relief. Leaning against his palm, she closed her eyes as he slid his other hand to her neck, just below her jawline. It felt as though he were touching her for the first time, and knew it was because walls no longer separated them. She wasn't fighting her feelings or holding back. Only pure and complete surrender on both sides. Freedom to be themselves, individually and together.

He traced her bottom lip lightly with his thumb and felt her body respond, but the reaction felt new and softer somehow. His touch remained light as a feather, and she shivered, her delicacy and raw vulnerability humbling him.

Sliding his hands down her arms, his lips trailed up the curve of her neck, then cheek, and stopping to hover over her mouth. His breath mixed with hers, quickening her heartrate with anticipation. She could have asked him for anything in that moment, and without hesitation, he would have given it to her. Whatever the cost or sacrifice, the world would be hers if she wanted it.

Everything changed between them in that moment, and as his lips and fingertips slowly roamed over her skin, he vowed to ensure she always felt safe with him. Before he could tell her as much, her hands grew impatient. Through the fog of desire, he felt them on his waist inside the sport coat, then on his chest. When she pinched the first ivory button of his shirt between her fingers and pulled, he took a soft hold of her wrists and drew back to see her face.

One look into her eyes, and he knew what she wanted. He'd seen those soft, emerald eyes darken with desire many times before. "Are you sure?" When she smiled and quickly moved to the second button, his grip tightened. "I don't want to hurt you… physically."

"Ben, you're not going to hurt me. I want to be with you. Do you want me?"

"More than anything, but—"

"No, buts. Forget everything else. Let's enjoy this moment and just be us." She rose to her toes for a kiss, but he held firm and kept her at a short distance.

"Not here," he decided. She deserved better, and he would not allow their first time together after confessing their love to happen on an office rug.

"What do you mean, not here?"

"I will not make love to you in his room. I want it to be special."

Her budding agitation with his easy rejection dissipated to complete admiration. "Okay. What do you propose?"

"We should go support our friends and let everyone drool over you in that marvelous dress. Then, we make love until dawn somewhere private and comfortable." He'd already planned it out in his mind. There would be candles, romance, plenty of slow caresses, generous offerings of pleasure, and unconditional love in every harmonious movement.

"Just until dawn?" She batted her eyelashes again, and his blood kicked up a few degrees.

"Did I mention that I love you?" Bending, he lingered lightly on her lips until they parted. She surprised him when she took a fistful of his shirt and yanked.

A moan oozed out of her when his tongue graced hers then left her wanting.

"I thought that would hold us over for a while, but—"

"Nope. Did just the opposite. Way to go." She sighed and sunk into his arms as they wrapped around her. "I have another idea. How about we sneak out of the party early and go to the spot I set up for such an occasion?"

"You made a place for us to be together tonight? Where?"

"Near the lake. There's a beautiful opening on a hill overlooking the water."

"You must have been pretty confident that I'd say yes."

"Not in the least, but it's a full moon tonight. I figured that meant anything could happen."

"Then that's what we'll do. When the time is right, we'll grab a bottle of wine and a blanket and—"

"Already there, waiting for us." Proud of her foresight, she smiled as he put the pieces together and realized all she'd done to plan for their reunion. "I wanted tonight to be special, too."

"Genevieve, every second I spend with you is special." He pressed a long kiss to her forehead. "Don't you ever forget that."

Chapter Fourteen

★ ★ ★

Genevieve

How did you find this place?" Ben asked once he'd finally pried his body from hers. He laid next to her, looking satisfied and in love, warming her more than the muggy summer night.

"I like to walk when I'm worried."

He shifted to his side and propped himself up on his elbow. "What have you been worrying about?"

"It's fitting that there's a full moon tonight. It explains that out-of-this-world performance you just gave." She offered, a weak diversion to his question.

"Genevieve."

"What?" She rolled her head to face him and smiled innocently. "I'm kidding." Popping up, she kissed him on the nose, then laid back down. It was all she could manage with what little muscle strength she had left.

"If we're going to give us another try, an actual try, we need to be able to talk to each other."

"I know."

"But my performance *was* spectacular."

"Yes, darling." She patted his thigh. "Yes, it was."

"Now, with that settled, what's been worrying you?"

She kept her eyes on the starry sky, trying to summon the courage to talk about her feelings. She'd spent two decades keeping them tucked away. Yet even she could admit, it was time to change that, especially if she wanted to hold on to him this time. It just didn't make it any easier. She hadn't known she had a comfort zone until Ben. Now, there was no escaping it.

Taking a deep breath, she began. "I was worried about seeing you again, about all the possible ways you could respond, and how I'd react to each one."

"Did you really think I could do something other than accept you?"

"I did." And the pain she'd felt when she considered it hit like a runaway train against her chest.

"Like I told you earlier, I will always choose you."

She turned to see his face and saw that he meant it. Taking his hand, she held his fingers to her lips. It was a simple gesture, one she'd received from him many times before, but she'd never been willing to share that part of her. It had always seemed too vulnerable, too risky. After surrendering to each other, it only felt like love.

"I'd like to know what helped you feel better, if you can tell me."

She studied his face and felt the nerves swell in her belly. "It was several things, really."

"Like what?"

"Seeing you with Samantha, for one."

He dropped his gaze, guilt taking over. "I'm sorry for parading her in front of you. It was incredibly insensitive. I regret it more than I can say." He brushed her hair off her shoulder and kissed her there.

"It's okay. I'll always remember how it made me feel, but I'm not innocent in this either. Seeing you with someone else and getting my heartbroken needed to happen. It snapped me out of the weak and pitiful funk I was in." She took a deep breath. "And when I came out of it, I realized what gave up."

Surprised by the admission, he leaned forward and kissed her. "You said several things helped you get better. What else happened?"

She sighed and thought about the two other things that ended her depression. Uncertain of how to tell him about the life growing inside her, she started with the easy one. "Jackson and his idea. VETS inspired me to get back to work and gave me something else to think about. I love the project."

"I'm sure he appreciates that. What else? I have a feeling there's more."

"I do have something else to— What was that?" She shot up, her eyes wide as she searched through the darkness.

"What?" Ben joined her.

"You didn't hear that growl?"

"No, I—"

"Shhh," she urged and slapped a hand over his mouth. For a full minute, they sat naked in the moonlight, listening, until footsteps on dry leaves had them scooping up their clothes and running in the opposite direction.

———

Ben

"Do you know where you're going?" he yelled and followed her into the forest at the edge of the clearing. The dark woods at night was the last place he ever wanted to go again. Her nude body, running away from danger, didn't help either and brought back memories he'd rather not relive.

"Stop," he yelled as they emerged from the tree line and doubled over. "I can't breathe."

"What is it?" She wrapped the blanket around her and rested a hand on his bare back.

"I don't care for the woods."

"Join the club, but it was either take that shortcut or be attacked by whatever animal was chasing us."

"Good point." He sucked in breath after breath, trying to relax his overburdened lungs. It felt like a panic attack, or was he just that out of shape? His eyes still blurry from fear and lack of oxygen, he could focus only on the black ground in front of him. "Are we close?"

"I can see the house."

"Fantastic, but we should probably get dressed."

"Nah. All the interior lights are out, so everyone's probably asleep. Come on, live dangerously. It's less to remove when we get to the bedroom."

"I like the way you think. Let's go."

With sex fresh on his mind, he took her hand and walked beside her to the back porch. He grabbed the knob on the back door, but it wouldn't budge. He tried again.

"Shit."

"Side door?" she suggested. It was also locked. "Last one." She cringed when they reached the front door and pushed down the old iron handle to no avail.

"Looks like our romantic night under the stars will have to continue a little longer than expected. Any more bright ideas, my beautiful queen?" he asked.

"We can use this blanket on the grass."

He considered it. "Nice flat surface, plenty of room to roll around. I like it."

"But there may be bugs and more wild animals."

"Not a fan of wild animals or bugs crawling up my ass."

"What about the car."

"Oh. We know how to make great use of a back seat."

"But there isn't enough room to lie down and sleep unless we spread out."

"I don't plan on doing much sleeping, but we do need some rest to keep the sex going." He thought about what he wanted to do with her that night, then shook his head. "Nope. The car won't work."

She smiled. "Back porch couch?"

"Now you're talkin'. Off the ground, away from anything with four or more legs, and a soft space big enough for two." His eyes smiled well before his lips did. "Race ya!" He gave her rear a loud smack before taking off down the walkway.

"Oh, I don't think so." She pulled up the blanket to free her legs and sprinted around the house in the opposite direction, reaching the back porch first.

"How did you get here so fast?" he puffed between gulps of air.

"I know the estate better than you do. Left is quicker."

"What? How?" He was sweating now, and, unfortunately for him, it wasn't from making love with a beautiful woman outdoors in the summer heat.

"No big ass garage." It was her turn to smack him on the ass. "The right side has the garage in the back, so the route is longer." She dropped her clothes on the table then sat down, crossing her legs under the blanket.

"I don't appreciate that smug look on your gorgeous face. Let's change that to something a little more…satisfied."

Before she could react, he'd joined her and dragged her into his lap.

Genevieve

Love. The word floated around in her head like embers in the wind, reminding her that despite all the sabotaging she'd done, *she* and *he* still turned into *they*. *Me* had become *us*. And because of her crushing need for him, she couldn't be the independent, fearless woman she thought she was— thought she needed to be.

For too long, she'd been masking her insecurities inside the shell of a woman pretending to have her shit together. That armor cracked the instant his tender heart stole hers and held her together.

"The sun's coming up," he whispered, lacing his fingers with hers. "What were you thinking about just now? Your facial expressions looked like a kaleidoscope."

Humming her contentment, she snuggled closer, enjoying the cozy feel of waking up next to him again.

"The me I was before you." She leaned back to take in the view of him in the orange glow of the early morning sun. "You changed me."

"I never wanted to change you, Genevieve."

"I know. You didn't mean to, but I don't want to be the person I was when we met. That person took advantage of others and wasn't very kind."

"I liked you then. You couldn't have been all that bad."

"You liked anyone with boobs," she teased.

"That may be true, but I liked your boobs the best." He pushed her onto her back, expecting her to play along.

She couldn't. Not yet.

"What is it?" he asked, his eyes searching her face for answers.

"I'm so grateful for you. You helped me see that I was worth loving."

"Genevieve, you're worth that and so much more."

Pulling him down for a kiss, she hoped he always felt that way. "You know what?"

"What, my Goddess?"

"Goddess? That's a new one."

"It's not. You've always been that to me."

Relishing the feel of his strong arms, she held him before continuing with her confessions and potentially ruining this sweet moment.

Her heart drummed fast. *Oh, God.* "Ben, I need to—"

The back door swung open, and Ms. Beasley stepped onto the porch, jostling her full coffee mug and breakfast plate when she saw them. Blushing, she turned away.

"Hi, Ms. B," Ben beamed.

She set down the hot dish and mug on the table, keeping her back to the couple. "What are you two doing out here?"

"We were locked out last night."

"Well, not anymore, thank goodness. How about you go inside and find some clothes?"

"Sure." Bounding up without a care, he reached around Ms. Beasley for their clothes, and her eyes darted in the opposite direction. "I'll just get these out of your way."

As he returned to her, that mischievous schoolboy grin she learned to love alights his face, and she can't stop her own from emerging.

She circled the blanket around her, keeping her eyes on him as she rose. His gaze lowered to her exposed cleavage, and she knew what he was thinking. Batting her lashes, she motioned for him to lean closer.

"Race you," she whispered and pushed him down onto the couch for a head start.

He didn't complain or try to stop her. He just followed her, streaking through Jackson's house without a care, and she loved him for it.

Chapter Fifteen

* * *

Genevieve

Waking with the mid-day sun on her face, Genevieve reached a hand over the bed beside her only to find it empty. Annoyed, she propped herself up on an elbow and looked around the room, hurt and disappointment that he wasn't there simmering deep within her.

"I thought I'd see a smile on your beautiful face this morning," Ben said from the doorway, confusion over her tragic mood evident in his expression.

Her eyes shot to his as he crossed the room and sat on the bed. "And I thought you left."

"Why?"

"You know why." His eyes hardened, and she suddenly missed the joy she saw in them only hours before.

"I'm not like all those other assholes you've been with. Do you really think I'd tell you I love you and leave?"

"It's not that." She couldn't look at him. She had thought exactly that. and she was ashamed. He'd done nothing to make her insecurities flare. "I just thought that maybe—"

"I had second thoughts?"

She nodded.

"I was famished, thanks to you, and went downstairs to get breakfast. But just so you understand, I'm going to say this out loud and as many times as you need to hear it."

"Ben," she whispered, but couldn't look at him.

"Genevieve." Gently, he placed a finger under her chin to lift her gaze. "I have zero interest in running or ever leaving you again. Like it or not, you're stuck with me." He tapped her on the leg and scooted off the bed. "Come on."

"Where?" She pressed her fingers to her eyes and took a deep breath. She still struggled with shame twisting in her belly, or was that... Oh, no. Not now, but the plea was a waste of time. Jumping up, she ran to the bathroom, slamming the door behind her.

"Was it something I said?" she heard him yell after her with a laugh.

After emptying her stomach, she emerged from the bathroom, feeling unsteady and weak. He swung his legs off the bed and covered her with a blanket in one swift movement. He was gentle, the way he'd been every time she needed him, as he helped her into bed. She would have swooned if she didn't feel so beaten from the inside out.

"I'm sorry," she whispered and drifted off to sleep.

———

"How are you feeling?" Ben asked when she awoke, thrilled to have company again.

She pulled herself into his lap. "Better now. Were you sitting here all this time?"

"I wanted to be here in case you needed me."

I always need you, she thought, then corrected herself. *We need you.* "Thank you."

"Should you rest today, or do you want to get out of the house?"

"I'd love to see your Richmond."

"What do you mean?"

She rolled onto her side to see him better. "I want to see your hometown through your eyes and the places you like to go. Other than a shopping trip for that dress—"

"It was the sexiest dress I've ever seen, and I'd like to see you in it again so I can watch you wiggle out of it."

"Later," she promised and gave him a little peck. "We've barely left this house since we arrived. Amazing as it is, I need to get out."

"Hold on. When did you get here?"

She waved it off. "A few days ago."

"A few days? Like how many exactly?"

"I don't know. I think it was last Friday."

"Friday?"

"What's the problem?"

"Why the hell did you wait an entire week to talk to me?"

Instinctively, she sat up and lifted the sheet as a shield against the familiar hurt flashing in his eyes. "Excuse me?"

"I'm sorry." He took her hand. "I'm just so happy to have you back and wish we could've had more time. I assume you're going back to Savannah soon."

Softening, she regretted waiting for that very reason. "Not knowing how things were going to turn out between us, I originally planned to leave tomorrow. I've neglected my clients for too long and with all the things required for VETS, I need get back to work."

"I see."

"Ben." Her belly churned again, and she waited for it to resettle before continuing. "There's something—"

"G, are you in there?" Emily called through the door.

She dropped her head to Ben's shoulder, irritated at yet another interruption. "Where else would I be?" After tossing on her robe, she marched to the door and yanked it open.

"It's lunchtime. Jackson and I are going out. Do you two want to join us."

Genevieve turned around for Ben's answer.

"Sure," he answered with a surrendering sigh.

"Give me a moment to get dressed."

"Great. See you downstairs in fifteen?"

"I'll do my best." Closing the door, Genevieve crossed the room to Ben, sitting on the edge of the bed. She stood between his legs and draped her arms over his shoulders.

"I don't want to go," he confessed, his hands trailing up the backs of her legs.

"Me either, but they're our friends and have done so much for us. We'll talk this afternoon, I promise. We have a lot to figure out still." New worry clouded his eyes, so she kissed him softly, hoping it would set his mind at ease and relieve hers in the process.

"I'll give you some space to get ready."

Before she could protest, he was out the door. Would she ever get to tell him about the baby? Every time she waded through the nerves and tried, something interrupted her, and she was beginning to think it was a sign. Maybe the universe was doing her a favor. Maybe the timing was off.

Letting out a long breath, she grabbed a pair of jean shorts and a T-shirt out of her suitcase before heading to the bathroom. She didn't have time to think about the pesky unknown, fate, or her dilemma. Everyone waited for her downstairs, and she still needed a quick shower to help her feel somewhat normal again. The previous night with Ben had been a dream, but reality hit her hard when she woke up, and she'd yet to recover.

After rinsing off, she pulled on the shorts but couldn't button them. *That settles it*, she thought and felt a few defenses activate. No matter how difficult it would be, she needed to tell Ben about the baby soon, or he'd figure it out on his own.

Standing bare in front of the mirror, she studied herself, turning from side to side and running her hand over her tiny bump. If only she knew how he felt about being a father. Their situation was infinitely more complicated now. He had a new business to think about, and there was the matter of their living in two different states. One of them would have to move if they were to raise the child together. Were either of them willing to uproot their life? Were they ready for an instant family? Could he be a father to a child that may not be his?

It wasn't a conversation she looked forward to having. Yet again, she had no clue how he would react, and she expected the worst—a blowup with him walking away for good. That's what people do, right?

Later that afternoon, there was a real possibility that their relationship could end before it even had a chance to begin.

———

Ben

The couples went in separate directions after lunch. Jackson and Emily had plans to view potential locations for VETS, while Ben took Genevieve on the tour of Richmond she requested.

"I'd take you to my place, but I've been staying with friends. I want to find a loft apartment that could also serve as a studio, but I haven't had a chance to look around." He was rambling, but a new tension developed between them on the way to the restaurant, and she sat uncharacteristically quiet beside him now. It made him uncomfortable, and he teetered on the verge of losing his temper again. After all, he just got her back. They should be enjoying their limited time together and talking about their future. Not... this.

Back at the estate, he took her hand. Instead of leading her inside, he headed toward the lake. Something drastic needed to be done to get her out of her head.

"Where are we going?" she asked, struggling to keep up. His long strides and swift pace were more than she could handle in flip-flops on the uneven ground. "Can we slow down? Ben!"

Ignoring her, he took hold of her hips and tossed her over his shoulder.

"Put me down!" She beat her fist on his back and kicked her feet, but he simply adjusted his arms and held her down.

"Not until we get there."

"Get where?"

"The only place we've ever been able to talk."

"If I throw up, I'm not going to feel bad about spewing it all over you."

Moments later, when he figured they were far enough away from the house to avoid distractions, he set her on her feet. Ready or not, they wouldn't leave this spot until they'd had the conversation she'd avoided all day. Why wouldn't she talk to him like she had the night before? And why was she so upset with him now?

She reared back, ready to let off some steam, but he caught her wrist before her hand reached his face. "I wouldn't do that if I were you."

"Oh, no? Well…"

"Well, what, Genevieve?" He dared and tightened his grip, unsure of what she might do next. The last thing he expected her to do was double over and lose her lunch right in front of him. Jumping back in time to prevent his shoes from getting soaked, he watched in disbelief while she convulsed and vomited over and over.

"I warned you," she said when her stomach had nothing else to give. Resting her hands on her thighs, she took several deep breaths.

He studied her as she reached into her purse and removed a tissue, a tiny bottle of water, and a mint. She'd come prepared.

"This is the second time you've gotten sick today." Concern quickly replaced frustration. She'd gone frighteningly pale.

"It's not just today."

"You seemed fine last night. Is it the diabetes?"

"No."

"How long have you been throwing up?"

"A few weeks."

"A few—Have you seen a doctor?"

"Ben, we should talk."

"That's what I've been trying to do all day." If he was going crazy before, it was nothing compared to what she was doing to him now.

She found a dry patch of grass, crossed her legs at the ankles, and lowered to the ground.

Joining her, he looked out over the smooth water, wishing for his erratic emotions and the tension between them to be just as calm. How could their relationship be this strained after the night they spent together? He wanted answers, and he wasn't leaving that spot until he got them. "Genevieve, I thought we were past all this."

"We are."

"It doesn't feel like it."

She plucked a blade of grass and twirled it between her fingers. Her nervous fidgeting made him feel the same.

"I'm sorry," she finally said.

"I don't want an apology. I want to know what's going on with you."

"You deserve that." She tossed the grass into the air and watched it twirl to the ground. "When you asked me about overcoming my depression, I didn't tell you everything."

"I know."

"You do?"

"You started to say the third reason last night, but we were interrupted. Plus, I know *you*." He nudged her with his shoulder and smirked.

Feeling more at ease, she leaned against him. "I guess you do. One of the few."

"What else happened, Genevieve? I know it's something big, or you would have told me already."

"Right again." She forced a grin, then shifted to face him. Taking his hand, she took a deep breath. "I'm pregnant."

———

Genevieve

She watched his face go blank with shock as he attempted to process what he'd heard. He shook his head slowly before pulling his hands free and standing.

"I think it's yours."

"You *think*?"

She stood, but it crushed her when he mirrored her steps, maintaining distance between them.

"You—" He struggled to say what she knew would be a concern of his and reminded herself to trust in his love. "You don't think it's his?"

"There's no way to know at this point."

"And you want to keep it?"

Fighting the hurt that snapped into place with the question, she urged herself to be patient. She, too, had been terrified when she found out. "I wasn't sure in the beginning, but he—"

"He?"

"I'm assuming it's a boy."

"Why?"

"It's not important. Look, Ben. I love you, but—"

"How can you add a but after saying that?"

"Ben," she sighed at the dismay in his voice. "Whether he's yours or not, I'm going to have this baby, and we're a package deal. I need to know if you still want me. If you do, can you accept this child as ours, no matter what?"

She watched him struggle to understand and process the potential life changes he never saw coming. She could relate, but she'd prefer to be in his arms instead of standing yards apart, cold and distant, while he contemplated whether he was ready. Whether he still wanted her with a child involved—a child that may not be his.

"If you don't want to be a father or take the chance on him not being yours, I'll go back to Savannah, and you'll never have to see us again."

"That's one hell of an ultimatum, and completely unfair."

"You can't have your freedom and me at the same time."

"That's not what I was thinking." He dragged his hands through his hair, then over his face. "What do you want?"

"I want it all. You, our family, all of us forever. That's why I'm here. I need to know if you want that, too."

"Genevieve."

"What?" If she wasn't already unraveling with unimaginable ideas of motherhood and potentially losing everything she'd gained over the past twenty-four hours, the shake in his voice would have been her undoing. "Is a family with me so hard to fathom?"

His shoulders dipped before he closed the awkward distance between them and pressed his lips to her forehead. "I need some time. Can you give me that?"

The word *no* tickled her tongue, but he deserved that much. "Yes."

They traveled in silence to the house, neither knowing what to say. Without a word, a kiss, or even a wave goodbye, he lowered himself into the car and drove away.

She managed to hold in the storm of emotions, battering her from the inside out, until the car disappeared behind the tree line. Too shocked and exhausted, she couldn't move.

"It's over." Her voice echoed in her ears as though someone else had said it. He wasn't coming back, and for the first time in her life, she didn't want to be alone. She wanted a partner, someone to cuddle with on the couch, and to count on to be by her side… always. She wanted that someone to be Ben.

An empathetic arm wrapped around her trembling shoulders and held her up as she crumbled.

"What's the matter, dear?" Ms. Beasley asked, tilting her head to see Genevieve's face.

"He doesn't want our baby."

"I can't imagine Benjamin turning away his own flesh and blood, or you. Did he say that?"

"It was in his eyes." Powerless to stop them, the sobs came fast and hard. She collapsed into Ms. Beasley's comforting embrace and didn't protest when she was her upstairs. She would wallow in her heartache until it was time to escape back to Savannah.

———

Hours later, Emily knocked on the bedroom door and let herself in.

Genevieve wasn't proud to be lying on the bed, clutching a box of tissues as if it were her favorite teddy bear, but she had nowhere else to be and no strength left.

"I heard you were upset. I assume you talked to Ben about the baby. What happened?"

Sitting up, she wiped her nose with a fresh tissue then let her hand drop into her lap. "Not much, really. He was too shocked to make a decision, and the fear in his eyes... I don't think he's ready. He may never be."

"I don't believe that. He loves you."

She shook her head. "It may not be enough. Anyway, I doubt he can make up his mind by tomorrow."

"Why tomorrow?"

"I need to get back to work, and there's no reason to stay if he's done." The possibility of going home rejected and alone was a hard pill to swallow, but with the way Ben reacted, reality tilted in that direction. The sooner she faced it, the sooner she could move on and start her new life as a single mother.

"I don't want you to go. Having you here with Jackson and me has been a dream."

"You're starting your life together. You don't need a third wheel hanging around. Plus, seeing you two together will only make me want to throw up all the time." It took everything she had to flash a grin.

"Funny."

"Emily," Jackson called from the other side of the door.

She patted Genevieve on the leg and crossed the room.

"I need to run out. Do you need anything?" he asked when she appeared.

"I don't think so. Where are you going?"

She stepped into the hallway when he motioned for her, probably so they could talk about *poor Genevieve* and her pitiful, stupid life without hurting her stupid, fragile feelings.

Returning moments later, Emily clapped her hands with an energy that made Genevieve nervous. "Get dressed," she commanded, putting an end to their earlier conversation and Genevieve's wallowing. "If this is your last day, we're going to make the most of it."

Chapter Sixteen

✲ ✲ ✲

Genevieve

Are you sure you have to leave?" Emily asked, folding the dress Genevieve wore during the party and placing it neatly inside the suitcase.

"Yes. I can't put my life on hold waiting for Ben to suddenly decide he wants us. I have a life in Savannah. I've come to terms with it, and if I'm being honest, it's what I expected." Sitting on the bed, she gathered the items she'd tossed there earlier from the bathroom and stuffed them into her red makeup pouch. "Being a single mom can't be all that bad. Women do it all the time."

"Sweetie," Emily started, before Genevieve held up her hand and stood.

"There's nothing you need to say. We all knew this could happen. I came here to tell him, and it's over."

"You came for more than an announcement about the baby. You came to also tell him you loved him, and that you wanted to be together."

"And look where that got me. Once a lifelong commitment was mentioned, love no longer seemed to matter. At least we can move on now."

She placed a stack of folded shirts in the suitcase and reached across the bed for the jean shorts that would collect dust in her closet over the next year.

"We have time for one last meal together, so I plan to treasure every minute." Emily went to the door. "Come on, Ms. Beasley is making your favorite."

"God, I adore that woman. I'm going to miss her cooking, especially her brownies."

Arm in arm, the friends strolled slowly down the stairs.

"Guess that means you'll have to come back often for a visit. I'm sure she would love to see you and make you a big batch."

"I will, but *after* I get rid of the baby weight." She laughed, and it echoed through the two-story foyer. "Anyway, I want my boy to spend time with his godparents."

Emily stopped on the last step, her hand clasped over her mouth. "Seriously?"

"Who else would it be? You're like a sister to me, my best friend, and my rock. I know you'll love him as much as I do." She grinned. "And Steamy Eyes is okay, too."

"Oh, you know I will, and Jackson will be so thrilled. Two godsons. What a blessing." She linked her arm with

Genevieve's again and headed down the hall. "I can't wait to see his face when you ask him."

"Me? I was hoping you'd just slide the news into conversation after I left. No need to make a big fuss over it."

"Absolutely not. It will be good for you both to have this moment."

"You suck."

She felt lighter than she had in the past twenty-four hours. A new life on her own without Emily or Ben would take some getting used to, but she could handle—

They both stopped in in the dining room entrance at the first sight of Ben. Looking him over, it was obvious he hadn't slept much the night before. And although he tried to clean up, his hair was a disheveled mess. She'd seen that look before and knew he'd been combing his anxious hands through it.

When she didn't move, Emily stepped forward to greet him. "Ben. It's so nice to see you this morning." She kissed his cheek, but his eyes stayed on Genevieve. "Will you be joining us for lunch?"

"Thanks, but I'm not hungry."

"If you need me," she said to Genevieve and pointed toward the kitchen, "I'll be in here."

With a determined nod, Genevieve placed her hands on the back of a chair, set her courage, and sharply turned her gaze on Ben. She had no interest in making this conversation easy for him. He'd caused her too much heartache to escape unscathed, and deserved to suffer the silent treatment, especially if he'd come for the reason she expected—to end their relationship forever.

"You're so beautiful."

"Why are you here, Ben?"

"What do you mean? I'm here to talk."

"I don't think we have anything left to discuss."

"I disagree. I, for one, have a lot to say." He pulled out a nearby chair and motioned for her to join him.

She did as he requested, making sure her crossed arms and blank stare told him her patience had already been spent.

"I'm sorry for leaving yesterday and for taking so long."

"Why was that?" she asked, feeling her protective walls reactivate. "You said you would always choose me—without hesitation."

"You dropped a pretty big bomb on me, and I needed some time. How long have you known?"

"Does it matter?"

"No. I just want to know."

"Since Orlando." It added more fuel to the fire, but she couldn't lie to him.

"Why didn't you tell me then?"

"You really have to ask that question?"

"Fine." He took a deep breath, understanding neither of them handled the last several weeks with much grace. "And you don't think the baby's his?"

"No, I don't, but I no longer care. Whether he was made with love or with force, it's not his fault."

"You loved me back then?"

"Ben, why are you here?" She'd run out of patience for this conversation well into the night while she hovered over the toilet, vomiting and cursing him.

Relenting, he took a deep breath. "When Jackson and I left Savannah, I really struggled to find my rhythm. He'd joke and ask why I wasn't flirting with the waitress or any other woman for that matter."

"So?"

Ignoring her, he continued. "I was so jealous when Emily showed up the night we left, and you didn't. That's when I realized that I wanted that kind of love, attention, and devotion, and only from you."

She continued to stare at him, wondering when *his* bomb would drop.

"I understand why you're mad," he said. "You think I don't want to be a father, and that I'm willing to give you up to avoid it. You're also determined to retreat to Savannah and raise him alone. That will show everyone how you don't need a coward like me in your life. How close am I?" He held her gaze, daring her to tell him otherwise.

"Sounds accurate." A flicker of hurt altered her stone expression, and she hated herself for letting him see it. "Am I right?"

He rested his arm on the table and showed her his closed fist. Slowly opening his hand, he revealed the ring sitting like a tiny grenade on his palm. "Does this answer your question?"

"What's that?" The lights from the chandelier above glittered in the large diamond in rhythm with her racing heart. She could no longer focus on anything but the love in his eyes.

Between his thumb and forefinger, he held up the ring by the thin gold band.

"Ben." She pushed to her feet to pace, unsure if what she saw in him was the truth or simply what she wanted to see. "I don't want to be your obligation, and I don't want a pity ring." It would upset him, but she didn't care. She needed to be sure this was what he genuinely wanted.

"Is that really what you think I'm doing?"

"I don't know. You say you loved me, then, as soon as you learn I'm pregnant, you leave."

"I just needed some time to think," he tried, but she continued to pace, lost in her own fears and doubts.

"Neither one of us knows how to raise a child or be in a committed relationship. We've both been on our own for too long. How can I trust you won't do that every time it gets hard?"

"Genevieve—"

"We have two separate lives hundreds of miles apart. Where would we live?"

"In Richmond."

She stops pacing to meet his gaze, his conviction surprising her. "What?"

"It makes sense for us to live here. And you're right," he began and rose from his seat. "We know nothing about being in a relationship, but it can't be that hard." He smiled when she glared down her nose at him. "We'll figure it out together. What else is bothering you?"

"Okay." She squared her shoulders, her arms still crossed over her aching belly. "Why do you want to marry me? Be honest."

"Seriously?" he said with an easy grin, and she wondered how that question could put him at ease after what he learned. "I'm in love with you, and you are the only woman I could ever be with. I want you today, tomorrow, and forever."

Melting, she dropped her arms. "But it's no longer just me. I have a baby growing inside me, and I'm not the same woman you met in Myrtle Beach."

"I know. I'm not the same either." Stepping around the table, he took her hand and held it to his lips. "I love you, and without a doubt, I know I will love this baby. I want to be your husband and his father if you'll have me."

"It took you a while to come to that conclusion," she finally said, pulling her hand free and adding the table between them again. She desperately needed some space to think and breathe.

"It's not a conclusion. It's how I feel," he said, determined. "I want you, him, us, all of it." Holding her gaze, he went to her and lowered to one knee. "Marry me, Genevieve. You are my world. Please let me prove it to you for the rest of my life."

Setting her tears free, she studied him. His dark eyes, glossy with his own mounting emotions, held steady. She had everything she wanted. He said exactly what she needed to hear but never thought she would, and a river of relief flowed through her.

"Can I see that ring again?" she whispered, but when he dropped his face into his hands instead, his own sobs taking over, she was lost. She fell to her knees before him.

Weak and overwhelmed with emotion, he pulled her into his lap. He held on tight and rocked her while they cried together in the silence.

"Ben," she said and sat up. He tucked her hair behind her ear then wiped the tears from her cheeks, melting any remaining doubt from her mind. She wasn't accustomed to being treated with such delicacy, but she wanted to be. She wanted to feel how much he treasured her, savor and appreciate it, and reciprocate it freely. "I want you to know…"

"What's wrong?"

She quickly took his face in her hands and kissed him to erase his worry. "Nothing's wrong. I just wanted you to know that I believe you. Last night and this morning, I thought I'd never see you again." She dropped her head, remembering how much it hurt. "But I'm so incredibly happy and thankful you came back."

Turning, he kissed the inside of each palm, then gathered her hands and held them to his chest. "I can't promise that I won't need a break to think when life gets hard, but I *can* promise, without question, that I will always come back. I will always choose you."

"I love you so much," she said and pressed her lips to his.

"Oh, wait!" He dropped her hands and dug in his pocket. "Let's make this official before you change your mind," he joked and held up the ring. "Genevieve Elizabeth Olsen…"

When that playful grin she loved emerged, she shook her head and returned it. "That's not my name."

"I know, but don't you think it's time you told me your real middle name?"

"It's Lynn."

"Finally." He rolled his eyes in dramatic jest, looking more like the man she met at the bar in Myrtle Beach. "That's been eating at me for weeks."

She smacked him lovingly on the arm. "No, it hasn't."

"You're right, but I am glad to know. I want to know everything about you." He kissed the tip of her nose then pulled her to her feet before kneeling in front of her again. "Let's try this again. Genevieve Lynn Olsen… Wait a minute. Your initials are GLO, like a star or a candle glow. It's the name of your business."

"Right again. Can we talk about that later? Weren't you about to ask me something?"

"Oh, right. Genevieve, the love of my life, will you marry me?"

"Yes," she yelled and watched in amazement as he slid the diamond ring onto her finger. "It's beautiful."

"Not as beautiful as you, my Goddess." Shooting to his feet, he wrapped his arms around her and lifted her up. "I love you, Genevieve, and I'm going to spend every day making sure you never forget that."

"Same here. I also promise to be less stubborn and set in my ways."

"Don't ever change. I adore you just the way you are." He was anything but patient and tender when he kissed her again. "Can we go upstairs and celebrate?"

"We better, or I may take you right here."

He hesitated, liking the idea too much, and she pushed him toward the door. Once in the hallway, he scooped her up into his arms and climbed the stairs to the guest bedroom two steps at a time.

———

Jackson

"I guess we aren't going to the airport today," Emily joked when she heard the guest bedroom door slam shut from the kitchen. "Did you have anything to do with this?"

"With what?" he asked before taking a big bite of roast. He and Emily had been sitting at the island trying not to eavesdrop.

"Sure, play innocent, but I know you helped talk him off the ledge yesterday."

"I'd love to take the credit, but all I did was listen. He figured it out on his own."

With an adoring smile, she placed a hand on his arm. "You're a good friend."

"But I did help pick out the ring," he confessed casually, making her drop her fork to stare at him—all adoration gone, and he was too amused with himself to miss it.

"What?"

"I helped pick out the ring. It's quite nice. Square diamond, gold band, we—"

She punched him on the same arm she touched lovingly only a moment before.

"Ow. What was that for?"

"You know exactly what that was for. Why didn't you tell me?"

"He made me swear not to."

She continued to glare at him with disapproval, then laughed. "I can't believe it. From denial to engagement in less than twenty-four hours. Hope he didn't get whiplash from the sudden turn of events."

"It wasn't as sudden as it appears. He was caught off guard and needed time to process. He's always loved her and has been dreaming of starting a family with her since we left Savannah. He just didn't want to admit it and ruin his reputation." He smiled over his shoulder.

"I wonder what this means. Did he mention anything about moving down there? Oh, I hope they both stay here with us."

"Wait, when you say here, you mean Richmond, not *here* in this house, right?"

"We do have plenty of room." A laugh squeaked out despite her best effort to appear serious. "Of course, dear. We can't have any more roommates. It would cramp our romance."

He leaned in and kissed her cheek. "Glad we're on the same page, but I doubt he's thought that far ahead. He just got her back two days ago. Yesterday, he found out he's going to be a father, and today, he's engaged. Quite the weekend."

"I'll say. I'd love to talk to her, but I don't see them coming up for air anytime soon."

"Good," he said and leaned toward her again. "More time for us. You're not still mad at me, are you?"

"How could I ever stay mad at you?" Placing her hands on his thigh, she pressed her lips to his and they parted instantly, sending his thoughts into naughty territory. "What's on the agenda for today, soldier?"

"Keep doing that, and we're going to christen this island whether everyone's here or not."

"Mmm, tempting." She trailed the curve of his neck with her lips and returned to nibble on his ear, his weak spot. "How about a walk instead?"

"You should have asked that before your lips touched me."

With a laugh, she hopped off the stool and placed their empty plates in the sink. "Come on. I've walked this beautiful place with Genevieve, but I want to see it with you and hear how you grew up."

"Alright," he surrendered with a groan and accepted the hand she offered. "But don't expect me to keep to myself."

Flashing a sultry smile over her shoulder, she led him outside. "I'm counting on it."

Chapter Seventeen

★ ★ ★

Emily

"Where have you been?" Genevieve demanded when she and Jackson entered the kitchen, but one look at their rumpled, grass-stained clothes should have answered that question.

Not in the least bit embarrassed, Emily winked at him when he stepped past her, his hand brushing across her lower back, then turned to Genevieve. "I could ask you the same thing. Aren't you supposed to be on a plane right now?"

"Change of plans."

"Oh, yeah?" she asked innocently. "What's going on?"

Genevieve's left hand flew up, and she rolled her eyes at Emily's dramatic surprise. "I know you know, so give up the act. Isn't it fabulous?"

Holding Genevieve's hand, she studied the diamond. "It is. And, yes, Jackson told me, but only after you two went upstairs. He kept his side of the bargain." Her brow pinched together in a playful *I'm not happy with you* look at him, but he continued to fill two glasses with ice as if he wasn't listening. "I'm so happy for you. Does this mean you're staying?"

"I don't know. It all happened so fast."

Emily accepted the glass of water Jackson passed her. Where's Ben now? I'm surprised he let you out of bed this soon."

"He's taking a shower."

"I can't wait to see him. I bet he's glowing."

Pink rose into Genevieve's cheeks. "Maybe just a little. It's not going to be easy at first, but we'll figure it out."

"Yes, you will, but I hope you stay in Richmond. Godparents should be close by, you know."

"Wait. Godparents?" Jackson asked.

"Oh, dang. I wanted you to ask him," she said to Genevieve before turning back to him. "This morning G asked us to be his godparents. Isn't that wonderful?"

"Wow. Didn't see that coming. I guess we're even."

"How?"

"I didn't tell you about Ben buying the ring, and you didn't tell me we're going to be godparents. We're even." Raising the glass of water to his lips, he patted her on the rear and stepped away.

"That man," she said absently to herself, her gaze following him out the door.

"Guess what?" Genevieve asked, impatient to keep her friend's attention.

"What?"

"I'm getting married." She jumped down from her stool, and the two friends hugged and danced around the kitchen. "Can you believe it?" Out of breath, she leaned her hand on the counter for support.

"Absolutely not. If someone had asked me a few months ago if you'd take the plunge, I would have said never in a million years. But love has the power to change everything."

"I never thought I'd do it either." She held up her hand to gawk at the ring again. "I can't stop looking at it."

"I'm so happy for you," Emily said again. "Now that you've stopped fighting it, how does it feel?"

"Amazing. Who knew?"

"I did."

"Yeah, yeah." She waved her hand, then returned to her stool and Emily followed.

"Isn't it amazing how we all came together at the same time?"

"I know. I'll never understand it. Both Ben and I despised relationships and avoided them our entire adult lives. You and Jackson weren't looking for love when you met."

"No, exact opposite, but our connection was undeniable from the start, and so was yours and Ben's."

"I wouldn't go that far. He disgusted me at first."

"Come on. You don't have to lie anymore. You know you were attracted to him. You just refused to admit it."

"I was attracted to how he felt, but I was not attracted to the man."

"You keep telling yourself that." Emily took a sip of her water and smiled. "Either way, you eventually saw the real man that he is, and he's yours now and forever. You lucky girl."

"She is lucky," Ben chimed in from the doorway, surprising them both. "Luckiest girl in the world." He crossed to Genevieve and dipped her head back with a kiss so long and steamy, Emily had to look away.

"What are you two going to do today?" she asked, when her friends came up for air.

"I was hoping my bride-to-be would want to go look at a few houses." Ben combed his fingers through Genevieve's hair, love pouring out of the motion and through his gaze. "What do you say?"

"Houses?" Emily turned to Genevieve, her eyes wide with excitement. "I thought you hadn't discussed where you were going to live yet."

"We haven't." Genevieve tilted her head at Ben and squinted at him in confusion.

"I'll leave you two alone. Seems like you have a lot to discuss." She scooted down from her stool, then stopped beside Genevieve. "I hope you stay," she whispered before exiting the room.

———

Genevieve

"You want to go house shopping? Like one for us to live in?" she asked cautiously. That was a giant, house-size step for them.

Ben leaned on the counter and took her hands. "Sweetheart, I beg you. Please don't go back to Savannah. Let's start our lives together here. Today."

"But I…"

"No buts. Your business can flourish in Richmond, and our friends are here. What does your heart say?"

When his eyes touched her soul like that, so passionate and pleading, there could be no denying him. *The old Genevieve*, she mused, *would instantly have thrown up walls, grown defiant, and done everything she could to not give in.* That was not who she was anymore or who she wanted to be with him.

"What I was going to say," she began and drew his fingers to her lips, "is that I still have to go back to Savannah to pack up my apartment and office."

"Hallelujah." He pulled her off the stool and into his arms. "How about we go together?"

"To Savannah?"

"Yeah. We'll fly down, and I'll while I pack everything, you can work on moving your business to Richmond. What do you say?"

"I say…" She smiled up at him, adoring his eagerness to help. "When do we leave?"

Happier than she'd ever seen him, he surprised her with a crushing kiss. "But before we can move your stuff here, we need somewhere to take it. Let's go find the perfect house for our little family."

"I'd like that." And surprisingly, it wasn't scary to say or imagine. She couldn't wait to move in with Ben, her lover, fiancé, and soulmate.

"You make me so happy. I love you."

"I'll never get used to hearing that, and it will never get old." She kissed him softly and leaned her body against his, igniting even more love and appreciation for the man that changed her life for the better. "Say it again."

"I love you, Genevieve, with all my heart."

———

Emily

As she and Jackson drove west away from downtown Richmond, the sun descended in front of them, casting a golden glow over the city beyond. Three weeks had passed since she moved to Virginia, and it already felt like home.

Jackson insisted that she redecorate the house how she wanted, but she couldn't do it. The house was already beautiful. However, she did take some liberties in his office to better represent the man who now used it.

She'd also made some friends. When they weren't working on VETS, she and Jackson spent time with Eleanor, Harrison and Sophia, or Sydney and William. It took a few visits for William to grow more comfortable with her and allow her to hold him. It was difficult getting him away from Jackson long enough to make any real progress, but that was okay. They were the cutest together. Next week, they planned to spend the weekend with Callie and Olan, who seemed to be on the mend.

But with so many tasks on the to-do list to get VETS launched, Jackson worked long hours with bankers, realtors, and City officials to find potential locations to fit his vision. He handled it with grace most of the time, his excitement outweighing the stress. Other times, he struggled to wrangle it all with his PTSD symptoms.

She watched him closely and learned both his signals and pressure points. Whenever he began to slip, she'd provide distractions and something positive for him to focus on. One afternoon after he'd recovered from another migraine following a long meeting with his attorney, she insisted he take a break and join her for a drive. They ended the trip in the one place she knew would put the stress into perspective—Will's gravesite.

They spent over an hour at the cemetery as Jackson recounted some of their escapades, both as kids and while serving. Afterward, he felt more energized, and for the rest of the evening, they made love as they had when he first visited her in Savannah. *A Lazy Saturday on a Thursday*, she called it.

On that day, Jackson held her hand as he drove to their destination. "Where are you taking me?"

"If I told you, it wouldn't be a surprise."

"I love surprises almost as much as I love you, but the anticipation is killing me."

"Sorry, you'll get no answers from me, at least until we get there."

Minutes later, he stopped in front of a sad, old warehouse at the edge of the city. The red brick, three-story structure had an eerie feel about it—the perfect backdrop for a horror movie. For all she knew, a monster lurked inside the cold, damp shell already. She shuddered at the sight before gladly returning her attention to Jackson.

"Please don't tell me this my surprise because I'm properly dressed for a game of haunted hide and go seek with a nasty, blood-thirsty villain."

"What?"

"Nothing. My imagination is getting the best of me. Why are we here?" She swallowed hard and continued to study the building, completely covered in shadows now that the sun dropped behind it.

"Welcome to VETS." He smiled wide and waited for her to match his excitement, but she only stared blankly at him. "What? You don't like it?"

"No, no, it's…" She paused, searching for the right words to describe what she saw, and leaned forward to get a better view out the windshield. "It's definitely… unique."

"It's okay. You don't have to love it yet, but it's a great location. This area is evolving, and VETS can help with the neighborhood's transformation. It's also close to downtown and other resources veterans might need. There's even a clinic that specializes in helping people suffering with PTSD around the corner. Isn't that perfect?"

"Yes, that is an added benefit for sure." She returned her gaze to the building, attempting to envision it as anything other than a crime scene. The roof had caved in on the south side, and the mortar between the bricks had cracks taller than she was.

"But?"

She adjusted in her seat to face him. "I just worry about how much it's going to take to get this dilapidated structure up to code and safe for use."

"I had both a contractor and engineer look it over. It has great bones, and the problems you see are mainly cosmetic." He held up his hands when her gaze snapped to his, her eyes narrowing with suspicion. "Yes, there are a few structural issues we'll have to patch, but it's built well. The other benefit is that we can design it from scratch. The entire interior has been gutted. It's primed for redevelopment. Look."

He reached behind her seat and pulled out a long cardboard tube. Removing the paper rolled up inside, he unfurled it across the dash. "The architect threw together a rough conceptual drawing to show the building's potential."

"Wow." She wished she had more words, but the drawing and all it represented took her breath away. "Jackson, it's amazing."

"I know. It's exactly how I pictured it."

She studied his changing expressions as he looked from the drawing to the building and back again. His vision was finally coming to life, and he'd brought her there so she could share the moment. "From everything we've talked about, it's perfect. I love it."

"Really?"

When she nodded, he dropped the papers to frame her face with his hands and kissed her until she melted with desire.

"Let's go inside."

"What?" Her eyes flew open. That was not the kind of foreplay she had in mind after that kiss. "No. Jackson!" Before she could protest further, he was outside, motioning for her to join him. Reluctantly, she opened the door and stood behind it for protection from whatever may jump out of the shadows. "You seriously want to go in there?"

"That's why we're here. Plus, this is nothing compared to the places I went overseas."

"No doubt, but it's getting dark." It was a feeble excuse, but desperation altered her brain.

Reaching around the door, he grabbed her hand and tugged, but she held on to the frame. "It's not that bad once you get inside, and there's electricity. It will be fine. I'll protect you from the—what did you call it?"

"Blood-thirsty villain."

"Right. He can't be all that bad. He wants to play hide and go seek." He smiled, and normally, that would fix anything that bothered her. Not this time.

"I wouldn't joke if I were you. He'll come after you first. You have more meat on your bones."

"Maybe, but I'm fast. He might prefer to have dessert first and come after you. You do taste mighty sweet." Pulling her close, he nibbled on her neck.

"Mighty sweet? I think you've spent too much time in the deep south during your trip." She leaned her head back, encouraging him to explore more, then straightened to put some distance between them. "Wait a minute. I thought you were going to protect me."

"Of course, I will. No imaginary villain is going to lay a hand on my woman," he added in an exaggerated southern drawl, bringing a smile to her lips. "There's my girl. Now, let's go."

He pulled her to the entrance and inserted a key into the lock. No code on a lock box or special instructions from a realtor taped to the window.

"Hold on." She covered his hand on the knob with hers and stepped in front of him before he could open the door. "You already bought this horror show, didn't you?"

"Maybe." He gave her a proud, goofy smile, and she surrendered.

"Alright. Let's see what we're dealing with."

Chapter Eighteen

✷ ✷ ✷

Genevieve

I'm sweating. Ugh, I hate sweating," she complained, fanning herself with a crumpled magazine. The fall leaves in Virginia were a stunning distraction. Humidity there was low in late October, and the temperature paled in comparison to what she was used to in Georgia. Yet, the waterworks under her arms spouted just the same.

"Relax," Ben urged and carefully pulled the magazine from her hand. "You're getting yourself worked up."

"For good reason."

"No. We're here to make sure the baby is growing and healthy. Whatever the ultrasound confirms or doesn't, changes nothing. I'm still going to love you and the munchkin."

He patted her firm, swollen belly, and she forced a grin. "I don't deserve you."

"Genevieve Olsen," a technician in perky pink scrubs called from the doorway.

"Oh, God." Her hand sprang into motion again, waving it in front of her flushed face.

"Stop that." Cupping her elbow, he tugged her out of the chair. "You're acting like Emily."

She glared up at him, knowing he said that to get a arise out of her. "Whatever. She would be a sobbing mess. At least my mascara is still perfect."

"For now." Before she could protest or stall further, he led her through the lobby and into the exam room. While they waited in silence for the ultrasound tech to set up her equipment, he held Genevieve's hand and noticed her pulse racing in tandem with her bouncing leg. "If you keep that up, you'll get a cramp," he joked and was saved from her retort by the technician spinning around on her rolling stool to face them.

"Before we get started, am I hunting for a tiny penis today?"

"Excuse me?" Ben squawked, narrowing his eyes at her through the dim overhead light.

"Sorry. My humor isn't for everyone." She snickered. "It's easier to confirm the sex when there's a tiny penis present. No tiny penis means…"

"Got it," he interrupted. "I don't think I've heard the word penis used that many times in my life."

"It's just another word around here. So, are we penis hunting today?" she asked again and patted the bed next to her machine.

"I already know it's a boy," Genevieve told her as she heaved herself up.

"Your mother's intuition kicking in already, huh?"

Ben rolled his eyes. "It would still be nice to get confirmation, though."

"Nothing's guaranteed until the baby's born, but we'll see what we can see." She smiled and raised her eyebrows as she squirted gel on the end of a wand. "Ready?"

Genevieve turned her head to check on Ben. When he nodded and kissed the top of her hand, she sighed. "I think so."

She moved the wand around Genevieve's belly, scowled, pushed a few buttons on the machine, then stopped. "Ha. There's the little bugger."

"What? Where?" Ben leaned over Genevieve for a closer look.

"See that fluttering. That's the heart. And this here is the head." She pointed at the screen.

He studied the shape, looking perplexed by the black and white blob. Then, his face lit up as he put it all together. "Look, Genevieve."

"I see him." Moved by his excitement, she wiped at the tear that escaped, but couldn't fully get invested in the moment just yet. The wand continued to move over her belly as the technician marked and measured her baby's limbs, head, and body. She'd read enough online articles to know what came next. She held her breath and waited for the answer that would either set her mind at ease or send her off the deep end.

"Alright. It appears that you're about twenty-two weeks along."

"Oh my God." She dropped her head back on the pillow.

"What?" Ben pulled her hands off her face, his eyes begging for an explanation. "Genevieve."

"I've done all the calculations multiple times."

"And? You're killing me. What does twenty-two weeks mean?"

"It means he's yours." She laughed, sheer relief consuming her sanity. "He was conceived in Savannah."

His sparkling eyes met hers, and she'd never been more in love. "Our first time together. I felt something change between us the next morning, and now we know what it was—a baby."

He shook his head then rested his forehead on hers. "Our baby. I love you so much."

"I love you, too."

Wrapping her arms around him, she held him tight, grateful for him. She kissed his hair and lingered there until a nearby sniffle sent a reminder that they weren't alone.

Ben straightened, and they both looked over at the technician. Her glistening eyes shone over the tissue she pressed under her nose.

"I didn't want to ruin it. This is why I love my job." She burst into tears and reached for Genevieve's hand. "You're so lucky to have a real man by your side."

Genevieve looked up at that man—her man—and smiled. "Exactly what I was thinking." With a wink, she turned back to the sniffling tech. "And my real man wants to do some hunting. What do you say?"

"Oh right. How could I forget?" She blew her nose into the tissue and tossed it in the trash can. "That's my favorite part."

They watched the screen as she moved the wand into position, readjusted and moved it again.

"What's wrong?" Ben asked when she puffed out her frustration and blinked hard.

"This is what I get for crying. My darn contacts are blurry."

She continued to move the wand, blink, and push buttons. "There! Target acquired."

They all leaned closer to the screen.

"That's it?" he asked. "That means it's a boy?"

"Like I said, tiny penis." She blinked again, reevaluated then flashed Ben a smile over her shoulder. "It's a boy."

"Was there really ever a doubt?" Genevieve complained and accepted Ben's hug.

"Not a second."

"Yeah, right."

———

A week had passed since the ultrasound and with her fears put to rest, Genevieve went shopping for baby items every chance she found. On that day, she and Emily finished lunch early and stopped by a downtown children's shop.

"Oh, you have to get this." Emily held up a plaid onesie.

"Nah. Never been a fan of the country style."

"But you love country music and line dancing."

"Yes, I do. Doesn't mean I have to look the part while I shake my ass."

"Fine. What about this little cutie?" She held up an outfit consisting of khakis, a white collared onesie, and a sweater vest already put together on the hanger.

Her face crunched, causing Emily to return the outfit to the rack with a sigh. "I can't wait until he stays at our house. Then, I can dress him however I want."

"Sure, so long as it isn't preppy like that last one. Anything that looks like the asshole doctor is off limits."

"G, I'm sorry. I wasn't thinking."

"Don't worry about it. Just no solid-colored collared shirts with khakis. That's all I ask."

"Done." Emily continued to browse through the little stacks of clothes while keeping an eye on Genevieve.

"Stop it. I'm good," she said without turning around.

"I know. It's just…"

Genevieve let out a long breath and looked over her shoulder. "What?"

"It's been five months. I thought we would have received at least an update from the prosecutor."

"He tried to call the other day, but I didn't answer." She held up a pair of socks, checked the price, then tossed them back into the display basket.

"Why not? There might have been news about the trial."

"I was having a good day and didn't want it ruined. I'll call him back later." Moving to the blankets, she ran a hand over one that matched the nursery theme. "I'm surprised he hasn't called you."

"Me, too. Maybe I'll reach out and see what he wants."

"Go for it, but I doubt it's important. He didn't even leave a message."

"Interesting. I bet it's—Oh! I almost forgot." Emily checked her watch. "I'm supposed to meet Jackson. Gotta run. I want to see everything you get later."

After giving Genevieve a quick hug, she rushed out of the store.

Chapter Nineteen

☆ ☆ ☆

Jackson

Whenever possible, Emily joined Jackson onsite at VETS. He consulted her on design decisions and included her in meetings with the architect. On this mid-November afternoon, he and Emily were meeting with the contractor to get a progress update on the construction.

"Mr. Vane, Miss Robertson, so nice to see you again," David Scott said, brushing at the sawdust on his black logoed T-shirt before reaching out his hand to shake theirs. "Little chilly out there?"

"You could say that," Emily managed through the shivers as she rubbed her hands together.

"It's just 45 degrees outside. You act like that's sub-freezing temperatures," Jackson teased and was met with a playful scowl.

"Forty-five feels different up here."

"Once you thaw out," David began and received the same disapproving eyes from Emily, "I'd like to introduce you to our new foreman. He's in the pool room."

"What happened to Bill?" Jackson asked as they moved in-stride behind David through the building. Crews were sanding drywall and installing electrical in the meeting and fitness rooms, while others were painting in the finished lobby.

"He fell off a ladder last week and broke a hip."

"That's terrible. Is he all right?" Emily asked.

"Yes, thankfully. He's at home recovering, but because he'll be out of commission for a while, he appointed one of his supervisors to take over temporarily. The new guy arrived a few days before the accident, so thankfully, we didn't lose much time."

"Arrived? Was he not already working here?"

"No. He and his team were finishing up another project in Georgia and came up to help to fill in. Unfortunately, we had a few more workers come down with the flu."

"Where in Georgia?"

"The Savannah area."

Emily turned to Jackson. "What are the odds?"

"Come on. He's been asking for you. He has some questions to help get him up to speed."

They followed David into a large room where bright blue tiles were being installed around the pool's edge.

"The new foreman must be tough," Jackson joked. "They've made considerable progress since our last visit."

"Mr. Vane, I'd like to introduce you to—"

"Cameron!" Emily interrupted when he looked up from a set of drawings.

"Hi, Emily."

"You two know each other?" Jackson asked, concerned by the way her confident and friendly demeanor had been dialed down to unsteady and uncomfortable.

"We go way back," Cameron answered with a tight smile but kept his eyes on her, his gentle tone making Jackson uneasy as well. "How are you?"

"I'm great, thanks. Um, this is Jackson." She motioned toward him, and he shook Cameron's hand while continuing to study him.

"Nice to meet you. Everyone else calls me Cam."

While Emily sunk into her thoughts, Jackson got down to business. The sooner they took care of this the sooner he could get an explanation. "I hear you have some questions."

"I'll leave you two to your work and go check on the progress in the sauna," Emily announced and made her escape.

They watched her leave before returning to their conversation.

"You two are involved?" Cameron wasted no time, putting Jackson on alert.

"Yes. And I take it you two were involved at some point."

He nodded. "It was a long time ago."

"Well, as long as that stays in the past, we'll be good."

"Understood."

"Now, what questions do you have about the renovation?"

———

Thirty minutes later, after a brief search, Jackson found Emily in the women's locker room discussing shower installations with a crew member. "How's it going in here?"

"They're ahead of schedule, but we've run into a snag with the floor tiles. They're on backorder," she explained.

"Do we know how long they'll be delayed?" he asked the young worker.

"No sir. They've provided no information."

"Are you comfortable waiting, or do you want to switch to something in stock?" Jackson asked her.

"I'd like to wait a little longer."

"Alright. We'll give it another week. If you're finished here, I want to show you something."

Exiting the locker room, they made their way across the large open room that would become the fitness area.

"How'd it go with Cameron?" she asked

"Ex-boyfriend, huh?"

"I'd hoped that wouldn't come up until I could tell you myself. It was a long time ago."

"So I hear." He smiled when her head snapped up to meet his gaze. "Don't worry. We talked it out."

"Oh, really? What did you talk out exactly?"

"Just that his past with you needs to stay there if he wants to keep working here."

She paused and grabbed his arm, causing him to stop mid-stride. "You're not worried that I still have feelings for him, are you?"

His fingers threaded with hers as he reached for her hand. "Not in the least."

"Good, but you should know that I covered one of his therapy appointments shortly before I left for Myrtle Beach last year, and he asked me out."

"I assume you turned him down?"

"Ignored him is more like it. He asked through text, so I just didn't answer."

"If it gets awkward or you're uncomfortable at any time, we'll have David replace him."

That option seemed to relax her before she changed the subject. "So, what did you want to show me?"

"It's right in here." Down a short hallway off the fitness room, he opened the set of double doors at the end. Stepping inside first, he watched her take in every inch of the bright, empty space.

The large room had been finished, painted a soft gray, cleared of all construction equipment or debris, and cleaned spotlessly. The early afternoon sun streamed in through the large windows on the left, showcasing the room and all its potential. There were three doors on the right side, and flipping on the lights, she examined each one.

"Is this what I think it is?" she asked, spinning around.

"If you're thinking this is the physical therapy area, then yeah. What do you think?"

Her breath caught and her hand sprang to her chest. "It's amazing," she breathed out as her enthusiasm burst through the shock. "I can see it so clearly. We'll put the weight equipment here." She rushed to the wall opposite the entrance. "The treadmills and bikes can go here, and the reception desk over there." She pointed to the space near where he stood then met his gaze.

"And your office is in here." He opened the door behind him and turned on the light before she stepped inside.

The room was small but larger than her last office, and the wide picture window added plenty of natural light, just like she wanted. "I can't believe this is finished already."

"They worked on this area first and kind of in secret." He grinned. "I wanted it to be a surprise. Happy birthday, my love."

Jogging to him, she jumped into his arms and circled her legs around him. "Oh, Jackson." She kissed him hard before he set her back on her feet. "But my birthday's not for another two weeks."

"I couldn't wait."

"I love it and you even more."

Feeling as though everything was coming together and happier than he knew was possible, he lowered his lips to hers.

Her eyes fluttered open when she drew back. "You sure know how to—Cameron!" She jumped back when she noticed him standing in the main room, watching them.

How long had he been there, and why hadn't he announced his presence?

Jackson spun around and took her hand in his, a possessive gesture, but he didn't care for the angry hunger in Cameron's eyes.

"My apologies, but we have an issue upstairs you need to see."

———

Emily

She let out a shaky breath as the door shut behind them. Crossing her arms against the cool brush of fear that lingered from the way Cameron had glared at her, she paced to work it off. He seemed to send her a message. What did he want, and why was she suddenly frightened of him? They'd had a long relationship, and she knew him well. Or had at one time. Why had her body reacted to protect herself?

She was being ridiculous. The fear she felt had to be residual emotions to her discussing Lucas and the trial with Genevieve recently. Cameron was harmless, and she'd overacted. Then again, of all the construction projects on the east coast that he could have been assigned, why this one?

Determined to put the strange encounter out of her mind, she laid out several options for her first and very own practice. A pleasant distraction since it was something she'd dreamed of doing her entire career. With her feet, she measured for the equipment and furniture needed to fill the empty space and got lost in the task, stopping only long enough to enter a few notes into her phone along the way.

When Jackson returned, she was lying on her stomach on the floor of her soon-to-be office.

"What are you up to?"

She looked up and smiled, glad to have him back. "I'm looking at the furniture options the designer sent. I hadn't ordered anything since I thought we were weeks away from finishing in here."

"So, you're shopping?"

"You could call it that." She patted the floor next to her. "Everything okay upstairs?"

Joining her, he crossed his legs in front of him and leaned back on his hands. "Yeah, it was something simple. Not sure why he felt the need to come get me. Are you okay?"

"Yeah, why?"

"Your expression changed when I mentioned him just now."

"It's my overactive imagination getting the best of me again." She touched his cheek. "He's not a bad guy. We just didn't end on a good note, and with everything that's happened recently…"

"Would you mind if I asked what happened between you?"

Emily shook her head then pushed to her knees. "When we met, he was struggling with depression. He always said I was the light that brought him out of it."

"Sounds familiar."

She grinned but her nervous hands demanded her attention. "As he felt better, he began drinking and going out a lot. I was focused on my studies and didn't have the time or the patience for partying. It didn't take long before he decided he needed a more exciting woman."

"He must have regretted it, since he asked you out when he saw you again."

"Maybe, but it was the last thing I wanted. I was also dealing with Lucas then. It was a difficult time for me and the reason Genevieve and I took the vacation to Myrtle Beach."

"Thank you for telling me. How about we get out of here and you can shop by a nice, warm fire?"

"That sounds amazing. You sure know how to make a girl happy."

"Is there anything else I can do for my happy girl?" He pulled her up and locked his arms around her.

"I am craving a hot bubble bath. The taste you gave me earlier made me want the full meal."

"I'm quite hungry myself. We better get home before I start on the first course."

"Hmm. The bubble bath could be dessert." She ran her fingers through his hair, took a fist-full, and kissed him hard.

"There are too many eyes and ears here to do it right. Let's go."

———

"What's wrong?" Ms. Beasley asked between deep breaths. She'd dashed to the living room from the kitchen when she heard Emily squeal and rested her hand on the back of a chair from the exertion.

"Sorry, Ms. B. I got a little excited. My equipment has arrived at VETS, and they're setting it up now."

"Wow. That was fast. Didn't you just place the order a couple weeks ago?"

"Yes. Isn't it amazing? The gentleman helping us design the fitness center, you remember Mr. Hamlett, don't you?" Emily closed the large plastic container of Christmas decorations she'd been rummaging through.

"Yes. I remember you and Mr. Vane mentioning him."

"He pulled a few strings to get the equipment since he recently placed a huge order for his fitness center expansion. Luckily," she clapped her hands in excitement, "the furniture I picked out was in stock."

"That's great news."

"Oh, I love it when a plan comes together. I wish I could be there."

"Why can't you?"

"Ms. B." She tipped her head and set her hands on her hips. "I can't leave now. Today was our day to decorate for the holidays."

"It can wait until you get back. I promise I'll leave everything out and untouched."

"But look at this mess." She looked around the room and chewed on a nail. They had only been decorating for a few hours and barely put a dent in it. Of course, that was her fault. She couldn't stop herself from pausing to admire and dust every antique or heirloom piece she removed from the boxes. She also took her time deciding on the perfect spot for each one. "There are boxes and decorations everywhere."

"Who cares? Go see your space, and we'll pick up where we left off when you get back."

Torn between two things she loved, decorating for the holidays—the estate was Christmas on steroids—and her physical therapy practice, she decided she could chance running into Cameron again if it meant getting to see her vision come to life.

"Okay. I'm going." She squealed and gave Ms. Beasley a hug. "Thank you. I'll return soon."

"Have fun!"

————

Arriving at VETS, she parked the car near the construction entrance and took a beeline to the physical therapy suite. There, she found large cardboard boxes and unassembled equipment placed haphazardly around the room. Her heart fluttered at the potential it represented.

"Looks like a hurricane happened here," she joked to no one.

"Nope." Cameron popped up from behind a box. "Just progress."

"Cameron," she slapped a hand over her now racing heart. "You frightened me. I didn't see any of the crew on my way in, so I thought I was alone."

"It's lunchtime."

"You didn't want lunch?" She was less than thrilled to know they were the only two people in the entire building.

"Not hungry. Plus, I knew you'd want these put together sooner than later."

"Yes, I'm very excited to see them set up." She searched for an escape. "Well, I don't want to get in your way, so I'll—"

"Actually, I could use some help."

When she hesitated, he put on a smile.

"Sure," she conceded, reminding herself to not let her imagination get carried away, but she still hoped the crew returned soon.

"How long have you and Jackson been dating?" He cut his eyes to her just in time to catch her blushing.

"About six months."

"Hmm. Not as long as we were together…before I screwed it up."

"Cameron." She didn't know what to say, only wanted him to stop. Their working together was awkward and uncomfortable enough.

"I'm sorry," he said, sitting back on his heels. "And I'm happy for you."

"Thank you."

"You see. I'm not such a bad guy."

"I never said you were. In fact, I told Jackson that after you two met."

"You did? Good to know." He flashed her a wide smile and secured the last screw on the treadmill. "Help me set this one up."

Reaching over him, she grabbed hold of the handles and pulled.

"This is awesome." She clapped her hands and swooned at the treadmill and other two pieces of equipment they assembled earlier. There were at least three more to go, plus the furniture still wrapped in plastic in the other rooms.

"Shall we get started on the next one?"

For the next hour, they chatted about nothing in particular as they worked. After the crew returned, the assembly and unpacking progressed much faster.

As she instructed and guided, the crew moved each finished piece to its permanent location until everything was set in place. She scanned the room—her space to grow and nurture others—from the entryway and marveled at another dream come true.

Cameron crossed the room to stand beside her. "What are you thinking about?"

"How grateful I am to not only have this beautiful space, but the opportunity to help so many people who need and deserve it." She took a deep breath before turning to him. "Thank you for all your hard work on this."

"No problem." When she looked back over the room, he continued to watch her. "You're glowing, like the first night we met."

Her gaze shot to his, and she couldn't believe what she saw. After all this time. After everything he knew about her relationship with Jackson. After all he'd put her through, he still had feelings for her. When he asked her out all those months ago, she'd been gullible enough to believe that it was done on a whim. That he simply needed a friendly face to soothe a few lonely days.

His eyes now told her how wrong she'd been.

"Cameron, you can't keep doing this."

"Doing what?"

"Bringing up the past. It's only making our working together more difficult than it already is."

"Emily, I—"

"There you are," Jackson called from the end of the hallway.

"Sweetheart, come see." Grateful for the interruption, she took his hand and tugged him into the room. "Isn't it wonderful?"

Chapter Twenty

✫ ✫ ✫

Emily

Emily grumbled as she lowered herself into the chair and laughed when Genevieve and Sydney scrunched their faces at her. "I can't remember the last time I felt this sore."

"Shut up." Genevieve gave her zero sympathy. "Until you've experienced incubating a human inside you, you have no right to complain."

"Fair enough."

"Why are you sore?" Sydney asked, picking up the oversized restaurant menu.

"We put together the fitness room equipment yesterday, and I spent today decorating the house. We emptied twenty boxes, and it still looks like we just started."

"It's a massive house."

"It will look like a magazine cover when I'm done with it."

"Ask her who helped set up the equipment," Genevieve suggested to Sydney and rolled her eyes back to her own menu.

"Why? I assume based on your expression it wasn't Jackson." Curious excitement had Sydney leaning over the table. "Who was it?"

Before Emily could answer, Genevieve slapped her hand on the table in disgust. "Her good for nothing, asshole of an ex."

"What? How? I'm so confused."

Emily scowled at her so-called best friend. "He works for the construction company Jackson hired. It's an unfortunate circumstance, but Cameron's a good person. He just had a drinking problem at the time that led to some bad decisions. I'm over it."

"You're not seriously making excuses for him, are you?" Genevieve's disgust with Cameron hadn't dissipated one iota since the breakup—over three years ago. True friends, even ones who hold grudges, are to be treasured, Emily mused.

Sydney turned to Emily, wide-eyed. "What did he do? Cheat on you?"

"With her roommate," Genevieve answered, and Sydney's jaw dropped open.

"I thought this was my birthday celebration, not a discussion about my embarrassing past," Emily complained.

"You're right." Genevieve sat back and sipped her water. "I'm sorry for bringing it up."

"No, you're not."

"Guilty as charged."

"Anyway," Sydney began. "I need more details."

"We'll talk later," Genevieve promised, making Emily growl her disapproval.

Satisfied, Sydney winked at her. "Our only goal for the rest of the night will be having a good time in honor of the birthday girl."

"Thank you," she said, despite Genevieve's promise to talk about her behind her back. Then again, it didn't matter. Her history with Cameron was nothing more than that, and they can talk about it all they want. So long as she doesn't have to hear it.

The waiter soon arrived to refill their glasses and take their dinner orders. When he stepped away, Emily looked out over the room. She adored the miniature chandeliers hanging above the tables, the deep burgundy walls, and the ornate framed art on the walls. It had quickly become her favorite restaurant for those reasons alone, but the food and service made it even better.

"That's odd," she said absently.

Genevieve's head whipped up to follow her gaze. "What's she doing here?"

"Looks like she's waiting for someone."

"Who?" Sydney turned and saw Will's cousin Avery sitting alone several tables over. "She didn't tell me she was coming here tonight. I'll go investigate." Popping out of her seat, she went to Avery.

"Don't even think about it," Genevieve protested as Emily watched the other two women talk.

"What am I not to think about?"

"You're thinking about asking her to join us, and it's a bad idea."

"Why?"

"You really have to ask that?" Her hand pops up as she ticks off her thoughts. "For one, she's still in love with your man. And two, she's still in love with your man. Do I need to spell anything else out for you?"

"I feel sorry for her. She looks so sad."

"That's probably because she can't have your man."

"Stop it. They're coming." Emily put on her best smile. "Hi, Avery. It's nice to see you again."

"Hi, Emily. Genevieve," Avery greeted, her tone reluctant as though she'd been forced to say it.

"Her blind date didn't show," Sydney informed the others.

"Oh, no. That's terrible."

"Story of my life."

"You should join us," Emily offered, despite the burning glare she felt from Genevieve.

"That's sweet of you, but I don't want to interrupt."

"You're not. The more the merrier, right girls?"

"Right. See, I told you," Sydney said, hooking her arm around Avery's, as all heads turned toward Genevieve.

She let out a long breath, then pushed out the empty chair across from her with her foot. "Right."

With everyone settled, Emily waved for the waiter, but he was already walking toward them, carrying a bucket with an uncorked wine bottle inside.

"What's this?" she asked when he set it down on their table.

"A gift for you, courtesy of another guest."

"Who?"

"He didn't provide his name. I'll bring another glass for you madam," he said to Avery.

"Thank you. Who could it be?" Avery asked.

"No idea." The anonymous flowers that appeared in her office during the Lucas drama popped into her mind. She spun around, expecting to see him sitting at the bar.

"What is it?" Sydney leaned over the table and placed a hand on her arm.

"It can't possibly be him," Genevieve insisted.

"Who?" Sydney sat back, her concern matching what she saw in them. "Why are you both anxious all of a sudden?"

Emily glanced one last time over the bar and surrounding tables, then settled back into her seat. "It's nothing. Remember the rule for tonight?"

"Only fun," Sydney answered.

"Right. Now, grab that wine. I need a drink."

"Let's get this party started."

———

"I don't know about you, but I'm not ready to go back to adulting," Sydney said to the others after their empty plates were collected. "How about some dancing?"

"I'm always up for that." Genevieve placed a hand on her belly. "But my little man has been doing gymnastics all night, and I'm ready for bed. Sorry."

"You don't even have to ask me. You know I'm in," Avery agreed. "Come on, say yes," she urged Emily when she hesitated.

"Clubs aren't my scene, and I've been to plenty enough to know. Thank you, G."

"You're welcome."

Sydney scooted up in her seat. "I haven't been out in over two years and tonight has been so much fun. I don't want to go home to dirty diapers, toys under my feet, and a cold empty house. Not yet anyway. Please."

With her heart strings successfully tugged, she caved. "Fine, but I can't stay long."

"Some is better than none. I'm ready to let loose and shake my ass."

"That's our cue." Genevieve rose first, then followed the others outside.

"Are you sure you don't want to come with us?" Emily asked after giving her a hug.

"Oh, yeah. It's past my bedtime. You go and have fun, before you're a tired, washed-up momma like me. As Sydney will surely tell you, you need to enjoy your freedom while you can."

"Funny, not funny."

She escorted Genevieve to her car, then walked with the others to their next destination.

Entering through the double doors at the club, the wave of electronic music pulsated through the dark room like a strong wind. Connected together, they found the bar, then made their way to the dance floor with cocktails in hand for Sydney and Avery and a bottled water for Emily.

Watching the mob bounce and move to the ear-splitting chaos masquerading as music, Emily's head pounded rhythmically with the speakers. The strobe lights flashed over the mob from every direction, but she could barely see Avery and Sydney standing beside her. It was the last place she wanted to be.

"I can't believe I've never been here before," Sydney said, tilting closer to Emily so she could hear. "This is exactly what I needed tonight. Thanks for coming."

"No problem." She sipped her water and tried not to despise that decision.

This club was no different than the ones Genevieve dragged her to over the years. Loud, dark, and dangerously crowded. As expected, florescent lights lined the edges of the room and bar, providing the main source of light— except for the random strobe or laser lights shooting overhead. She should be used to it, but places like this would never fit inside her comfort zone.

Her name sounded between the beats, and she spun around with Sydney and Avery following.

"Cameron?"

"What a coincidence seeing you here," he yelled over the music and ran his eyes over her. "I thought you hated dance music."

"What?" she yelled, regretting it immediately since it caused him to lean closer.

"I thought you hated dance clubs."

"I do. With a passion."

"Out celebrating your birthday?"

She leaned back, surprise surely taking over her face. "I can't believe you re—"

"It's tomorrow, right?"

"Yes."

"Happy birthday."

Straightening, he focused on the other girls. "Who are you celebrating with?"

"My friends, Sydney and Avery."

"Nice to meet you. This is Robbie." He pointed to his friend and reached out his hand to both as the music lowered.

"Oh, thank God." Emily sighed and smiled at Cameron's co-worker and friend. "Hi, Robbie. Nice to see you out outside of the construction zone."

"Yes, it is, Ms. Robertson."

"Please call me Emily," she insisted, but he wasn't listening. Robbie could only see Sydney.

"Genevieve already on the dance floor?" Cameron asked.

"No. She wasn't feeling well, so she went home."

"She didn't drink all the wine, did she? No." He waved a hand. "That couldn't be it. I remember her boasting that she never gets drunk."

"Were sent the bottle at the restaurant?"

His smile widened. "Was it good?"

"Were you there? I didn't see you."

"No, but I knew that's where you were going tonight."

"How?"

"The walls at VETS are still a little thin."

"We were just on our way to get a drink," Robbie mentioned. "Can we get you anything?"

Sydney held up her full glass and smiled sweetly at him. "I'm good. Thanks."

"Me, too," Avery said.

"Maybe we'll see you later?" Cameron added before Robbie pulled him into the darkness.

"At least the wine mystery is solved, but out with it," Sydney turned on Emily. "I can't wait for story time with Genevieve. I need all the spicy details and now."

"About what?"

"Don't play dumb with me," she fussed. "What's up with you and Cameron?"

"There's a you and Cameron?" Avery tuned in.

"No, there is not. We dated in college, and it ended badly, but we both got over it and moved on. That's all there is to tell."

Avery took a sip of her fruity cocktail. "How long were you together?"

"Two years."

"They broke up because he cheated on her with her roommate." Sydney caught Avery up on what she'd missed at dinner.

"Sydney, I really don't want to talk about this. It hurt then, and it's awkward now."

"You forgave him?"

"Yes. We were very different people back then, and he apologized."

"He seems nice."

"He is." *When he isn't drunk,* she thought.

"Finally!" Avery interrupted when the music revved up again. "Let's go."

"You go ahead. We'll be there in a minute," Sydney promised and accepted the glass Avery handed her.

"I can't believe you two are friends," Sydney said to Emily and set Avery's drink on a nearby table. "Don't get me wrong. I adore her. She's like a sister to me, but she's Jackson's ex."

"So? She's done nothing to me, and I appreciate how she helped him."

"She hasn't let him go."

"I know, but it doesn't matter. Maybe she needs to see us together to give her a nudge."

"Wouldn't that be nice?" She turned to set down her drink and discovered Robbie had joined them. "Hello again."

"I was hoping I could entice you to dance with me," he said shyly.

"That isn't necessary. I'd love a dance." Sydney linked an arm with his when he offered it, and flashed Emily a playful smile over her shoulder.

"You have the prettiest eyes I've ever seen," Emily heard him say, and swooned. *What a sweet—*

"Cameron!" She slapped a hand over her racing heart. Why was he always catching her off guard?

"Didn't mean to scare you. Robbie left me at the bar, so I figured he came back this way. He has the hots for your friend."

"They went to dance, and it's obvious how he feels about her." She took a sip of water and searched for Avery, hoping she'd return soon. "I didn't thank you for the wine earlier. It was very tasty."

"You're welcome. How's your house in Savannah? I heard someone broke in and did some damage."

"How did you know about that?"

"Word travels fast."

"I didn't tell anyone about it, other than G and my neighbor. How did you hear?"

"I don't know. Maybe your realtor told someone."

"My realtor?" She shifted to face him, familiar concerns resurfacing. "The house isn't on the market yet."

He held up his hands. "I'm sorry, Emily. I didn't mean to upset you."

"I know." She made significant effort to keep her nerves under control. "I'm the one that should apologize. It's a touchy subject."

"Do you have an idea who did it?"

"No. My dad's working with the detectives, but they haven't found any clues."

"That's too bad."

"Emily." Avery bounded up, snatched her drink off the table, and tossed it back. She was breathing rapidly, tiny beads of sweat forming around her hairline.

"Having fun?" she asked, relieved to have female company.

"Yes. You must come dance."

Finally, she had a way out. "Sure."

"You should come, too," Avery commanded Cameron and grabbed them both by the arm.

"Why don't you two go? I'll stay with the drinks." Her desperate attempt to back-track fell on deaf ears.

"Come on. I love this song!"

She dragged them into the center of the floor and danced beside them for a moment, before bouncing off into the crowd. Suspecting she'd been set up, Emily looked for someone to save her. She located Sydney lip-locked with Robbie. She'd be useless.

The music slowed and the crowd density thickened, trapping Emily where she stood. Cameron held out his hand with a charming and gentle grace, but Emily had the urge to slap it away. Why had she come?

While she frantically searched for an excuse to leave, an exuberant dancer bumped into her from behind, pushing her against Cameron. She hadn't meant to, but she'd gripped his shoulders for balance, and before she knew it, his arms had circled her waist, holding her upright.

Embarrassed and flustered, every muscle in her body was on alert and screaming at her to run.

"Relax, Emily. We used to slow dance in your apartment all the time." He leaned down subtly and breathed in as he swayed, pushing her hips to the beat of the music. "You'd play those ridiculous Whitney Houston and Mariah Carey songs until—"

"No," she yelled and stepped back. "I don't want this."

"What do you mean? I wasn't—"

"I know what you're doing, Cameron. Please, just leave me alone."

In a few steps, she was swallowed by the crowd, desperate for the quiet solitude of her car. She gave Sydney a hug on the way by without giving her a chance to ask questions and zeroed in on the glowing exit signs. Once outside, a cold wind smacked her across the face, making her wish she'd brought a jacket. But she had no time for regrets. All she could think about was getting out of there and going home. She fumbled for her keys with frozen fingers, finally locating them at the bottom of her purse, and pushed the unlock button.

Letting out a long, visible breath, she cranked up the heater and leaned back against the headrest. How had such a laid-back night out with friends taken such a hazardous turn? Stupid question. She knew exactly why.

"Cameron!" He surprised her by stepping in front of the car, the headlights painting him in a beam of white. Motionless, as if frozen in time, he stared at her through the glass. Her pulse raced, beating like the club's speakers still sounding off in her ears.

He moved forward, and she jumped, startled by the sudden movement. With each step he took closer, her stomach rose higher into her throat. Her mind spun with possible things he could say or do and none of them were good, but it didn't stop her from pushing the button when he motioned for her to roll down the window.

"What is it?" A gust of wind blew through the open window, flinging her hair off her shoulders and sending a shutter down her back.

"My truck won't start. Can you give me a ride?"

"What about Robbie?"

"I don't want to disturb him. He's having a good time with Little Red."

"Her name is Sydney."

"Right. Can you give me a ride back to my motel?" When she hesitated, he crossed his arms against the cold. "Come on. It's freezing out here."

Her temper came bubbling back to the surface along with the memories. When they were together, she'd held on to their relationship longer than was healthy to avoid conflict and heartache. With Lucas, she wasn't firm enough with her wishes, and look at the damage he caused. Both were significant mistakes, and she refused to make a third.

"Seriously?"

"What?"

His pinched brow told her he hadn't expected her to do anything but back down.

"It's just a favor for a friend."

"We're not friends, Cameron. I didn't want to dance with you earlier. I don't want to give you a ride or do you any favors."

A vein in his neck pulsed. Although she needed to make him understand, she also worried about her safety. Vulnerable out there alone with him, she was all too familiar with what that thick vein of his meant. If he went off, she had no way to defend herself... again. Hadn't she learned her lesson?

"What do you think I'm doing here, Emily?"

"I see the way you look at me, Cameron. I'm not the person you remember, and what we once had is ancient history. I've forgiven you, but I don't want to talk about our time together or make new memories. Understand?"

He shoved his hands in his pockets as Lucas would when he was amused by her attempts to be stern, and she had to remind herself that they were not the same person.

"I understand perfectly. You are my customer, nothing more. The years we spent together mean nothing to you."

"Cameron."

He turned to walk away, and although she wanted to feel bad for hurting him, she couldn't locate the emotion. Instead, she took off with a screech of the tires, relieved the conversation ended and proud of herself for saying what needed to be said. Her body may have cowered and trembled in fear—that disgusting habit would be a hard one to break—but she'd overcome and did what she'd always struggled to do.

She didn't let him manipulate her or walk over her. At the time, it felt amazing to face a conflict head-on. Especially after all that she endured with Lucas, and despite her obliging nature. But now that she'd had time to reflect on the out-of-body experience, she hoped to never have to do it again.

Chapter Twenty-One

✯ ✯ ✯

Jackson

S he's bringing a date?" Emily asked when he told her Sydney wasn't only bringing William to dinner that night.

"Yep. Apparently, she's been secretly seeing someone and wants to go public with their relationship."

Joining her on the couch by the fireplace, he rested a hand on her leg. A winter storm left a deep chill in the air, and the furnace constantly labored to keep the old house warm. "Any idea who it is?"

"I may. Remember when G, Sydney, and I went out for my birthday?"

"Oh, yeah. You said she hit it off with Robbie. He does great work and seems like a good guy."

"The way he reacted to her reminded me of when Ben first saw G, except with less primal lust and more sweetness." She grimaced then giggled. "She hasn't mentioned him since then, but that night, their lips were inseparable."

"Not sure I need those details, but I look forward to getting to know him better. Check out who will be hanging around my boy."

"Good idea." Emily glanced at her watch. "Crap! Aren't they coming at six?"

"Yeah."

"I didn't realize it was this late." Throwing the blanket off her legs, she jumped up. "I need to get ready."

"They won't be here for at least an hour," he called after her, but she was already running up the stairs.

Resigned to waiting alone, he turned on the television, something he hadn't done in years, and flipped through the channels. After a second pass through, he switched it off as Emily's phone rang. He checked the Caller ID and answered it.

"Hi, Charlie."

"Jackson. How are you, son?"

"I'm great. Thanks. How's Florida?"

"Better than up there. I hear you got some snow last night."

"Nothing a little sun and snowplow can't handle. Want me to get Emily for you?"

"Actually, I'd rather talk to you."

"What's up?"

"I may have a lead on who was breaking into Emily's house."

"That's great news. Is it anyone she knows?"

"Not sure. Has she mentioned a guy named Cameron Reid?"

"You're shitting me?" He stood and paced the room. "Are you sure?"

"No. Not yet. Do you know him?"

"Yes. He's an ex of hers from college."

"I thought the name sounded vaguely familiar. The old noggin' isn't what it used to be."

Jackson shoved a hand through his hair as his stomach knotted into angry fists. "Why do you think it might be him?"

"The letter she found."

"I never asked her what it said. Didn't want to upset her again."

"It didn't say much and most of the sentences were illegible. Almost like he wrote it drunk."

Jackson thought about the damage done to her house in Savannah, and his temper began to beat on his temple. "Or during a blind rage."

"You're probably right, but we were able to make out one clue to point us in a direction, whether it's the right one or not. We did some digging on this guy. I didn't want to alarm Emily before we knew more, but…"

"But what, Charlie?"

"We found out that he recently moved to Richmond. The coincidence is something we can't ignore."

"He's working at VETS."

"You're joking."

"I wish I was. It doesn't feel like a coincidence anymore."

"What is he doing there?"

"He was appointed as the foreman after his predecessor was injured. He works for the contractor I hired."

"I see."

Jackson returned to pacing. How could this be happening again? First Lucas and now Cameron. "Charlie, I don't like all these supposed coincidences."

"Me either. Has Emily mentioned anything to you about how he's acting around her?"

"Not really. She doesn't love having him here, but she seems to be fine." He stopped mid-stride. "Wait, she told me that she ran into him at a nightclub a few weeks back. He sent her wine at the restaurant, hung around her group at a club, and left when she did. Could he be following her?"

"We're probably reading too much into it, but I wouldn't rule anything out at this point. Keep an eye on him and keep her close. If he does or says anything suspicious, let me know immediately."

"Of course, but I can't promise I won't take care of the situation first."

"I would expect nothing less."

"And if you learn anything…"

"You'll be the first one I call."

"Thanks, Charlie." After hanging up, Jackson threw the phone onto the couch as fury and fear sunk their claws into his head. "Not now."

"Jackson, are you okay?" Ms. Beasley rushed to his side when he dropped to sit on the fireplace hearth, his head in his hands. "Come."

She led him into the kitchen, filled a glass with water, and disappeared into the pantry. Soon, she placed the glass, now filled with a light pink liquid, and three Tylenol in front of him. "Take this now before it gets worse."

He did as she instructed and took slow, deep breaths with his head resting on the cool stone counter.

"I'll get Emily."

"No," he managed through the blinding light and pain. "I'll be fine." He didn't want to worry her, and he needed to think. While Ms. Beasley returned to her work, reluctantly, of course, he closed his eyes and ran through the last several months in his mind.

He replayed how Cameron looked at Emily the first time at VETS. It bothered him, but it seemed harmless at the time. Now, he wasn't so sure. It was too similar to how Lucas looked at her when she introduced them at the deli in Savannah. They both seemed to want her, but in different ways. Lucas wanted to possess her. Cameron longed for her and what they once had. That didn't necessarily mean he was dangerous.

Then, he pictured what was left of Emily's house. If Cameron had been the one to destroy it, they couldn't have him at VETS, much less in Richmond, or anywhere near

Emily. He needed to find the truth. The only option he had until uncovering more evidence was to get to know him better. If he felt comfortable, he may reveal more over time.

With the pain receding, he sat up and sucked in a deep breath. Thank goodness for Ms. Beasley and her strange concoctions.

Pushing off the stool, he stalked to the office and looked out at the sea of white in the front yard. He needed to keep his mind just as blank. The tranquil scenery and nerve dousing brew worked to keep his mind in safe territory until a truck rolled through the gate. Their guests had arrived. After the news he'd learned from Charlie, he looked forward to the distraction William and getting to know new friends would provide.

Once in the foyer, he called for Emily from the foyer.

"Are you feeling okay?" she asked, noticing the change in him. She watched him closely these days, and he loved her for it.

"I'm fine. Just a little headache." He kissed her forehead, grateful to have her safe by his side, and swore she would stay there. When the doorbell rang, he lifted her chin with his finger and kissed her one last time.

"What are you doing here?" he asked Cameron directly when he opened the door and noticed him standing behind Sydney with a smug grin.

"I was invited."

Emily's hand tightened around his, reminding him of his manners. But she didn't know what her father found. She didn't know the man in front of them might not be who she thought him to be. That she may be inviting someone dangerous into their home, when she said, "Why don't you come in out of the cold?"

He hugged Sydney after they entered through the door and accepted William when he jumped into his arms.

"I couldn't pass up the opportunity to see the great Vane estate," Cameron added and removed his coat. "Sydney's told me so much about it."

Sydney smiled at him then wrapped her arms around Emily. "You okay? You look like you've seen a ghost."

"I thought you were bringing Robbie," she whispered.

"Surprise," Sydney joked, releasing her. "Is it awkward? I know you two used to date, but you said you were over it."

"No. It's fine. Let me take your coats."

She helped Jackson unzip and peel William out of his jacket. Then, she gathered the others and tossed the pile onto the parlor couch.

"Emily, this place looks like it was decorated for a holiday *Southern Living* cover. It's gorgeous!" Sydney looked around, her mouth gaping open as she took it all in.

"That was the goal. Ms. Beasley and I had a lot of fun with it. It took forever, but I loved every minute," Emily beamed, and Jackson loved how much joy the estate brought her. It had started rubbing off on him the more she settled in and made the home theirs.

"How about we get out of the foyer and get a drink?" Jackson suggested and put William down. "Cameron, do you like Scotch?"

"Yes, I do."

———

Emily

"You two enjoy your bro time," Sydney said, grabbing William's hand. "I want to see the living room."

Once William recognized his surroundings, he took off toward the basket of toys kept in the corner of the living room just for him.

Stopping in the doorway, Sydney clasped her hands over her mouth. "Oh my."

"I know. Isn't it magnificent?" Emily was especially proud of how the living room turned out. She'd combined traditional Vane decorations with those she'd used in her home in Savannah. Her Christmas decorations were some of the few items that survived the destruction since she kept them in the attic.

The sixteen-foot pine tree was freshly cut from a tree farm about thirty miles outside Richmond. It took over an hour to find one that matched her vision, but it couldn't be more perfect for their first Christmas together.

Sydney examined each item on the fireplace mantle before turning to face her with tears in her eyes. "You know, I've been in this house many times now, and it always takes my breath away. This," she ran her hand over the carvings in the wood fireplace, "is my favorite." She smiled, but it strained.

"Mine, too."

"The house is so beautiful, but seeing it decorated for Christmas, for family gatherings, and making happy memories, it's more of a home. He deserves that."

Emily's eyes blurred with tears at the sentiment. "I love how much you care for him."

"I do. If Will was still here, I have no doubt that we'd be married by now because I would have gotten tired of waiting and proposed to him." She laughed. "Jackson would have been his best man, and just like that, I'd have a new brother."

"I know you still miss him."

"Every day. Sometimes it's suffocating, especially when I think of what could have been." She took a deep breath to stay in control of her emotions. "He was Jackson's best friend and mine. The four of us would have done everything together. Raised our children, taken vacations, and celebrated birthdays and holidays together. It should be Will in there with Jackson right now."

Sobs suddenly burst from her throat. She cried in Emily's arms until being led to the couch.

"I'm sorry," Sydney said, accepting the box of tissues Emily passed her. "I've been trying to not do this so much. It's been two years, for goodness' sake."

"You'll probably always miss him, but when you fall in love again, those memories won't hurt as much."

Sydney sniffed, lost in her thoughts, then slumped back against the couch.

"What is it?" Emily asked. "You look like something came to mind."

"What if I can't love again? What if Will was my only shot at it? My heart feels like it's dead. The only thing keeping me going is my son—our son." Sydney looked over the back of the couch at William, playing contently in the corner.

"I know you're frustrated and lonely, but it will get better."

It probably wasn't the great advice Sydney hoped to hear, but it was all she could provide. She had no experience to draw from and tried to imagine having to move on if something ever happened to Jackson. She couldn't. It would feel impossible. *Would* be impossible.

"Are you happy with Cameron?" she asked to keep the *what ifs* from taking over her good mood.

Sydney shrugged. "He's been a nice distraction. He's cute—love his blond curls—and makes me laugh."

"That's something, but I have to know how this happened."

"Me and Cam, you mean?"

"Did another surprise walk through our door tonight? Yes, I mean you and Cameron. Last time I saw you, your lips were glued to Robbie's."

"Robbie's a great kisser, the sweetest guy I've ever met, and so not my type. I like men with a wild side." She winked, looking more relaxed.

"So, tell me. How'd you two come together?"

William running up to the couch and handing her a truck interrupted her explanation. "We bumped into each other at the grocery store of all places."

"Really? When?"

"The day after your birthday party when you watched William for me so I could study for finals. I needed a break and went there for comfort food."

"Ice cream?"

"What else? And cookies and pie to go with it. I think I gained five pounds that day."

"I can't believe you didn't tell me," Emily complained.

"It started casual—a meet up for coffee or lunch here or there."

"But it's more serious now?"

"Getting there." She grinned. "He's a pleasant distraction at least."

———

Jackson

While their girlfriends talked, Jackson worked extra hard to not declare Cameron guilty without the necessary details. They sat in awkward silence in the office, sipping scotch in glasses etched with the Vane family insignia, and he'd yet to pull it off.

"So, Jackson. What do you want to know?"

"What?" He lowered the glass he'd raised to his lips.

"I know we're here so you can get the dirt on me."

"Alright." He took a long drink then set the glass aside. "I assume you know how much Sydney and William mean to me."

"I have an idea, but we haven't been together long enough to get into our pasts. Is she an ex of yours?"

"No."

"Darn. That would have made us even."

"Not funny."

"The boy yours?"

"No." Jackson stood quickly, his rising blood pressure pulsing behind his eyes.

To release the pressure, he plucked his glass from the table and stepped to the bookshelf. As he sipped, he noticed a new framed picture Emily must have added recently—a photo of him holding William by the lake at sunset. His tiny arms were wrapped tight around Jackson's neck as they both laughed. He loved William as he would his own and must do what was needed to protect him.

"Since you asked, I guess that means you haven't heard what happened to his father."

"Sydney hasn't mentioned anything."

"His father was my best friend, and he died before William was born." He turned to meet Cameron's gaze. "I wasn't looking for dirt on you. I just wanted to get to know the man hanging out with my godson and his mother. Plus, you're in charge of the construction at VETS. I'd be stupid not to learn more about you."

"Fair enough. So, I'll ask again. What do you want to know?" A little too at ease for Jackson's liking, Cameron leaned back in his chair, his eyes challenging him.

"Will you return to Savannah when the project is over?"

"I'm not sure. It all depends on my next assignment and if I have any reasons to stay."

"Sydney?"

"Not ruling it out, but we just started seeing each other. It's too early to be planning our future together, don't you think?"

Jackson thought of the first time he saw Emily and shrugged. He knew she was the only woman for him before he even spoke to her.

"You don't agree?" he asked when Jackson didn't respond.

"No. I think you're right." Time to build some trust, he decided. The conversation hadn't started the way he intended. A detective he was not. Although, he'd gotten plenty of training and experience reading body language in the military. He'd mastered the skill, but, to his frustration, Cameron remained a mystery. "You're doing a great job at VETS, by the way."

"Thank you. It's an interesting project." He took another sip, watching Jackson over the rim. "Emily seems excited."

"Yes. She's always wanted to run her own practice."

"I remember. She must be very grateful to you for making it happen."

"I believe she feels more than gratitude." What was it about this guy? His blood raged at boiling again, and he had to tap into his training to keep from taking Cameron by his collar and throwing him against the wall. Beating the truth out of him sounded like a better idea than befriending him at that moment.

He held up his free hand. "I wasn't trying to imply anything."

"I'm sorry. I've been a little on edge lately." He decided to try another tactic.

"Why? Stress from VETS?"

"That doesn't help, but it's something that happened to her in Savannah. We're still trying to figure out who did it."

"What happened?"

Jackson paced the room. "Someone broke into her house and destroyed it this past summer. Not sure what message the coward was trying to send, but it didn't work." He whipped around to face Cameron sitting in the chair— the height difference added to his advantage. "Have you heard anything about it?"

"We don't run in the same circles anymore, but I heard grumblings."

"Really? From who?"

"I don't remember. I was back and forth a lot over a few assignments, so this year's mostly a blur."

Convenient. "What projects did you work on?"

He hesitated as if he had to think it through before answering or come up with a story that would sound believable. "There was an office building in Macon and a rec center in Tallahassee."

"Oh yeah, I remember talking about those with David during our interviews. I thought those finished up last spring." *Gotcha*, he thought, but Cameron's body language remained unaffected.

"Maybe I'm getting my projects mixed up. I travel so much I'm rarely in one place very long." He drained his glass as Sydney stepped into the room.

"Dinner's on the table, boys. Come eat."

Chapter Twenty-Two

✵ ✵ ✵

Jackson

L ater that night, after tucking William into his crib in the guest bedroom and Emily had fallen asleep, Jackson retreated to his office. He sat by the window in the dark, watching snowflakes dance in moonbeams as they fell to the ground. The silence allowed his mind to process and analyze all he'd learned that night, and unfortunately, travel back in time.

"There you are," Emily said to announce her presence. "It's three o'clock in the morning. Everything okay?"

"I'm not sure."

"What's going on? Is it your memories?"

"Not so much." Touched by her concern, he took her hand and tugged her into his lap.

"Then, what's bothering you?"

"How do you feel about Cameron and Sydney dating?"

Caught off guard, she drew back to see him. The moonlight reflected off the snow outside and streamed in through the large windows, highlighting her face in pale light. "They seem happy, and she likes him."

He shook his head. "I want to know how *you* feel."

"I don't love it."

"Does he make you uncomfortable?"

"Jackson, why are you asking these questions?"

"I need to know, Emily. Are you uncomfortable being around him, or has he done anything to make you uneasy?"

She held his gaze and understood how serious and gravely worried he was. "Yes. He makes me uncomfortable. I think he still has feelings for me, or at least he did before he started dating Sydney."

"What makes you think that?"

"It's the way he looks at me. He's also said a few things that could be taken in that way, but I could just be reading too much into it. I'm a little skittish since… You know." She placed a hand on Jackson's cheek. "What's going on, sweetheart?"

"I wasn't supposed to say anything yet, but now that he and Sydney are dating, it's more complicated now."

"What weren't you supposed to tell me? You're scaring me." She shifted to the other side of the window seat to face him and crossed her legs under her.

"I'm sorry. I don't mean to." He held both of her hands. If anything ever happened to her, he wouldn't survive it. "Your father called while you were getting ready earlier."

"Are they okay?"

"Yes. He and your mother are fine. It's about the break-ins. He may have a lead."

She sat back, shock and fear taking over her body.

"He didn't want me to tell you until he had more evidence, but now more people are at risk. More people I care about."

"More people? Who?"

"Sydney, William, all of us."

Her hand clasped over her mouth when her brain translated what he was trying to say. "Cameron?"

He nodded.

"Oh, my God. Oh, my God." She dropped her head into her hands and rocked.

"I know this is hard to—"

Her head popped up, her eyes finding him through unshed tears. "Why does Dad think it's him?"

"There was something in the letter that pointed him that way."

"What letter?"

"You found a letter in your room. Don't you remember?"

"No. What did it say?"

"I don't know. You handed it to Charlie, and then you fainted. You don't remember?"

"No. Well, I remember fainting and remember waking up on the couch with you, but not a letter."

"You must have been in shock. I think you read it before joining us in the living room. Can you remember anything about it?"

Her eyes cut to her lap, and he bent to see her face.

She shook her head as the tears came. "Destroying the house is one thing—anyone could do that. Leaving a letter after painstakingly tearing apart my home is personal. The officer I talked to had been right. This is about me and what I mean to whoever did this."

"Do you think Cameron is capable of doing it?" He swiped her tears with his thumb, trying his best to stay calm for her benefit.

"I don't know. I didn't think Lucas could do what he did either. Look where that naivety got me." She started to drop into his lap for his comforting embrace, then straightened. "Oh, God. Sydney. We have to tell her."

"We will. We'll try to steer her away from him, but we can't tell her any details until we know for sure. What if it's not him?"

"Do you think she and William are in danger?"

"I wish I knew. I couldn't get a read on him tonight."

Not willing to let either of their minds to wander to the unthinkable, he took her in his arms and focused on what was most important. "We need to figure out if he did this. Now that you know he's a potential suspect, think back on your previous interactions with him, the graffiti, and the break-ins. Does anything jump out at you?"

Sitting back, she thought for a beat. "No. There's nothing," she admitted with a sigh. "If it is him, I can't understand why. Why would he break into my home and follow me to Richmond? He broke off our relationship, and I've done nothing to make him think I want anything to do with him. Although he gave it, I didn't want an apology. I don't want to talk to him, or see him, or get back together."

"That's good news," he joked, and flashed her an uneasy smile when she looked his way.

"I never wanted anything to do with him. You do know that, right?"

With a nod, he raised her hand to his lips. He knew he didn't have to worry about her feelings wavering, but it still felt good to hear it. "Maybe he's romanticized what happened between you and wants you back. What?" he asked when her eyes widened.

"You may be right. I thought nothing of it before." She stared into the darkness surrounding them, focusing on her thoughts.

"What? What happened?"

When she stood and began pacing the room, alarms went off in his head. Shooting off the window seat, he grabbed her arms and turned her to face him. "Emily, what did he do?"

Her eyes glistened as she searched for the words to begin. "I'm sorry, Jackson."

Softening his grip, he stepped back, unsure of what she was about to say and confident he didn't want to hear it. "Sorry for what, Emily?"

"I didn't keep my promise to you. I didn't tell you everything that happened the night we ran into Cameron and Robbie at the nightclub."

The walls were closing in on him, and he feared the worst. Had something happened between them after all? A few hours of reminiscing evolving into a moment of passion. He tried to stay calm, but his mind raced faster than his pulse, and he stumbled backward.

"Jackson, it's not what you think."

Despite the low light, he couldn't hide his pain and anger. She crossed to him, took his hand, and led him to the dual chairs in front of the window.

He sat, but only because his legs were too weak to pace. "What is it then? Because the images in my mind are making me sick."

She took another long, shaky breath. "At the club after dinner, Avery dragged both of us onto the dance floor. The next thing I knew, she was gone, and the music switched to a slow song. I tried to get away, but I was knocked into him."

The thought of Cameron's hands on her had blood gushing recklessly through his veins. "Go on."

She felt his muscles tense and swallowed hard, bracing for his reaction. "He grabbed hold of me like we were slow dancing and held on."

"What did you do?"

"I pushed away and told him to leave me alone."

"But he didn't."

"No. I left immediately, and by the time I got to my car, he was there. It was as if he hadn't heard a word I said."

"Why didn't you tell me about this when you mentioned him asking for a ride?"

"The more I thought about it, the more I second-guessed his intentions and my reaction. When he asked me for a ride, he said we were friends. After I left and calmed down, I began to wonder if I'd misread him. Maybe he wasn't trying to do anything, and his intentions were innocent. Maybe he just wanted to dance. I felt bad for being rude."

"You're too nice. Do you still feel like you overreacted?"

"I don't know. He kept bringing up moments we spent together, or things he remembered about me." She combed her fingers through her hair and stood. "I never should have gone."

She took his hand. "Jackson, no matter what I did or didn't do, please know that I didn't keep it from you to hide anything."

"I understand, but we've already been through this."

"I know, and I'm sorry."

He rose and stalked to the bookshelves, trying not to fall apart. "He's playing with your emotions. Either he wants you back or wants his way with you, and he's willing to say whatever is needed to keep you close." Stalking back to the bottle of scotch he shared with the asshole just hours before, he yanked out the crystal top and poured a double. "It's the fucking doctor all over again."

She placed a hand on his rigid back as he tossed back the shot and poured another.

"I'll kill him if he touches you again. I won't be able to stop myself this time."

"I won't let him."

"How?" Knowing he may not be able to save her a second time, no matter how hard he tried, he sunk deeper into the quicksand of hopelessness. "You didn't want Lucas to touch you, but that didn't stop him." Leaning his hands on the serving table, he fought the migraine, the fear, his unstable and flaring temper. "Damn it!"

"Jackson, I—"

"We have nothing on him—no proof. He owns us and is just waiting for the right moment to crack the whip." His knuckles went white from gripping the edge of the small wooden table for support.

She wrapped her arms around him from behind. "Jackson," she said to get his attention, but his eyes couldn't raise to hers. "Jackson, we'll be okay. Look at me, sweetheart." Placing a hand on his cheek, she turned his face and pressed her lips to his until his heart rate slowed. "I love you, and he can't do anything to us that we can't handle together."

"I'm sorry," he managed and buried his face in her hair. Through the rage, he saw the fear in her eyes, and it tore him in half. The last thing she needed was to fear him too.

"There's nothing you need to apologize for. *I'm* sorry."

His head spun from the potent mixture of alcohol and stress. "I didn't mean to frighten you."

"You didn't," she whispered, but he surprised her when he straightened. In his eyes, she saw what he was thinking. "I wasn't scared of you," she clarified. "Just where your mind might go next. I hate how much trauma I've caused you since we've met."

"Trauma?"

"In the hospital with G, Jacksonville, and now Cameron. I don't want to be the reason you slip backward."

He laughed for the first time that night, and all tension melted from his body. "My love, you're why I fight to stay out of that hell." He took her hands. "You are my reason for living, and you have been since before I left for Orlando."

Tears filled her eyes. "Before? I don't understand."

He motioned for her to sit, and he did the same opposite her. "I felt an urge to leave Richmond long before I had the idea for the memorial run. It was telling me to go find you, but I didn't know that until I saw you."

She shifted into his lap and curled around him, allowing him to relish the feel of her in his arms.

"You're right, as always," he added and kissed her hair. "We will get through this. Nothing could ever tear us apart."

Chapter Twenty-Three

☆ ☆ ☆

Jackson

I need to warn you about something," Jackson said one night while he and Emily lied in bed, enjoying the quiet after a long day of meetings and errands.

"You do?" She rolled over and placed a hand on his chest. The snow clouds blanketing the sky shadowed her face, but he could hear the worry in her voice. "This doesn't sound good."

"There's a certain day in December where I struggle more than others, and I want you to be prepared."

"Okay. What happens?"

"My blood pressure spikes, and I have a panic attack. It usually ends with a black out, or at least it has the last two years. There's nothing I can do to stop it or control it."

"Oh, Jackson, that sounds terrible. Do you know why?"

"It's the explosion's anniversary—December twentieth." He swallowed back the memory. "I was hoping this year would be different, but after what you said the other night, I wanted you to know in case it happens again."

"What did I say?" She pushed to her knees and switched on the lamp beside the bed.

"You said you don't want to be the reason I slip backward. I didn't want you to think it was your fault. It's never your fault."

She nodded, empathy softening the fear in her eyes.

"And I didn't want to scare you. Ms. Beasley and Eleanor have both been through it with me, so if you need to talk to someone…"

"I'm sorry you suffer with this, sweetheart." She leaned down and pressed her lips softly to his. "Thank you for telling me. There's not anything we can do to prevent it?"

"I'm not sure. If there is, I haven't found it yet. Then again, you weren't here the last two times." She matched his smile. "Maybe you're the antidote."

"I want to be, but I don't think I have that kind of power. Do you get a warning? Do you know when it's coming?"

"No. The first time, I had no idea it was even happening. My father casually mentioned the day, and my body reacted. The second time, my mind wandered into it. That was once a hazardous thing for me. Still is sometimes."

"What if we made love all day? Would that keep your mind occupied enough to stop it from happening?" She grinned.

"I'm willing to try anything."

"I bet. You know the twentieth is this week, right?"

"Yes. That's why I brought it up. I made sure not to schedule anything at VETS that day."

"Then, it's decided. We'll spend the day together doing whatever makes you happy, and if your mind starts to wander, we'll just have to find a distraction."

"I like the sound of that."

———

Emily

"Can we stay here all day?" Emily sighed and snuggled closer to Jackson between the warm sheets. The sun peaked through breaks in the clouds, casting a muted light through the sheer curtains. Since they stayed up late talking, she wasn't ready to start the day. Plus, the Sydney and Cameron situation waited for her at VETS, and she wasn't looking forward to dealing with that either.

"We have a lot of work to do if we're going to open by April first," he answered lazily without opening his eyes. "It sounds like it's a long way off, but it will be here before we know it."

"It would be worth it. Having Lazy Saturday on another Thursday sounds pretty good right about now."

"Mmm." He sighed. "Ms. B is probably wondering where we are."

She propped herself up on his bare chest and studied him. Relieved to see amusement on his face, she wanted to hold on tight and keep that gorgeous smile on his face. "Are you actually trying to get out of spending a day in bed with me?"

"Absolutely not. Now that you mention it, that's suddenly all I want to do."

Giggling, she snuggled under his arm and dozed off until his cell phone rang, shocking her out of a gratified slumber.

He snatched it off the bedside table with a grumble and checked the I.D. "It's your father," he announced and sat up to answer it. "Hello, Charlie."

"Did I wake you?" he asked with a touch of amusement in his voice. "It's after ten."

Jackson confirmed the time using his grandfather's antique clock on the dresser and scowled. "Is everything all right?" Holding the phone up to his ear with his shoulder, he slipped into a pair of shorts.

"I wanted to check in since our conversation yesterday. I think we should tell Emily."

The events of the previous night flooded his thoughts and made his stomach churn. "Funny you should say that."

"Oh yeah? Did the little fucker do something?"

"I'll let Emily tell you." To maintain his sanity, he passed her the phone, kissed her on the forehead, and padded to the bathroom to take a shower.

She waited for the bathroom door to close before giving her attention to her father. "Hi, Daddy."

"Sweetheart. It's so great to hear your voice. Everything okay there?"

"Yeah. I think so, anyway. Jackson told me you think Cameron is the one breaking into the house." She expected him to backtrack, but he didn't skip a beat.

"Has something happened since I called?"

"You could say that." She told him about Cameron's actions when they ran into each other at the club.

"Is that it?"

"Isn't that enough?" She tried to laugh it off, and then it hit her. "Oh, shit." It was such a red flag. How could she have forgotten about it?

"What?"

"Somehow, he knew about the break-ins, and my putting the house on the market. I swore my neighbor and realtor to secrecy, and I know G wouldn't gossip. Have you told anyone?"

"Who would I tell? He could have gotten the break-in information from the daily call reports on the S.P.D. website or happened to see the moving trucks."

"If either of those is the case, I'm even more worried."

"It's definitely suspicious."

The water in the shower shut off. "He's seeing Sydney."

"Who's Sydney?"

"Sorry. Jackson's godson's mother. We've grown close, and we're now worried about both of them."

"Why is he seeing her if he's after you?"

Feeling on edge again, she sighed. "We don't know he's after me. I'm just going on a gut feeling and a lot of circumstantial evidence. All I'm concerned about now is making sure Sydney and William don't get hurt. She's been through a lot already."

"Don't worry. Your old man's on the job, and we'll figure this out."

She laughed and realized she needed it. "Thanks, Daddy. Are you calling for a reason, or were you just checking in?"

"Is Jackson still with you?"

"No. He went to take a shower. What's wrong?"

"Get him, sweetheart, and I'll tell you."

"Hold on." Setting down the phone, she opened the bathroom door and found Jackson at the sink preparing to shave, a towel wrapped around his waist. She motioned for him to join her in the bedroom.

She sat beside him on the bed while she held up the phone, her father now on speaker. "Go ahead, Dad. We're here."

"I searched Cameron's apartment in Savannah last night."

"What? How?" she asked, surprised but not shocked. She knew her father would stop at nothing to find the person responsible for tormenting her.

"Tricks of the trade, my darling."

"I don't even want to know." She sighed. "And?"

"I found some photos."

"What kind of photos?" Jackson asked when Charlie stalled.

"Of Emily."

"That's to be expected. They once dated, and he seems to still have feelings for her. I'd imagine he would have kept some—"

"Not some." Charlie interrupted and took an audible breath. "An entire bulletin board full and some were recent."

"How recent?"

"From both of your social media pages."

"Then that proves he's the one," Jackson said, his body hardening with fury.

"Not so fast, son. All this proves is that he had an unhealthy obsession when he was here. He hasn't done anything to tip us in that direction since, and there's no proof that he's set foot inside her house. Maybe he's over it now with seeing you two together."

"What about the letter?" she asked and raised her eyes to Jackson when his head whipped around. Her lips curved to tell him she was okay, and she was... for now. "How did you get clued into Cameron from the letter?"

"It was written in mad riddles. None of it made much sense, but he included something that stuck with me. I kept churning it over in my brain until I thought to ask your mother. She knew exactly what it meant." He chuckled. "That woman has an elephant of a memory."

Emily's mouth went dry. "What did it say?"

"I'm surprised you didn't see it. Your mother said it should have instantly registered."

"I don't remember reading the letter."

"Oh. That's odd. You're the one that gave it to me when you—"

"Daddy, please. What did it say?"

"I couldn't decipher all of the sentence but clearly written, as though he wanted to be sure you saw it, was the name, Melanie."

Her hand suddenly weak, she dropped the phone and folded her arms over her stomach. Fear and confusion balled in her belly as she rose to slip on a robe.

"Charlie," Jackson began after picking up the phone. "What does this mean?"

"It means whoever wrote it knew Emily's roommate in college."

Jackson sent her a puzzled look across the room, but she couldn't hold his gaze. As she paced, she listened to their conversation and tried to hold her ragged emotions together.

"And?" he asked.

"Cameron cheated on Emily with her roommate. That's why they broke up."

"Oh." When she mentioned Cameron wanting another woman, she didn't say it had been her roommate. Neither of them had been excited to have that conversation and discuss details. "This mention plus the photos has to be enough to arrest him."

"Well, he's in Virginia now, and the S.P.D. have their hands full with other more pressing matters."

"This seems pressing to me."

"No doubt, but until we have more definitive proof linking him to the break-ins—"

"This letter wasn't mailed. It was in her house. That isn't proof enough?"

"No. He could have put it in her mailbox and Harry would have brought it in with her mail. We need more. The S.P.D. have pretty much set the case aside for now, but you and I won't. Keep your eyes and ears open. He'll slip up, and when he does, we'll be ready."

"I may not be able to wait for him to show his hand. Emily's upset, and I want him gone. Locked up with that other asshole."

"If he's the one, I'm right there with you. But for that to happen, you need to keep your cool. If he gets comfortable, make no mistake, he'll get messy. They always do, and we'll have the proof we need. Don't let Emily out of your sight."

"Already planning on it."

"I knew you would."

When he hung up, Emily spun around. "We need to tell Sydney. She should understand who she's dating."

"We'll talk to her today, but we'll have to be delicate. We still don't know for sure it's him and these are big accusations."

Chapter Twenty-Four

☆ ☆ ☆

Emily

"This day could not possibly get any more beautiful," Sydney sang to anyone who would listen when she walked into the spacious two-story lobby at VETS. "And there are my two beautiful best friends."

She hopped over the short counter at the reception desk and wrapped her arms around Jackson and Emily as they hunched over the new computer.

"You're in a good mood this morning." Emily studied her. Sydney was practically glowing.

"That's what good morning sex will do for a girl." She nudged Emily with her shoulder.

"Wow. Okay. Didn't need that information."

"Sydney, we need to talk," Jackson interrupted, having heard enough.

"About the candidate interviews? I've got four lined up today, and the first one should be here any—"

"They can wait." When several workers walked into the room with ladders and buckets of paint, he motioned for Sydney and Emily to follow him. He turned into the office behind the reception desk, designated for the accountant he expected to hire that day.

Once inside, Sydney sat on a box of unwrapped furniture.

"I don't know how to do this delicately, so I'm just going to say it." He closed the door. "We think you and William should stay away from Cameron. He could be dangerous."

Sydney's eyes jumped between Jackson to Emily before she threw her head back in a wild burst of laughter. Her eyes glistened with amusement until she noticed no one else in the room found the advice funny. "Wait. You're serious?"

"Deadly."

Struggling to understand, Sydney took a deep breath and let it out slowly. "Mind telling me why?"

"It's a long story." Twisting at the knock on the door, Jackson opened it to find one of the painters on the other side. "Yes?"

"Your appointment is here, Mr. Vane, and we need your guidance on something before we can get started."

"I'll be right there." He looked to Emily, who motioned for him to go. "Please listen to her," he instructed Sydney and closed the door behind him.

"Emily, what's going on? Why is Jackson so upset?"

"He's just frightened, Sydney. We both are."

"Why? You two are making a pretty big accusation, saying Cameron is dangerous."

"Until we can confirm what we suspect, we're begging you to be cautious."

"I trust both of you with all my heart, but you sound like lunatics." Sydney stood and stalked to the window. "You don't think Cameron is being honest with me?"

Emily shook her head. "We're just trying to keep you and William from getting hurt."

"Why does it feel like you're not talking about emotionally?"

"Because I'm not."

Sydney crossed her arms and stared at her friend. "Emily, I'm sorry, but you're giving me nothing to go on, and I'm having a hard time getting on board with this. He's sweet and gentle with me. He's done nothing but make me feel special, and you know I need that right now."

"I do. Sydney, please sit." She patted the box Sydney vacated earlier. "I didn't want to tell you this yet."

"If it's serious, I deserve to know."

Emily nodded and took a deep breath. "We think he's the one that destroyed my house in Savannah."

"You're kidding?"

Emily straightened in response to Sydney's sharp tone and spoke smoothly, hoping not to agitate her further. "I wish I was."

"Why would you think that?"

"He has said and done a few things that make me think he still has feelings for me, and—"

"When was this? Was it before or after we started dating?"

"Before, but—"

"Forgive me, Emily, but when we're together, he doesn't seem to be pining after you, or anyone else. Where is this coming from? It seems a little out of the blue."

"It's not. There was no need to include you in the drama from Savannah until now, and we found some new evidence. I'm worried he may be unstable."

"He seemed pretty damn stable last night and this morning." She tossed up her arms and let her hands drop into her lap. "I thought we were friends."

"Of course, we are. That's why I'm telling you all this. I care about you, and Jackson's beside himself, worrying about you and William."

"It doesn't feel like it." She hopped off the box again, her good mood nonexistent now. "Are we done here? I need to get the interviews started."

"Yeah, we're done." Feeling as though she'd lost a battle, Emily stalked back to the lobby. Since Sydney wouldn't listen to anything she had to say, all she could do was hope they learned the truth about Cameron before she or William got caught in the crossfire.

On the reception desk computer, she launched the new membership software. Although Jackson and Sydney were down the hall in the management offices and a small crew worked nearby, she couldn't keep from looking over her shoulder. Cameron was somewhere in the building, and after the new information they learned about him that morning, she feared he would sneak up on her when she least—

A large box dropped onto the counter, causing her to jump and slap a hand over her chest.

"What the heck, G?"

"Sorry, but this nice fella needed some help, and you were in La La land." Genevieve leaned on the box with a wide smile and pointed her thumb at the thin, short man standing beside her. "He's looking for the person in charge of this joint."

He looked up at Genevieve with admiration before reaching a hand over the box to Emily. "I'm Joel. I'm here to install the security system."

"Right. My apologies. It's been a crazy morning already." Emily shook his hand. "I can show you around." She circled the counter to join them. "Did you need something, G? You shouldn't be wandering around town in your condition."

"My condition? I may not be able to walk without waddling like a drunken penguin, but I'm not dying." She chuckled with the others. "And I needed to drop off the new business cards, brochures, and posters we had printed."

"That's so exciting. Can you stick around for a bit? This shouldn't take long."

"I have some time. I'll rest my marshmallow ankles over here until you get back."

"Ha. While you're at it, figure out how to get that program up and running. It's been a thorn in my side for days."

In less than twenty minutes, Emily gave Joel a high-level tour of the three-story facility. She was proud of how far they'd come since purchasing the horror show, yet the tour provided a frightening reminder of how much work remained. With Jackson's target date for the grand opening only a month away, she worried they wouldn't make it.

Returned to the lobby, she found Genevieve typing away at the computer. "What are you doing?"

"Entering information into that thorn of yours," she answered without missing a beat. "But now it also has beautiful roses like the awesome logo I designed. You're welcome."

"No way."

"Yep. Wasn't that difficult either."

"I hate you."

"No. You're so grateful I saved the day that you want to buy me lunch later." She smiled over her shoulder when Emily joined her behind the counter.

"Love to, but there's too much to do today. I'm sure we'll be working through lunch. Rain check?"

"Fine. But if you wait too much longer, we'll have to get a table for three."

"Aww, I can't wait. Now, show me what you've done."

Chapter Twenty-Five

☆ ☆ ☆

Emily

Before dawn on the twentieth day of December, Emily shot out of bed soaked in sweat and short of breath. She looked over at Jackson, who, to her relief, slept soundly beside her. Her vivid dreams of what the day might bring lingered in her mind and had her on edge.

All night, when she managed to sleep, her dreams manifested into nightmares so real she felt them in every muscle. She woke up each time crying and on the verge of screaming from having to watch Jackson suffer through one agonizing PTSD episode after another. No two episodes she conjured in her subconscious were ever the same, and she was helpless every time.

Since Jackson told her about the day, her anxiety held steady at a high and unmanageable level, fueling her nightmares. All she could do was worry about what he might go through, how useless she would to be, and how unfair it all was.

The worst part, she decided, was not knowing if or when the symptoms would strike, like waiting for a bomb to drop with no warning sirens. At least they'd planned for it and would be working from home that day. Maybe a break from the chaos would prevent the bomb from being launched in the first place.

She looked forward to the uninterrupted time. They needed it. So far, their life together in Richmond had been too hectic to enjoy fully. The few blissful moments they'd found here and here didn't overcome the stress of construction, paperwork, and threats. It didn't help that Jackson was the center of attention everywhere he went, overwhelming him at times. He constantly being pulled in various competing directions, putting out fires, making quick decisions, and managing people, projects, and expectations. With Genevieve's upcoming delivery and the Cameron and Sydney situation mixed in, she was surprised more symptoms hadn't resurfaced along the way.

She checked the clock and tried to control her frazzled nerves by taking deep breaths. He needed her to be a calming force that day, not a stressed-out mess. Careful not to wake him, she rolled out of bed, slipped on her robe, and tiptoed downstairs.

Throughout the night, after she calmed down from another nightmare, she'd think about soothing activities they could do that day. Making a list and memorizing it helped untie the knots in her stomach and allowed her to fall back asleep. That brutal cycle repeated itself at least three times.

She recited the activity list as she headed to the kitchen. First, they'd start with breakfast in bed, then lovemaking for dessert. A short jog for some fresh air and exercise followed by a long bubble bath. *Or,* she thought with a sly grin and a shiver, *they could take a long, hot shower* as they did in Savannah after a run.

Once in the kitchen, she gathered the few ingredients she needed for breakfast and continued to roll through her list. She cracked an egg into a bowl. They could take a canoe out on the lake and do some fishing on the dock. Another two eggs. If he was up for it, they could visit Josh, Billy, and Will's graves. Then again, she considered whether the cemetery would be a trigger on this day. Based on what she knew and witnessed herself, it didn't seem to be. It usually grounded him and reset his focus on the positive and present.

Firing up the stove, she added the whisked eggs to the pan and added a dash of salt and pepper. After the trip into town, they would have a late lunch at home and snuggle on the couch while watching a classic Christmas movie. She would bet Jackson hadn't seen any of them. A complete tragedy she was happy to remedy. Afterward, they could share holiday memories and hang their stockings on the mantle. It was the only thing left to add to the room before Christmas, and she'd saved it for them to do together.

She gave the eggs one last toss, turned off the burner, and removed a bowl of freshly cut fruit from the refrigerator. Once everything they needed for breakfast in bed sat perfectly on a serving tray, she carefully climbed the stairs, making sure not to jostle it.

Despite still having nerves about what Jackson might endure that day, she looked forward to spending it with him. It would be like their first day together in Savannah when his journey detoured for a visit—just a relaxing time together, enjoying easy activities. No adrenaline, no excitement, only love and simple pleasures.

With her foot, she pushed on the door, but it wouldn't open all the way. *Odd*, she thought and tried again. No improvement. Peering over the tray, she looked through the slender opening and saw Jackson's arm on the floor.

"Oh no!" Setting down the tray, she squeezed through, and collapsed to her knees beside him on the floor. "Jackson! Sweetheart, wake up." He didn't respond, and she checked his heart. It worked harder than usual, but at least it was beating. She checked his head and body for injuries and found nothing.

Relieved, she sat back on her heels, dropped her head, and waited. She needed the panic racing through her body to settle so she could breathe and think. He wasn't hurt, or at least she hadn't found any blood or swelling. He didn't seem to be in any danger or pain. He just blacked out, as he told her he would.

She wanted to move him to a more comfortable location, but there was no way she could get him back in the bed alone. Ms. Beasley was out of town visiting Brian at the farm, and it was too early to wake Ben. Anyway, she doubted Jackson would want anyone to see him like this. He'd cleared his schedule and wanted to stay home that day for privacy. As she expected, she was helpless, useless, and at a loss for what to do next.

Seeing him like this and not knowing what he went through tore her to pieces. He'd been alone when the attack struck, meaning she broke another promise to him. Tears threatened, but she wasn't ready for them. There was more to be done and feeling sorry for herself would be of no use to him.

She looked around the room, then jumped up. She snatched several pillows and a blanket from the bed and adjusted him so his arms, legs, and neck could rest in a normal position. When he awoke, he may be sore from lying on the hardwood floor, but hopefully, a pillow and a warm blanket would help prevent some of his discomfort.

When she'd done all she could think of to make him comfortable, she laid another blanket and pillow on the floor and snuggled against him, her arm draped over his chest.

"I'm sorry, sweetheart," she whispered and pulled the edge of the blanket over her.

The air was chilly in the large room thanks to the winter weather and old drafty house. The sun should help bring some heat into the room, but it wouldn't stop the guilt from taking over.

With no distractions or anything to occupy her mind, she let the tears come. He'd counted on her to be there for him, just as Eleanor and Ms. Beasley had been, and she let him down.

Until the doorbell sang through the house, she hadn't realized she'd fallen asleep somewhere during the merry-go-round of cursing herself and soaking her pillow with a river of tears. She ignored it at first, unwilling to leave Jackson alone, but it rang again before a key inserted into the lock and the door opened.

Rolling out from under the blanket, she rushed to the top of the stairs. "Eleanor?" As fast as her legs would carry her, she ran down the stairs and into Eleanor's arms while her sobs returned with a vengeance. "I'm so glad you're here."

"My darling, is everything okay?"

"No." Emily gulped for air. "It's Jackson."

"What's wrong?" Eleanor pushed the hair from Emily's face and wiped the stream of tears from her cheeks. "Oh, no. Did it happen again?" When Emily nodded, she sighed and said a quick prayer. "I had hoped you being here would have kept the demons at bay."

Sobs burst from Emily's throat again. She was too weak to stop it and dropped her head to Eleanor's comforting shoulder.

"Tell me, dear. What happened?" She led Emily to the parlor couch.

"I wanted to be there for him." She sniffed and wiped her nose with the back of her hand. "I'd planned out the entire day to keep his mind occupied with happy, pleasant things, but…" The guilt weighed too heavy to say it.

"But what, dear?"

"I went downstairs for a few minutes to fix breakfast, and when I came back, he'd already collapsed. Oh, Eleanor, he was alone."

"Don't beat yourself up, sweetie. If I know Jackson, and I *know* Jackson, he will prefer it that way."

Emily raised her sad, red eyes, and Eleanor's smile was a small comfort.

"Darling, the last thing he wants is to scare you with it all. He remembers how bad it can be, and I bet he'd rather you not see it."

"He warned me the other night, and I could tell he was embarrassed by it."

"You see. The way it happened was the way it was meant to be."

"But—"

"No buts. He will be thrilled to have it over with when he wakes up and even more grateful that you didn't have to see it." She patted Emily on the thigh. "I'm sure you haven't eaten yet today. Come. I'll fix you lunch and keep you company for a while."

"What about the grandkids?" She rose to follow Eleanor to the kitchen.

"They're in school. It's their last day before the holidays. Don't you love this time of year?"

She climbed onto a stool and watched Eleanor move around the kitchen with the grace and expertise of someone comfortable in the space. "Our first Christmas together is going to be so special."

"He's been alone for too long. I'm glad he found you on that crazy trip of his. You saved him, you know?" Eleanor said over her shoulder as she filled a pot with water.

"From what I've heard, you hold that honor."

Eleanor shook her head. "No. I kept him alive. You brought him back and gave him a reason to stay that way."

"I often think about where we'd both be if our paths hadn't crossed when they did. So many things had to fall into the place at the right time."

"You're both very lucky. Not everyone finds a love as strong as yours."

"I know. I couldn't imagine my life without him."

With a satisfied grin, Eleanor set the pot on the stove and turned lit the burner. "What does that life look like in your mind?"

"Everything I dreamed of when I was a little girl—a strong, fulfilling marriage, a load of kids, plenty of time with family and friends, and a career that gives me purpose. All of it I want with Jackson."

"That sounds wonderful. I've seen you two together. You'll have all that and more." She smiled over her shoulder as she gathered the ingredients she'd need for spaghetti.

"Eleanor, can I ask you something?"

"Sure, sweetie." She continued her search through the kitchen now organized for another cook.

"Is there anything I should be or could be doing for him right now?"

"Don't you feel guilty for being down here with me," she scolded. "He'll be asleep for at least another…" She checked the clock on the oven. "Fifteen hours or so. He'll need you when he wakes up disoriented and famished."

"Oh, Eleanor. I've been so selfish. Was there a reason you stopped by? I doubt it was to cook me lunch."

"I do apologize for letting myself in. When you didn't answer, I figured you both were out. I should have called first," she added while she stirred the sizzling beef.

"No need for that. This is your home, too."

"Thank you, dear. Isabelle had asked me to stop by and—"

"Isabelle?"

"Isabelle Beasley."

Emily's palm smacked against her forehead. "How could I not know her first name?"

Eleanor laughed. "Ms. Beasley, is it?"

"Yes, even Jackson calls her that. G calls her Ms. B. Brian calls her Grammie. It hasn't come up, and I haven't asked."

"Such a horrible friend you are." Eleanor clicked her tongue then laughed. "Stop beating yourself up. You've had to learn and adjust to a lot lately."

After draining the meat, she poured in the homemade tomato sauce she canned and dropped off a few weeks prior. Jackson loved her spaghetti sauce, and she couldn't bear the thought of him using someone else's, or God-forbid, sauce from the store. Remembering how her face scrunched at the notion of store-bought sauce like it contained manure, Emily smiled to herself.

"Well, Isabelle," she said and resumed stirring, "asked me to check in on the house and do a few things."

"That's not necessary. I can—"

"Yes, I know you can, but we have a way about us when we're in charge of this household. You could call it being particular, stuck in our ways, or stubborn, but no matter what, we're going to personally make sure it gets done our way."

"Message received loud and clear." Emily held up her hands, happily surrendering.

When the delicious meal, complete with garlic bread and salad, was ready, the pair ate at the kitchen table and continued their conversation. Having Eleanor all to herself, it was easy to see why Jackson adored her. Their bond was special, and so was Eleanor.

"This is just heavenly," Emily sighed out before taking another bite of spaghetti.

"Thank you. Whenever Jackson allowed himself a few carbs," she said, playfully rolling her eyes, "he always wanted my spaghetti. No bread, of course."

"Of course. But I'm not surprised he made exceptions for it. It's the best I've ever had, Eleanor."

"Glad you enjoyed it, dear."

Emily set down her fork and leaned back, her stomach full and protesting another bite. "Will you tell me about Jackson when he was young? What was he like growing up here?"

Pride bright in her eyes, Eleanor grinned. "Rambunctious and happy. He was always outside getting into something. It gave me so much laundry and scrubbing to do—the stains were endless." She shook her head, remembering. "But sweet. Lord, that boy was the sweetest, most loving child. He'd melt your heart with a smile or a hug. He would often bring me a flower or something pretty he found while exploring—a rock or colorful leaf. It didn't matter to him if they were in the middle of playing war or a game." Her eyes filled with tears again. "If he found something special, he'd bring it to me immediately and would never leave without a kiss. Oh, I miss that little boy."

"Jackson said you raised him. He didn't spend a lot of time with his parents?"

"It made me so angry the way they disregarded him. They had the most precious gift, and they tossed him aside for parties, money, and material possessions. His father was cold, always, but his mother Jackie would love on him when she was here, which wasn't very often. She had her volunteer work, and…" Eleanor scowled. "Other things."

"Other things?"

"I shouldn't be talking about this. Jackson should be the one."

"But he doesn't. He's only mentioned he and his parents were estranged, and that you and Harrison were his parents in every sense of the word."

"How sweet."

"I had to ask about his mother. He doesn't seem to want to talk about her. What was she like?" Emily took a sip of water and waited, hoping Eleanor would tell her more.

Eleanor sighed. "She was a beautiful woman. Stunning and elegant. She had the same eyes and energy as Jackson, but there was a deep disturbance inside her."

"What do you mean?"

"She had everything a woman could ask for. A husband who adored her, although Grayson wasn't perfect either, mind you. He had his own faults as we all do, but before she got pregnant with Jackson, he was in love with her and showered her with everything her heart desired."

"Until she got pregnant? Did something happen between them?"

Eleanor pinched her lips and scowled. "She didn't want children and blamed Grayson for the pregnancy. I don't think she ever truly loved him as a wife should. She loved the prestige of his name more than she loved the man, and when Jackson was about ten, she tried to leave him for another man."

"No," Emily gasped. "What happened?"

"While she was pregnant, and after he was born, she and Grayson had many loud and dangerous fights. They'd throw things and yell for hours. It got so bad that whenever they were here together, I would get Jackson out of the house or pack him in the car and leave. It would take me half the day to repair or clean up what they destroyed. Made my blood boil."

"I bet."

"Thankfully, by the time Jackson figured out what was going on, they were better at hiding it. They stayed away from each other, and usually that meant away from Jackson. Grayson had a revolving door of women he entertained at his downtown apartment, and Jackie had her young boyfriend. But neither wanted to give up the act that was Grayson and Jacqueline Vane—the most exciting and powerful couple in Richmond." She shook her head. "Keeping their status was more important than the family they created."

"That's heartbreaking. Does Jackson know about all this?"

"He knew some and figured out a lot through the years before he left for the military. The details weren't revealed in all their gruesome glory until Grayson and Jackson had an argument soon after he moved back home."

"Oh no. How did he handle it?"

"In true Jackson fashion, he pushed it aside and was more worried about me."

"Why? Did Grayson do something to you, too?"

"Just the usual verbal demands and disgust, but Jackson knew I would be upset by the horrible things Grayson told him, more so than he was. I had always wanted them to be friends, and he knew I would be disappointed." She shrugged her shoulders. "And I was, but you know the worst part about it all?"

"What?" She held Eleanor's hand when she began to cry.

"The altercation started because Jackson stood up for me. Grayson arrived ready to tear apart anyone who got in his way, and I was the first person he saw." She tried to laugh about it. "Jackson didn't take it too kindly."

"No doubt. He loves you too much."

"He does, and I love him as though he were my own flesh and blood. He has my heart."

She patted Eleanor's hand. "Speaking of that, I've been meaning to thank you."

"You have? For what, sweetie?"

"For being there for Jackson when he needed you all those years. If you hadn't, who knows what would have happened to him. He definitely would have been a different person, and he may have taken a different path in life. We may never have met."

Eleanor dabbed at her eyes with a tissue she pulled from her apron pocket. "My dear. Everything happens according to God's plan. I was meant to be here for him. A long military career wasn't his destiny, and you two were meant to be together. We're all here for a reason. All we're supposed to do is enjoy the ride."

———

Fourteen hours.

That was how long Emily entertained herself after Eleanor left while Jackson slept. To pass the time, she read an entire romance novel, reorganized their closet, took several short naps beside him, and continued the routine of rotating and massaging his legs and arms every two hours. The only thing that comforted her in the silence was how peaceful he looked.

As she sat beside him, and ran her experienced hands over his legs, she watched his smooth, rhythmic breathing. At the fifteen-hour mark, she'd lit some candles to add a soft glow around the room. If he awoke before sunrise, she didn't want to shock his system with bright overhead lighting or have him come back to her feeling alone in the darkness.

Expecting the wait to be over around six, she hadn't allowed herself to doze since 3:00 AM. It was few minutes after five, and she was exhausted.

Shifting her focus to his upper body, she carefully picked up his right arm. She slowly bent and straightened his elbow before rotating and massaging his shoulder. Using her phone, she switched on a light classical music station and moved to his fingers.

"I didn't know you liked this kind of music," he said hoarsely, surprising her.

Grateful to hear his voice again, Emily took a moment to enjoy the relief that flooded her body before pressing her lips to his. "How do you feel?"

"Back's a little sore, but overall, not too bad. How are you?"

"Better now that you're awake. I missed you."

His hand rose to the base of her neck and pulled her down for a kiss. "What time is it?"

"Around 5:30 in the morning. Eleanor said you'd sleep for 24 hours."

"You called Eleanor?"

"No, she stopped by soon after I found you here."

"You weren't in here when…"

Lowering her eyes, she took his hand. "I was cooking breakfast. When I left the room, you were sleeping in bed."

"I see."

"I'm so sorry, Jackson." Even with Eleanor's advice, regret filled her again. "I wanted to be here for you—"

"I'm glad you weren't." He kissed her fingers and smiled when she did. "What's that smile for?"

"Eleanor also said you'd feel that way."

"She's a smart woman, and I bet you're why I'm not sore." He placed a finger under her chin and raised her eyes to his. "Thank you."

Needing to feel his arms around her, she snuggled up against him. When his stomach growled, loud and fierce, she laughed. "Alright, alright. You don't have to yell at me."

"I have no idea what you're talking about." He grinned when she lifted her head to see him. "Who's yelling?"

A giggle escaped as she pushed to her knees. "Come on, soldier. Let's get you something to eat. Eleanor made her famous spaghetti. Would you rather have that or some—"

"Yes!" Thinking only of his empty stomach, he shot up to his knees, freezing when his eyes rolled back. He reached for her hips and held on for support while his woozy head rested on her shoulder.

"It's okay. I've got you." She ran a hand over his back and encouraged him to breathe. "Better?" she asked when he straightened.

"You always make me better."

Swooning, she kissed his hair. "I have an idea. How about I start you a hot bath? While you soak those sore muscles, I'll make you a plate, and you can eat while you relax."

"Then, will you join me?"

"Absolutely."

Chapter Twenty-Six

☆ ☆ ☆

Jackson

H oney, they're on their way," Emily called through the back screen door.

With an uncharacteristic warm winter day, Jackson took advantage and exercised in the backyard. With the opening of VETS just over a month away, he'd been working indoors more and not running as much as he used to. It had taken a toll on him mentally.

"Already?" He checked his watch, surprised to see he'd been at it longer than he thought. He jogged to the porch and up the steps.

"I think Ben's excited to have someone else to entertain G for the afternoon."

"She still complaining about everything?"

"Back, hips, ribs, skin. You'd think she was growing Big Foot in there. Ben even shaved her legs for her the other day because she complained about not being able to reach them herself."

"Sounds sexy." He kissed Emily on the cheek.

"Doesn't it? But I don't think it worked out that way for him." She opened the screen door, and he followed her inside.

"She does seem more miserable these days. Let me take a quick shower, and then, I'll be ready to entertain whoever needs it."

"You're the best." She patted his rear as he stepped past.

Twenty minutes later, he entered the kitchen as Genevieve and Ben did.

"What took you so long?" Emily joked.

Ben glared down his nose at her as he helped Geneveive lower into a chair at the table.

"Bad day?"

"They're all bad when you're the size of a house." Genevieve pushed on the side of her belly and grimaced. "Anyone who has more than one child is insane."

"You're going to live. Just one week left, and once you see that sweet baby, you'll forget all about this."

"I doubt that."

Emily smiled down at Genevieve when she groaned. "I know you're not feeling great these days, but I'm glad you could make it. We've barely seen you two since the holidays, and we've missed you."

"Anything for Ms. B's brownies."

"And she made an extra batch for you to take home."

"God, I love her." Genevieve glanced around the room. "Where is that lifesaver?"

"Visiting with Eleanor. It's so cute how close they've gotten since volunteering together at VETS."

Jackson pointed at Ben. "How about a drink?"

"Only if it's a strong one."

"Got just want you need in the office."

"You guys have fun," Emily told them. "I'm going to take Miss Grump here to the living room where she can prop up her cankles."

"Ha. Ha."

"Come on." Bending down, Ben lifted her arm and draped it across his shoulders. "I'll help you up first."

Bracing herself with a hand on the table, she helped heave herself up. As she got to her feet, her knees buckled, and she sucked in a long breath through clenched teeth.

"Is that a contraction?" Emily asked, suddenly panicked.

"She's been having them all week. Braxton Hicks the doctor called them and said they were nothing to worry about."

"He's full of shit because they get stronger every day." Genevieve panted through each word then straightened. "And more frequent." She loosened her grip on their shoulders, her muscles relaxing as the pain subsided.

"Better?"

"Yeah, but if it gets worse than that, it's going to kill me."

"I guess we better say our goodbyes now because it gets far worse… Or so I hear."

"Not funny," Ben scolded.

"Sorry. Just setting expectations."

"When we make it to the living room sometime today," she teased, "how about a back rub?"

"Only if you bring that tray of brownies I see over there."

"Deal." As Genevieve clung to Ben and the counter, she grabbed the brownies. By the time she returned, Jackson had replaced her as Genevieve's other crutch, but as they shuffled out the door, another contraction took over her body.

"I think we should get you to the hospital," she suggested when Genevieve could breathe again. "Just to see if you're dilating. These contractions are too close for my comfort."

The guys carried Genevieve to Jackson's new truck. No one trusted Ben to drive safely in panic mode and Genevieve needed both Ben and Emily to keep her calm through the contractions.

As they rolled through the gate, Genevieve reached for Emily from the back seats. "I'm sorry, Em."

"For what?"

"I think the epidural will be my new best friend."

————

Genevieve and the others endured three more contractions before parking and locating the labor and delivery unit.

After check-in, the on-call obstetrician arrived and confirmed that Genevieve was indeed in labor. "You're at eight centimeters, so we'll get everything set up."

"Oh God." She gripped Emily's hands. "Don't forget to send the drugs."

"Understood."

"Oh no."

"What?" Emily asked.

"No. No. No!" Another contraction vibrated through her body. "Where's that damn doctor?"

"Right here," the anesthesiologist announced, walking into the room with a pep in his step. "I finished up next door and heard I was needed in here. I'm Dr. Rhinehart. Are you the father?"

He reached a hand out to Jackson, who laughed and pointed to a frantic Ben behind him.

"Absolutely, not. He is."

"Got it. Congratulations." Dr. Rheinhart shook Ben's hand. "I'll set up over here and wait until Ms. Olsen is ready."

"I'm ready," she announced through gritted teeth and rode the last wave, releasing her grasp on Emily.

"You really need to breathe through those contractions," she urged Genevieve, shaking out her sore hands, but her sound advice was met with a hard scowl.

"Please, Doc, before the next one tortures me."

"Alrighty." He rolled the little metal table beside the bed opposite Emily, put on a smile, and reached out his hand. "Can you sit up, Momma?"

She answered by rolling her head from side to side on the pillow and poking out her bottom lip.

"Come on, you big baby." Emily held up her arm, then motioned for Jackson to take the other. Instead, he slid an arm under her shoulders and set her up.

"Don't you be looking at my ass, Jackson."

Dr. Rhinehart raised his eyebrows. "She's a feisty one, isn't she?"

"You have no idea."

———

"Ah, would you look at that?" The beeping machine next to the bed caught Genevieve's attention. The little black line going across the screen was trending up.

"What's that mean?" Ben asked, sitting on the bed next to her.

"I'm having a contraction."

"And that's good?"

"It is when you can't feel it. It's the worst pain I've ever experienced, and I never want to go through that again."

"Guess that means having enough kids to fill a basketball team is off the table," he laughed, and she slapped him across the chest with the back of her hand.

"What do you think?"

"Yeah. I—"

"Are we ready to start pushing?" the obstetrician asked as she entered with a nurse and went directly to the sink to wash her hands.

"You tell me."

"I will." She dried her hands as she crossed the room. "I'll also be delivering your baby. Your regular O.B. is out of town today."

"That's fine. Just get him out of me."

She sat on a stool at the foot of the bed and waited for Emily and Jackson to turn away before lifting the sheet.

"Well," she began after completing the exam. "I was right. It's time."

"Our baby's coming." Ben squeezed her hand with excitement, and Emily swooned. She knew he would be everything Genevieve needed and then some. "I can't believe it."

He bent down to hold Genevieve when uncertainty and fear flickered in her eyes. "You're going to do great. Be the powerful and fearless warrior that you are."

"We'll be nearby waiting to meet our godson." Emily kissed her forehead.

"I love you."

"Love you more."

While she and Jackson sat in the waiting room, she bounced with nervous energy. As the minutes ticked by, energy balled inside her, making her feel like a full balloon on a hot day.

"She needs to hurry up and have that baby. I can't take much more of this," she complained.

"Stop worrying. They'll be fine." He draped an arm around her shoulders. "That kid's going to slide out with so much flare the doctor isn't going to know what hit her."

She giggled and relaxed into him. "He'll probably pop out, smile, and wink at her instead of crying."

"I wouldn't be surprised if he did."

———

"You're joking," Emily accused when Ben found them an hour later and delivered the news. "She had a girl?"

"Yep. She's so beautiful."

"I'm speechless."

"So is Genevieve. First time I've ever seen her not have something to say." He laughed, giddy with pride for both of his girls.

"The delivery went smoothly?" she asked.

"Far as I could tell. I got to cut the cord. That was gross, but I did it."

"I'm happy for you." Jackson patted him on the back but soon found himself in Ben's arms. "I can't breathe," he announced when Ben didn't seem to be releasing him any time soon.

"Oh, sorry, man. I'm just so… freakin'… terrified."

Emily smiled at Ben's sudden mood swing. He no longer gushed with excitement, panic draining his face of color. "Everything will be great. Once you hold her and learn how to do a few things, your instincts will kick in."

"But she's so tiny and fragile. She's going to be relying on me for literally everything."

"That *is* terrifying," Jackson joked, flinching when Emily's hand smacked against his abdomen.

"She's a very lucky girl," she countered, "because you understand that she needs you. You're going to be an amazing father."

"Thank you, Emily."

"When can we see her?"

"Soon. I'll text you when she's ready." He hugged them both then trotted off.

"What am I going to do with you?" She turned to Jackson and crossed her arms.

"What?"

"Under normal circumstances," she grinned, then cleared her throat, "that little joke of yours would have been funny, but—"

"Admit it. You wanted to laugh."

She studied him, then gave him a quick peck on the lips. "Oh, absolutely."

———

While waiting for an update from Ben's, Jackson and Emily made phone calls and answered emails to keep the work at VETS progressing. The touchup painting in the lobby moved along ahead of schedule. The cleaning crew had arrived to finish dusting and scrubbing the locker rooms and fitness room, which were the last to be completed. Once those rooms are spotless, the painters could get to work in there, and just in time, too. The City inspectors were scheduled to stop by in the next two weeks.

With slight irritation in her voice, Sydney reported that she had one more interview to go. Although, she suspected she wouldn't find someone she preferred more than the first person they interviewed that morning.

"After the last interview, if you still feel that way, make the offer. I'll probably be here for a little while longer, and I don't want to wait," he told Sydney.

"Are you sure? It's your organization, and you're the one that will have to work with them. Maybe you should do a second interview."

"I trust you. If you think they're the right person for the job, make the offer. Just let me know how it goes."

"Sure. I'll take care of it. Also, a couple of small packages came for you today, not addressed to VETS. Were you expecting something?"

Jackson stood and pretended to look out the window. "Where are they from?" he asked, lowering his voice.

"Ugh, hold on."

He heard her rustling in the background.

"Looks like Florida and South Carolina."

"That's what I figured. Please put them in my desk drawer, but don't open them."

"Didn't plan to. What's so important that you want them hidden away?

"It's a surprise I'm planning for Emily," he whispered.

"Fine. I'll put them somewhere she can't find them."

"Thank you."

As he disconnected, Emily raised her eyes to him. "Did she still seem upset with us?"

"Her tone was still short and dripping with annoyance." He patted Emily on the knee. "But she's smart. She'll see

Cameron for who he really is now that she's heard our side."

"I hope you're right. She wasn't happy when we talked."

"She'll get over it, and if he continues to behave, I'll get over it… eventually."

———

Ben soon word that Genevieve and the baby were ready for visitors, and the pair hurried through the corridors. When they arrived, Genevieve was sitting up in the bed, relaxed, smiling, and snuggling with her newborn.

"Oh, G. You're glowing." Emily crossed the room to get a better view of her new goddaughter. She had a head full of dark hair, and her pink skin was smooth and spotless. Sliding her finger under the baby's tiny hand, she let the tears flow. "What's her name?"

"Madelynn Emily Stevens."

Her eyes shot to Genevieve's. "I can't believe you named her after me."

"You're my best friend. Where would I be in this crazy life without you?"

"I love you both so much. Can I hold her?"

"Of course."

Genevieve lifted the baby into Emily's arms, and she bounced to settle her on the way to Jackson. "Look how beautiful she is."

"As expected." He fell the moment her tiny fingers curled around his. "So, not a boy."

"Go figure." Genevieve smiled at him, pleased to see the love he felt shining in his eyes. "I guess even I can be wrong, once in a while."

"Don't forget the tiny penis ultrasound," Ben reminded them and laughed.

"True. I wasn't the only one who got it wrong."

"Oh! We should call Mom and Dad," Emily said, and Jackson reached for his phone.

"Let's send a picture first."

"You want to take a picture?" she teased, remembering all the complaining he did when he posed for photos with fans.

"It's a special moment."

"True."

Everyone crowded around Genevieve with the new addition to the family and smiled for the camera. He quickly added it to a text, sent it off to Charlie and Eden, and began the countdown.

It took only ten seconds for the phone to ring. He'd predicted less. Amused, he answered the video call.

Chapter Twenty-Seven

★ ★ ★

Emily

Two weeks remained until the grand opening of VETS, and the buzz around Jackson's journey and mission had revved up again. Reporters stopped by often to get a glimpse of the progress, and to talk with Jackson—a product of Genevieve's work, no doubt.

Phone calls and emails from supporters and investors, families of veterans, and potential members never stopped, causing Emily to ask the new front-desk staff to start early.

Because they understood the profound significance the day held for Jackson, everyone they knew pitched in to get VETS opened by April first—the day, twelve months prior, he started the journey that changed his life. Whatever it took, he was set on closing the loop and marking the official completion of his Memorial Run with the reason he started it: helping, serving, and potentially saving as many veterans as possible.

"Where's Jackson today?" Sophia asked as she, Sydney, Eleanor, and Emily unpacked office and medical supplies for the physicians' suite.

"He ran to Adam's office to sign some paperwork, and then he had meetings at City Hall to finish up more there," Emily answered with a cringe.

"Ugh. I bet he hates that."

"You know him well. He'd much rather be building or fixing something here rather than running errands." Emily removed several boxes of latex gloves from the crate then wiped her forehead with the cloth she kept in her back pocket. Although the air conditioning worked smoothly, the manual labor of lifting heavy boxes, unpacking them, and breaking them down for recycling had her sweating.

She glanced over at Sydney and watched her remove plastic from around a few metal trays. Although they were talking again, she'd been quiet that day, and Emily worried it might have something to do with Cameron.

"Those are for the front desk," Emily informed her when she opened another box and removed the contents. "I ordered custom clipboards with the division logo for in here."

"OK. I'll set them on the counter."

"Thank you."

"Everything okay between you two?" Sophia asked after witnessing Emily's posture deflate.

"I hope so. Something's been going on with her, but she won't talk to me about it."

"Maybe she's just tired or overwhelmed. The days get long and hard when you have a child that won't sleep through the night."

"I hope that's all it is."

Sophia leaned over the table to whisper. "You think this has to do with Cameron, don't you?"

"Yes. Both have been distant and moody lately, and I'm worried he's drinking again. I hear him and Robbie talking about their late nights out, and he's not a loveable drunk."

"Are you saying he could hurt her?"

"Based on some things we've learned about him recently, yeah. I'm scared for her."

"Does she know you feel this way?"

Emily nodded. "She thinks we're overreacting. I'm worried he may be unstable. All the usual signs are there and amplified with the added pressure of getting VETS finished. He's drinking more to compensate. I just know it."

"Emily." Sydney entered the room with a pronounced frown. "These came for you."

Twisting to see Sydney, her eyes zeroed in on the small bouquet of white, pink, and yellow flowers she held. A chill ran over her skin, and she shuttered. "Please," she attempted. "Please tell me there's a card."

"What? Yeah, there's a card." She plucked it from the plastic holder and held it up.

"What's wrong?" Sophia asked, placing a hand on her back.

She shook the reminder of Lucas from her thoughts, and cautiously accepted the tiny envelope. Pinching the thick paper, she lifted it out, and her hand sprang to her lips. She dropped the card as if it had burst into flames.

"What does it say?"

Emily couldn't answer. Fear had taken over her body.

"Sit down. You look like you're going to pass out."

"I can't breathe."

Eleanor pushed a chair behind her and gently pressed on her shoulders. "Sit, sweetheart. Sophia, what's it say?"

Reaching under the table, she snatched up the card. "It says, 'I miss you,' but there's no name."

"Sydney," Sophia began. "Get Jackson on the phone."

"No. He doesn't need this." Emily stood, but too quickly. Her eyes blurred with the motion, and her stomach churned, causing her to return to the chair.

"Who could have sent this, Emily?"

"I don't know."

"Yes, you do," Sydney accused. "You think it's from Cameron, don't you?"

"Cameron?" Sophia asked, shocked. "Why would she think that?"

"As you know, they dated a long time ago, but she thinks he has unresolved feelings and is using me to get to her."

"Sydney, please," Emily begged. Now was not the time to air out their grievances.

"That's what you think, isn't it?"

"I don't want to, Sydney. I'm not trying to sabotage your relationship. I'm trying to protect you." The ground moved under her, and she reached for the nearby table to steady herself.

"Since the burden seems to be too much for you to handle, I'm relieving you of your responsibilities. I am fully capable of protecting myself and my child. These," she said and held up the flowers, "are not from my boyfriend." Tossing the bouquet onto the counter, she spun and stalked out of the room.

———

"I'm not leaving until someone is here to stay with you," Sophia said when Emily insisted she go home and rest.

"You've yawned four times in the last ten minutes."

"That's because I'm old." She laughed but Emily didn't join in. "I'm sure Jackson will be back soon. Until then, you're stuck with me."

"You're a great friend."

"So are you." Sophia continued to study her while she organized a cabinet in the storage room. "Emily?"

"Yeah?"

"Do you want to talk about what happened earlier with Sydney?"

"Not really. I just want to get this room finished and move on."

"Ms. Robertson? Are you in here?" a volunteer called from the doorway.

"Yes, I'm here." She stepped out from around a cabinet and forced a professional smile. "Hi, Beverly. What can I do for you?"

"Someone's in the lobby asking for Mr. Vane. He says he's a friend."

"Did you get his name?"

"Yes. Logan Carter."

"Logan? Really?" Emily dropped the empty spray bottles she'd unwrapped and rushed toward the door.

"Wait a minute." Sophia stepped in front of her and grabbed her shoulders to stop her. "Thank you, Beverly."

"Sophia, you don't need to worry."

"I don't know who this guy is. Do you?"

"Jackson told me about him last year. He's a friend, and a veteran who's still struggling, like Jackson."

"But…"

"No, I don't *know* him, but every ounce of me says his presence here is a good thing. He needs VETS, and I have a feeling, we need him, too."

Sophia let out a long surrendering exhale. "Okay, but I'll be nearby if you start to feel uneasy about this."

"Thank you. I won't." She patted Sophia's hand. "I'll be right back."

Once she reached the lobby, she searched through the commotion. Crews were moving in furniture, touching up paint, and cleaning windows, floors, and cabinets. Under other circumstances, she would have taken a moment to appreciate what the chaos meant, but when someone laughed by the entrance to the food pantry, she turned that way and saw him.

His dark hair was cut short, but not shaven. His T-shirt, shorts, and sneakers were tattered and dirty. A sleeve of black and gray tattoos covered his left arm, and although he was thin, he still had muscle definition. She wanted to go to him, but the way he looked up at the large American flag hanging from the ceiling, both warmed and broke her heart. What he endured as a Prisoner of War and every day since was etched into the bags under his eyes.

He lowered his gaze and noticed her watching him from across the room.

"Hi, Logan," she said, crossing the lobby to him. "It's so nice to finally meet you. I'm Emily." He took her hand when she offered it, but his expression told her he was unsure of how she knew him. "Jackson's girlfriend," she explained.

"That's right. Sorry. It was a long journey to get here, and I'm a little tired. Jackson told me about meeting you on his way to Orlando."

"He told me about you, too, and how much he's missed you. He's going to be so thrilled you're here. Did he know you were coming?"

"No. I didn't know how long it would take, so I just thought I'd surprise him."

"How far did you have to travel?" He'd obviously walked there, she decided, by the condition of his clothes and sunburnt skin.

"About a month. I left as soon as I heard what he was doing here, but I move at a much slower pace than he does." His laugh sounded unsteady, tugging at her caretaker instincts.

"Most people do. Please, come in and make yourself at home. Can I get you some water and something to eat?"

"Some water would be great. Thanks."

"Sure." On the way to the kitchen, she showed him around and told him about Jackson's vision and goals along the way. When they came to an exam room, she was happy to find Sophia and Sydney working together again. Sydney's expression remained blank as she greeted Logan, but Sophia was cordial and welcoming, despite her earlier concerns.

"Logan, please rest in here, and I'll be right back with that water." She rushed back out to get several bottles from the kitchen, and when she returned, Logan was breaking down boxes.

"We put him to work," Sophia confessed with a wide smile.

"Logan, you don't have to do that. You must be exhausted." She handed him a bottle and set the rest on the counter for the others.

"I don't mind, and the company is much better than what I'm used to." His eyes cut to Sydney then back to Emily before he smiled.

"Well, you must stay with us tonight. I know Jackson will want to catch up."

"Thank you, but I couldn't impose. Plus, I've already set up camp nearby."

"You're staying outside? It still gets a chilly at night," Sophia chimed in, her motherly nature kicking in.

"I'm used to it. I was in Pennsylvania for most of the winter." Logan sliced through the tape on a box with a pocketknife, folded it, and tossed it on the pile with the others. "It's a lot better than desert heat."

"No doubt. Are you sure I can't convince you to stay at the house with us? We have plenty of room."

"I'll think about it, but really, I don't mind."

"Alright, and feel free to use the facilities here whenever you like. There's a locker room with showers, a kitchen, and if there's anything else you need, just let us know."

"Thank you. That's kind of you."

For the next several hours, the group continued setting up the remaining rooms. With Logan taking over both the heavy lifting and the box disposal, the task moved much faster.

"Are you sure you'll be okay here?" Sophia asked after Sydney left to pick up William.

"Jackson should be back any minute, but maybe I can bribe Logan to keep me company until then." She smiled at him over her shoulder.

"Happy to."

"See. Things are good. Will you be here tomorrow?"

"I've got nothing else to do," Sophia said with a laugh and gave her a hug.

Once they were alone, Logan set a box on the counter and leaned his elbows on the top. "Can I ask why she's concerned?"

She sighed. Since she asked for his protection, he deserved to know the truth. "It's a long story involving one of the contractor's staff."

"Did he approach you?"

"Something like that." Picking up the spray bottle of cleaning solution, she wet a rag and ran it over the counter. "I promised Jackson I would never be here without him or someone he trusts. Tag, you're it."

Clicking his heels together, he spun the broom in a circle then stopped it sharply at his hip. "Lieutenant Sergeant Logan A. Carter at your service, ma'am."

"Wow." She giggled. "Aren't I lucky?"

The sound of footsteps running down a nearby hall echoed into the room, followed by a slamming door.

"Does that happen often?" he asked, suddenly on alert.

She checked her watch. It was well after 5:00 PM. "No. There shouldn't be anyone else here. By now, it's usually just me and Jackson."

Raising the broom like a weapon, he crept toward the door and peeked his head out. "I can see a shadow moving."

"Maybe it's Jackson?"

"I don't think so. I'm familiar with his massive frame." He motioned for her to join him. "Stay close behind me, and don't leave my side."

She gripped the back of his shirt and mirrored his slow, cautious steps. They moved in tandem down the hall toward the moving shadows. "Someone's going through the drawers ahead."

Emily nodded. Somehow, she'd heard it, too, over the sound of her pounding heart. With every step, she grew more thankful for Logan showing up when he did. She had no idea who the shadow belonged to, and her imagination had free reign. A burglar. A serial killer, Cameron.

Emily's hand slapped over her chest when Sydney appeared at the end of the hallway. "What are you doing here?"

Sydney glanced at Logan, leaning casually against the wall with a broom, then at Emily. "I was about to ask you the same thing."

"We thought you were an intruder."

"Nope. Just little ole me. But did you know the front doors were still unlocked?" She tossed a thumb over her shoulder toward the lobby.

"That's odd. I thought Cameron locked those when he left for the day."

"Maybe he hasn't left yet."

"Oh." Emily glanced behind her, worried he'd sneak up when she least expected it. "Are you here to meet him?"

"No. I came to get something I left in the office." She held up a small red leather wallet. "William's in the car, so…"

"Okay. Please give him a kiss for me. Thank you for your help today."

"No problem." Sydney forced a grin and stepped away.

"Well, my imagination conjured up all kinds of things, and none of them were Sydney," she laughed and leaned against the wall, opposite Logan.

"Is she always like that?"

"Like what?"

"Indifferent."

"No. Actually, she's quite charismatic and..." She searched for the right word. "Colorful, I guess is the right description. She's not thrilled to be in my presence these days."

"Ahh. Tension can build when you have this much going on. Do you have a way home, or were you planning to stay and wait for Jackson?"

"I have a car here, and I think I'm going to—" She stopped and listened when animated voices could be heard from the lobby. "That's Sydney."

"Are you serious?" Sydney said.

A male voice responded, but Emily couldn't make out any words.

"I can't talk to you like this... No. I don't want to."

Distress coated her words, and Emily took off with Logan on her heels. They arrived to find an empty lobby.

"Do you see her?"

He jogged to the window. "No, but there's a car leaving the parking lot."

She followed his gaze. "That's her car. What about the other person?"

"Don't see him."

Emily whipped out her phone and called Sydney. It went straight to voicemail. "Damn it. She's not answering."

"I'm sure it's because she's driving."

"Yes, but it could also be because she's in danger."

"She said she's going home, right?" Logan asked, opening the doors off the lobby and checking down hallways.

"Yes. I need to make sure she got there safe."

"Alright. Let's get your keys and go check on her."

Chapter Twenty-Eight

✷ ✷ ✷

Emily

T hat's her car," Emily confirmed as she pulled into
Sydney's driveway. She turned off the engine, but
when she went to grab the door handle, Logan
placed a hand on her arm.

"We need to—"

"Not right now." Climbing out of the car, she ran across
the yard.

"Emily!" He followed her onto the front porch, and she
pushed open the unlocked door before he could stop her.
Rushing into the living room, she found Sydney lying on
the couch watching an animated movie. A pile of crumpled

tissues and an empty wine glass sat on the coffee table. William laid across her lap, asleep.

"What are you doing?" she asked, twisting to see them in the foyer.

Emily glanced through the dark room. "Are you here alone?"

"Yes. What's the problem?"

"We heard you arguing with someone at VETS, and I assumed it was Cameron. We wanted to make sure you were okay."

Sydney's phone lit up, indicating she received a call, and spotlighted her face. She checked the I.D. and sighed.

"Don't answer that," Emily warned when she saw Cameron's name.

"Wasn't going to."

"Do you know where he is?"

"No."

"You shouldn't leave your door unlocked."

"Normally, I don't. My hands were full when I got here, and I've been distracted ever since. But if he wanted in, a locked door won't stop him."

"I know and that's why we're here." She sat on the coffee table, facing Sydney. "What happened with Cameron earlier?"

Her eyes shifted to Logan before dropping to William. "I don't want to talk about it, but as you can see, we're fine. He won't come here."

Her phone lit up again with a text message, and Emily glanced at the message.

"I'm going to check around the house," Logan said.

"Thank you." She took Sydney's hand. "The text was from Cameron. He said he's sorry and wants to talk to you tomorrow."

"Not interested. I broke up with him."

"You did? Why?"

"Don't try to act like you aren't happy about that." Sydney forced a side grin.

"I'm not happy about seeing you upset or what he might do in retaliation or to get you back."

"He won't."

"He's not the type to give up so—"

"You were right." Sydney ran a hand over William's hair and followed with her eyes, now full of unshed tears. "I should have listened to you."

"About what?"

"You know. He still has feelings for you, and I don't think it's a coincidence that he's at VETS."

"That's what we believe, too. I didn't tell you this before, but there was a letter in the pile of rubble at my house. It was from Cameron."

"Oh, no. What did it say?"

"I don't know. He must have written it while drunk because most of it was illegible, but there was enough to scare me. I went into shock after finding it, and I don't remember what it said."

Sydney placed a hand on her knee. "I'm so sorry."

"And I'm sorry you got caught up in this mess. We still don't have any hard evidence that he was the one that did it. So, we have to go on like nothing's happened. It's so frustrating, and working with him every day, seeing him with you and William, we've been a nervous wreck not knowing if or when he's going to blow next."

"I got a glimpse of that tonight. When I saw just your car and his still at VETS, I confronted him about the flowers."

"What did he say?"

"He denied it, of course, but he couldn't deny that he watches you all the time. I've caught him several times, and his answers tonight were the last straw. Or I should say lack of answers. He got very defensive."

"He didn't do anything to hurt you, did he?"

"No. Just bruised my ego a bit." She laughed it off, but her smile quickly faded. "For the first time in years, I got a small reminder of what it was like to be happy again. I didn't want to lose that—not so much him, but the happiness." She reached for a tissue and wiped at the tears now coating her cheeks. "I don't think I'll ever be able to love or trust again."

"Yes, you will. Don't give up."

"Too late." She sniffed and let her shoulders droop.

"I don't like you being here alone. Why don't you come stay with us?"

"That's sweet of you, but I'm not scared of him. We argued, but he looked more sad than angry. I don't think he'll do anything."

"Sydney…"

"Emily…" she mocked then smiled. "I promise to call or come to your house if anything happens or if I see any warning signs. I promise."

"I still don't like this."

"And I love you for it, but I'll be—"

The back door opened, startling them, and Logan entered. "Other than all the doors being unlocked, there's nothing to be concerned about outside."

Emily pinched her lips and glared at Sydney.

"I know, I know. I should lock my doors."

Chapter Twenty-Nine

✯ ✯ ✯

Emily

"Has the inspector arrived yet?" Jackson asked the first person he saw when he and Emily entered VETS the following day.

"Yes, sir."

"Is the foreman with him?"

"Mr. Reid's not here, sir."

"Where is he?"

"I haven't seen him yet this morning."

"Go. I'll check on her." Emily quickly dialed Sydney's number then heard the familiar ring sounding off behind her.

"Are you looking for me?" she asked, canceling the call.

Emily let out a sigh of relief as she wrapped her in a hug. "Yes, actually. What are you doing here so early?"

"I have class in a couple of hours, so I thought I'd help get the rest of the finance offices ready for your new staff starting next week."

"That's sweet of you."

"Why were you calling?"

"Cameron didn't show up for work this morning, and we were—"

"Afraid he was with me." Sydney slumped onto a nearby bench.

"Yes. You haven't seen or talked with him, have you?"

"He came back late last night."

"Oh no. Why didn't you call us?"

"I didn't need to. Logan was there."

"He was? Why?"

"After you dropped him off, he said he couldn't relax and needed to walk. Emily, he walked all the way back to my house to check on me, and by the time he got there…"

Sydney's shoulders trembled, and Emily pulled her into a hug. "Oh, thank goodness. I knew he was sent here for a reason. What happened?" she asked, releasing her.

"I watched Cameron rant and pace on the porch from the window. I'd never seen him like that. He had this look in his eyes, almost like he flipped a switch, and something had taken over his body."

"He was drunk, I bet."

"Very and it scared me. I was about to call the cops when Logan showed up."

"What did he do?"

"He just yelled something from the yard, and Cameron took off. He chased after him but didn't want to go far in case he came back."

"Oh, Sydney. That must have been awful."

"After everything you said about him and what you suspect he's done, yeah, it was terrifying. Logan stayed the rest of the night and kept watch outside. I'm so grateful for him."

"Me, too. Where is he now?"

Sydney shrugged. "He rode with me here but didn't come in."

"He has a camp nearby. Sydney, I'd like for you and William to stay with us until we figure out what's going on." Emily thought about the damage done to her little house in Savannah and shuddered at the thought of that happening to Sydney.

"I appreciate that."

"And you might as well move in tonight since you're coming over for our prep party."

"I was hoping you'd say that. While I was up last night, worrying about Cameron coming back and Logan's safety, I packed up everything."

"Good. When Jackson has some free time this afternoon, I'll have him stop by with the truck."

"I can't ask him to do that. He's so busy and overwhelmed with everything here."

"True. Do you know anyone who might be able to help?"

"I have a few friends I can ask."

"Okay, and I'll do the same. Come on." Emily tapped Sydney on the leg and stood. "There's a lot to get done today."

"Let's do it together."

"I'd like that."

———

"Sorry, Em," Ben answered when Emily called and asked him for help. "Genevieve and I are visiting my parents before she goes to your house for the… What did you call it?"

"The Pretty Prep Party."

"Yeah, that. Sounds girly."

"Better get used to it. I bet there will be plenty of Barbies and tea parties in your future."

"I'm fine with that."

"Never doubted it for a minute."

"Wish I could help. Why don't you call Avery? Maybe she can get Brett or Henry to help."

"That's okay. I'm sure they are nice people, but I really want someone I know and trust for this job." Her chiming phone indicated she received a text. "That's probably Sydney. Talk to you later."

Disconnecting, Emily checked the message. Sydney said she, too, had no luck finding someone to help on such short notice. Frustrated, Emily dropped the phone on the counter and pinched the throbbing space between her eyes. A stress headache threatened to ruin her day, and it was the last thing she needed.

"Hi, Emily."

Her eyes flew open at the sound of Logan's voice. He looked freshly showered and clean-shaven. "Logan, so nice to see you."

"You seem a little tense. Is there anything I can do to take the load off?"

"Here to save the day again, are you?"

"If I can."

She waved a hand, feeling guilty for even considering asking him. "I can't. You must be exhausted after what you did for Sydney. Thank you."

"No problem. I hadn't planned on going back, but something didn't feel right, and I needed to check on it."

"Thank goodness you did, but I can't ask you for another good deed."

"I have nothing else to do." He grinned. "What is it?"

"After last night, I thought you might stay far away from here."

"I don't scare easily."

"Alright, then. I'm looking for someone I trust to help Sydney. She and William will be staying with us until we get this Cameron thing figured out, and I want to make sure they get there safely."

"Good. I was worried about them."

"That's sweet of you." She stood and tucked her phone in her back pocket.

"What time?"

"She gets out of class at three, then picks up William. How about four?"

"Works for me."

"We really appreciate this, Logan. Have you had a chance to talk with Jackson yet?"

"No. I don't want to bother him. I'll be here until after the grand opening, so we'll connect eventually."

"Were you planning to go back to Pennsylvania?"

"I don't have any plans."

"Just going where the wind takes you?"

"Something like that." He rocked back on his heels, looking as though the future caused him discomfort.

"Well, I hope you stay and take advantage of our services for a while."

"That's the other reason I'm here."

"Good. Thanks again for helping, but I should get back to work."

"Is there something I can take care of for you? Boredom is a dangerous pastime."

"Understood." She considered her long to-do list. "Know anything about landscaping? A load of flowers and mulch should be delivered in the next hour."

"Consider it done."

Although he seemed to be grateful for something to do, she didn't want to take advantage of his generosity. "You don't have to volunteer, you know. We're still hiring for a lot of positions, and we'd love to have you stay in town longer."

"I'll think about it." He turned to head outside, stopping when she called for him.

She jogged closer. "Do you have a way to get to Sydney's house?"

"I'll figure something out."

"You will *not* walk there again. Stay here." Before he could object, she took off down the hallway and soon returned with a set of keys. "Take Jackson's truck."

"I can't do that."

"I insist. You're doing us a huge favor, you're volunteering to help around here, and you were there for us yesterday. You're going to take the truck, and you're going to stay for dinner tonight. I won't accept no for an answer."

"I—"

"Can't resist?" she finished for him.

"You did say that wasn't an option."

"Yes, I did." Satisfied, she handed over the keys and left him. "See you tonight," she called without turning around.

———

For the rest of the day, Emily inspected each room, making a list of the remaining items and tasks needed before VETS officially opened. More towels in the barbershop, additional shelving in the food pantry, soap for the men's locker room. There was also a leak in the sink in an exam room, and marks on the wall in the laundry room that needed repainting.

While she searched, she made a mental list of the things she needed to do before Sophia, Avery, Sydney, Eleanor, and Genevieve arrived at the estate later that night. They were planning for the grand opening decorations and catering, while enjoying a much-needed girls' night. With that group, it should be a good time, and she couldn't wait.

"There's the love of my life," she said, finding Jackson assembling shelves for the water aerobics barbells in the pool area. "These look great."

"Thanks." He stood and kissed her on the cheek. "I needed something mindless to do."

She took hold of the end of the rack when he motioned, and together, they slid it into place.

"Voila." He stepped back, wrapped an arm around her waist, and appreciated his work.

"It's very sexy."

"The shelves are sexy?"

"Not exactly." She nudged him with her shoulder. "Watching you put these together was sexy."

"Really? I've got another set to do if you want to stick around."

"As hot as that sounds, I've got a few more rooms to inspect, then I need to get home. The girls will be there soon."

"Sounds like a good day for me to work late."

"What?" She let out a gasp. "You don't want to search countless websites for decoration ideas for the grand opening?"

"As hot as that sounds..." He winked on his way to collect the screwdriver and hammer from the floor.

"That's fine, but you wouldn't be the only man there."

"Oh yeah? Who is the brave soul crashing girls' night?"

"I kind of forced Logan to come for dinner. He looks like he could use a good meal, and he's been helping me a lot. Speaking of that, I also gave him your truck to use tonight."

"You did? For what?" He slid over the box containing the disassembled shelves and ripped open the top.

"He's making sure Sydney isn't alone after class and helping transport her and William to our house. She's agreed to stay with us for a while."

He straightened to face her squarely. "Did something happen?"

She stepped closer and lowered her voice. "Cameron was at her house last night drunk and out of control. Now he's missing."

"What the hell? Why didn't she call the police?"

"Logan showed and ran him off."

Jackson's hands pushed through his hair. "She should have come over then."

"Agreed, but Logan stayed through the night and kept watch. She felt safe. I think he has a soft spot for her."

"Is he still here? I'd like to talk to him."

"He's helping with the landscaping outside. When you talk to him, try to convince him to take a job. I love that he wants to help out around here, but I'd rather help him get back on his feet."

"I imagine he likes to not be tied down."

"I guess. I still don't like it. He seems to be doing okay, but he needs help and that's why what we do here."

He circled an arm around her waist, touched by her concern for his friend. "I'll talk to him."

"Thank you." Rising on her toes, she pressed her lips to his. "I miss you."

"I miss you, too, but soon, all this will be finished, and we can focus more on each other."

"Can't wait."

He kissed her forehead. "I'll call for a ride when I'm done here."

"Or I can come to get you. It's not that far. Just text or call me when you're ready."

"Sounds like a plan. If I haven't already told you, I love that we're doing this together. All this is as much yours as it is mine."

She leaned back to see his face. "VETS mean so much to me, as do you." She tugged him into a hug and lingered until she had her fill.

Chapter Thirty

* * *

Emily

How was Logan when he was at your house?" Avery asked Sydney with a smirk after he left, and girls' night had officially begun.

"Quiet."

"A rugged, sexy, gorgeous man shows up on your doorstep to save the day for the second time, and you didn't talk to him?"

Sydney shrugged. "He's nice, but I've sworn off men, so small talk wasn't necessary. Anyway, I like a man with more personality."

"Give him a break," Emily chimed in. "I bet he has plenty of personality when he's healthy. He's still dealing with a lot."

Genevieve puffed. "Wounded puppy."

"What?"

Avery raised her hand, her smile wide. "I love puppies."

Ignoring her, Genevieve explained. "Emily has a soft spot for and attracts all things wounded."

"That's not true," she attempted but quickly surrendered. "Okay, fine, but my hunches are usually right about those sweet things."

Genevieve glared down her nose at her and frowned. "Cameron?"

Emily shrugged. "Nobody's perfect."

Without a word, Sydney left the room, and Emily smacked Genevieve across the arm.

"Way to go."

"How was I supposed to know she was going to flip out? The guy's a psychopath. I figured she'd be over him already."

"It wasn't a pleasant breakup, and it's only been twenty-four hours."

"More time than the jerk deserves."

———

After all the arrangements were determined for the grand opening and the to-do list divvied up, Emily topped off her glass of tea and raised it in a toast. It was almost ten o'clock, and she'd long ago traded in her wine glass to be ready to pick up Jackson.

"To my girls. Thank you for all you've done for VETS. We're going to make a difference for so many thanks to all your hard work and dedication."

"Damn, right," Genevieve added and raised her glass.

"I thought you were enjoying girls' night," Sophia whispered when Emily checked her watch and frowned.

"I am. I just thought Jackson would have called by now. He's been at VETS for over thirteen hours."

"He probably fell asleep on an exam table." Sophia giggled at her joke, but Emily couldn't join in.

"Or something's wrong. All that's happened lately has me suspicious and anxious all the time. I don't like him being there alone."

"Now you've got me worried."

"I need to call him." Emily grabbed her phone and stepped out of the living room to find a quiet place to talk. With one click, she dialed his number and listened as ring after ring fueled her fear. She tried again, and when he didn't answer, she texted. No response.

"You should go check on him," Sophia suggested a few minutes later. Emily may have rejoined the group, but her attention and thoughts were elsewhere.

"I'm sure I'm overreacting, it's a nasty habit of mine, but something's off."

Sophia leaned back in her seat with an over-exaggerated yawn. "Goodness. It's well past my bedtime. Harrison's probably wondering where I am. Emily, would you mind giving me a ride home?" she asked, giving Emily an excuse to leave the party. "I've had a little too much to drink."

"Sure." With a wink, she rose to address the group. "I'll be back soon. Feel free to keep the party going for as long as you want," she offered to the others.

She glanced over at Sydney sitting on the couch, her legs tucked under her and her gaze distant. Clearly, she was in her head, and Emily had to fight her instinct to soothe. She could talk with her tomorrow. Right then, she needed to get to Jackson and set her mind at ease.

After dropping off Sophia, Emily arrived at the entrance gate to VETS as the clouds overhead began to spit raindrops on the windshield. The gloomy night only added to her jitters and charged her imagination. She climbed out and headed for the lock only to be startled by a figure stepping out of the shadows.

"Sorry, Emily. I didn't mean to frighten you."

"Logan?" She squinted through the darkness until he stepped into the beam from her headlights. "What are you doing out here in this weather?"

"I was going to ask you the same thing."

"I came to check on Jackson. He's working late and isn't answering his phone." She punched in the gate code, and it screeched into motion.

"He's probably with the guy that showed up a little while ago."

"What guy?"

"I couldn't get a good look in the dark, but he was about my height, curly hair. He carried a toolbox, so I assumed he worked here."

"Oh my God!" She took off toward the building with Logan following closely behind.

As they entered, shouting voices echoed through the empty building. She ran toward the noise, but Logan grabbed her arm and yanking her to a halt. "Wait. What's going on?"

"Jackson could be in danger." She jerked her arm but couldn't free it from his firm grasp.

"What the hell are you going to do if he is?"

"What?"

"No offense, Emily, but if you're right, you'll only be adding yourself to the situation." With caution, he slowly released her. "Let's go together."

He had a point. She let Logan lead the way, but the sound of a single gunshot had them sprinting toward it. Shadows and patches of moonlight from the skylights flashed by as she ran toward her worst nightmare.

As they approached, the voices grew louder, and Logan dragged her into a nearby office. Beams from the parking lot lights shone through the windows and lit his face. His calm eyes soothed the sharp edges of her panic.

"We need to be smart about this," he whispered.

"What if he shot Jackson? We need to help him."

"We will, but that's why we need to be careful."

She nodded, fighting back the tears she had no time for, and kept her eyes locked on Logan's. He gave her the strength she needed to keep from collapsing to the floor.

"What does he want with Jackson?"

Between gulps of air, she explained. "To get to me."

"Okay. We can't just walk in there. We need a plan. He obviously has a gun, maybe more, and we don't know if it's just the two of them." Logan stepped into the doorway and looked down the dark hall toward the men's locker room where a deep voice could be heard yelling obscenities and banging something hard against the metal lockers. "Do you have your phone with you?"

Quickly, she patted her jeans pockets. "Shit. I left it in the car. Do you have yours?"

"No. Do the desk phones work?"

She shook her head. They were scheduled to be set up tomorrow, and Cameron knew that.

"Guess it's up to us."

"This can't be happening." She dropped her face into her hands, fighting back tears and panic.

"You can do this." He grabbed her by the shoulders and waited for her eyes to find his. "Let's go see what we're dealing with."

Taking her hand, he rechecked the hallway before leading her to the side entrance of the men's locker room. With his back pressed against the wall, he glanced inside.

"Can you see him?" she whispered, needing to know Jackson was okay but afraid for the answer.

"Yes. He's beat up bad, but I don't think he was shot. Must have been a warning."

"Thank God. What do we do?"

Before Logan could answer, another rant started.

"Emily will want nothing to do with you when I'm done with your pretty face," he added proudly and punched Jackson somewhere, making a bone-crunching sound, and Emily gasped.

Logan's hand went to her mouth and held firm.

"What was that?" Footsteps headed their way. "Emily, is that you? I'd know that sexy voice anywhere."

Logan shook his head slowly, a warning for her to say nothing.

"I wasn't quite ready for you, but since you're here, you might as well join us. It's time for you to say goodbye."

"No, Emily," Jackson pleaded.

Fresh tears flooded her eyes, and with both hands, she peeled Logan's fingers from her face.

"It's not him," she wheezed, tears of fear now pouring down her face in streams.

"What?"

"It's not Cameron. It's—"

"Did you get my flowers, Emily?"

A hard punch to Jackson's body made him groan.

"He's going to kill him," she whispered. "I have to do something."

"No," Logan mouthed and took hold of her hands, but she tugged free and stepped into the light.

"Lucas, please stop hurting him," she pleaded, and Jackson's head snapped up at the sound of her voice. She fought the urge to drop to her knees and sob at the sight of him strapped to a chair, his arms tied behind his back. His hair was down and in his face, slick with blood. Swelling had already plumped his lips and cheek. Blood also pooled on the floor between his feet and another large splatter colored his white shirt.

"Emily, run!" Jackson demanded only to receive another blow for it. He spit a mouthful of blood at Lucas's feet.

"It's about time you showed up," Lucas said, turning toward her. "My arms were getting tired. Your boyfriend has some impressive endurance." He snatched the gun off the bench for added insurance and crossed the room.

"If you touch her..." Jackson growled through the pain.

"Oh, I'm going to do more than that." He trailed his knuckles lightly over Emily's cheek.

"Untie me, coward, so we can settle this like men."

"Nah. I like you right where you are. You'll have a great view of the show."

"You're fucking insane."

At that, Lucas's temper boiled over. He stepped back and pointed the gun at Jackson, his finger wrapped tight around the trigger.

"Stop! Please," she begged. "I'll do anything."

"Anything?" Lucas asked, looking satisfied with the promise.

"Emily, don't do this."

"Shut up!" Lucas pulled the trigger, and a twinge of satisfaction flashed across his face when Jackson flinched. "Tell me, Emily. What will you do to make sure the next one doesn't miss?"

With the barrel still pointed at Jackson, more tears spilled, but she held strong. Getting him away from that deadly weapon was all that mattered. "What do you want?"

"Besides having my way with you? I want him to suffer for what he did to me."

"Lucas, I—"

"How's that whore friend of yours? Did she come with you? I've missed her." He motioned for her to come closer. "But I've missed you more."

"How did you get out of jail?" she asked, stalling, and praying Logan was still nearby, but hoping he went for help at the same time. She couldn't handle seeing Jackson tortured another second longer.

Catching her off guard, Lucas lunged and hauled her further into the room by the arm—the force of it sending her body crashing against his. She stumbled but located her balance with the help of his hand around her neck. Sucking in a breath through her teeth, she focused on his face and despised the pleasure she saw in his eyes. He enjoyed seeing her frightened, but at least his attention had shifted away from Jackson, the pistol now tucked in his back pocket.

"Emily," he began and tightened his grip. "I'm not here to talk. But if you must know, I was released in December on a bail appeal. The justice system is a joke."

"December?" How could she not have known?

His finger trailed across her collar bone. "And it took a matter of minutes to locate you. You really need to do a better job of protecting yourself, Emily."

"Get your hands off her."

She shifted her gaze to Jackson, and her heart shattered. Blood still dripped from his hair and around his swollen left eye. He slumped over from the pain and exhaustion, but his gaze never left her face. His crystal blue eyes, now bloodshot, begged her not to comply. Not to give in.

"Are you ready to give yourself to me?"

"Don't do it," Jackson tried again, but she closed her eyes and slowly nodded.

"Good. But first, we're going to teach 'ole Jackson here a lesson."

"What? No."

"Stay here." He shook free when she grabbed hold of his arm and pushed a bench over to Jackson. With a foot propped on top, he rested an elbow on his thigh. "I had hoped your girlfriend would have made this more of a challenge, but then again, she's always been easy to manipulate." Lucas leaned down next to Jackson's face. "Like when I told her I lost a patient. She was all over me after that Emmy performance."

"Fuck you."

"When I had her whore, she would have given me anything, like she will tonight."

"Touch her and I'll kill you."

"You're not in a position to make threats, Jackson." Lucas dropped his foot to sit on the bench. "I am, without a doubt, going to touch every tantalizing inch of those legs and curves until I'm satisfied. Which, after all these months, should take a very, very, very long time." He breathed out slowly. "Speaking of those sexy curves, tell her we want to see more."

"Never, asshole."

Ripping the pistol out of his back pocket, he pressed it to Jackson's temple. "As you're aware, I'm not a patient man. When I tell someone to do something, I expect immediate action. Do it!"

Emily shuddered at the demand and grabbed hold of her shirt. "It's okay, my love," she said to Jackson before dragging it over her head.

Lucas clucked his tongue. "You disappoint me, Emily. What's with the bra today? Has your man suppressed your edge?"

He pushed at Jackson's head with the barrel, and sobs burst from her throat. The sound of her crying had Jackson retaliating and yanking at the restraints to get to her. To get to Lucas.

"You'd be better off to remember that I always win, Jackson. I'm in charge here, and Emily is my prize. There's nothing you can do to change that. Go on," he urged her.

This is Jacksonville all over again, she thought. He was one step ahead, ruthless, and cunning, and she was helpless as usual. But did she have to be? Suddenly tired of being a coward and the victim, she swatted at the weakness streaming down her cheeks. If it was a challenge he wanted, she would give it to him. Anything to get him away from Jackson.

"Now, Emily."

She shook her head, and Jackson dropped his gaze. He wouldn't agree with her next move. "Make me."

Straightening, the corner of Lucas's mouth twitched up in amusement.

"No weapons. No violence." She coated her tone in sensual sugar. "If I'm going to do what you know I can, I need a different kind of... motivation."

Jackson's head shot up. "Emily! No."

"Shh," Lucas demanded and set the pistol on the bench. "The situation just took an intriguing turn." He stepped toward her. "I know what you're doing."

"What am I doing?"

"You're trying to trick me into forgetting about Muscles here."

She shrugged, ran a hand over her abdomen, and watched his eyes drop to her exposed skin. He took another step. "I'm not sure you have it in you. Jackson's quite skilled."

He grinned, his eyes covering her before meeting her gaze. They stayed on her face as he hooked an arm around her waist and pulled her close. His breath burned hot on her neck as he leaned down to press his lips there.

"You have no idea what you're doing, but if it's a game you want." He tilted back to see her reaction. "Run."

"What?"

"You better run, Emily." Lucas lunged at the bench and snatched up the pistol, his voice rising. "I'm going to enjoy hunting you like you say I do, and when I catch you, *I'll* decide how we finish this. Not you."

"Don't you dare touch her!" Jackson yanked at the restraints.

"Oh, Emily." Lucas placed a hand over his heart. "He dared me. You know what that means."

He stalked to her at a pace she hadn't anticipated, and she stumbled backward, hitting hard against the doorframe. The impact knocked air out of her lungs, and when she sucked in a breath, all she got was his mouth on hers. With his hands on her hips, he pushed her against the sharp corner of the frame, and it dug into her skin, bruising the bone underneath.

His tongue and teeth mashed with hers, trapping her beneath him. As his hands loosened their grip to move up her sides, she shimmied her hands to his chest. She could only move him a few inches, but it was enough to free her only defense. Her knee connected between his legs, and he doubled over, dropping the pistol.

Stunned, she held onto the wall and gulped for air as he groaned and muttered obscenities through the pain. Another voice registered in the distance despite the haze of fear clouding her thoughts.

Oh, God. Jackson. She rushed to his side and fumbled with the plastic ties around his ankles.

"Get the gun, Emily. Hurry," he whispered.

Spinning around, she found Lucas standing with one hand on his hip, the other holding the pistol. Beads of sweat glistened on his forehead. As he raised the barrel in their direction, she stepped in front of Jackson.

"Leave him out of this."

"I can't. He's the reason I ended up in the hospital with a broken nose and concussion. He's why I went to jail."

"No. You did that when you raped G."

"I did no such thing. She gave herself to me."

"To save me."

"And it *almost* worked."

She shuddered at the almost—almost safe, almost free, almost living without fear.

"Every moment of every day since I was locked up in that cell, I've thought about, dreamed about seeing you both again. Maybe I'll stop by—"

A loud clash of something heavy hitting the floor down the hall made him pause.

Logan. She took off toward the back exit of the locker room. The sound of heavy footsteps on the tile floors followed her.

Reaching for the wall to guide her through the dark hallway, she turned toward the lobby, grateful to be familiar with every inch of the building. Her hand hit a light switch, and she remembered the panic button under the welcome desk. Connected to the security system, it would activate a response from the police.

She could see the lobby, lit in a pale, white light by the moon, shining through two levels of windows. Moving closer, the corner of the reception desk and their saving grace appeared at the end of the hallway, and she picked up speed. In her blind determination, she didn't see the ladder leaning against the desk until she tripped over the leg. Stumbling forward, she reached for the counter to catch herself, but her momentum carried her passed it into a pair of arms instead.

Her feet continued to kick as she swung her fists. Whatever it took to get away and find that button.

"Emily, it's me."

Pausing, she looked up. "Cameron?" She pushed at his arms circled around her waist. "Let me go. I have to go."

"Calm down." Setting her on her feet, he held her arms. "Where are you going?"

Before she could break free, Lucas emerged from the dark hallway behind her, the moonbeams highlighting his face and empty hands. Where was the pistol?

"There you are," he said, approaching slowly.

"Cameron, let go of me."

"Are you looking for her?" Cameron asked as if he and Lucas had passed casually on the street.

Her bones ached from the pressure of his fingertips, which grew possessively tighter in Lucas's presence.

"Help me, Cameron. Please. He's trying to kill us."

A deep laugh bellowed out of Lucas's throat, and he slapped a hand over his stomach. The sound traveled through the two-story foyer on repeat. "Emily, why would I do a thing like that? She's been a little stressed lately with—well, you know," he said to Cameron and waved to the space around them.

"Please, Cameron. If you have any care left for me—"

"But Emily…" Cameron twisted her around to face Lucas and drew her back against him. An arm wrapped around her mid-section, and his other hand pressed firmly over her mouth to keep her still and quiet. "Shh. Relax. You're going to like this part."

Lucas looked Cameron over, considered the intrusion. Intrigue hovered in his eyes as the corners of his mouth twitched into a grin. "Who are you?"

"Cameron Reid, ex-boyfriend."

"Interesting. Why are you here?"

"I'm the foreman for this build."

"What a coincidence. Or was it?" He squinted in amused suspicion. "Doesn't matter. I bet she wasn't excited to see you. She doesn't like surprises."

"You know her well. She'll tell you otherwise, but she really does hate them."

"And flowers, apparently."

"Oh, really? That's a new one."

Lucas's fingers curled around his chin before he pointed at Cameron. "Do I know you? You look familiar."

"I don't think so. What's your name?"

"Lucas. Doctor Lucas Oliver. Emily and I worked together. I swear I've seen you before."

"Oh. I remember. Emily and I reconnected when she took my appointment last year. Broke my ankle."

"That's it. I've seen you in the office and you two on River Street." He waved a finger in their direction.

She twisted in Cameron's arms in another unsuccessful attempt to free herself.

"Yeah. That was the second time she turned me down. I thought it was because of you."

"Me?" Lucas asked with a chuckle.

"I thought you two were hookin' up."

"Ha! Well, we almost did, but—"

"She rejected you, too? I've lost count of how many times she's done that to me. She has a way of—"

"Leading you on, teasing you, making you do stupid things?"

Her screaming only made Cameron tighten his grip, muffling the sound. Her throat and lungs burned from the effort, her muscles felt non-existent in comparison to his, and she could see no way out. With Cameron's help, her role in Lucas's scheme was sealed.

"Same for you, huh?" Cameron empathized.

"I'm surprised my balls don't turn blue just at the sight of her."

"Ha. That's funny. So, what business do you have with Emily at this late hour?"

"We were, ugh…negotiating a contract for my services. She was practically on her knees begging me to join her. Guess she's missed me." He smiled then let his eyes wander over her. "We need to further discuss my…payment if you know what I mean."

"I do. I do. Well, when you're done, I'd like a moment with her. A chance to remind her of what she gave up, if you know what I mean."

"Sure. But let me ask you this." Lucas shoved his hands in his pockets. "How do you feel about that piece of muscle she calls a boyfriend?"

"Jackson? A massive roadblock. Why?"

"Thought you'd like to give him a piece of your mind while I settle up with her. He's in no position to talk back, so you should enjoy the time spent."

"Interesting. I think I'll take you up on that offer."

"Great, but not too much. I get the final word."

"Understood."

When Cameron didn't budge, Lucas rubbed his hands together, then nodded to Emily with his arms out. "Now, if you don't mind."

"Oh, right. Let's get to it, shall we?"

She screamed and kicked when Lucas took a step forward. How could Cameron just hand her over, knowing she was in danger? How could he join in? Then, she thought of the letter he wrote her, the things Sydney learned about him, and his recent actions. If he was truly the person they thought he was, she and Jackson were as good as dead. They would have no defenses against two of them.

As he came closer, she prepared herself to give them one last fight. They'd have to hold her down or knock her out if they wanted—

A loud crash sent sharp and jagged pieces of something flying around them. Before Cameron whipped around and covered her with his body, she saw Lucas collapse to the ground.

"Don't move," he demanded and removed his hand from her mouth."

"What was that?" she panted, frantic and unsure.

"Logan, you got him?" Cameron yelled over his shoulder.

"Yeah. I got the asshole."

Pushing back on his heels, he stood and held out a hand to her. "It's over."

Chapter Thirty-One

★ ★ ★

Emily

"What?" Emily sat up to take in the scene that unfolded after she closed her eyes. Logan had Lucas on the ground, face-down with his hands tied behind him and Logan's knee in his back. He looked unconscious.

"Great job, Cameron."

"You two were…" Emily was too exhausted to think. Getting to her feet, her eyes darted between Logan, Cameron, and Lucas, trying to understand.

"While you were distracting this asshole in the locker room, I went to find Cameron. I knew he was somewhere in the building."

"How?"

"I saw him come in, remember? The person I saw enter didn't match the guy in the locker room."

"But…"

Cameron placed a hand on Emily's back. With her nerves still in survival mode, she flinched at the touch, and he stepped back to give her space. "I had an embarrassing night and felt bad about not showing up this morning. I thought I'd get some projects done while the building was empty. I had in ear buds and didn't hear anything until Logan found me. You didn't deserve this, Em. I'm sorry."

"Cameron, where's your phone?" Logan asked.

"Upstairs in the storage room."

"Okay. I'll grab it and call 911. You guys go help Jackson. This piece of shit can lie in his own blood until the cops arrive."

"Logan." Every bone and muscle in her body ached, but she wrapped him in a hug. "Thank you. To both of you," she added awkwardly, turning back to Cameron.

"I wish we could have intervened sooner," Logan said, removing his T-shirt and handing it to her. "We were keeping a close watch but couldn't do anything until his weapon wasn't a factor. That was some quick thinking you did to get it away from him."

After slipping on the shirt, she placed a hand on his shoulder for support. "Thanks. It worked for a minute."

"Come on, Emily," Cameron urged softly. "I'll take you to Jackson. He's probably worried sick."

Jackson

At the sound of approaching footsteps, Jackson's head shot up. He could do nothing but listen to his raging heartbeat after Lucas took off, terrified he got what he wanted.

Then, she appeared, covered and whole, and his unsteady control broke. In her absence, the fight to get out of his restraints and save the woman he loved held him together. Now that the war appeared to be over, he wept with relief.

Emily knelt in front of him and cut the ties from his ankles and wrists with the scissors she brought.

"I'm so sorry, my love." She carefully brushed his matted hair from his face, then pulled him into her arms.

As he held her, he promised she'd never live another day in fear for the rest of her life. "Where is he?"

"Unconscious."

He sat up to see her and set his wayward thoughts at ease. "How?"

She turned to Cameron waiting in the doorway. "It's a long story, but Cameron distracted him while Logan knocked him out. He's tied up in the lobby."

"Logan's here?"

"Yeah. We came in together."

He nodded to Cameron. "Thank you."

"Glad I was here," he said before stepping away to give them privacy.

"Are you okay?" Jackson asked as she pulled the bench closer to sit beside him.

She took his hands. "Shaken but glad you're alive. How are you feeling?"

"Sore. I'm sure I look worse than I feel. He didn't touch you, did he?"

"No."

"Where'd you get the shirt?"

"Logan's now the shirtless one."

"Good."

Leaning against him, she inspected his hands, applying pressure to a gash on his left wrist with her palm. "This one might need stitches."

"Sweetheart." He kissed her forehead when she didn't look up. "You were so brave tonight. Watching him torment you destroyed me, but I was proud of the way you fought back. He'll be locked away for a very long time after this. No more unexpected releases or visits."

"We thought that the last time. I'm so scared he'll find another loophole." She wiped her nose with the back of her free hand.

"Emily, I need to tell you something."

With a sniff, she reached for a towel on the counter nearby and held it to Jackson's wrist. "I don't know if I can take any more."

"This can't wait." He placed a finger under her chin to lift her eyes. "Lucas confessed. He was the one that destroyed your house."

"What?" How could it have been Lucas all this time?

Her shoulders drooped as she accepted all the blame. He wouldn't allow it.

"What about Cameron's letter?" she asked, lifting her teary gaze to his.

"Purely coincidence. I guess Charlie's speculation had been right. Harry must have brought it in with the mail."

"I don't know what to say."

"I'm glad it wasn't Cameron. He may be a bad drunk, but this means he isn't dangerous."

"He did seem to regret his actions lately. He needs help." She sat up when the sound of footsteps traveled down the hall. "Someone's coming."

"They're in here," Logan said from the hallway before he and two officers and two EMS personnel entered the room. "I briefed them on the situation," he told Emily and Jackson.

"Lieutenant Hardy with Richmond Police," the officer introduced himself and motioned to his partner, "and Officer Unger. I'd shake your hand but looks like you need some bandaging."

"This is Emily Robertson," Jackson told them as she moved the bench to make room for the EMTs. "And I'm—"

"I know who you are, Mr. Vane. It's a big city, but word of what you're building here is well known. We have many veterans on the force."

Jackson nodded in appreciation, trying to ignore the pulsating pain in his head and abdomen.

Hardy leaned against the counter and removed a small notebook from his pocket. "Mind if I ask you a few questions?"

"Sure." He held out his arms for the EMTs to clean and wrap his wounds while another checked his vitals.

"The name of the suspect in the lobby is Lucas Oliver?"

"He's no suspect, Lieutenant. He's a sick and demented criminal."

"That may be so, but he's a suspect until convicted. When did you first come in contact with him?"

"I met him in Savannah, Georgia last May, but Emily has known him longer." He looked over his shoulder at her and offered a grin for encouragement.

"We were co-workers, and he was supposed to be in jail."

"What was he in for?" Lieutenant Unger asked.

"For assaulting me and raping my friend."

"I'm sorry to hear that. What about tonight? What happened before Mr. Carter and Mr. Reid intervened?"

"I was working late alone. He snuck in and hit me with something. When I came to, I was tied to this chair. In between his tirades, he tried to knock me out again with his fists."

"How about you, Ms. Robertson. When did you arrive, and what happened?"

She took a deep breath and filled him in. Then, Jackson added Lucas's involvement in the break-ins.

"So." Hardy pushed the pencil back through the metal spiral of the notebook. "All of this was to take you out of the triangle."

"And to punish me for what I did to him in Jacksonville."

"I saw cameras on the way here. Do they work?"

"Yes, but there are no cameras in here."

"That's fine. I'll take whatever you have."

"We've done all we can do here," the EMT mentioned. "You'll need stitches for the gash in your wrist and above your eye." Blood still dripped down his cheek from under the bandage. "We need to get you to the hospital for a few tests and x-rays."

"I have all I need for now," Hardy said. "When Mr. Oliver is stable, we'll interview him and get his confession."

"Don't count on it."

Hardy crossed to Jackson and held out his hand. "I'll be in touch. I hope you feel better soon. Ma'am." He tipped his head to Emily as he and the other officers headed out.

"Ready, Mr. Vane? An ambulance is waiting outside."

"I'm fine. I don't need—"

"Please, my love," Emily pleaded. "Let them check you over. For my peace of mind."

"Alright. For you."

The EMTs helped Jackson to his feet, but he refused the gurney waiting for him in the hallway. He shuffled toward the door with Emily close behind.

"Before you go, I thought you might want this," Logan told Emily and passed her a photo. "I found it in the asshole's pocket."

She recognized it instantly. It was the one Ben took of her and Genevieve on the beach. The same one she couldn't find in the rubble after returning to Savannah from

Orlando. Lucas had taken it as a trophy, reminder, or promise.

"Emily, come sit," Jackson urged, recognizing her signals. "You're going to pass out." He led her to the bench when she didn't move and knelt in front of her. "He's in custody and no longer a threat. This doesn't matter."

She nodded, her eyes blinking faster than he was comfortable with, and her breathing remained erratic.

"Look at me," he instructed to ground her as she'd done for him so many times. "You're safe. The people you love are safe."

Her teary eyes flew open and focused on him, burrowing into his soul, and leveling him.

"There's nothing we can't handle together, right?"

With a weary grin, she cupped his face and let the tears fall, setting her fear free. "We're unstoppable."

"Unbreakable."

"Forever and always."

Chapter Thirty-Two

✩ ✩ ✩

Jackson

S tanding in the center of the lobby, he looked around at his vision in full color and surround sound. Hustling staff and volunteers rushed this way and that, hanging banners and streamers and shining windows and equipment. Excited chatter came from every corridor with every room full of people and activity. It was a glimpse into what a typical day at VETS might be like after it opens. He adored it all.

"Only a few more days," he said, wrapping an arm around Emily's waist as she joined him. He watched her soak in the moment and what they built together as he had, filling him with a pride he'd never experienced before. The hard work, long days, frustrations, and relapses—all had been worth it.

"It's going to be amazing."

"When do your parents arrive?"

She checked her watch. "Any minute. They're excited to pitch in, so they're coming straight here from the airport."

"I'm excited to see them again." He searched the lobby and the areas he could see. "Still no sign of Logan?"

With a long sigh, she took his hand. "No, and I'm worried. It's been three days."

"I tried calling him again this morning. Still no answer."

"Do you think he's avoiding us?"

"I don't know why he would."

"Maybe what happened triggered an episode. I'm scared something may have happened to him, and he's alone."

When concern pooled in her eyes, he drew her close.

"After your parents get settled, I'll try to find his camp. Keep asking around. Someone may have seen him."

With a nod, she wiped her cheeks, rose to her toes, and kissed him softly, careful around his tender bruises.

"Emily." He tipped his head toward the door and smiled. "They're here."

She spun around, her long hair circling around her before she took off and threw herself into her mother's arms. "I'm so glad you made it."

"Wouldn't miss it for the world," Eden squeezed her daughter, then opened her arms to Jackson. "Sweetheart, this place is mind-blowing."

"Thank you, Eden. Charlie, it's great to see you." He accepted a gentleman's embrace from her father.

"Come," Emily urged. "I want to show you everything."

"You go ahead, sweetie," Charlie said to his wife. "I want to talk to Jackson a bit."

Emily blew them a kiss before escorting her mother through the lobby.

"It feels good to see her happy again," Charlie said. "How are you doing?"

"Little sore and stressed about the opening, but otherwise like a weight has lifted. We can finally start our lives together."

"You deserve that. How's your friend doing? The one that helped catch that asshole?"

"Actually, I was about to go look for him."

"Look for him?"

"We haven't seen him since the cops left that night, and we're worried about him. He set up a camp nearby, and I want to see if I can find it."

"I've got some tracking experience. Want some help?"

"That would be great." Jackson led the way outside.

"I talked to the Richmond investigator on the case," Charlie mentioned as they walked the property. "They got a search warrant for the doctor's hotel room and found more weapons, mostly handguns, and some drugs. Antidepressants and pain killers. Nothing too dramatic," he added when Jackson's head snapped to face him. "The place was a complete disaster. He'd refused room service for weeks."

"Weeks? How long had he been here?"

"Based on the evidence, a while. So, why does your friend camp out? Is he homeless?" Charlie asked to change the subject and motioned toward a worn trail near the edge of the parking lot.

Jackson had felt his demeanor switch from casual to rigid at the mention of Lucas, and surely Charlie noticed.

They continued down the path, pushing past shrubbery and low-lying tree limbs before Jackson answered the question. "Logan was held captive for six months by some terrorists two years ago. He's still struggling to deal with the aftermath. He wanders around searching for healing and working when he can. He walked here when he heard about VETS."

"Walked, huh? From where?"

"Pennsylvania."

"I had a good buddy back in the day who was captured right before the end of the war. He was never the same after that."

"I'm hoping he'll stay long enough to let our team help."

"Your mission with VETS, it's—" Stopping, Charlie pointed toward something silver shining in a patch of sunlight in the distance. "There."

Picking up the pace, they rushed toward a tent in a small clearing, calling for Logan. He unzipped the tent, when they reached the makeshift camp, only to find it empty.

"Damn it. Where are you?" Frustrated, he spun around to continue his search. Moving toward a shallow ditch, he saw clothes and shoes through the tall grass and didn't hesitate. As he approached, he recognized the dark gray T-shirt with thick, black lettering. He'd had one himself not too long ago. The sun seemed to shine only on the U.S.

Marines symbol on the front—a guiding light for Logan's rescuers.

Sliding to his knees, Jackson took hold of Logan's shoulders and shook him. Nothing. He patted his sunburnt cheek, but his head only rolled with the motion.

"Don't you go and die on me, too," he muttered as panic started a war with his control. Scooping his arms under Logan, he tried to stand, but stumbled backward with the weight of Logan's body falling on top of him. Air escaped his lung on impact.

"Wake up," he strained. "We have to get out of here." His heart raced, and fear snapped his wavering grasp on reality and held it hostage.

As he laid trapped on the ground, he knew he needed to move, but he was paralyzed, struck powerless by memories he hadn't seen in months. His throat felt dry, like he'd swallowed a cup of sand. A bass drum pounded in his head, and the blinding sun burned his eyes as the explosion had. He had to get out of there before—

A hand on his shoulder snapped Jackson's gaze to the figure kneeling beside him. It took a moment, but Charlie's friendly face and the quiet woods around him were a welcome sight. There was no desert. No sand in his throat. No missiles or assault rifles raining down around him. Just someone lying motionless on his chest.

Logan.

Charlie lifted Logan's torso, allowing Jackson to crawl out from under him.

"Are you all right?" he asked.

"I'm fine. Help me get him up."

When Jackson was steady, he and Charlie wrapped an arm around Logan's waist, and together, they carried him to the parking lot.

"My car's parked on this side of the lot," Charlie mentioned between breaths.

They reached the small SUV quickly, and after securing Logan in the backseat, Charlie tossed Jackson the keys. "We'll get there faster if you drive."

Within thirty minutes, they had Logan loaded onto a gurney in the Emergency Room and answered the doctor's questions. Jackson was added as his emergency contact and sent to the waiting room for further instructions.

"I need to call Emily," he mentioned and brushed at the dirt and leaves on his shirt. "She'll want to be here."

"I'll do it. Go get cleaned up and take a moment to gather yourself. You clicked into survival mode in the woods, and you don't need it here. Remember that."

———

"Talk to me, son."

At the sound of a voice nearby, Jackson jumped. Rubbing his hands over his face, he looked around and tried to remember how he got to the waiting room. He had no recollection of anything that happened after arriving at the hospital.

"When I saw him lying in that ditch…" He shook his head and sighed. "It took me back to the desert. Bombs and bullets were piercing the ground all around me, and as

I got closer, I saw myself. It was me, lying in a pool of my own blood and that of my fellow Marines again. My best friends." Closing his eyes, he tried to erase the memory. "I was wearing the same shirt under my uniform that day."

He rose and stalked to the windows.

"I thought I was over this."

Joining him, Charlie placed an empathetic hand on his back. "Triggers, my boy. You'll find them here and there. Some diminish over time while others won't. You've been stressed lately, and I'm sure that played a role. Hang in there and focus on the present whenever you can."

"Thank you, Charlie."

"Speaking of hanging in, I believe she can help with that."

Jackson spun around in time to catch Emily as she lunged into his arms. Burying his face in the curve of her neck, he held her there until the crashing waves of desperation subsided, and he could breathe once more.

"Are you okay?" she asked, cupping his face in her hands. He searched her eyes for the peace he always found there.

"Yeah." Taking her in his arms, he stayed there until a doctor called for him from the entrance.

"There you are." The doctor, short in stature with a full head of curly black hair and matching glasses met Jackson halfway into the room. From under the sleeve of his white coat, oversized for his small frame, he thrust out his hand with a wide smile. "What a pleasure it is to meet you, Mr. Vane. I saw you on the news the other day and—"

"How is he, Doctor…" He looked down at the red, embroidered name on his coat, "Bradley?"

"He's resting. We've got a long caravan of I.V. liquids lined up. He was severely dehydrated, but nothing else seems to be wrong. There's a small bump on the back of his head, probably from when he collapsed. All the x-rays, blood tests, and scans came back normal."

"That's good."

"Any idea how this happened?"

"No. Can we see him?"

"Come back tomorrow. He will be better able to receive guests after he's accepted a few more truckloads of fluids." He snickered before pivoting and scurrying away.

"Odd fellow," Eden commented.

"He'll be okay." Relieved, Jackson slumped into a nearby chair.

Sitting next to him, Emily reached for his hand. "I guess we'll have to wait for visiting hours tomorrow. Until then, what do you want to do, sweetheart? Go home?"

"No. There's too much to do at VETS, and it will be a nice distraction."

Despite exhaustion and embarrassment weighing on him like a freight train, he felt better knowing Logan would recover. They both had a temporary, unforeseeable lapse in sanity, but at least they had returned to reality mostly unscathed. He would prefer to never lose track of that again.

———

"Hospital food is awful, isn't it?" Jackson asked as he, Emily, and Sydney entered Logan's hospital room.

They found him sitting up in bed, scooping a spoonful of instant mashed potatoes and letting the slimy heap slide off the spoon onto the plate with a scowl.

"The worst. I much rather eat tree bark. Which is not that bad after you cook it," he added with a smirk when Emily and Sydney's faces crinkled in disgust. "Don't knock it until you try it."

"It warms my heart to see you smiling," Emily said. "We've been worried about you."

"No need for that but thank you." Dropping the spoon, he moved the tray to the foot of the bed. "You all are looking relaxed and happier than the last time we were together."

"Lucas is locked in jail for good. This morning, Cameron apologized for his freakish behavior of late and entered rehab. VETS is almost finished." Emily placed an arm around Jackson's waist and smiled up at him before turning to Sydney. "And…"

"William and I are moving back home later today," Sydney finished.

"All good news."

"Speaking of good news, do you know when you're able to break free of this place?" Jackson asked.

"They said possibly tomorrow." Logan grimaced. "If I eat."

"How about we bring you something tasty from Ms. B's kitchen to help with that."

"Good idea," Emily said, loving the idea. "How about her famous vegetable lasagna? Would that be more appetizing than runny potatoes?"

"I can bring chocolate chip cookies for dessert," Sydney added. "They won't be from scratch like Ms. Beasley's, though. Pre-mades are all I can handle and still make them edible."

"Those are my favorite," he said with a wink then turned to Emily. "Make it beef lasagna and you've got a deal."

"Done. Dinner will be at your place tonight," she said to Logan with a laugh. "We'll bring the fixin's, fatten you up, and break you out of here all before the doctors can say mashed potatoes."

Chapter Thirty-Three

☆ ☆ ☆

Jackson

"Good morning," Emily whispered when he opened his eyes.

He rolled over to face her, still groggy from finally getting some sleep, something that had eluded him for months. "The sun's not even up yet."

"It'll be here soon enough." She kissed his cheek and ran a hand over his bare bottom. "I'm ready to get Lazy Saturday started. How about you?"

"I think you missed the lazy part of what today is all about."

"Nope. Somehow, in that gorgeous head of yours, *you've* forgotten. There was very little sleeping on the inaugural Lazy Saturday."

"Hmm. You're right. Sleeping *was* rare." Taking hold of her hips, he dragged her on top of him. It was their first free weekend alone since she joined him in Richmond, and he planned to make the most of every minute. "It's all coming back to me now. We've spent too much time apart lately, and I plan to make up for lost time this weekend."

"I love that and you."

No matter how busy their lives became or how their relationship changed through time, they would always have their connection—a rare, powerful, and profound love that could never fade.

And as drew her close, he knew this was only the beginning.

———

While Emily slept, he wished to do the same, but his wandering mind refused him the luxury. He'd spent weeks getting ready for this day to ensure there were no unexpected detours or distractions. Every detail had been mindfully considered. He'd prepared and planned, but still couldn't stop this thoughts from running rampant.

Earlier that week, he sent Ms. Beasley on a mini vacation to see her other grandchildren in Tennessee with two motives. For one, she deserved it. She'd worked hard both around the estate and at VETS since he and Emily returned, and he wanted a meaningful way to thank her.

But the trip didn't come without some convincing. She wouldn't accept the gift at first—she hated when Jackson spoiled her—but she agreed to go on one condition: she must be back for the grand opening. Touched, he couldn't refuse her.

The second motive was personal. For his weekend plan to work the way he envisioned, he needed an empty house.

To help with that, Harrison and Sophia graciously took Emily's parents on a winery tour through the Shenandoah Valley. They planned several stops with at least two overnight stays out of town.

With all the preparations complete for the opening on Monday, he and Emily could finally enjoy that Lazy Saturday they'd dreamed about since she moved in. But he had more than sex on their itinerary that day.

"I can't believe it took us ten months to do this. What were we thinking?" She all but purred the words as her eyes fluttered open.

"We knew it wouldn't be a true Lazy Saturday with all the chaos."

"True. The dust has settled. Finally." Her giggle—his favorite sound—was unbridled and giddy, and nothing made him happier. "Until Monday at least."

"Let's not think about Monday. All that matters is today."

"I like that." Combing a hand through his hair, she leaned in for a kiss. "What *do* you want to think about, my love?"

"I only want to think about you." He snuggled her tighter, ready to start a long bout of foreplay, but his stomach growled and shifted the mood. "And food, apparently."

"You better keep your strength up. We haven't christened the island yet like you promised."

He had promised that back before she moved in and looked forward to following through. "Or the couch."

"Your office."

"The back porch."

She ran a foot up his leg. "We did say we wanted to break in the entire house."

"It's a big house."

"Mmm. And if we do it right, it's going to take a very long time."

"We always do it right."

"Yes, we do. If we're going to do all that and hopefully more, we better get started."

"I'm convinced. Where shall we go first?"

Emily didn't hesitate. "My favorite."

"The kitchen island it is, and if you touch that robe, there will be consequences."

"Oh, yeah? What kind of consequences?" Her hand found his inner thigh, and he sucked in a breath. Before he could react, she threw back the blankets, snatched her robe off the chair in the sitting area, and bolted out the door.

"Hey! I said don't touch that." With a laugh, he took off after her. He didn't want to miss her graceful, naked body running down the stairs.

By the time he caught up, he found her standing by the island with the small pink gift bag he'd placed there.

She looked up and smiled sweetly. "What's this?"

"Open it." He leaned on the stool beside her for a better view.

"You're something else." She touched her lips to his then reached inside the bag. "Is this what I think it is?" She didn't wait for his answer and yanked out her hand. Holding it up on her palm, she squealed as it sparkled in the light. "You got me a glass slipper?"

"Every princess should have one." He laughed when she launched herself into his arms and dotted his face with kisses. "Does that mean you like it?"

"It's the most adorable thing I've ever seen. You, my Prince Charming, couldn't have given me a more perfect gift. I love it."

"And I love you."

He saw the change in her eyes and accepted the invitation by softly taking the slipper from her hand and placing it on the counter a safe distance away. Without a word, he lifted her and placed her on the counter. Her legs circled around him, drawing him close as he lingered on her lips. A breath oozed out of her throat, and she was ready for him.

This time, he would savor the moment and her.

———

He felt her cheeks move with a grin against his neck as they clung to each other in recovery. "What are you smiling about?"

"Just that I love you and this island." A chuckle bubbled out or her.

"I think I love it, too and want to do that again soon."

"Yes, please." She took his mouth and kissed him hard.

Somehow, he managed to put some distance between them and dislodge himself from her. "Food first. You shred me, and I need to recover before starting over."

"I can live with that, but refueling my energy is only going to make me want you more."

"And I can live with that." He gave her a peck on the nose, careful not to ignite the flame again. If he didn't eat soon, he would be useless to her for the rest of the day. And that would be a damn shame.

———

"I don't think I've ever seen you eat that much," she teased when he set his fork on the empty plate.

"I was starving, thanks to you. But now that my stomach is no longer a priority, I have to say, seeing you naked at the dining room table has so many ideas running through my head."

"Oh really?" She propped an elbow on the table, her chin resting on her palm. "I'm all ears if you're willing to share."

"Nah. I have another surprise for you first."

"You do?" She sat up. "This is my lucky day."

"Lazy Saturdays are lucky for us both." He leaned over and kissed her forehead before standing. "Stay here. I'll be right back."

———

Emily

She watched him sprint out of the room in a tan blur and sighed. It shouldn't be possible to love someone this much, but every day, her love for him expanded beyond her comprehension. After all they'd been through, she planned to appreciate and take advantage of every second they had together that day and for the rest of their lives.

He soon returned, wearing shorts and a sweet smile. This casual, relaxed view of him, like the one she got when he visited her in Savannah, was another she wanted to remember always. All strength and power, with every gorgeous muscle on full display. He was her protector, her inspiration, and all man. But most importantly, he was her forever.

In his hand, he held a thin piece of fabric she didn't recognize and her robe. Holding his gaze, she didn't take the robe when he held it out for her. "I thought you said there would be consequences if I put that on."

"I'm making an exception because it's only for a minute. I will be glad to remove it myself after your surprise."

"Works for me."

Slowly, she stood and slipped an arm in one sleeve of the robe then lifted her arms to pull it around her back. She knew he watched her, and she could almost hear his heart slamming against his chest. With her other arm now in place, she fluffed the wrinkles out of the silk, making sure her breasts and torso remained exposed for an unnecessary amount of time.

"I know what you're doing, and I'm holding out."

"What?" She batted her eyelashes and frowned. "You don't like the view?"

"I like it more than you know, but we're never going to make it outside if you don't put that on."

"Maybe that's the plan."

Determined, he shook his head. "No. It's early, and we have plenty of time for that."

"There's never enough time." She trailed a finger between her breasts and waited impatiently for his hands to return to her body.

"You win." Stepping out of his shorts, he crossed the room faster than she'd expected, and used the element of surprise to yank the robe off her shoulders. He pressed her against the table, tossing away all niceties or pretenses. Just a pure unbridled drive to take what she offered and give what she demanded. Her fingernails dug into his back, and she was right there with him.

———

Pure satisfaction in the aftermath of all he'd just done to her—given her—awakened her senses. She could hear her uneven breaths, the grandfather clock ticking in the hallway, and a liquid dripping into a puddle nearby.

"Ms. Beasley is going to be so pissed," Jackson muttered against her throat and a happy laugh snorted out.

"She'll just have to understand, because this table is now my new favorite."

"Mmm. I don't think she'll appreciate naked breakfast time either."

"Not one bit." She kissed his cheek and tried to sit up, but his arm draped heavy over her stomach. "Do you hear that dripping noise?"

"Yeah. Another reason she's going to be pissed. We may have just ruined the rug."

She rolled her head to the side to see their glasses had tipped over in the commotion and were leaking orange juice onto the floor. "Whoops. We better clean that up."

A low loan rumbled in his throat, and she sat up, slapping his thigh as she hopped off the table, suddenly energized. "Come on, you big baby. Didn't you want to show me something?"

"Yeah, but now I can't remember what." He pretended to mull it over. "Hey, what are you doing?"

"I'm putting on my robe for my surprise as you instructed."

"Ugh. I did, didn't I? What was I thinking?"

"You weren't. That's the problem."

"You tend to do that to me." Sitting on the table, he grabbed hold of the silk belt and pulled her between his legs. "You grab a towel for the spill, and I'll put away the plates. Then, I'll take you to your next surprise."

"I thought you couldn't remember what it was."

Kissing her softly, his hands pushed inside the robe. "It's all coming back to me. Hurry up. I can't wait to show you."

———

Jackson

"Is this really necessary?" she asked as he led her slowly down the hall blindfolded with the mysterious fabric.

"Yes, it's necessary."

"Fine, but if I stub my toe, it's on you."

"I'll take my chances." Opening the screen door leading to the back porch, he helped her down the steps, his excitement for this moment boiling over. "Stand right here," he instructed and positioned her with her back to the house. "Now you can look."

She ripped off the blindfold and immediately burst into tears. Not the reaction he'd expected or hoped for.

"Oh, Jackson."

He glanced at the freshly painted wooden swing, swaying softly in the breeze. "What's wrong?"

"Absolutely nothing. It's perfect." Stepping across the porch, she ran her fingers over the smooth, white finish before sitting. "How? When did you have time to hang this?"

"I had a little help." After joining her on the swing, he pushed it into motion. "An experienced swing installer had come into town, so I hired him."

"Dad?" she asked and teared up again. A gift from her two favorite guys. "It's better than the one I had in Savannah and exactly where I would have hung it, facing the sunrise." She threw her arms around his neck. "Thank you, my love. I can't believe you thought of this."

"I remembered how much you loved your old swing, and since we weren't able to bring it with us…"

"You're too good to me."

He shook his head. "I'll never be able to show you how much you mean to me."

"You don't have to show me. I feel it when you look at me." She kissed his hand, turning it over to kiss his palm. "In the way you kiss me, touch me, hold me."

"And I'll never stop."

———

"How do you feel about a walk?" he asked after a short nap on the couch with Emily lying limp on his chest. It was two in the afternoon, and he had more surprises to unveil.

"Mmm. They're nice," she answered without opening her eyes, making him laugh.

"I mean, would you go for a walk with me?"

She propped her chin up on a hand and found his eyes. "I'd do anything with you."

"You keep resting, and I'll get us something to wear."

"No. It's my turn to serve you." She pressed her lips to his and reluctantly rose. "I'll be back before you know it."

Once they were ready, he took her hand and led her across the yard toward the lake, his growing nerves altering every movement. They chatted casually while walking around the lake and through the edge of the forest before finding her surprise. She blinked hard, crunching her eyes closed and opening them over and over like she couldn't believe what she saw was real.

The colorful Ferris wheel he'd rented stood tall in the center of the clearing. Pink, blue, and purple blinking lights glowed bright, despite the sunlight, and all he could do was marvel at the sight along with her. Memories of their first date in Myrtle Beach and their Ferris wheel ride flooded his thoughts. But he didn't bring it here to decorate the property.

He turned to her. "Want to take a ride?"

"More than anything."

Opening the door, he nodded to the operator before closing them inside. The wheel jerked into motion, and she braced herself with a hand on his thigh until their compartment steadied. From the top, they could see the house in all its wonderous glory, the lake, glittering with the sun's reflection in the water, and the surrounding property. At this vantage point, he gained a new appreciation for all he'd gained over the last three years.

Correction—all *they* had—and he wanted her to understand that.

"All this is yours, too," he said. "Ours and our children's."

Her eyes filled instantly, riveling the sparkle of the lake. "How many?"

"What?"

"How many children?"

"However many God gives us."

"That's what I want, too. Tell me more," she said, shifting in her seat to drape her legs over his.

"We'll take long family vacations and visit your parents in Florida often. Family time during the holidays will always be events to remember, and our children will have the freedom to be who they want to be. Most of all, they will be loved and know it."

"I can't wait." She leaned in when he kissed her, then rested her head on his shoulder while they rode in romantic circles.

On the third loop, she sat up, and pointed to something in the distance. "Is that what I think it is?"

He followed her gaze to the rainbow beach umbrella he installed in a truckload of sand near the lake. "If you think our little Myrtle Beach paradise has been moved here to Richmond, then yeah, it's what you think it is."

"Oh, Jackson." She placed a hand on his cheek. "I can't believe you did all this."

"It's not quite our anniversary yet, but today was a day we could celebrate with no distractions or responsibilities getting in the way. I wanted it to be special."

"It's more than special. It's everything. Will you lay under the umbrella with me like we did at the beach?"

"Nothing would make me happier."

While he texted the operator to stop the Ferris wheel and let them off, his mind wandered to the turning point in their new and unexpected relationship—the day they spent at the beach after Genevieve and Ben's scare at the club. He and Emily had known each other for less than forty-eight hours, but as they relaxed in the shade under that beach umbrella, it was the first time he admitted he was falling for her. Their connection had been instant, their love easy, and neither had faltered since.

A loud screech of metal and a gentle tossing of the cabin interrupted his reminiscing.

"Can we ride again later?" she asked as they headed across the clearing toward the lake. "I'd like to sit it at the top and watch the sunset."

"Of course. Whenever you like."

After arriving at their own private beach, they spread a blanket on the sand and snuggled together as they had last summer. Content in each other's arms, words were unnecessary. Gentle caresses and tandem heart beats said it all.

"Emily," he whispered, breaking the silence. "Will you dance with me?"

Caught off guard, she raised her head to see his face. "You want to dance?"

"I do." After pulling her to her feet, he started the song he picked for this moment on his phone, and it began playing through a speaker hidden on the beach. He smiled when her hands sprang to her lips, proud of himself for moving her to tears. "I guess that means you remember?"

"How could I forget?" She dropped her arms in surrender. "It's the song we danced to at that country bar the night we met."

"It was also when I knew that I could never live without you." Despite meeting her only an hour before, he knew he'd never be the same. She saved him and gave him something to fight for.

Taking her hand, he wrapped his other arm around her back and drew her close. She rested her head on his shoulder as she did that night at the bar, but this time, he wasn't worrying about what she was thinking or trying to figure out how she silenced the war in his head. Instead, he simply swayed to the music, enjoying the way she fit in his arms.

"I knew you were the one when I first saw you. You changed me with your touch on the dance floor, and I swore never to let you go after we kissed." And as time went on, she showed him that he was capable of love and deserving of it in return.

When the song ended and started again, he stepped back, taking her hands in his. She looked up at him with absolute love in her dark blue eyes.

"I'll never find the words to adequately express how much you mean to me." He took a deep breath, looked down at their hands together, and fought against more emotions than he'd prepared for. "It wasn't always easy getting here, but nearly one year later, we've started the most amazing life together. I didn't know I could be this happy until I met you." Framing her face with is hands, he pressed a kiss to her forehead. "I have one more gift for you."

Before she could react, he reached behind a shrub and held it up for her to see.

"Oh, Jackson."

"I had it shipped here from Myrtle Beach. You deserve the original."

She accepted the little blue beach house she didn't get the chance to buy while on vacation and examined every adorable corner. It had a round clock trimmed in gold for a door. Sand and seashells covered the roof and base, and tiny flowers decorated the boxes under each window. Running a hand over them and the shiny shells, she noticed the latch on the side and released it. The clock door swung open and revealed the hollow inside, but he made sure it wasn't empty.

She peeked inside, then turned it over to shake out the contents, and a small black box tumbled out. Staring at it perched on her palm, her breathing paused.

"Emily," he began, surprising her, and her eyes shot to his. He couldn't keep his pulse from jumping as he waited for her to comprehend what the box meant "You are my everything, and I'm ready to build the life we dreamed about. You are the best part of me, and my heart will forever be yours."

Gently, he removed the box from her hand, lowered to a knee, and opened it. "My love, will you marry me?"

Her fingers went to her lips as she nodded, spilling streams of tears. "I love you so much."

On her left hand, he slid the ring into place and stood to accept her embrace, lost in the moment and in her. She was his light in the darkness, the center of his world, and his reason for living. Soon, they would fill the estate with children, laughter, love, and family, making it the home he wanted and never knew he desperately needed.

Twelve months ago, his life had no meaning. He followed a hunch and left Richmond in hopes of finding a purpose and an explanation for why he'd been spared in the explosion. Holding Emily now, it was strikingly clear that his journey and months spent on the road hadn't been about searching for answers, getting away from Richmond, or outrunning his past.

The journey had always been about coming home.

Leave a Review

If you enjoyed Book 3 of The Journey Series, *A Journey Home*, please consider leaving a review at any or all of these platforms: Amazon, Goodreads, BookBub, Barnes & Noble, social media (remember to tag me), and others. Reviews are so important to new authors and help us reach more readers.

Continue the series and find out what happens next with Sydney's story (book 4), *A Journey Beyond*.

About the Author

Since she was a young girl, Alexandra Grace has dreamed of writing a book. She started out with emotional poetry but writing a novel that made readers feel and appreciate was her passion. It wasn't until her 40s that Alexandra fulfilled that dream, and she had so much fun, that her first novel evolved into a series. She likes to combine her appreciation for military service men and women with her heartfelt approach to storytelling. All her novels and short stories are heartwarming, sweet with heat stories that give lovable veteran heroes the happy ever after they deserve.

Alexandra lives in Virginia with her family and is a proud full-time public servant for a local government. She enjoys reading, binge watching TV action series with her husband, and being her kids' biggest cheerleader.

Alexandra Grace

Let's Connect

Instagram: @authoralexandragrace

Facebook: @authoralexandragrace

TikTok: @authoralexandragrace

Goodreads: @authoralexandragrace

BookBub: @authoralexandragrace

Visit my website to subscribe to my newsletter:
https://authoralexandragrace.carrd.co

Printed in Great Britain
by Amazon

44268976R00239